Lyn Andrews is one of the UK's top one hundred best-selling authors, reaching No. 1 on the *Sunday Times* paperback bestseller list. Born and brought up in Liverpool, she is the daughter of a policeman and also married a policeman. After becoming the mother of triplets, she took some time off from her writing whilst she raised her children. Shortlisted for the Romantic Novelists' Association Award in 1993, she has now written twenty-seven hugely successful novels. Lyn Andrews divides her time between Merseyside and Ireland.

lyn andrews

Days of Hope

headline

First published in 2007
by HEADLINE PUBLISHING GROUP

First published in paperback in 2008
by HEADLINE PUBLISHING GROUP

7

Cataloguing in Publication Data is available from the British Library

ISBN 978 0 7553 3197 0

Typeset in Janson by Avon DataSet Ltd,
Bidford-on-Avon, Warwickshire

Printed and bound in the UK by
CPI Mackays, Chatham ME5 8TD

Headline's policy is to use papers that are natural, renewable and
recyclable products and made from wood grown in sustainable
forests. The logging and manufacturing processes are expected to
conform to the environmental regulations of the country of origin.

HEADLINE PUBLISHING GROUP
An Hachette Livre UK Company
338 Euston Road
London NW1 3BH

www.headline.co.uk
www.hachettelivre.co.uk

My grateful thanks go to Julia and Peter Leonard of Ballinastragh, Rahan, for their time and hospitality. You were both an enormous help to me with your knowledge and experience of post-Emergency (World War II) life in Ireland, particularly in Rahan and Tullamore. As there are only a certain number of facts that can be obtained from reference books, without your help many of the background details in this book would be missing and therefore the sense of authenticity would sadly have been lost, to the detriment of the novel. Thank you both for those pleasant hours and your remarkable memories.

Thanks also, as usual, to my friend and neighbour Michael Guinan for additional local information.

Lyn Andrews
Tullamore 2007

Chapter One

—◆—

LIVERPOOL
May 1945

'IT'S OVER, MAM! IT'S really over!' Chrissie Devlin's cry rang through the small kitchen as she burst into the room. Her pretty oval face was glowing with excitement; her blue eyes were dancing with pure joy. 'Switch the wireless on, Mam! Go on, Mr Churchill's going to speak. I was just talking to Mr Shiells from number eighteen and he told me and he said he'd heard there are huge crowds out on the streets in London and there's fireworks and floodlights too. Oh, I just can't believe it's true!'

Chrissie, panting a little after running home, sank

down into the chair beside the range, her hands to her flushed cheeks. Tendrils of light brown curly hair clung to her forehead.

Sadie Devlin put down the pan she had been scouring and stared wordlessly at her youngest daughter. Her thin shoulders slumped and she was overcome by a wave of great weariness. As she glanced around her shabby kitchen she thought how hard, how exhausting it had been to keep a home going through years of war. Trying to put decent, nourishing meals on the table when there was nothing in the shops and what little there was available was rationed and had to be queued for. Trying to keep the place clean when even carbolic soap was in short supply; trying to keep it warm when there was never enough coal for heating never mind to boil up water. Trying to make clothes and household linens last by patching and mending. And throughout it all she had had to try to bolster everyone's spirits.

She wiped her hands on her faded and stained floral pinafore and thought with a strange detachment that the garment was just like herself. Once she had been considered pretty. Like Chrissie she had had thick curly hair and laughing blue eyes. She'd had a pink and white complexion and been plump like Chrissie too. Now all that had gone. She was worn out and thin, her hair was limp and dull, her eyes had lost their sparkle. The freshness of youth had gone and she was old before her time.

It was Grace who, with fingers that trembled slightly, twiddled the knobs on the wireless set that stood on a small table in a corner of the room. Of course they'd heard that the Germans had surrendered in a school-house in France last week, she thought, but it hadn't been announced officially that at last the war that had raged in Europe for six long years was over.

'Hurry up, Grace. We'll miss it,' Chrissie urged, jumping to her feet like a jack-in-the-box, seemingly unable to sit still, and jostling her sister in her eagerness.

'If you'd stop pulling and poking at me I might be able to find the station. Wait, I think this is it,' Grace replied in a voice that held both mild irritation and excited anticipation. At twenty she was two years older than Chrissie, taller and slimmer with dark brown curly hair, but she had the same blue eyes as her sister. Eyes that, like Chrissie's, were full of relief and joy.

The wireless crackled a little but then the unmis-takable voice of the Prime Minister came through, the voice that had given them all courage and fortitude and hope over the long, dark and dangerous years.

Japan had yet to be subdued, he told them, but the war in Europe would end officially at midnight. 'Advance Britannia! Long live the cause of freedom! God Save the King!' he finished in ringing, stentorian tones.

Chrissie threw her arms around her sister and hugged her, her eyes bright with incipient tears of relief. 'Oh, Grace, it's finally over! There'll be such a party! We'll have the time of our lives. There'll be dancing and singing and we can have every light in the house on and every streetlight in the city will be on again too. Just think, soon we'll be able to get decent jobs and not have to slave away every day in that damned munitions factory. We can have pretty clothes, good food – all the things we've had to do without. And there'll be no more flaming ration books or queues!' She could hardly believe that what had just been dreams were about to become reality. She'd been a child of twelve when war had broken out and had had no idea of what it would entail. Those years, which should have been so happy and carefree, had been stolen from her. She'd been deprived of a part of her youth. But she was grown up now – eighteen – and she was going to enjoy the rest of her life. She would seize every opportunity that presented itself, come what may.

Grace laughed and hugged her exuberant sister and let herself be danced around the kitchen until she realised that her mother wasn't joining in. She had sat heavily down in the chair Chrissie had recently vacated and was just staring into the fire in the range, her face pale and drawn. Grace disentangled herself from Chrissie's embrace and squatted down beside Sadie, taking her hand.

'Mam? Mam, are you all right?' she asked gently.

Chrissie stared at them, puzzled. Wasn't Mam delighted? Why was she sitting as if she was carved from stone? As if she still had the cares of the world on her shoulders?

Sadie looked at her two daughters and shook her

6

head slowly. She felt empty and bowed down with misery. Her gaze slipped away and focused again on the faded wallpaper, chipped paint and shabby furniture of her home. The sight only lowered her spirits yet further.

'Ah, Mam, it's just the shock, you'll get over it. Come on, can't you give us a bit of a smile?' Chrissie was determined that nothing was going to mar this day. She couldn't wait to go out and celebrate, as she was certain everyone would soon be doing.

Before Sadie could reply the kitchen door burst open and Mary, Kate and Ellie Nelson from next door crowded into the room. The three over-excited young girls grabbed Chrissie and dragged her laughingly towards the lobby.

'Chrissie, everyone's going out in the street. People are bringing bottles of beer and spirits – God knows where they got them from – and me da is helping Mr Bradshaw get their piano out on to the pavement,' Ellie screeched delightedly.

'Come on, Grace!' Kate Nelson urged.

Grace shook her head, still holding her mother's hand. 'Later, Kate. I'll be out later,' she promised as they all clattered down the lobby, through the front door and out on to Royal Street where the occupants of nearly every house were spilling into the road, laughing, cheering and hugging each other. Through the open door came the sound of church bells – silent for six years – now pealing joyfully out across the city.

When the girls had disappeared, a hush fell on the kitchen, despite the bells and the sounds coming from the street.

'What's wrong, Mam? What is it?' Grace pressed. She had always been more sensitive and sensible than Chrissie. She understood, as her sister did not, how heavily the burden of the last six years had weighed on her mother.

Sadie looked at her and slowly shook her head. 'Oh, Grace, what have I got to celebrate?' The tears that had welled up in her eyes spilled over and trickled slowly down her thin cheeks. 'I've lost your da, not only a good and caring husband but the best friend I ever had, and I've lost Harold. My poor lad is lying somewhere at the bottom of the Atlantic Ocean. Not even in a proper grave, just the rusting hulk of that old merchant ship. My firstborn and him not even as old as you when he died, Grace.'

Grace nodded slowly and put her arm around her mother. She would never forget the day they'd heard that her eldest brother had gone down with the *Southern Cross* when the convoy had been attacked by submarines. She glanced at the photograph on the mantel of the dark-haired young lad, proudly wearing the uniform of the Merchant Marine and grinning widely. She still missed him terribly; she would never forget him. His death had aged her parents, her da in particular, and then there had come that terrifying week in May 1941 when the city had been bombarded night after night and her da, an ARP warden, had been killed trying to rescue a family from their bombed home. A wall had collapsed on him. Grace brushed away her own tears and the painful memories.

'But, Mam, just think, our Georgie will be coming home from the Army soon and now Billy won't have to go and fight. They're both safe and we have our house, we didn't get bombed out, and I can go back to work at Porter's and Chrissie can get a decent job. You won't have to go out cleaning offices any more. We have some things to be thankful for.'

Sadie managed a sad little smile and wiped her eyes with the hem of her pinafore. 'I suppose so, Grace, but with half the cities in the country in ruins and all the men coming back from the forces, there isn't going to be a wave of prosperity. Things aren't just going to go back to the way they used to be, no matter what our Chrissie thinks. I remember what it was like after the last war. We'll all have to work and work damned hard too. Six years. We've all suffered for six long terrible years and now it's over and I'm asking myself was it worth it?'

'Oh, Mam, of course it was! Think what it must have been like for all those people who had to live under Nazi rule? At least we never had to suffer that.'

Sadie sighed heavily. 'At a cost, Grace, at a terrible cost.'

'I know, Mam, but now at least we can look forward to the future. We've all *got* a future. Georgie, Billy,

Chrissie, me and you too. The city will be rebuilt; people will get new houses, better houses and decent jobs. We've got *hope*, Mam!' Grace smiled. 'You remember that story you used to tell us when we were little, about Pandora and her box?'

Sadie looked wistful, remembering the days when her children had been young and had clamoured for a bedtime story. She'd grown tired of repeating the same fairy stories over and over and had resorted to the myth of Pandora's box. 'That seems a lifetime ago, Grace. It was one my mam used to tell me; I don't know where she heard it because she never had time to read. I didn't understand it fully until I was grown up. It's not a story for children really.'

Grace nodded. 'You'd tell us about all the dreadful things that came flying out of that box after she opened it. War and famine and death and pestilence, although we didn't know what half those words meant then, and I always thought she was really stupid to have opened it at all when she'd been forbidden not to, but what was the last thing out of that box, Mam?'

Sadie squeezed Grace's hand. 'Hope. That was the last thing out of the box.'

'And the best, you always used to say, and now after war and death we still have *hope*.'

Sadie made a huge effort to try to pull herself together. Grace was trying so hard. 'You're a good girl, Grace, and wise beyond your years. I'll be fine now. You're right. The two lads I have left will be safe, we all will. No more dreading the news on the wireless or the wail of the air-raid siren. No more sitting in the shelter wondering if we'd survive the night and if we did would we still have a roof over our heads. No more dreading the lad from the Post Office knocking on the door with a telegram or the police coming with bad news. We have to try to look forward now. You go out and enjoy yourself like the rest of the young ones, I'm all right now, luv, truly I am.'

Grace got to her feet with relief but she wouldn't leave her mother alone, not tonight. 'I'll go up and bring Ada McMurray down to you. She won't be in much of a mood for celebrating either.'

Sadie nodded. Frank McMurray had been killed on the Tuesday night of the May Blitz when the fire engine he'd been driving had plunged headlong into a bomb crater. Ada had also lost two sons in North Africa. No, there wouldn't be much celebrating in number four Royal Street tonight either. She stood up and filled the kettle. 'And if you see our Billy, tell him I don't want him falling in the door drunk. Sixteen is too young to be drinking – even tonight!' she called as Grace left to fetch their neighbour.

'I'll tell him that – if I see him,' Grace called over her shoulder.

By the time she had persuaded a tearful Ada to keep her mother company, made them both a cup of tea and gone back outside the celebrations were well under way.

Mrs Bradshaw was playing a spirited version of 'Roll out the Barrel' on their piano, which had been dragged into the middle of the road. People had brought tables and chairs and stools out from their houses and all the women had brought what food they could scrape together. The pub on the corner of Royal Street and Walton Lane that went by the rather grand name of the 'Brontë Hotel' had generously supplied a barrel of beer and from the depths of cupboards and sideboards the precious remaining 'drops' of spirits, usually obtained on the black market, had been unearthed. Red, white and blue bunting was being strung from the lampposts and Ellie Nelson had draped a huge Union flag from the front bedroom window of their house.

Grace had a glass thrust into her hand by Maggie Molloy from number fourteen.

'Get that down yer, Grace! We've plenty ter celebrate terday!' Maggie laughed.

Grace grinned and sipped it; it was rather weak home-made lemonade but at least a dash of port had been added.

Mrs Bradshaw had now launched into 'We'll Meet Again' and young Tommy Milligan from the bottom of the street dragged Grace into the crowd of singing and dancing neighbours.

'Have you seen our Billy?' she shouted over the noise.

'His bike had a puncture; he went to get it mended, like. Said he'd need it for tomorrow but I don't reckon he will now. I can't see many people getting in to work at all tomorrow,' he yelled back.

Grace nodded. Both lads worked for the Post Office as messenger boys.

'Well, if you see him before I do, tell him Mam says he's not to be getting drunk.'

Tommy rolled his eyes expressively. 'She's got ter be kiddin'! Who's goin' ter stay sober ternight? I'm not and neither are me mam and da and your Chrissie's half cut already. Them Nelson girls managed to persuade that feller from the pub ter give them a bottle of Empire sherry.'

Grace pulled a face. 'It tastes like paint-stripper, that stuff, and she's not used to it, none of us are. Oh, well, on her own head be it.'

Tommy grinned. 'She'll have a head as big as Birkenhead in the mornin' but she said she's determined ter enjoy herself.'

Grace laughed. She couldn't blame Chrissie – she couldn't blame any of them. They all wanted to forget the last six years, if only for today. She wondered if she should try and get a couple of glasses of something halfway decent for her mam and Ada.

She begged two tiny glasses of port wine and took them into the two women. She found them sitting talking quietly but at least the tears had stopped, she saw with relief. They seemed more composed as they thanked her for being so thoughtful.

At a few minutes past ten, aided by Kate Nelson,

Grace half dragged and half carried a thoroughly inebriated Chrissie up the stairs to the bedroom the sisters shared. The light in the long, narrow lobby was dim, barely illuminating the brown varnish on the doors and the cream and brown wallpaper that had darkened with age, which helped hide Chrissie's state from Sadie – until she broke into a very tuneless version of 'White Cliffs of Dover'.

'For God's sake, Kate, put your hand over her mouth! Mam will go mad if she sees the state of her,' Grace hissed.

'I can't. It's taking me all my time to keep her from falling down the flaming stairs!' Kate hissed back. 'I don't know where she got the second bottle of sherry from.'

Sadie appeared in the kitchen doorway, having heard the racket. 'Grace, what's going on?' she demanded.

'Oh, God! Now we're for it!' Kate muttered. She raised her voice: 'It's all right, Mam, Chrissie's just had a bit too much sherry. We're getting her to bed.'

Sadie tutted and folded her arms. 'Trust that little madam! Well, no doubt she'll suffer for it tomorrow. Did you see our Billy?'

'I did, Mam. He's all right, he's with Tommy Milligan. I think he's staying with them tonight so as not to disturb you,' Grace called back.

'Well, the pair of them will have to report for work in the morning just the same,' Sadie said a little curtly before returning to her conversation with Ada.

Kate and Grace exchanged glances and then Kate burst out laughing. 'I can't see Tommy Milligan "reporting" for anything tomorrow. The last time I saw him he was sitting in the big basket on the front of the butcher's delivery bike, singing his head off.'

Grace laughed with her. 'And our Billy was pedalling it and the pair of them were heading straight towards the lamppost at the bottom of the street. They'll both be in a heap on the floor by now but I couldn't tell her that. One drunk in the family is enough.'

At last they'd hoisted Chrissie up to the bedroom. It was rather cramped, containing as it did two single beds covered with heavy blue and white cotton bedspreads, a narrow wardrobe and a chest of drawers on top of which was a small lamp. They heaved the now unconscious girl on to the bed and Grace began to pull off her shoes.

'It's been a day to remember all right and it's not over yet!' Kate grinned.

Grace smiled back. 'It's just a pity madam here won't "remember" half of it or even if she enjoyed herself. Well, I'll turn this lamp off and we'll get back to the dancing.'

Kate bent and pulled the bedspread up over Chrissie and Grace smiled at her. Kate Nelson was by far the most attractive of the three Nelson girls. Her glossy dark hair was styled in a fashionable pageboy and she had wide hazel eyes, fringed with thick lashes.

'She'll feel terrible in the morning,' she whispered as the two girls went back downstairs.

As they stepped out into the crowded street Agnes Milligan caught Kate's arm. ' 'Ere, Kate, I'd go an' get a grip of your Mary if I were youse.'

'Oh, now what?' Kate demanded a little irritably.

'She's got 'erself draped all over that 'Arry Bently from number twenty and iffen yer mam sees 'er she'll 'ave a blue fit. Course she's 'alf cut, like, and so is 'e, but that won't cut no ice with Polly.'

'God, aren't younger sisters a bloody pain! Well, I'm not interested in what our Mary is up to – let Mam sort her out. We've just had to put Chrissie Devlin to bed and Grace and me want to enjoy ourselves, not play nursemaid.'

'And don't even mention our Billy,' Grace added.

Agnes laughed. 'Suit yerself. I was just tryin' ter be 'elpful, like. But don't you worry about Billy, Grace. I'll cart 'im and our Tommy 'ome to our 'ouse later on. Oh, aye, there'll be a few thick 'eads in the morning all right!'

Chapter Two

———◆———

THERE WERE MANY PEOPLE who did have thick heads, including Chrissie and Billy Devlin. Chrissie had never felt so ill in her entire life. Her head felt as though it would explode every time she moved it even a fraction of an inch and she felt horribly sick and shivery.

'Oh, God! I'm dying!' she groaned to Grace who was getting dressed.

'Don't be daft; it's just an almighty hangover. Kate and I had a terrible job getting you to bed, you insisted on singing. You shouldn't have drunk so much of that terrible stuff. Where did you get it?' Grace looked without much pleasure at the creased cotton dress, printed with small blue and yellow daisies, she'd carelessly thrown over a chair the previous night. She'd been too tired to hang it up.

'I don't remember. I don't remember much at all after Ellie said we should go up to the Brontë for another bottle,' Chrissie moaned, pulling the sheet up over her face for Grace had drawn back the curtains and the shafts of sunlight streaming in through the window felt like piercing white-hot needles.

'I'll bring you up a big glass of water; try and drink it all, then go back to sleep. You'll feel better as the day goes on.'

When Grace reported on the state of her sister's health Sadie just raised her eyes to the ceiling and nodded. 'I suppose she's suffering enough. Let that be her punishment and I hope it'll teach her a lesson.'

'I'd say it's something she won't forget for a while, Mam. She looks terrible,' Grace replied.

Sadie sighed. 'It's a good job you don't have to go to work today.'

'They'll probably be closing the place down now. They won't need so many anti-tank shells.'

'Thank God.' Sadie crossed herself devoutly.

'I was wondering, Mam, should I go to Porter's on my way to work tomorrow? I'd like my job back. I know I'd only been there a little while before I had to go to munitions, but I did enjoy it there.'

Sadie looked thoughtful and then nodded. 'I don't suppose it would do any harm. There's going to be a rush now for good jobs, best to get there first.'

* * *

The following morning Grace kissed her mother and determined to call into her previous employers before going on to the munitions factory. She really couldn't see that there would be much activity there from now on.

The premises of Porter Bros were on the Old Dock Road and as Grace walked towards them she remembered how the area had looked when she'd first come here for an interview. Then huge warehouses had lined both sides of the road, the docks had been full of ships of all sizes and the traffic had been heavy: mainly horse-drawn carts but also lorries and trams; and above the road the Overhead Railway had transported hundreds of dock and factory workers to their places of employment. Now many of those warehouses had gone, reduced by bombs to piles of rubble, which had been cleared to leave vast empty sites where weeds now straggled between broken, blackened foundations. There were still ships in the docks but not as many, the U-boats had taken a heavy toll on shipping, and the carters still drove their carts pulled by heavy horses along the cobbled roadway, but there were very few lorries. Petrol was still in short supply. Even on such a bright May morning the place looked depressing, a shadow of its former self, as did the entire city, she thought. Battered, broken, shabby and run down – but not defeated, never that.

She turned into a yard and went through a small door that led into a sort of reception area. A middle-aged woman was sitting at a desk, sorting through a pile of papers.

'Mrs Middleton, am I glad to see you!' Grace cried as she approached the desk.

The woman looked over the top of her glasses and then her face broke into a smile. 'Gracie Devlin! I haven't seen you for years!'

Grace smiled and looked around the room. 'Isn't it great that the war is finally over? I've come to see if I can have my old job back. I loved working here, everyone was so friendly.'

Myra Middleton nodded. 'And you were one of the best workers we had, Gracie. You showed great promise, everyone said so. But the place has changed, I'm afraid. Most of the men went off to the Army, a lot of the younger girls and women – like yourself – had to go to munitions.'

'But we'll all be coming back now so I thought I'd be one of the first.'

The woman stood up and smiled. 'Come along with me and we'll see Mr Alfred. There'll be plenty of work now, everyone will be clamouring for flags and don't we make the finest?'

Half an hour later Grace had left the building with a skip in her step. She'd been promised her job back. As soon as she was released from war work she would recommence as a cutter in the workrooms of Porter Brothers, the oldest established firm of flag-makers in the city, and if she was as efficient and skilful as she had once been, then there would be the chance of promotion. She just hoped that she would be released soon; she hated the dirty, smelly and dangerous work of filling anti-tank shells and the long, arduous trek out to the factory in Kirkby, beyond the furthest city suburbs. It would be great to work with the brightly coloured materials again, for there was very little that was bright and colourful in life these days. Everything around her seemed to be drab and grey, tired and dilapidated from over-use, even her clothes and the second-hand, scuffed canvas shoulder bag that was the only bag she possessed. How she longed for something sunny and new to wear. Something that could be purchased without having to save up the necessary coupons. Still, she was sure it wouldn't be long now before the hated ration books could be torn up for ever and the shops would once again be full of lovely, stylish things to buy. She'd smiled to herself as she'd quickened her steps to catch the tram she saw trundling down the road towards her. She didn't care now how late she would be getting to work.

Billy hadn't arrived home until midday. He was a gangly lad and today his usually pale face was even whiter making the freckles across his nose more noticeable. His light brown hair was standing up at odd angles and he looked decidedly sheepish. He found the kitchen untidy and his mother reading a telegram.

'Ah, so you've finally shown up! I don't suppose

Tommy Milligan went to work either? Aren't the pair of you a living disgrace! At least some of the lads working for the Post Office behaved themselves last night otherwise I wouldn't have had this delivered.' Sadie waved the buff-coloured paper at him.

'Sorry, Mam, we . . . er . . . sort of overslept,' Billy muttered, pushing a lock of unruly hair from his forehead.

'Oh, I heard about the carry-on out of you and Tommy Milligan and the butcher's delivery bike. The front wheel is buckled beyond repair and he'll want paying for it!'

'Ah, Mam, it *was* VE Day!' Billy protested. 'What does the telegram say?' he asked to divert his mother's attention from the transgressions of himself, Tommy Milligan and obviously Chrissie. He presumed Grace at least had gone to work.

Sadie's manner softened and she smiled. 'Our Georgie is getting demobbed. All being well, he'll be home in about a month, thank God.'

'Ah, Mam, that's great! I bet lots of lads will be home soon – will we be having a party for him? For all of them?' Billy was truly glad his older brother was coming home. He hadn't seen him for nearly two years.

'I expect so although where we'll get enough food I don't know. We'll scrape some sort of a celebration meal together. Now, you can get from under my feet. There's hardly a tap of work been done in this house all morning and before I know where I am I'll be having Grace and Chrissie home tired and hungry. Billy, you can get the yard brush and go out and help clean up the mess that's been left in the street. The celebrations are over for now and if I have anything to do with it, the next street party will be far more orderly.'

Grimacing, Billy headed for the scullery to locate the yard brush.

Grace didn't feel in the least bit tired when she got home for there hadn't been much work done at all. Those people who had turned in had stood around in groups, talking until some sort of effort had been made to tidy things up.

'I see our Billy finally arrived home then,' she commented to her mother, having seen her brother and half a dozen other lads brushing the remains of the rubbish into wheelbarrows. He'd grinned and waved to her and she'd waved back.

'He did and he'll be back at work tomorrow and then he and Tommy will be paying Mr Granby the butcher a few pennies a week towards the new wheel for that bicycle.'

Grace laughed. 'That should teach the pair of them. What's for tea, Mam?'

Sadie sighed. 'Cottage pie, although there's not much meat, it's all potato.'

'I'll set the table,' Grace offered, taking the cutlery from the drawer in the dresser.

'How did you get on today?' Sadie asked, returning the pie to the oven.

'I went to Porter's on the way and I'm to have my old job back and maybe even a promotion if I get on well. And what's even better news, it was announced that munitions are winding down, we're to be released gradually but anyone who has a job to go to can apply to leave first, so I did and I'm finishing on Friday so I'll be starting back at Porter's next Monday.'

Sadie smiled at her. She knew just how much Grace had hated leaving Porter's. 'You'll get on well there, luv, I know you will. They're good people to work for.'

Chrissie got to her feet. 'Mam, I couldn't face anything to eat, honestly.'

Sadie nodded. 'I've had some great news today myself.'

'What?' Grace asked.

'Our Georgie is going to be demobbed. Oh, I can hardly believe he'll be coming home soon.'

Grace hugged her. 'Mam! That really is great. Isn't that wonderful, Chrissie?'

Chrissie smiled. It *was* the best thing that had happened all day. 'If you don't mind, Mam, I'll go up and tidy the bedroom, it's a bit of a mess.'

'I'll go up too and take off this dress, it's so grubby.'

'Don't be up there too long, Grace, tea's nearly ready,' Sadie advised.

As Grace stripped off the offending dress Chrissie sat down on the bed. 'I suppose I'll have to find myself a decent job too. I've only ever worked in munitions.'

'I'd be quick if I were you, there's going to be hundreds of girls looking for alternative work. And don't expect to be paid as much.'

'I always thought I'd like to work for T. J. Hughes, the department store in London Road,' Chrissie mused. Of course she'd miss the company of the girls and women she'd worked with for so long but she was bound to make new friends in a place like 'T. J.'s' as it was commonly called.

'It's as good as anywhere with both Blackler's and Lewis's having been bombed out.'

Chrissie looked wistful. 'Oh, Grace, wouldn't it be great to work in the dress department or the millinery department? I'd get to see all the latest fashions as soon as they come in. I might even be able to buy them, maybe at a discount.'

'I wouldn't hold out too much hope of that. I can't see them selling new stuff cheap to the staff before it's on offer to the customers at full price,' Grace warned.

Chrissie nodded; that made sense. 'Well, I think I'll try there first. I'll go down first thing in the morning before work and if I'm in luck and get taken on I can get an early release too. Oh, I'm so sick of all these old rags!' She picked up the faded brown and cream check skirt she'd been wearing the day before.

Grace smiled at her. 'I know. There's been nothing new or pretty for what seems like years. The only stuff you could buy was dark and serviceable and the skirts had to be short to save on material. Everything was skimped and you couldn't get a decent hat for love nor money! I'm going to treat myself to something really frivolous – if I can find anything – with my first week's wages from Porter's.'

'We'll need something nice to wear for when our Georgie gets home. He'll be home in about a month and then there'll be a party for him, and the other lads in the street.'

Grace hugged her. 'Oh, I'm so glad he's coming home, I really am! It might make Mam a bit happier. It's been so hard for her, Chrissie, losing Harold and then Da and having to bolster our spirits and keep going every day.'

'I know, Grace. I'll be glad to see Georgie too and know he's safe and well. I do miss Da and Harold, though – even now the house seems strange without them. But I feel as though I've never really *lived*. Before the war started I was just a bit of a kid and then all the years I've been growing up we've been at war. I'm fed up doing without so many things and "making do". I want to enjoy myself, see what life and being grown up is really all about. But I'm looking forward to the future now, Grace, I really am. I want pretty clothes and make-up. I want to go to dances, to the cinema and meet a nice lad and—'

'Fall in love? Don't we all? Still, there'll be plenty of lads coming back from the forces and things are bound to get better. The country will get back on its feet in no time.'

Sadie's voice came up the stairwell and Grace smiled.

'And we might even get decent food again. Oh, for a nice pork chop and oranges and even bananas! I can't remember the last time I tasted one.'

Chrissie grinned. 'And we'll have a bonfire with the flaming ration books! Do you think there'll be decent things to eat by the time our Georgie gets home?'

'There's bound to be. There are no more U-boats so there'll be stuff coming in from all over the world. We'll have a great time and I'll be able to get all the flags from Porter's. I'm sure they'll let me use the off-cuts to make yards and yards of bunting *and* I know someone else who'll be delighted he's coming home.'

'Mags Draper?' Chrissie queried.

Grace nodded. 'She's been writing to him for years and she's never been out with anyone else while he's been away fighting, although I know she's often been asked.'

'Do you think they'll get engaged?'

'Probably. I hope so, I like her.'

Chrissie looked a little doubtful. Margaret 'Mags' Draper lived in Westminster Road, near the police station. She was a pretty girl with dark curly hair and big brown eyes but she could be a bit sarcastic and on the few occasions when Chrissie had been in her company she had felt that the older girl thought her a little self-centred and vain and giddy.

'Grace, this pie is getting cold and it's not very appetising even when it's piping hot!' Sadie called up again.

Grace grimaced. 'What I wouldn't give for roast beef and all the trimmings!' she sighed as she left her sister sitting on the bed, frowning slightly.

Chapter Three

━━◆◈◆━━

CHRISSIE WAS DELIGHTED WHEN she was offered a job in the dress department of T. J. Hughes, a department store that was renowned throughout the area for its bargain prices. It might only be as junior assistant and on a month's probationary period on what she considered to be a very low wage, but, as she remarked to Grace, it would be wonderful to be surrounded by lovely clothes instead of smelly chemicals and metal shell casings.

Both girls started their jobs the following Monday and Grace slipped easily and effortlessly back into the routine of the workshop. The work was so much easier, she thought as she measured and cut the squares and strips of brightly coloured material that were then pinned and passed to the machinists to make up. There were off-cuts and she begged to be allowed to use them to make bunting during her lunch break.

To her disappointment Chrissie found that there still wasn't very much in the way of pretty, stylish clothes and that the despised ration books were not yet being scrapped. In fact Miss Perkins, the Departmental Manageress, had been very sceptical about things when Chrissie had broached the subject.

'It will be months and months, if not years, before things are in any way back to normal, Miss Devlin. It is a huge undertaking to get this country back on its feet after what we've been through. Food and fuel supplies, housing, roads, transport, communications, the care of the wounded and jobs for the returning servicemen are the government's priorities. Not fashions or cosmetics or perfumes or entertainment,' had been the depressing reply. Still, there were some lovely fresh-looking and quite inexpensive dress materials in the haberdashery department, Chrissie'd thought, if you could sew or pay a dressmaker – although she could do neither. She had brightened up when she remembered that Kate Nelson had gone back to her old job as a seamstress in Bold Street. If she had enough coupons she'd get a dress length and beg Kate to make it up for her, then at least she'd have something new for when Georgie got home.

As the weeks went by Sadie received more definite news from Georgie about the date he was to be demobbed but she was finding it just as hard to get things for the 'Welcome Home' party that was being planned. He was amongst the first group that consisted of seven lads returning to their homes in Royal Street; the remaining men and boys would not arrive until later in the year.

'I'm so glad he'll be amongst the first to get home, Polly, it will be such a relief, but I would have thought that at least some tinned foods would be coming into the country now,' she confided to Polly Nelson from next door whose own son was also returning.

'Why don't you have a word with Charlie Dawson from number twenty? He works on the docks: those fellers always know what's coming in and when. His lad, Joe, is being demobbed too so it's in his interest as well. And I know for a fact that Ted Granby, that butcher down on Walton Road, opposite the Astoria Cinema, keeps stuff under the counter for special customers, so I'll be asking him for a bit of something to make a few pies and as many sausages as he can provide. If we cut them up small we should get a couple of dozen sausage rolls out of them,' Polly advised.

'And there'll be sandwiches and jellies and hopefully a few cakes. Oh, I suppose it will have to do. I just wish we could have laid on a slap-up feed for them, they've been through so much.'

'I've a feeling it's going to be a good while yet before any of us can put a "slap-up" meal on the table, Sadie. At least next Christmas we should be able to get a goose or a turkey or even a capon and not be having to make do with whatever we can get our hands on as we've done in the past.'

'Well, our Grace is going to make sure that the street is decorated and Chrissie and your Ellie are making a huge banner to string right across the road with the words "Welcome home all our brave lads!" printed on it.'

Polly nodded. 'Although not all of them are coming home. Young Freddie Chambers is still a POW in Burma.'

'And my poor Harold is lying at the bottom of the ocean.'

Polly patted her hand. 'It's been a terrible time, Sadie, luv, and we'll never forget them, but let's be thankful for the lads that are coming home and give them a real Liverpool welcome. I suppose young Mags Draper will be at the station to meet your Georgie?'

Sadie nodded, pushing away her grief. 'She's a good girl. Steady and loyal. I hope they decide to make a go of it.'

'So do I, it will be good to have a wedding in the street.'

'Let's not go jumping the gun, Polly. Let them get to know each other again, he's been away over two years and God knows what terrible sights he's seen. I hope he hasn't changed.'

'He'll have grown up, Sadie, stands to reason, but maybe that's for the best. Marriage isn't something anyone should go rushing into.'

Sadie nodded and they returned to the list they were making.

Towards the end of the month Mags Draper, Georgie's long-standing girlfriend, came to call on Sadie bringing with her a bag of currants and two pound-bags of flour.

'I managed to cadge them off the boss, I thought they'd come in handy, Mrs Devlin,' she said, placing them on the kitchen table. Mags worked in Peegram's Grocery Stores.

'They will indeed, thanks, luv. I'll make some scones. Every little helps. Sit down and have a cup of tea. I've got to go out to work soon but our Grace is in, you're not in a rush, are you?'

Mags shook her head. It was hard on Georgie's mam to have to go out cleaning offices, she looked so tired and pale but with Mr Devlin now dead she knew they needed the money. 'Then let me put the kettle on, you sit down for a bit and tell me how the "party food" is coming along.'

Sadie smiled at her. She was a pleasant and thoughtful girl from a decent family. She was attractive too but certainly not flighty. 'We're doing the best we can, although all our Chrissie seems to think about is the new dress she's managed to persuade Kate Nelson to make for her. It's all we ever hear about.'

A frown creased Mags's forehead. That was typical of Chrissie Devlin. Always thinking of herself. If she had money to spare for new dresses surely she could afford to turn up a bit more to her mam and then maybe Sadie could work fewer hours scrubbing floors. She liked Grace who was the same age as herself but she didn't have much time for Chrissie. Still, who wouldn't want a new dress for such an occasion? And she was Georgie's sister – if everything went well she would become her sister-in-law.

'I wanted to ask you, do you mind if I come to Lime Street Station with you to meet Georgie? If you'd prefer it to be just family I'll understand, truly I will,' Mags asked a little hesitantly as she handed the older woman a cup of tea.

'Of course I don't mind, Mags! You'll come along with us, he'd go mad if I said you had to wait for him at home. Besides, I'm hoping that eventually you will become "family".'

Mags blushed but said nothing.

'Well, here's our Grace now. I'd better be off. The sooner I get the work done the sooner I can get home to my bed.' Sadie quickly finished her tea as Grace came into the room.

When Sadie had left the two girls cleared and washed the dishes.

'I'm glad you came round, Mags, our Chrissie is next door with Kate having a fitting and she'll probably be there for hours, she's being so fussy over this dress. I didn't much feel like going out so I'm glad of your company.'

'I heard about the dress. Your mam told me,' Mags

replied a little curtly, then she sighed. 'I wish I had something new to wear when I meet Georgie but I'm trying to save up.'

Grace smiled at her. Mags wasn't as tall as her but she was slim and attractive. 'Is there anything of mine you'd like to borrow – not that I've anything brand new either? My pale pink blouse is fairly new by today's standards. I've had it six months but I've only worn it a few times.'

Mags looked thoughtful. 'Well, I've a decent navy skirt and if the weather holds I won't need a jacket.'

'Our Chrissie could get a bit of navy ribbon from T. J.'s and we could tuck it under the collar and tie the ends in a bow at the neck, that might dress it up a bit. Make it look a bit different. Our Georgie hasn't seen any of the clothes we've got, he's been away so long.'

Mags grinned. 'And probably wouldn't really notice what we have on, you know what fellers are like! But I do want to look my best. Oh, Grace, I've missed him so much and I've been terrified that something awful would happen to him!'

'We all have, especially after our Harold, but nothing did and now he's coming home. You really do love him, don't you?'

Mags nodded, her eyes shining.

Grace looked at her enviously. 'What's it like? I mean how does it really feel?'

Mags fiddled with the edge of her cardigan and looked shyly at Grace. 'It's wonderful. It's exciting and yet sometimes you feel . . . nervous and at the same time so happy you could burst. And it's being . . . cherished, looked after, sharing all your hopes and dreams. Oh, I can't really explain it, Grace, but you'll know what it's like when you meet the right lad. You'll never want to be parted from him, not even for a few hours. That's why it's been so terrible to have been separated from Georgie for so long.'

'Will you get married then?' Grace hoped that one day she would indeed feel about someone the way Mags felt about her brother.

'I hope so, Grace. He . . . he's hinted in his letters – the bits that weren't censored – that he was going to ask me.'

'Then knowing our Georgie he will. We can have a double celebration. You will say yes?'

'Of course I will!'

'Would you come and live here? So many houses have been bombed that it's nearly impossible to get anywhere of your own and with Da and Harold . . . gone, we've a bit more room.' Grace would enjoy having Mags's company and maybe then with the extra money coming in Mam wouldn't have to go out to work.

'I don't know, Grace. I think I'd better wait until Georgie asks me to marry him first.'

Grace nodded, wondering if she had been too pushy.

'There's going to be a wedding in our street in December and I'm so glad Georgie will be home in time for it. It's been planned for ages; it's Eileen Kilroy who lodges with the Graysons who is getting married. Half the street has been invited and she even has relations coming over from Ireland. She's Irish. She came over to be a nurse; that's how she met her fiancé. He was wounded in France, just after the D-Day landings last year. He walks with a bit of a limp but he's fine apart from that.'

Grace smiled at her. 'You'll be able to get some ideas from her then. Is she having a proper dress?'

'Mrs Grayson says so. I heard the material is being sent over specially from some shop in Dublin as you can't get much here.' Mags sounded a little despondent.

'Oh, things are bound to have improved by the time you and our Georgie set a date and our Chrissie will be able to help.'

'Help with what?' Chrissie demanded, entering the room in time to hear her name mentioned. 'And why are you two sitting in the dark? The war's over, remember? You can switch the light on and not have to draw the blackout curtains now.' She was surprised to see Grace sitting in the semi-darkness of the summer evening with Mags Draper. She hadn't known she was coming round this evening.

Mags cast Grace a warning look. She didn't really want to talk about weddings, after all Georgie hadn't asked her to marry him yet.

'With the welcome home party. We'll all be doing our bit,' Grace answered and then decided to sound her sister out – cautiously. 'Mags was just telling me that a girl in their street is getting married in December and is having a long white dress. She's having the material sent over from Dublin.'

'Isn't she the fortunate one! Well, we've certainly no white satin or white *anything* in our haberdashery department, people are making do with a nice costume or borrowing dresses.'

'But things will be getting better, surely? I mean doesn't that Miss Perkins get to know when new stock is expected?'

Chrissie laughed cuttingly. 'According to her it may well be *years* before anyone can get a decent wedding dress or any kind of stylish outfit.'

'But she would be the first to know, wouldn't she?' Grace pressed, seeing Mags's disappointed expression.

Chrissie shrugged. 'I suppose so. I'm just so lucky to have got that lilac and white cotton. Kate's doing a great job *and* I'm having the skirt made longer. I'm fed up wearing skirts that come above my knees, I look and feel as though I'm still a kid in short socks.'

Grace raised her eyes to the ceiling and Mags pursed her lips.

'Mags is coming with us to Lime Street to meet Georgie,' Grace announced to divert her sister's attention from the much-discussed new dress.

'That's great. Well, I'm tired so I'll be off to bed,' Chrissie excused herself.

Mags rose. 'I suppose I'd best go too, I told Mam I wouldn't be long.'

'See you a week on Wednesday evening then, the train is supposed to get in around seven o'clock,' Grace informed the girl.

When she'd gone Grace began to lay the table for breakfast to save Sadie a job in the morning.

'Do you really think our Georgie will ask her to marry him?' Chrissie probed.

'I do and I know she'll accept and that we'll all be made up,' Grace replied emphatically, glancing at her sister. 'What's wrong with you? Don't you like her?'

Chrissie shrugged. 'I suppose so. It's just that . . . well . . . sometimes I think she doesn't really like me.'

'What makes you think that?' Grace demanded. This was news to her.

'Oh, she's just made the odd remark about being "giddy". She's so serious, Grace! She never goes *anywhere*!'

'She doesn't go anywhere because she's been waiting for Georgie to come home and she's saving up. You can't save up and go out, Chrissie, and if you loved someone you wouldn't want to go places without them.'

'Oh, don't you start, Grace! All I'm saying is that she's too serious for her age.'

Grace sighed. 'Aren't you forgetting something, Chrissie? Our Georgie has been away fighting for over two years. He could have been killed or badly wounded or taken prisoner at any time and poor Mags has been worried sick about him. Isn't that enough to make anyone "serious"?'

Chrissie at last nodded. She supposed Grace was right.

Grace sighed again as her sister left the room. Chrissie had obviously got a bee in her bonnet about Mags and that didn't bode well for the future when Georgie decided to bring his new wife to live with them. Or rather *if* he did.

Chapter Four

————◦✦◦————

ON THE APPOINTED WEDNESDAY EVENING Sadie,
accompanied by Grace, Chrissie, Mags and young
Billy, made her way to Lime Street Station. They had all
made an effort with their appearance but Grace thought
that Mags looked particularly smart and attractive in the
borrowed pink rayon blouse with its navy satin ribbon at
the neck and the box-pleated navy skirt. She had to
admit though that it was the glow of pure happiness that
seemed to emanate from the girl that made Mags look
positively radiant.

She had persuaded Chrissie not to wear the new
lilac-and-white-flowered dress; it wouldn't be fair to put
Mags in the shade today, she'd urged. Chrissie had been
reluctant to agree, arguing that she too wanted to look
her best for her brother's homecoming, but Sadie had

added her comments to Grace's and she'd finally agreed. She comforted herself with the knowledge that she would be the best-dressed girl at the party on Friday night.

They travelled on the tram with the relations of all the other lads from Royal Street who were due home and as they alighted opposite St George's Hall Sadie hurried them forward, holding on to Billy's arm.

'There's going to be a right crush inside the station! Just look at these crowds. We should have got down here earlier.'

Grace linked both Mags and Chrissie. 'Well, it's not just the lads from our street that are coming home, Mam, there's a whole trainload of them and they're the first so everyone has turned out.'

'That being the case wouldn't you have thought they'd have made more of an effort? I thought there would at least be a band and loads of flags and that maybe even the Mayor would have come,' Chrissie said, feeling a little disappointed. The lack of festivity had diminished her excitement a little. It didn't seem very celebratory at all, she thought.

'Don't let that spoil the occasion, Chrissie. I expect the City Fathers know they won't be able to afford all that fuss for every train because there's going to be an awful lot of them over the next months,' Mags replied.

'And you have to remember that there are thousands of lads who aren't coming home at all,' Sadie reminded her.

Chrissie nodded, knowing that her mam was thinking of Harold.

'At least there're plenty of flags in Royal Street and that great banner you and Ellie made. They'll all appreciate that,' Grace said to bolster her sister's spirits.

The station concourse was full to overflowing with anxious-looking people and Billy was perturbed. 'Oh, Mam, we'll never be able to pick him out in this crowd. Which platform is it?'

'Ask that feller over there what platform it's expected in on?' Sadie indicated with her head towards a harassed-looking porter.

To Billy's shouted request the man pointed to the furthest platform and mouthed, 'Number seven.'

Sadie elbowed her way ruthlessly through the crowd until they were fairly near the front. Many people were checking their watches or turning to glance at the big clock on the back wall of the station.

'Oh, Grace, I'm so nervous! What if he doesn't recognise me?' There was a hint of panic in Mags's voice.

Grace laughed. 'Of course he will, Mags! You sent him photos, didn't you? You haven't changed that much!'

Mags grimaced. 'Yes, but . . . Oh, it's just nerves! I'm a wreck!'

Grace squeezed her hand. 'You look lovely, you really do, and he'll be delighted to see you.'

'He'll be delighted to see us all.' Sadie smiled, feeling

happier than she had done for a long time. 'And I'll be even happier when I get him back to our house.'

They didn't have long to wait before the train pulled in, the engine sending clouds of steam upwards to the vaulted roof. Men and boys were hanging out of the carriage doors in their eagerness to greet loved ones and the crowd surged towards them.

Sadie held on tightly to both Billy and Chrissie and Grace edged forward, pulling Mags with her.

'I thought they'd all still be in uniform,' Billy shouted over the din.

'They've given them new suits! Georgie said in his last letter that they were going to.' Mags's eyes were shining now and her cheeks were flushed.

As the ex-servicemen began to leave the train and hurry towards the barrier it was Grace who spotted the tall figure with the curly brown hair and tanned face. 'There he is! Mam, there he is!' she cried, pointing.

'Georgie! Georgie, lad! We're over here, luv!' Sadie's arms were waving like windmill sails and tears were streaming unheeded down her cheeks. There he was, in the flesh. Her beloved son was finally home, safe and sound, and he'd never have to go away again!

George Devlin's face lit up as he caught sight of them and he rushed towards his mother with open arms. 'Mam! Mam, it's so good to see you!' He hugged Sadie tightly before turning to Grace but Grace shook her head and pushed Mags towards him.

'She's been getting into such a state of nerves, thinking you wouldn't recognise her!' she laughed.

'Mags!' Georgie was fighting not to break down as he took Mags in his arms and kissed her. There had been so many times when he'd been afraid he'd never see her again, afraid he'd never see any of them again, afraid he'd never come home.

Sadie wiped her eyes as Georgie finally released Mags and turned to hug his sisters and then his brother.

'You've certainly shot up, Billy lad! You were just a scruffy kid when I last saw you.'

Billy positively glowed with pride. 'Mam wrote and told you I started working for the Post Office, it was just after you went away. It's great.'

'I'm hoping they'll have me back. I'll need a job now.' He winked at Mags who ducked her head, feeling a flutter of excited apprehension. He too had worked in Victoria Street before he'd been called up; it was good steady employment.

'They're bound to. Now, come on, let's get out of this infernal crush and go home,' Sadie urged.

As they walked to the tram stop Georgie held Mags's hand tightly and all the way home Sadie couldn't restrain herself from continually reaching out and patting his arm. He looked older and seemed to have much more self-confidence and the new navy pin-striped suit looked good on him. If only Tom had been here to see him, and Harold too, then her happiness would have been complete, but she pushed the thought away. Georgie had come through safely and for that she must thank God and His Holy Mother. There were women far less fortunate than herself. Women who had lost fathers, husbands, sons, brothers and their homes.

All the lads were hugged and kissed as they made their way to their respective homes and they were all loud in their praise of the gaily decorated street. Rows and rows of red, white and blue flags were strung between the lampposts. From every upstairs window fluttered Union flags and garlands of paper flowers decorated doorways. Chrissie and Ellie's huge white banner with the bold black lettering was attached to the railings of the Methodist church at the top end of the street where everyone could see it.

'And there's going to be a great party for you all on Friday night. We've all been hoarding and scrounging food for weeks,' Chrissie informed her brother. 'And I've got a new dress for the occasion. It's just gorgeous!'

'I kept a bit of stuff back for your supper tonight,' Sadie interrupted before Chrissie could comment further for she'd seen the swift look of disappointment that had crossed Mags's face.

Georgie grinned at her. 'That's great. I'm starving, Mam. I'm really looking forward to some home cooking, there's nothing to beat it!'

It was late when finally and reluctantly Mags said she would have to go home. She'd not had a minute alone with him but then she supposed it was only to be expected.

Georgie got to his feet. 'I'll walk you home, Mags. I'll come in and say hello to your mam and dad.'

She smiled at him. 'They'll be glad to see you.'

Sadie began to clear away the dishes; every scrap had been eaten and Georgie had declared it was the best meal he'd ever tasted. It had been well worth the hours she'd spent cooking just to hear him say that. Alf Nelson had called in with a jug of beer he'd got from the Brontë. Billy had been delighted when his brother had insisted on sharing it with him, despite her protests.

'Leave that, Mam. Chrissie and I will clear away and wash up. You're worn out,' Grace instructed while Chrissie sighed and reluctantly got to her feet.

'You can tell them you're giving in your notice, Mam. I'm home now, I'll get my job back. No more going out scrubbing floors,' Georgie said firmly. He'd been quietly shocked at how thin and tired his mother looked – she'd aged so much. Now that he was finally back home the loss of his father and elder brother had hit him forcefully, as had the realisation that now he was the head of the household and must shoulder all the added responsibilities that position brought. He bent and kissed her cheek. 'I won't be long. You go on up to bed and get a good night's sleep.'

Sadie patted his arm and smiled. 'I will, son. For the first time in years I'll sleep well. I've nothing to worry about now.'

* * *

Georgie put his arm around Mags's shoulder as they walked down towards Walton Lane. 'I've finally got you to myself.'

She leaned her head against him. 'I've missed you so much, Georgie. I'm so happy you're home. Your mam isn't the only one who's been worried sick.'

'You're all I ever thought about, Mags – when there was time to think, that is.'

'Was it . . . was it very bad?' she asked hesitantly.

He nodded. He would never tell her of the sights he'd seen; like so many others he would always refuse to be drawn on his experiences. If his da or Harold had been alive then maybe he would have opened up to them but Billy was too young and there were things that women should never be told. 'It's all over now, Mags. I want to put it behind me. I want to look forward to the future and I want my future to be with you. I'd like to ask your da for his permission to marry you – if you'll have me?'

Mags stopped and threw her arms around him. 'Oh, of course I'll have you! I'll be delighted! I love you so much, Georgie! I've never even looked at anyone else, you know that!'

He kissed her for a long time and when he finally drew away he felt a sense of peace and happiness fill him. It was for her that he'd endured the hardships and the horror but it had been worth it. They'd be happy from now on; he could put the war behind him. The days ahead were days of hope for them all.

Mr and Mrs Draper greeted him with cries of delight.

'Welcome home, lad! If you'd come a bit earlier I'd have taken you off to the pub for a drink,' Mr Draper said, shaking his hand warmly.

'Yer would not! There's plenty of time for all that, he's only just got home and it's our Mags he wants to spend time with, not you and yer old cronies,' Ethel Draper intervened but she was smiling.

'I do want to spend time with Mags, a lot of time. In fact I want to spend my life with her,' Georgie announced, feeling a little knot of anxiety in his stomach, despite the fact that he knew both her parents liked him.

'Am I hearing you right, lad?' Mags's father asked, thinking it was a good job his wife's sister Flo and her kids had all gone to bed.

'You are indeed. I want to marry her. I came to ask you for her hand.'

Ted Draper beamed at Georgie. 'You can have it and with pleasure, lad, and the rest of her as well!'

'Well, that's a nice way to answer the lad, Ted Draper, I must say, and him doing it all formal and proper, like! But I'm delighted. Our Mags thinks the world of yer, don't yer, luv?'

Mags nodded, blushing shyly before being enveloped in a bear hug by her mother.

'Now, the pair of you sit down while I see if I can find a drop of something halfway decent for us to drink to celebrate,' Ethel instructed.

'I knew we should have gone to the pub,' Mags's father muttered, winking at his future son-in-law.

'I heard that, Ted Draper, and thank God they're shut. There's a bit of port left in this bottle, that will have to do.'

Ted grimaced but Georgie grinned at him. He wouldn't have minded drinking tap water to celebrate.

Georgie was surprised to find that Grace was still up when he got home. 'Grace, it's really late! You'll not get up in time for work.'

She smiled. 'I know but I wanted to see you, talk to you, without Mam and Billy and Chrissie listening.' She was very fond of him and anxious for his happiness. 'Mags is such a thoroughly nice girl and she's missed you terribly. She's never looked at anyone else and I really like her and—'

He laughed. 'Stop fishing, Grace! Mags and I are getting engaged, we're announcing it at the party on Friday. It's all above board: I asked her da's permission tonight.'

Grace threw her arms around him. 'Oh, I'm so glad for you both! And I know Mam will be, she likes Mags too.'

Georgie became serious. 'I know she does. Mam isn't looking very well, Grace. I didn't say anything to her but she's so pale and thin.'

Grace bit her lip. 'I know. It's been hard for her, Georgie. I've done my best to help out but I can't take away the constant worry, the shock and grief over Harold and Da, the sheer grind of just getting through another day. Look around you, look how shabby everything is. We've been doing without and making do for so long and it wears you down. I know we shouldn't complain, we've not had to go and fight and we didn't get bombed out but it hasn't been easy either.'

He took her hand. 'I know, Gracie, but at least she can give up going out to work now and take things a bit easier. We'll all get back on our feet soon and maybe I could give the place a fresh coat of paint. That might cheer her up.'

'I'm sure it will, if you can get any paint, that is. Will you and Mags live here after you're married? The housing situation is desperate, there's three and four families having to share a house.'

Georgie shrugged. 'I suppose so, there's no room at the Drapers' house. They've got her Aunty Flo and her family living with them.' He grinned at her. 'No sign of you getting yourself a feller then and taking yourself off, or our Chrissie?'

Grace grinned back. 'No, but our Chrissie says she's determined to enjoy life now so you don't know whom she'll meet.' She laughed. 'She got absolutely legless on VE night! Kate and I had to put her to bed and she kept singing her head off.'

Georgie frowned. 'I don't suppose you can blame her for that but she needn't think she's making a habit of it. I intend to keep my eye on her now Da's not here to do it. Mam's had enough to worry about.' He sighed heavily. 'It wasn't until I actually got in the house, Grace, that I realised what not having Da or Harold here meant. It means I've got to take their place. I've got to shoulder the responsibility of looking after everyone and it's not something I've really given much thought to.'

Grace nodded. 'I hope it won't be too difficult for you. It will be good to have a man in the house again, someone to take charge of things.' You couldn't call Billy a man, he was still only a kid, she thought. Unlike Georgie. He'd only been home a short time but she could see that he had really grown up.

There hadn't been time to go and buy a ring so Mags's mam had lent her hers. It was a bit big but Mags bound rows of sewing thread around it so it wouldn't slip off. The party was again being held in the street and Georgie had announced the engagement after Mr Bradshaw had made a formal speech on behalf of all the neighbours, welcoming the lads home and praising them for their courage. This latter praise had been met with some rather embarrassed shuffling of feet by those to whom it was directed and there were a few mutters about 'just doing their duty for King and Country'.

Georgie's news was met with a huge cheer and much backslapping and hand-shaking. Mags was hugged and kissed by all the girls and women and Sadie looked on as pleased as punch.

Then the party really got under way. Plates of sandwiches, sausage rolls and sliced-up meat pies were brought out and laid on the tables that had been set end to end down the middle of the street, each covered with either a cloth or a clean bed sheet. Plates of fairy cakes and scones and various coloured jellies in assorted bowls followed these. All the younger kids and some of the adults wore paper party hats painstakingly made from old newspaper painted over. The Bradshaws' piano had again been manhandled into the street and the generous licensee of the Brontë had once more provided the beer. Polly Nelson had produced a bottle of port and a bottle of dry sherry, obtained from Charlie Dawson, via the docks, and had cast a withering look at both Chrissie and her own daughter Ellie.

'These are for those who won't go making pigs of themselves!' she remarked while Ellie looked pained and Chrissie grimaced, vowing to stick to soft drinks. Chrissie had received many compliments on her new dress and she fully intended to show it off to best advantage during the dancing. Of course she knew all the lads who had arrived home, she'd grown up with them, but she had secretly hoped they might have invited a few friends they'd been in the Army with. To her chagrin there were no strange faces, no one new or interesting at all, and she soon began to think that the whole affair was a bit of a disappointment.

Grace and Kate Nelson were leaning on the top of the piano as Mrs Bradshaw launched into her repertoire and Georgie led Mags out to start the dancing.

'You made a good job of that dress for our Chrissie, Kate,' Grace remarked, catching sight of her sister.

Kate rolled her eyes expressively. 'I hope to God she never asks me to make her another one! The fuss and performance! She doesn't look very happy about having to help your mam clear away the dishes.'

Grace nodded her agreement. 'It won't hurt her, she'll have plenty of time to enjoy herself and it really is Georgie and Mags's night, and the other lads too, of course.'

'Will he buy her a ring of her own? She keeps telling everyone she's borrowed her mam's.'

'He's taking her to town tomorrow to choose one.'

A lot of the neighbours were now dancing but Kate frowned as she saw Chrissie appear in the doorway of the Devlins' house. 'What's up with your Chrissie now?'

Grace looked confused as Chrissie was waving frantically. 'I'd better go over and see what's wrong with her.'

She was concerned to see that Chrissie was pale and her eyes were wide with fright. 'What's wrong? What's happened?'

'It's Mam! I was bringing the last of the plates in and I nearly fell over her! Oh, God! She's just lying on the floor in the kitchen, Grace! She looks awful!'

Grace rushed past her and into the kitchen and dropped to her knees beside the prostrate form of her mother. 'Mam! Mam, what's wrong?' She lifted Sadie's head gently on to her lap. 'Go and find Polly Nelson and get our Georgie! Go on, Chrissie! Hurry!'

Chrissie fled and Grace felt for a pulse. She breathed a sigh of relief at feeling the faint movement beneath her fingers.

Polly bustled into the kitchen. 'I told her she's been doing too much! Lift her up a bit, Grace, while I get this cushion under her head. She's collapsed with exhaustion, I bet. She's been on her feet since first light.'

Georgie and Mags appeared, both looking worried and anxious. 'Will I go for a doctor? How bad is she?' Georgie queried.

To Grace's intense relief Sadie's eyelids fluttered open and she raised a hand weakly to her head.

'Lie still, Sadie, luv. You passed out and it's no wonder. You're going to have to rest and take things easier,' Polly instructed firmly.

Grace helped her mother into a sitting position. 'You must have fainted, Mam. Thank God you didn't hit your head on anything. Chrissie, go up and turn down the bed.'

'There's no need for that. I'm fine now,' Sadie said rather shakily. She'd never fainted in her entire life but she didn't feel well at all. She was dizzy and sick and bone weary.

'No you're not, Mam! Our Grace and Polly will help you upstairs, you're to rest. It's all been too much for you and from now on our Chrissie and Billy can do more to help. I know Grace does her share and I'm home now to do my bit.' Georgie's voice was firm; he would brook no argument.

Slowly Sadie got to her feet and nodded. He'd sounded so like Tom that she felt a sense of relief wash over her. She *could* rest now; Georgie was home to take charge of things.

Chapter Five

MUCH TO EVERYONE'S RELIEF, with rest Sadie recovered and as the weeks of summer passed into autumn and then winter, life settled down into an easier routine. Mags often came round to the house in Royal Street as plans for the wedding were made. Georgie had gone back to work for the Post Office and they were both saving hard, for as Mags had said they couldn't expect Sadie to bear any of the cost, she just didn't have the money to spare. They had set a date for the following spring when they both hoped things would be easier to obtain.

Chrissie was becoming more and more dispirited with both her job and the fact that life did not seem to be improving at all. Everything was still dull and drab, there were the same shortages, rationing and queues, and Georgie insisted that she do more in the house and even take her turn at queuing, something her mam had never demanded of her. In fact there had been a few arguments over it, arguments in which Grace had always been the peacemaker. The worst and most recent one had occurred when Chrissie had come home from work bitterly disappointed and annoyed. The first shipment of nylon stockings had come in and she had been certain that she'd be able to procure a pair. All summer she'd had to resort to painting her legs with watered-down gravy browning and then draw a seam up the back with pencil as nearly everyone else had to do. She'd gone on and on about the new stockings and had the money safely tucked in a handkerchief in the top drawer of the chest in the bedroom. The news had quickly got around and that morning there had been a huge queue outside the shop that had stretched halfway down London Road. They had sold out in an hour for everyone had had sufficient coupons hoarded. Even though supplies had been restricted to one pair per customer there were many women who'd been disappointed and there had been none left for the staff.

'It's not fair! It's just not fair! I really wanted a pair to go to this wedding of Eileen Kilroy's. We're the ones who slave away all day and we get *nothing*!' she'd raged, flinging herself down in a chair in the kitchen.

'You didn't expect they'd keep it quiet, did you? Half the women in the city knew they were on their way and you know what it's like when *anything* new comes in,' Grace reminded her. She herself had had no expectations of getting the time off to go and queue. 'There'll be more in soon, I'm sure.'

'And we'll have no chance of getting them either! Oh, I'm sick of that place and that snooty Miss Perkins, she's always moaning and nagging at me! She says I don't pull my weight, that I've no "initiative", whatever that is!'

Georgie had looked up from the *Echo* he was reading. 'You'd better pull your socks up then, Chrissie, or you'll be getting the sack and there's plenty of girls who'd be more than willing to take your place.'

Chrissie had glared at him. He was getting far too big for his boots these days, she thought. He was only five years older than her. 'I don't care!' she'd snapped back.

'Well, I do! Mam needs your bit of a wage and don't you go upsetting her with your tantrums. A right song and dance over a pair of flaming stockings! You don't hear Mags carrying on about such trivial things.'

Chrissie had lost her temper for she suspected that Mags often made unfavourable comments about her to Georgie. 'Oh, no! She's a walking saint, isn't she? St flaming Mags! She can do no wrong!'

'That's enough of that! I won't have you talking about Mags like that!' Georgie had yelled at her.

'What's all the shouting about? What's going on now?' Sadie had demanded, coming into the kitchen with an armful of washing she'd just taken off the line in the back yard.

'Nothing much, Mam. Chrissie is upset that she wasn't able to get a pair of those stockings. They all sold out in an hour,' Grace had informed her mother, hastily shooting warning glances at both her brother and sister.

Sadie had shaken her head but tutted sympathetically. 'Well, they were always going to, luv, but I don't see the point of getting all het up about it. Now, give me a hand to fold these things. I'll put them on the rack to finish them off and I'll iron them tomorrow.'

It was Grace who'd stood up to help; Chrissie had continued to glare at her brother.

Georgie had returned to his newspaper. 'Put that pan on the stove, Chrissie, and make a start on the supper. Mam's been busy all afternoon.'

'And I don't suppose *I* have? Put it on yourself!' Chrissie had cried and had flounced from the room.

Sadie had stared after her in astonishment. 'What's got into her?'

'Oh, she's tired and disappointed, Mam. Take no notice, I'll have a word with her,' Grace had promised.

She had tried to talk to Chrissie later that evening but Chrissie had been tearful and uncommunicative and Grace had eventually given up. She hadn't known that Chrissie wasn't happy in her job but she was fully aware that Chrissie seemed to be disappointed with everything these days. Maybe she was just hoping for too much, hoping that things would change overnight and Grace at least was aware that that wasn't going to happen. And she conceded that Georgie could be high-handed and moody at times but she put his moods down to his experiences over the last few years. He was finding it difficult to adjust, as were many men. She had also begun to wonder if Chrissie was a bit jealous of Mags. She'd sighed. She supposed all families fought and argued at times.

She herself was quite contented at work and at home. She sometimes went out with Kate from next door when they could afford it. They went to the Astoria Cinema, which was near enough to walk to, and occasionally they went to a dance, neither of them complaining too much that they had to wear the things they'd had for months, even years. Kate was quite good at altering things, adding a lace trim here, a couple of rows of braid there, a bit of velvet on a collar, and she was fortunate in being able to bring odd bits of trimming home from work. Sometimes Grace too managed to get bits of leftover material that could be used to brighten up their clothes although they were only made of cotton. It was only Chrissie who continually complained that she had nothing new and stylish to wear.

Both Grace and Chrissie had been invited to Eileen Kilroy's wedding. It was the talk of the neighbourhood for Eileen's fiancé was an only son who came from a family who were not short of money, and no expense seemed to have been spared. It was Mags who had got them the invitations.

'I was chatting to Eileen about you and she said why don't you come too? Come along with us, Grace, you'll enjoy yourself.'

Grace had looked thoughtful. 'Thanks, I'd like to but . . .'

'But what?' Mags had probed.

'I was wondering what our Chrissie will say, you know what she's like about enjoying herself and she hates to be left out.'

Mags had frowned. Chrissie was developing into a spoiled little madam who always wanted to be the centre of attention. But then she sighed for she realised that Grace would be loath to come without her. 'I don't suppose Eileen will mind if she comes too. It's only to the evening do.'

'We didn't expect to be invited to the church or the wedding breakfast,' Grace had reminded her.

'There's enough going to that too! But I'm really looking forward to the evening bit; I heard there's going to be a really good spread. His da seems to be able to lay his hands on all kinds of things. God knows where from,' she'd said enviously. Then she'd shrugged. 'Still, I suppose if you've got plenty of money . . .'

Grace had nodded. The fiancé's father was one of the largest coal merchants in the area.

The news had cheered Chrissie up at first and she had plagued Mags wanting to know every single detail of the arrangements, but then she had become despondent, complaining she had nothing decent to wear.

'Wear your lilac-and-white dress, that looks lovely on you,' Grace had advised.

'It's a summer dress and now it's winter. I'll freeze. I'd like a nice crêpe-de-Chine or a fine wool bouclé.'

'Wouldn't we all!' Sadie had commented cuttingly. 'You'll have to make do with that dress, it's in the parochial hall when all's said and done, not out in the street! You'll be plenty warm enough.'

But Chrissie hadn't been satisfied and had trawled the shops in her spare time; something neither Grace nor Mags had the time, energy or inclination to do. Finally she had managed to find a sage-green needle-cord dress that was a 'second' and for which she had enough coupons. It was very plain with no trimmings at all and the skirt was the much-despised wartime short length. Still, she intended to persuade Kate to trim it for her and she'd put her hair up to show off the pearlized clip-on earrings she'd borrow from Ellie Nelson. She would have liked new shoes but she'd have to make do with her black courts. She would also have liked a pair of nylon stockings. The thought of all those pairs sold in an hour still rankled deeply.

'I don't know why you're getting into such a state about your clothes, Chrissie,' Grace commented as they both dressed for the big event.

Chrissie was fiddling with her hair, which she had piled up on the top of her head and fixed with pins; she was pulling a few curls down over her forehead. 'We don't want to go looking a mess, do we?'

Grace had left her hair loose and Mags had lent her a white blouse with a lace collar to wear with her good black-and-white dogtooth-check skirt. 'We don't look a mess. I think we both look very smart.'

Chrissie glanced at her sister and thought that Grace looked rather plain and ordinary in the skirt and blouse but she didn't say so. She went out more than Grace, mainly with Ellie Nelson and a few other girls from the street, but she hadn't met anyone she liked yet, although there were hundreds of servicemen returning now.

'Mags was saying that she's sure Eileen will look *gorgeous*. The dress has been made in Bold Street.'

'I bet Mags will be jealous, you can be sure she won't have a dress like that.'

Grace stared at her sister; sometimes she didn't understand Chrissie. 'Why do you say that? I don't think Mags has a jealous bone in her body. She's delighted for Eileen; we both are.'

Chrissie shrugged. 'I'd be dead jealous if I was engaged and had to listen to every single detail of someone else's *fabulous* wedding dress.'

'She didn't say it was fabulous,' Grace pointed out.

'It's bound to be. Oh, come on, let's go and see for ourselves. Is our Georgie coming down with us?'

Grace nodded. 'He's waiting downstairs. We're picking Mags up on the way.'

The parochial hall, which was the venue for the evening reception, was further down Westminster Road towards the County Road end and Georgie and Mags walked on ahead, followed by Grace and Chrissie. When they arrived they handed their coats into the small cloakroom and received a ticket in exchange.

Grace looked around. A big effort had been made to decorate the place with pink and white crêpe-paper flowers and chains and there were balloons hanging from the ceiling lights. Small tables covered with white cloths had been set around the perimeter of the room, which was packed with people.

'I can't see the bride!' Chrissie commented, peering into the throng.

'Look, she's over there. Oh, doesn't she look gorgeous?' Mags cried as the crowd parted slightly and the new Mrs Bateson came towards them, smiling.

'Eileen, you look like a princess! Congratulations!' Mags caught the girl's hands, thinking she looked radiant. She'd known Eileen ever since she'd come over from Ireland to do her training at Walton Hospital. She'd found lodgings with one of the neighbours and as she was cheerful and outgoing they'd soon become friends. Eileen was tall and slim with thick auburn hair, green eyes and the alabaster skin so characteristic of her Celtic origins. She had come from a small farm in the Irish midlands and was the next to youngest in a large family. Her parents were dead and all her older brothers and sisters had emigrated to America and Australia.

Eileen laughed. 'Thanks, Mags, but sure I think the "princess" is a bit over the top! I'm delighted with the dress just the same, so I am.'

Chrissie stared open-mouthed as Georgie and then Grace congratulated the girl. Eileen did look *gorgeous*. She'd only seen her once or twice before and then she'd been in her nurse's uniform, her hair scraped back into a bun beneath the starched cap. Now she was dressed in yards and yards of gleaming white satin, trimmed with ribbon and lace. Eileen's thick auburn hair now fell in a cascade of curls around her shoulders, over which was a long veil attached to a small Juliet cap. She looked like an illustration of a princess in a child's storybook.

'So, where's the lucky feller?' Georgie asked and Eileen linked both Mags and himself and propelled them towards her new husband.

Grace directed Chrissie towards a table where a couple of girls about their own age were sitting and asked if they could join them.

'Sit yourselves down. We're just taking in all the fashions. Where did all his relations get those frocks and hats?' one girl wondered enviously.

Grace followed her gaze and was astonished to see a group of women of various ages all dressed in very fancy floral dresses with matching hats. 'Maybe they've had them for years and were saving them for an occasion like this,' she suggested.

'I did hear that one of his sisters married a Yank and went to live in America. Maybe she sent them over,' her companion surmised. 'You certainly can't get stuff like that here. They look very modern and sort of different, if you know what I mean.'

Grace nodded. 'I've never seen material like that before and the skirts are much longer, so you could be right. They look very stylish – but not as glorious as Eileen's dress.'

'I couldn't believe it was her! *Sister Kilroy* with her hair all flowing around her shoulders! We work with her at Walton Hospital. I'm June and this is Iris.'

Grace smiled. 'I'm Grace and this is my sister Chrissie. Mags Draper and our Georgie are engaged, getting married next spring. Maybe by then Mags might be able to get a decent wedding dress.'

Iris nodded. 'Surely to God things will be better next year. It's rumoured that there's to be a great buffet later on. Apparently all kinds of food has been sent over from Ireland.'

Grace became engrossed in conversation with the two nurses and Chrissie sat looking around. Even though her dress was new she felt it was very plain beside the outfits of the bridal party. The George Davies Quartet who were providing the music struck up and she caught a glimpse of Georgie and Mags amongst the dancing couples. It would be just her luck to sit here all night with Grace and the two nurses and be bored stiff.

Eventually, Georgie came over to them with two glasses of port and lemon as Mags had gone to sit with her mam and some neighbours.

Grace introduced them. 'Georgie, this is June and this is Iris. They're nurses who work with Eileen. This is my brother, Georgie.'

'Sorry, girls, I only got drinks for these two. I'll go back and fetch you something.'

Iris looked at him hopefully. 'I wouldn't mind a gin and tonic, it's ages since I had one.'

June grimaced. 'Just a lemonade for me, I'm on duty at seven in the morning.'

'Mags will be over in a bit,' Georgie promised.

'Oh, tell her we're all right! We're all getting on famously.' Grace didn't want to monopolise either Mags or Georgie.

Chrissie sipped her drink and looked around until her gaze was caught and held by a tall, well-built young man with the same colour hair as Eileen and grey-green eyes. Chrissie felt a little shiver of excitement run through her as he smiled at her. He was quite handsome. This looked promising.

Chapter Six

❦

'OH, I SAY, HE'S A handsome-looking lad!' Iris commented as the young man made his way towards their table.

'He is and he looks nice,' Grace agreed. He seemed to stand out from the crowd of men and boys with his colouring and his easy carefree manner. His clothes looked different too. His jacket was of soft grey tweed and his shirt cream linen: both looked new.

'He must be Eileen's youngest brother, Pat. I heard he came over especially. All the rest of them are in America or Australia and obviously couldn't make it,' June informed them. 'I think it's you he's interested in, Chrissie,' she added in a whisper.

Chrissie felt the shiver of excitement run through her again. He was very handsome and self-confident and it was obvious that he only had eyes for herself.

He had reached the table and he smiled at them all. 'Good evening, ladies.' Then he turned his attention to Chrissie. 'Do you think I could have the pleasure of this dance, miss?'

Grace nudged her sister and Chrissie recovered her composure.

'Yes, I'd like that. And my name's Chrissie. Chrissie Devlin.'

As he took her hand and guided her on to the floor she glanced from beneath her eyelashes at him. He was by far the best-looking man in the room and she was aware of the envious glances cast in her direction by many of the other girls. She was delighted that he'd chosen her.

'Would you be a friend or a relation of the bridegroom for if you were related to me I'd have known it?' he asked, smiling down at her. She was a very pretty girl and not over-dressed as many of the Bateson clan seemed to be.

'Neither. I don't know either the bride or groom very well. My future sister-in-law is a friend of Eileen's and Eileen was kind enough to invite me as well. Are you her brother?'

'I am so. Patrick Kilroy, usually called just Pat. I'm the youngest in the family. Our parents died years ago and everyone else took the emigrant ship; I stayed on to help Uncle Conor with the farm of land that's belonging to us.'

He was holding her firmly around the waist and Chrissie felt a little light-headed as she smiled up at him. 'Is this your first time in Liverpool?'

He laughed, revealing white, even teeth. 'Sure, 'tis my first time anywhere and wasn't that crossing so desperate rough I thought we'd surely sink! I wasn't sure I would be able to come but Uncle Con said I couldn't miss this wedding for who else was there to give her away? She looks grand, so she does, and he's a decent-enough lad.'

Chrissie smiled. 'She does look "grand" and she's done well for herself. They're not short of money and he'll get the business eventually. Not that she doesn't deserve it. It's not easy being a nurse,' she added quickly for she didn't want him to think she was being mercenary or critical of his sister. Never in a million years could she envisage herself entering that profession, having to deal with wounds and blood and all kinds of other equally horrible and more base, disgusting things.

He nodded. 'Ah, wasn't she always the sensible one? And what do you work at, Chrissie?'

'Oh, nothing very exciting. During the war I worked in munitions – everyone did – but now I work in a shop. A department store,' she corrected herself, hoping it sounded a bit more interesting. 'In the ladies' fashion department,' she added, thinking it sounded more superior to the dress department.

He smiled at her again. 'Ah, couldn't I have guessed that? Aren't you the most stylish girl here?'

Chrissie blushed prettily and her heart beat a little faster. He thought she looked better than everyone else. She laughed a little archly. 'Oh, this is nothing special.' Lightly she dismissed the hours of trailing around the shops and the fear that she would have nothing new to wear. 'It's so very hard to get anything decent, the country is still in a terrible state.'

He looked serious. 'I saw that when I arrived on the ferry. Sure, half this fine city is in ruins from the bombs. We heard all about it but thanks be to God the Emergency is over now.'

Chrissie frowned. 'You wouldn't think so sometimes. We still have rationing and queues and lots of people haven't got a decent roof over their heads. But tell me, where do you live? Near Dublin?' She didn't want to sound gloomy or pessimistic and run the risk of him finding someone more cheerful.

'I do not. Why would anyone want to live near that place, isn't it a kip? No, I live down in the country where you can breathe fresh air and sleep soundly at night without all the noise of the traffic and the comings and goings.'

He danced with her for the next four dances and she began to like him more and more. He was amusing, attentive and disarmingly open with his compliments. At last it was Georgie who came over to split them up.

'You're getting talked about,' he informed her as they waltzed.

She was indignant. 'So? I'm doing nothing wrong! I'm free and so is he.' She had already ascertained that.

'I'm not saying you are doing anything wrong but don't make yourself too . . . available,' he warned.

She cast her eyes to the ceiling. 'I'm eighteen! And if you're going to carry on like this then you can go and get Grace up to dance, she's been asked a couple of times but mostly she's just been chatting to those two nurses. I don't want to listen to any of your lectures!' She wondered if Mags had had a hand in this.

'All right. I'm only thinking of you. You can be a bit naïve at times and now that Da's gone, I have to keep my eye out for you.'

Chrissie tossed her head. 'I'm not a complete fool! He's very nice and he's Eileen's brother and they own a farm, so he's bound to be respectable.'

Georgie let it go. He had heard from Mags that Pat Kilroy was returning to Ireland on the Monday night ferry.

'He looked very taken with you, Chrissie. He didn't want to let you go. He hasn't danced with anyone else,' June commented when she rejoined them and the buffet interval was announced.

Chrissie glared at her brother's disappearing back as he returned to Mags. 'He's a real gentleman, despite what some people think!'

Grace looked at her with mild amusement. Chrissie's cheeks were flushed and her eyes were bright and it wasn't just because she was annoyed with Georgie. No, she had obviously taken quite a liking to Pat Kilroy.

He danced with her again after the buffet interval and she was delighted when he asked if they could meet the following day.

'I'd love to see you, Pat. I can show you around the city, if you like?'

'Wouldn't that be grand. Are there any parks?' He was captivated with her. He'd never met anyone like her. In fact the whole experience of being away from home, travelling to another and very different country and meeting so many new people was almost intoxicating. He squeezed her hand.

'Plenty. Stanley Park is the nearest. It's got a Palm House, a boating lake, a bandstand and a bowling green and lots of open spaces as well. It might be a bit chilly though?'

'Well, maybe I could take you for some tea afterwards?' he suggested, wanting to show her that he could be generous.

She smiled up at him. 'If we can find anywhere open.'

'Ah, there'll be somewhere. We'll have a grand time. And now you're to promise me every dance – no going off with anyone else, not even your brother.'

'I won't, Pat. I don't want to be with anyone else,' she said a little shyly.

She said nothing to Georgie on the way home but

she did confide in Grace. 'I really like him, Grace. He's so different to all the other lads I know. He makes me feel special.'

'Don't go getting too fond of him, Chrissie, he isn't going to be here long.'

Chrissie sighed heavily. 'I know, more's the pity. I wish he was staying longer.' Then she had a thought. 'Maybe I could go and work in Ireland?'

Grace looked at her in astonishment. 'Are you mad? Can you see Mam letting you do that or our Georgie either? They'd say you had completely taken leave of your senses and so would I, to go chasing after someone you've only just met. And what would you do for a job? Where would you live?'

Chrissie had to see the sense in this. 'Oh, it was just a thought. I didn't really mean it. Don't you go saying anything to either of them about it.'

Grace was relieved; sometimes Chrissie said the most outlandish things. 'I won't but you'll have to tell Mam you're seeing him again. You don't usually go out on a Sunday afternoon, not at this time of year.'

Chrissie nodded but she wasn't worried. She could easily get round Mam and hopefully Georgie would be going to Mags's house after dinner tomorrow.

Sadie was relieved that she would get a bit of peace and quiet that Sunday afternoon. Grace always helped her to wash up after the dinner and with both Georgie and Chrissie out she could possibly have a little nap. Billy was always off somewhere with Tommy Milligan. Grace had assured her that this Pat Kilroy was a decent-enough lad.

Chrissie took extra care with her appearance, brushing her hair until a cloud of shining curls framed her face, then she placed her navy blue beret over them at what she considered a jaunty angle. She had borrowed Grace's red wool jacket, which she wore over her navy skirt and a clean white blouse.

'You look very patriotic!' Sadie had remarked sleepily when she'd come downstairs so she'd gone straight back up and changed the blouse for a navy blue jumper. She didn't want to look like a walking Union flag, she thought. At least the red jacket brightened the outfit up.

He was waiting on the corner of Fountains Road and Walton Lane leaning against the wall of a house, his hands thrust into his jacket pockets. He grinned delightedly as he caught sight of her. He hadn't been able to stop thinking about her.

'Don't you look very smart and elegant and you're early!' He tucked her arm through his.

'Mam always insists we're punctual. She says it's rude to be late, unless you can't possibly help it.' She didn't say that she'd been ready half an hour early. 'It's not far to walk.'

'So I heard and Herself, Mrs Grayson that I'm staying with, tells me we should be able to get a cup of tea at a little café just a piece from the park gates. She said they'd drop dead of shock if I took you into a pub and we'd both be shown the door.'

'Oh, I couldn't go into a pub! I'm only eighteen and besides . . . I really don't drink.'

He nodded. He'd wondered if women were allowed in pubs over here at all. No decent woman would be seen in a pub back home. He'd wanted to give her a little treat and had heard that it was very difficult to find somewhere for afternoon tea with all the shortages. Back home, although certain things were still in short supply, tea and scones and butter and jam certainly were not.

Chrissie thought the park didn't look its best, even though it was a lovely bright December day and the morning's heavy frost had now melted away. The railings around the bandstand had long gone towards the war effort. The paint on the Palm House was peeling and as there had been no coal to spare to heat it for years most of the plants had been removed or had died. The trees were bare; their branches gaunt and black against the sky and the unswept leaves on the ground made the paths look untidy. It was just another example of how shabby everything was.

'It used to look really lovely,' she said wistfully. 'The bandstand had brightly painted railings and there were all kinds of exotic plants in the Palm House, but what with the war . . .'

'Ah, 'tis no matter. There're plenty of trees and open space. Sure, I could never get used to living all cramped together in those narrow streets.'

'No, I suppose you must find it odd and I have to admit I'm getting very depressed with it all.'

He looked down at her with increased interest. 'Are you really?'

Sincerity shone from her eyes as she nodded. 'It really is *so* depressing! After six long and really awful years I expected life to get better, but it isn't. Our Georgie was reading in the newspaper that Mr Attlee, who is the Prime Minister now, has said that goods produced for the home market will now have to go for export so there'll be less of everything and that food that was to be used for American forces will have to be given to us. Is it like this in Ireland?'

'It is not. Ah, sure, there's places in Dublin that are desperate and there was rationing but not in the country areas. In the country we have meat and plenty of fresh vegetables and fruit and butter, cream, cheese and eggs in plenty.'

They sat down on a wooden bench and Chrissie listened mesmerised as he described his home and what seemed an idyllic life in rural Ireland.

'Of course we're not a rich country, like you here,' he finished.

'We're far from rich! I'd say we're flat broke. We've had to take a huge loan from America. Does that sound like a rich country? I'd say you are better off in Ireland.' She was fascinated by his tales of home.

'You really think so?' He looked down into her eyes, his mind working quickly. She was an absolute delight and was finding life here depressing . . .

Chrissie nodded. Suddenly she felt very miserable.

'I have to go back on the ferry tomorrow night, Chrissie. Uncle Con can't spare me for longer. He's getting on a bit now but he's a grand man. Hard-working and God-fearing and he has strong political beliefs.'

Chrissie felt even more dejected at the thought that she'd never see him again. He wouldn't be here to make her laugh or take her out or compliment her on her looks. 'I . . . I wish you didn't have to go, Pat. I'll miss you.'

He put his arm around her and drew her closer. It was now or never. 'I've never met anyone like you, Chrissie, that I haven't. I wish . . . I wish I could take you back with me. I know you'd love it. Tullamore is a grand town. I could take you to dances or to one of the hotels for tea and wouldn't I be the envy of the place with someone as gorgeous as you on my arm? I . . . I'd like to spend the rest of my life with you, Chrissie.'

Chrissie gasped. She was enthralled. He must love her if he wanted to spend the rest of his life with her! How she would love to be seen with him at dances and at big hotels for tea. She was thinking of the Imperial and the Adelphi. And she was sure you could get lovely clothes in Ireland; Eileen had had that wonderful wedding dress. 'Oh, do you really mean that, Pat?' she breathed.

'I do so. I know we've only just met, Chrissie, but I

knew from the minute I set eyes on you that you were the one for me.'

'I felt that too.' Utterly carried away by his words, she really meant it. 'I wish . . . Oh, but . . . I hardly know you.'

'I know that but I've fallen in love with you, Chrissie, and I was hoping that it was the same for you,' he said softly before kissing her.

Her lips parted beneath his and a wave of what she could only describe as ecstatic happiness washed over her. She *did* love him. She *must* love him. This was how everyone said being in love felt. She pulled away and gazed into his eyes. 'I do love you, Pat, but Mam would never let me go back with you.'

He stroked her cheek. 'Sure to God, I wouldn't ask you to do anything . . . sinful, Chrissie! I'd want to marry you.'

Her heart was thumping against her ribs and she could hardly breathe. He wanted to marry her! Oh, wouldn't it be wonderful to go back with him? To a land where there had been no six years of war, no bombing, no death or destruction. Where everything was fresh and green and there were no shortages and she would have lovely clothes, be taken out and admired. 'Oh, Pat, what can we do?'

'I'll come back for you, Chrissie, I swear I will! I'll write and I'll get everything sorted out. I'll come back with you now and speak to your ma and your brother so they'll know I'm serious.'

Chrissie was swept along with his enthusiasm. 'When we've both had chance to explain everything, I'm sure they won't refuse. I don't want to stay here, I want to be with you!'

He held her and kissed her for a long time.

Chapter Seven

As they walked back to Royal Street hand in hand Chrissie felt that the whole purpose of her life had changed. She had sworn to seize every opportunity and now, instead of the disillusionment of the past months, there really was something new and exciting to look forward to. She had no doubts at all that Pat's powers of persuasion would overcome any misgivings her mother might have and Sadie was bound to like him.

Even though these feelings for Chrissie had swept over him so suddenly, Pat had no doubts about them. She was the woman for him. Yet he felt very apprehensive about facing her family. They knew nothing about him, he was a complete stranger – to her mother at least. He'd met her brother and sister only briefly but he intended to do everything in his power to win them over.

Sadie was dozing before the fire and Grace was reading an old copy of *Woman's Weekly* that Kate had given her when Chrissie and Pat arrived. Grace was startled to see Pat Kilroy follow her sister into the kitchen.

'This is a surprise,' she said, getting to her feet and gently nudging Sadie awake.

Chrissie could hardly contain her excitement. 'Mam, this is Pat. We . . . we've got something to tell you.'

Sadie was a little confused to be confronted by such a tall, handsome young man in her kitchen but quickly regained her composure. 'Well, sit down the pair of you and have a cup of tea. If you've been out in the park all afternoon you must be frozen.' She poked at the fire and added to it a small amount of coal from the brass scuttle on the hearth.

Grace rose to put the kettle on. She had guessed at once that Chrissie was up to something. She hadn't seen her sister so animated for quite a while.

Pat took a deep breath. He was no fool, he knew that this wasn't going to be easy; but he was certain too he could win Sadie over in the end. Now that he'd taken the bull by the horns and asked Chrissie to marry him, he couldn't bear to let a girl like her slip through his fingers.

'Mrs Devlin, ma'am, I know Chrissie and me haven't known each other very long at all but . . . but the truth of it is that it was love at first sight for both of us. I want to do the right thing, ma'am. I want to marry Chrissie. I'll make a good husband. I work hard, I don't drink or gamble and I'd provide for her. We have a farm of land and she'd be very comfortable and would want for nothing. I have to go back tomorrow night, I can't be spared for longer, but if you agree, I'll make all the arrangements and then I'll come back for Chrissie. It's just your permission that's needed, ma'am. I really do love her and I'll mind her well.' It had all come out in a rush and he wondered if he'd sounded like an eejit? Perhaps he should have taken it a bit slower.

Grace stood clutching the teapot to her chest, unable to believe her ears while Sadie just stared in dumbfounded silence at both Pat and Chrissie.

Grace recovered first. 'Chrissie, do you realise what you're doing? You only met him for the first time last night, you've only spent a few hours together! How can you both know that you want to spend the rest of your lives together?'

'I *do* know and I really *do* love him! I just can't bear the thought of him going back and leaving me here. I'll miss him so much!' Chrissie clung to Pat's arm as if to emphasise her words.

Sadie found her voice. 'You want to get *married* to someone you've only just met? Someone we don't know a thing about? You want to up stakes and go and live in another *country*? Chrissie, have you gone mad? No disrespect to you, lad, but you're a stranger, we know nothing about you at all.'

Pat could understand her concerns. 'I know that and I can understand your fears, ma'am, but I swear I'll take care of her and she'll want for nothing. Sure, you can ask my sister Eileen what sort of a lad I am and what kind of a place we come from.'

'You can, Mam! Eileen will tell you everything you want to know and you can trust her, can't she, Grace?' Chrissie interrupted, appealing to her sister.

Grace could only nod. This all sounded like sheer folly to her. Oh, he appeared to be a nice, genuine lad but it was all too sudden. Chrissie hardly knew him! Her sister was so naïve, impetuous and impatient, she wasn't surprised at her behaviour, but she also knew that Chrissie became easily disappointed if things didn't go her way. Grace was afraid that this conversation was going to end in a terrible row.

'Mam, please say you agree, please? Oh, it will just break my heart if I'm never to see him again. It *will*!' Chrissie pleaded.

Sadie didn't know what to say. She was seriously worried. Chrissie was so very young and impressionable and marriage was for ever, for better or worse. Sadie had to admit that she was quite impressed with this Pat Kilroy, what little she had seen of him, and it wasn't that she had any particular doubts about his sincerity. It was Chrissie that concerned her. Heavens, the child had never even had a serious boyfriend! And now she wanted to marry a stranger? 'I'll have to think about it, Chrissie, I really will. And I'll have to have a long talk with Eileen Bateson.'

'But, Mam, there's no time to *think*, he's leaving

tomorrow!' Chrissie cried, on the brink of tears.

'Mrs Devlin, if you give your permission, I'll buy her a ring tomorrow so you won't be doubting my commitment and then I'll telegraph a date when I'll come back for her. I really do love her and my intentions are honourable, I swear to God and all His Holy Saints that they are!' Pat exclaimed. He didn't want to leave Chrissie without getting this settled.

'Oh, Mam, *please*?' Chrissie begged. Oh, why was Mam being so difficult? She hadn't expected it to be this hard.

Sadie was weakening a little but hearing the back door open she breathed a sigh of relief. Georgie was home.

Georgie looked curiously around at the occupants of the kitchen. His mam looked worried, Grace looked concerned and Chrissie looked as if she was on the verge of tears. When he caught sight of Pat Kilroy he began to feel uneasy.

'What's going on? What's she been up to now and what's he doing here?' he demanded of his mother.

Pat stepped forward before Sadie could answer. 'I've come to ask your ma's permission to marry Chrissie. I love her and she loves me. Sure, I know it's very sudden but it was love at first sight for both of us. I've sworn I'll take good care of her and at least you'll be after knowing what kind of a family we are, your own fiancée being a good friend of Eileen's.'

Georgie shook his head in utter disbelief. 'Is this true, Mam?'

Sadie could only nod.

He turned back to Pat. 'Look, lad, I'm saying nothing against you or your family but you don't know each other. She's only eighteen, barely old enough to know her own mind and she's a bit on the frivolous side. She doesn't really think about things too deeply. Half the time she doesn't look any further than her nose. She gets an idea in her head and doesn't think about the consequences.'

Chrissie gave an outraged cry. 'I do know my own mind, Georgie Devlin! I *do* think about things, *serious* things that is, and I'm not frivolous! I love Pat, I really do! You should understand that, you love Mags and you're going to marry her!'

'Chrissie, I've known Mags for four years. I really *know* her. Mags waited for me for two years, she wrote me countless letters; all the time she knew there was a risk that I'd never come home but she was faithful to me. We've talked for hours about our hopes and dreams and our plans for the future. You two can't know anything about each other!'

'We'll learn, haven't we years ahead of us?' Pat pleaded.

Georgie shook his head and looked to Sadie for support. 'I think she's too young and it's all too sudden. Wait three years until she's twenty-one, lad, and won't need Mam's permission. Give her time to grow up. If you both truly love each other you won't mind waiting. You can get to know each other.'

'And how will we do that, with me in one country and her in another?' Pat asked quietly, disappointment clearly evident in his voice.

'Write to each other and Chrissie could pay a few visits, with Grace, of course. And you'll be more than welcome to visit us at any time. I like you, Pat, but give yourselves a chance. Marriage isn't a step to be taken lightly.'

Sadie had made her decision. 'I think Georgie's right, Pat. She's just too young for me to give my consent now. She does need time to grow up and it's not a decision to be made in a rush. Marriage is for life. You do need to get to know each other.'

Chrissie burst into tears and threw her arms around Pat. She hated them all! They were all determined to ruin her life. 'I don't want to wait for three years! I love you! Take me with you?' she begged.

He sighed as he tried to calm her for he was bitterly disappointed himself. 'I can't, Chrissie, not against your mam's wishes. But I'll wait for you, I promise.'

Chrissie sobbed harder, seeing her dream of a new and exciting life disappearing. 'You won't! You'll meet someone else and forget all about me!'

'Ah, Chrissie, how could I ever forget you?'

Grace glanced enquiringly at her mother; she did feel sorry for her sister. 'Pat, why don't you take Chrissie into the parlour for a little while? You deserve some privacy.'

Sadie nodded and Grace ushered them out. As she

opened the parlour door she laid a hand on his arm. 'I'm truly sorry, Pat, but I'm sure it's for the best in the long run.'

'Thanks, Grace. 'Twas thoughtful of you to suggest some time on our own,' he replied with sincerity.

'Oh, I hope I've done the right thing,' Sadie said, sitting down heavily as Grace returned.

Georgie ran a hand distractedly through his hair. 'You did, Mam. This marriage idea is just ridiculous. You know what she's like. She changes her mind like the wind. She's impatient, and she's just too young! I know she's been through six years of war but it doesn't seem to have steadied her down. One minute all she's interested in is buying clothes, dolling herself up and going out and enjoying herself, wanting to be the centre of attention. The next she wants to get married and go and live in Ireland! She has no idea what her life would be like or what would be expected of her. Let them wait until she's twenty-one when she'll have more sense.'

Grace felt she had to agree with him. It was utter madness on Chrissie's part, even though she declared she loved Pat Kilroy. But did Chrissie even know what love was? Was Pat just a passing fancy because he was a handsome stranger who had flattered her? And what about him? She wasn't sure how deep his feelings for Chrissie were. He'd never been outside Ireland in his life before, Chrissie was a very pretty girl and he was obviously entranced by her, but was that enough to build an entire future on? Only time would tell. Georgie and her mam were right to make them wait. 'I'll put the kettle on, Mam. We could all do with a cup of tea,' she said with resignation.

Pat had managed to calm Chrissie down a little. 'Aren't I disappointed and hurt too, Chrissie? I hate leaving you, so I do, but I'll write and I'll try and visit and you and Grace can come over.'

'But that won't be for ages, Pat, and I'll miss you so much! Oh, I hate it here, I do, and it will be even worse now without you!'

He kissed her gently. 'I know, alannah, I'll miss you too.'

She felt as though her heart was breaking. How could they do this to her? Force her to stay here for three interminably long years while her youth was slipping away? She hated her job and the way they had to live and the knowledge that this wouldn't improve in the very near future. The winter months stretched ahead of her, miserable and bleak, with nothing to look forward to. She loved him, she *knew* she did! She wanted to be with him now, not have to wait three long years. Well, she wouldn't stay here. She would die of boredom, frustration and heartache if she did. She would follow him. The more she thought about it, the more determined she became. She would save up enough money for her fare and then she'd go. She'd tell no one. No, she decided, not even Pat, in case he tried to talk her out of it. It would be a wonderful surprise for him when she arrived. Mam wouldn't travel all that way to drag her back and, besides, she'd be married by then.

As her determination strengthened she became calmer and they sat and talked for a while until at last, reluctantly, he had to leave.

Grace tried to comfort Chrissie later that night. Chrissie was refusing to speak to either Georgie or her mother and had gone upstairs and was lying on her bed.

Grace sat down beside her. 'Chrissie, I know you are really upset and miserable but try and see it from Mam's point of view. She's thinking about your happiness, she really is. She doesn't want you to rush into something you'll spend the rest of your life regretting and neither do I.'

'You've never been in love, Grace, so you don't know how I feel!' Chrissie replied sullenly.

Grace sighed. 'I know I don't but I can try to imagine. Chrissie, you are very young and you're always saying that you've never really "lived", because of the war years, and that now you just want to enjoy yourself.'

'But I *would* enjoy living in Ireland with Pat,' Chrissie replied stubbornly.

'I'm not saying you wouldn't but you would be a married woman, not a single girl and that would make a difference. You would be expected to keep house, to look after your husband, not be going off to dances and the like.'

'I know that but he said he would take me out and he promised I wouldn't want for anything! I'm so fed up here, Grace, and things aren't going to get any better for years – everyone says so.'

'They will get better, you're just being too impatient. Oh, try to look on the bright side? We can start to save up and maybe we could go over for a few days at Easter, that would be something to look forward to, wouldn't it?'

Chrissie nodded slowly. If they both started saving Mam wouldn't be suspicious. 'I'll start putting some money into the Post Office,' she agreed.

Grace smiled at her. 'That's it. The time will fly, just wait and see, and if we can get the material I'm sure Kate will make you a new outfit for the occasion. Did he leave you his address?'

'Yes and he left a phone number too, for emergencies. It's the local Post Office but apparently they're the ones with the nearest phone.'

'So you can write and tell him that you'll see him at Easter. It's only a few months away and January and February are usually so cold that it's not worthwhile going out – except for work – and Georgie and Mags aren't getting married until the beginning of May, so Easter is the perfect time,' Grace enthused, noting that thankfully Chrissie looked far less unhappy.

Chrissie nodded and Grace felt relieved. If Chrissie really did love him and hadn't changed her mind, then Easter would present the perfect opportunity for a visit and she could then report back to her mam what kind of a life Chrissie could expect as the wife of Pat Kilroy.

Chapter Eight

———••✦••———

OVER THE NEXT WEEKS both Grace and Mags made a special effort to bolster Chrissie's spirits.

'It's Georgie's first Christmas at home and I want it to be special. I hope it will cheer Chrissie up a bit too,' Grace had confided in Mags who had heartily agreed. They'd all put a great deal of effort into shopping for small gifts, making home-made decorations and trying to put a decent meal on the table, but Chrissie had remained despondent.

'I hate to see her miserable but I'm sure she'll get over it in time. Patience was never one of Chrissie's virtues,' Grace observed as they both walked up Royal Street one bitterly cold evening. Grace was on her way home from the corner shop and Mags was on her way to pay a visit to Sadie with a new tea cosy she'd made for her. She'd unpicked an old scarf and had washed the wool and knitted it up.

'I think she was just swept off her feet by him. You've got to admit he is a bit of a charmer,' Mags replied.

Grace nodded. 'I hope he's sincere and not just stringing her along, but he seemed genuine enough. And she's had a few letters from him already.'

Mags looked thoughtful. 'It was the best thing all round for your mam to make them wait.'

'Chrissie doesn't think so at all and three years is a long time at her age.'

'If everything goes well and they really do love each other then maybe your mam will let her get married sooner.' Mags was sceptical about this but she tried not to show it.

'She might. We've both opened a Post Office Savings account for the trip to Ireland at Easter and Mam is being helpful too. She said Chrissie could give her a couple of shillings less a week as long as she saves it. I'm going to ask Kate Nelson if she'll make Chrissie something to wear. She swore she'd never make her anything again after the last fuss and performance but it will cheer Chrissie up to have something nice for when she sees him again.'

'Well, if I see anything halfway decent in the way of material in Frost's or the Co-op on County Road I'll let you know and I don't mind giving her something towards the cost,' Mags promised.

Grace thought that was very generous of Mags,

'That's good of you, Mags, but you'll need all your savings for your own wedding.'

'I can spare a bit and, well, I feel sort of responsible for all this, Grace. If I hadn't asked Eileen if Chrissie could come to the wedding too, then she would never have met him. And Georgie says your mam doesn't need anything else to worry about, she still isn't looking well and I agree with him.'

'She's better than she was now she's given up that job and I don't think she's too worried about Chrissie now that all the drama is over. Even though she's far from happy, Chrissie isn't throwing tantrums or weeping and wailing all the time. She does seem to have calmed down and accepted things. I'm still a bit doubtful myself about it all but I hope Chrissie will be happy with him.'

Mags nodded. 'Well, it's done now. She did meet him and she says she's fallen in love with him and maybe it's true. Only time will tell. I hope too that she'll be happy, I really do.'

'She has his letters tied up with a piece of ribbon and I know she writes at least three times a week, although what she finds to put in them I don't know. All she does is go to work and sit around at home in the evening. There's nothing very exciting in that.'

Mags smiled at her. 'It's easy to see you've never written a love letter. It's amazing what you can find to tell someone, even things that to other people seem trivial and boring and not worth mentioning are interesting when you're in love.'

Grace smiled at her. 'I was forgetting you had plenty of practice.'

'At least Chrissie won't have her letters censored. Half the time it was difficult to know just what Georgie was saying because so many bits had been blanked out.'

Grace thought it must be awful to have your private correspondence read by total strangers. 'Well, there's no more of that, thank God. How are all your arrangements coming along?' Both she and Chrissie were to be bridesmaids and before the appearance of Pat Kilroy it had been one of the foremost topics of interest in Chrissie's life.

'Mam has started hoarding anything tinned she can get her hands on and my Aunty Flo says she knows a woman who's got some parachute silk which will make some lovely underwear. She says you've got to have something decent for under the dress and for the wedding night and all I've got is boring, serviceable cotton. I'm still hoping to find something that will make a proper wedding dress, but if I can't then Eileen says I can borrow hers.'

Grace nodded. She knew Mags really wanted a new dress of her own, not something borrowed. 'That's very generous of her.'

'It is.' Mags tried to keep the note of disappointment out of her voice for she was grateful to Eileen for the offer. She sighed. 'Well, at least by the time Chrissie comes to finally get married life should be almost back to normal. And what about you, Grace? Still no one on the horizon?'

Grace laughed. 'No one special. Oh, I get asked to dance often enough when I go out with Kate and I really don't want to end up the old maid in the family, but I'm not in a hurry.'

'You just don't go out enough, Grace. You should, you know. Try different places. Go over to Birkenhead or out to Bootle Town Hall, they have dances there sometimes.'

Grace pulled a face. 'I can hardly afford to be going out very often now what with saving up for this trip at Easter.'

Mags looked at her thoughtfully. 'Maybe you'll meet someone when you're over there.'

They had reached the house and Grace frowned. 'I'll have my work cut out chaperoning Chrissie and don't for goodness' sake go saying anything like that in front of Mam. She won't want the pair of us deserting her!'

'You have to think of yourself, Grace. Georgie and I will be here to look after her and keep young Billy under control. You can't live your life always putting others first.'

Grace sighed. She knew Mags was right but she seriously didn't think she would meet her Mr Right on a quick trip across the Irish Sea – nor was that the purpose of her visit.

* * *

Once Chrissie had made up her mind to 'follow her destiny' as she romantically called her plan, she had to be careful about her demeanour – at least at home. She was supposed to be miserable and heartbroken and pining for Pat. In reality she was missing him and she waited eagerly for his letters and read them over and over. Sometimes she longed to write and tell him of her decision but always she told herself it had to be a surprise. What if he took it upon himself to inform her mam? He was very honourable about such things. No, she couldn't take that chance. She couldn't be separated from him for three years. She had worked out that by the end of February she would have enough money for her fare with a bit left over for additional expenses. In her lunch break she had taken a trip to the offices of the British and Irish Steamship Company and the clerk had been very helpful.

'Will you be requiring a cabin, miss? The weather can be bad at this time of year and it's far more comfortable in a cabin than crowded into the public saloon with everyone else. You don't look the sort of girl who should be sitting up all night.'

She had smiled at him. 'And how much extra would that cost me?'

'Five shillings, seeing as you're only travelling one way.'

Her smile had faded. She wanted to do some shopping in Dublin and she would need her money. 'I'm afraid it's a bit too expensive. You see, I'm going over to get married, so I'll need every penny,' she'd confided.

'He's a very lucky feller, if I might say so, miss. Will you be living in Dublin?'

'No, it's somewhere in the country. Near a town called Tullamore in County Offaly.'

He shook his head. 'Can't say I've heard of the place but you're bound to be able to get a train there or is your fiancé going to come to Dublin to meet you off the ferry?'

'We haven't sorted that out yet but I'll probably get a train.'

'Most of them go from Kingsbridge Station or Heuston Station as they call it these days, so I've heard. You ask for directions when you get to Dublin.'

She'd taken the small printed list of sailing times and fares that he'd given her and tucked it carefully into the zip pocket of her bag.

What was occupying her now was how to get her clothes out of the house without arousing suspicion. Of course she wasn't going to take everything she owned, most of her stuff was old and tired-looking, but she'd need to take a few things. She was sure there would be a much better choice of apparel in the Dublin shops. She wanted to look her very best when she arrived to surprise him. In the meantime she needed somewhere to hide the small case she'd bought in a second-hand shop. At length she decided to risk leaving it in a dark corner of the stockroom at work; she had covered it with a piece of heavy felt so it wouldn't be easily spotted. Now she could take things out of the house, item by item, without raising her mam's suspicions. There was absolutely nowhere she could hide a case at home without the risk of it being discovered for Mam and Grace turned the whole place upside down every week to give it a good clean. Polly Nelson did the same, so there was no use asking Ellie to hide it for her. Besides, Ellie couldn't keep a secret to save her life.

The ferry sailed at ten o'clock at night from the Pier Head and, weather permitting, it arrived in Dublin at seven the following morning. Once she had asked directions to the station she would find her way to the biggest General Post Office, where they were bound to have public telephones, and she would telephone the Post Office at Rahan and they would pass a message on to Pat. He would know what time the train would arrive in Tullamore and come to meet her. Every time she thought of how utterly delighted he would be to see her, her heart beat faster. He would sweep her up in his arms as she alighted from the train and then all this tedious waiting would be over. They would be married as soon as possible, for how could he prevaricate about such things as 'permission' when she'd made such sacrifices just to be with him? Of course Mam would be worried when she didn't come home and she wondered should she leave a note, but it might be found too soon and then Georgie would come storming after her. She really didn't want to cause her mam such anxiety but there was no help for it. She'd send a telegram as soon as she was married.

She would have liked a new outfit as Grace had suggested. Grace had even cajoled Kate into agreeing to make it, but it couldn't be helped; she cheered herself up with the thought that her savings might stretch to something stylish in Dublin. One of the girls she worked with who had relations in Dublin had told her there was a big department store there called Cleary's where the prices weren't too expensive. There were two other smart shops, Brown Thomas and Switzer's, but they would definitely be beyond her pocket.

It was very hard not to reveal even a hint of her plans in her letters to Pat. She wrote that she was saving hard and was counting the days to Easter; that she loved him and missed him dreadfully; that life was so dull without him. But as she posted each letter she hugged to herself the thought that long before Easter arrived she would be in his arms. By the time she had settled in with him on the farm spring would be on its way with the summer to look forward to and a whole new life ahead of her. Oh, she could hardly wait for the weeks to pass. Each day as she arrived for work she thought thankfully that it was one day less in the hated job but a little more money to save towards what she secretly thought of and optimistically called her 'trousseau'.

Chapter Nine

———◆———

At last the time had arrived and Chrissie could hardly contain her excitement. She was to sail on Friday night, which was the first of March: as the first official day of spring she thought that had to be a good omen. Even the weather seemed to be in her favour. It was unusually mild and as she sat on the tram on her way to work she caught glimpses of the parks and gardens where the first daffodils and purple crocuses were appearing and here and there a bright splash of yellow forsythia. She had withdrawn all her savings from the Post Office and they were safely in her purse in her handbag, which she never left out of her sight. The few things she was taking with her were packed in the little case in the stockroom, which she checked daily.

She had decided to travel in her working dress over

which she would wear a cardigan and her coat. She would take her coat off – the ferry was bound to be warm – for she didn't want to wear anything decent: it would get creased and grubby by the time she arrived. Whatever she bought she would change into. There would be a Ladies in this Cleary's department store. After she had paid her fare she would certainly have enough for a new skirt and blouse and maybe a hat. Of course she had no idea how much her train fare would be but she wouldn't worry too much about that and after she arrived in Tullamore she wouldn't have to worry about money at all. Pat had promised she would want for nothing.

She informed Sadie that she would be late home on Friday night, that she was going to the cinema in town with a friend, straight from work.

'Which friend is this then?' Sadie enquired.

'Avril, she's new. She only started last week but we get on like a house on fire,' Chrissie lied. She couldn't stand Avril Green who was very quiet and dull.

'I thought you were supposed to be saving up?' Sadie remarked. She wasn't really paying that much attention since she was making sandwiches for Georgie and Billy to take for their lunch and the small jar of Shipham's meat paste wasn't stretching as far as she had hoped it would.

'Oh, Mam! I haven't been out for almost two months! I'm not going to go spending a fortune, we're only going in the cheap seats. It's Celia Johnson and

Trevor Howard in *Brief Encounter* and everyone who's seen it says it's so romantic but sad! I'll be saving on my tram fare too. If I came home first I'd just have to go back into town and it would be a waste of money.'

'I would have thought it was cheaper to go to a local cinema.'

'I've been dying to see this film and besides, Avril lives on the other side of the city so there isn't a cinema that's local to us both,' Chrissie informed her. That at least was true.

Sadie nodded, scraping the bottom of the jar with the blade of the knife. She supposed Chrissie was right and indeed she hadn't been over the doorstep for weeks, except to go to work. It might do her good to get out a bit, instead of moping around of an evening. 'And you don't mind going in your working clothes?'

'No, but I intend to wear my good coat, not the old thing I usually wear for work.' She had already thought out the excuse for that circumstance in case her mam remarked on it.

'Well, you wear a headscarf or a turban. That's a real lazy wind that's blowing out there. It goes through you instead of going around you.'

Chrissie laughed. 'Honestly, Mam, you do have some odd sayings.'

'And see you're not too late coming home. I don't like you travelling on the tram on your own late at night.'

'I'm not a child, Mam! I'll be all right. There's always

a conductor on board and quite often a copper will stand on the platform for a few stops, just to keep his eye on things.'

Sadie nodded as she wrapped the sandwiches in greaseproof paper and put them on the dresser. Georgie would be through any minute now. There was always a rush in the morning to get Georgie and Billy off to work. Georgie was most particular about his appearance – she put it down to having been in the Army – but you had to virtually haul Billy out of bed. Thankfully both Grace and Chrissie were less trouble. They saw to themselves and neither of them took sandwiches. They got something at work. Only when they'd all gone did she make herself a cup of tea and sit down to drink it before starting the daily chores and then going out to do the shopping.

'Chrissie, will you get a move on, we're both going to be late!' Grace urged as Chrissie searched in a drawer of the dresser for a headscarf.

Both girls kissed their mother just as Georgie came out of the scullery, freshly shaved, his hair slicked down with Brylcreem.

'Will you tell Mags that I'll see her after work tomorrow? We're going to have a look in the window of Frost's. I heard they've got some new curtain material and she wants some for curtains in that bedroom you'll be sharing after you're married,' Grace asked him. He always went to Mags's house for his tea on a Friday.

Georgie nodded and grinned, shrugging on his jacket. 'She wants a new eiderdown and bedspread set too but I don't think we'll have enough coupons to stretch that far, even if she can find a shop that's got a set in.'

Grace cast her eyes to the ceiling as she left. It wasn't the ideal way to start married life, she thought, living with your in-laws, but there was no help for it. She was aware that Sadie didn't mind, she herself had started married life in her mother-in-law's house but Mags had expressed some reservations.

'I know we'll not get anywhere else, too many houses were destroyed in the bombing, and I get on well with you all but . . . but I'll be a bit embarrassed, sleeping in the next room to your mam.'

Grace had understood. 'Don't worry too much about it, Mags. I know you'd like some privacy but maybe it won't be for long.'

Mags had nodded but she didn't hold out much hope of a place of their own for a good while yet.

For Chrissie the day dragged interminably. Miss Perkins seemed to be constantly picking on her: she hadn't dusted the glass cases properly; the price tickets she had written out were not neatly done; she had been off hand with a customer. Chrissie had thought the lady was being very unreasonable over the limited choice of dresses that were on offer and when the woman had demanded to know when exactly the spring stock would come in, Chrissie had been annoyed. How was she supposed to know that? she'd thought to herself. There was very little of any kind of stock, spring or otherwise.

'I've no idea, madam. Things are still in very short supply. We all have to make do with what we can get,' she'd replied. It was the simple truth and in her opinion she hadn't been at all off hand, but the woman had complained about her 'tone of voice'. Chrissie'd stood tight-lipped during the lecture she'd received on 'civility'. Only a few more hours to go and then she would leave this place and Miss Perkins for good!

It was still light when she finally left and a cold blustery wind was blowing down London Road. She intended to walk to Lord Street and have something to eat at the Kardomah Café. She would linger there for as long as she could and then she would make her way slowly down to the Pier Head.

By the time she'd had a pot of tea and some cheese on toast she had begun to feel a little apprehensive. She had never travelled out of Liverpool in her life before and now she was to cross the sea to a different country – all on her own. When she arrived in Dublin she wouldn't know the city. 'Oh, for heaven's sake, Chrissie Devlin, you've a tongue in your head!' she told herself firmly. She would look on it as a big adventure and at the end of it all Pat would be waiting for her with open arms. By this time tomorrow she would be installed in the farmhouse in the little village of Rahan. Safe and sound in the arms of the man she loved and would soon marry. Mrs Chrissie Kilroy. It had a certain ring to it, she thought.

At half past nine she finally arrived at the Pier Head, bought her ticket and joined the queue of people waiting to board the ferry. She hadn't thought there would be so many people travelling but she couldn't blame anyone for wanting to escape the dreariness and austerity of life here. When she finally boarded she found a seat in the public saloon and placed her case beneath it. Her bag she tucked securely under her arm. Thankfully a middle-aged woman and her daughter sat beside her; most of the men made straight for the bar. She tried to find a comfortable position on the rather hard seat. She'd better see if she could get some sleep; it was going to be a long night and she didn't want to look pale and heavy-eyed tomorrow, for tomorrow would be the first day of a new and wonderful life.

It was Grace who discovered that Chrissie'd gone. She had gone to bed early on Friday night knowing Chrissie would be late. Chrissie had promised she'd be quiet when she came in and would not disturb her. Those had been her sister's parting words as Chrissie's tram had arrived ahead of hers. When she woke Grace turned over and saw at once that her sister's bed had not been slept in. She sat up with a start. Oh, God! Where was Chrissie? She could make out sounds coming from the kitchen below so she realised that her mam was up. Getting up she quickly dragged on her dressing gown and went downstairs, hoping and praying that she would find Chrissie sitting half-asleep in the chair beside the range.

'I've just made a pot of tea, Grace. You're up early, luv, you don't have to be in work for ages yet,' Sadie commented, glancing at the clock on the mantelshelf.

Grace's heart dropped like a stone. There was no sign of Chrissie. 'Mam, what time did you go to bed?'

'Not long after you, luv. I wasn't a hundred per cent, I felt tired and shivery, and our Billy was in. Georgie has a key and so does Chrissie and she said she was going to be late.'

Grace bit her lip. A flash of concern crossed her face.

Sadie suddenly realised that there was something wrong. 'What's the matter, Grace?'

'Chrissie didn't come home, Mam. Her bed hasn't been slept in.'

'Holy Mother of God! I knew I should have waited up for her! Oh, Grace, what's happened to her?' Sadie clutched the edge of the table for support. Suddenly she felt sick at the terrible thoughts that were racing through her mind.

Grace rushed to her side. 'Sit down, Mam. I'll go and wake our Georgie up.'

Within a few minutes Grace had returned, followed by a grim-faced Georgie.

'Grace, luv, pour us all a cup of tea,' Georgie instructed, seeing the fear in his mother's eyes.

Grace did as he bade her but her hands were shaking.

'Whom did she say she was going to the cinema with, Mam?' he queried.

'A girl called Avril, one she works with.' Sadie passed a hand over her eyes. Her head was beginning to ache.

'Where does she live, this Avril? Did Chrissie say what her surname was?'

Sadie shook her head. 'No, and she just said she lives on the other side of the city, I don't know where. Oh, do you think we should go to the police or try the hospitals first?'

'Not just yet, Mam. Grace, go and see if any of her clothes are gone.' A suspicion was growing in Georgie's mind.

'Surely you don't think she's run off?' Grace asked incredulously.

'You know how pig-headed she is and she's never forgiven us for making her wait to marry Pat Kilroy.'

'Jesus, Mary and Joseph! You don't think she's run off to him?' Sadie cried.

Grace ran upstairs and rummaged through her sister's clothes and then returned.

'I can't see that there's anything missing, except of course her good coat but we knew she was wearing that to go out last night. Surely if she'd run off all her clothes would have gone? And she seemed to have become resigned to waiting. She was looking forward to the trip at Easter and she's been saving hard.'

Georgie nodded gravely. It didn't seem as though his suspicions were founded. Now things really did look bad. 'I'm not going into work this morning, Mam. I'll give Billy a note to take in, explaining.'

'Oh, Georgie, what's happened to her? My poor girl!' Sadie covered her face with her hands and began to weep softly.

Grace put her arm around her. 'Don't upset yourself, Mam. I'll go round all the hospitals and—'

'I think the first place to start with is T. J.'s. I'll speak to this Avril, see what she has to say and then . . . then . . . I think we'll have to inform the police. I'll get Polly Nelson to sit in with you, Mam, and I'll see if their Ellie knows anything.'

Polly was very sympathetic but a tearful Ellie swore she could tell them nothing that would be of any help. Georgie and Grace both got dressed and Grace informed Billy of what had happened and that he had to go into work, taking a note explaining Georgie's absence.

'We'll both go and see this Avril, Grace. There's no sense you traipsing around all the hospitals until we've heard what she has to say,' Georgie pronounced grimly as they went for the tram.

Grace nodded, praying that something had prompted Chrissie to spend the night at Avril's house. Maybe they'd been late out of the cinema and had dawdled and missed the last tram? Oh, please God, let her be safe! she prayed silently.

They had to wait for the store to open, and Grace stood biting her lip while Georgie paced up and down, deep in thought. At last the doors opened and they both made their way towards the ladies' dress department. Chrissie had described Miss Perkins in detail in the past, always detrimentally, so Grace had no trouble picking the woman out.

'Miss Perkins, would it be convenient for my brother and me to speak to you, please?' she asked as they approached.

Beatrice Perkins looked a little startled but nodded.

'I'm Grace Devlin and this is my brother George. Chrissie is our sister and I'm afraid—'

'Has something happened to her? She has not reported for work this morning,' Miss Perkins interrupted, noting the grave looks on both their faces.

Georgie spoke. 'We hope not, miss, but she didn't come home last night. She was supposed to be at the cinema with a girl called Avril who works here. We'd like to speak to this Avril, please?'

'Avril Green? I wasn't aware that those two were friendly.' The woman turned away and scanned the sales floor. Then she beckoned a girl over to them. She was a small, pale and rather plain girl with straight brown hair and grey eyes. She didn't look the type of girl to be friendly with Chrissie, Grace thought.

'I believe you went to the cinema with Chrissie Devlin last night, Miss Green?' Miss Perkins queried.

The girl stared at her, confused. 'No, Miss Perkins. I went straight home last night. I don't think Chrissie

Devlin likes me much, she hardly ever speaks to me so she wouldn't ask me to go anywhere with her.'

Grace's heart plummeted like a stone; she had been hoping against hope that this girl knew something of Chrissie's whereabouts.

'Thank you, Miss Green, you may return to your work.'

'Just a moment,' Georgie interrupted. 'Did you see Chrissie leave work last night? I'm her brother.'

Avril nodded. 'Yes and she walked down towards Lime Street; she looked as if she was going into the centre of town. And she was carrying a small case. I did think that was a bit strange.'

Grace and Georgie exchanged glances. 'Thank you both, you've been very helpful,' Georgie said in a voice full of suppressed anger.

'Can I expect your sister to be back at work soon? Is there something I should know about? What has she done?' Miss Perkins probed. She had always thought Chrissie Devlin was utterly unreliable.

Georgie shook his head; he certainly wasn't going to enlighten the woman about what Chrissie had done. 'There's nothing for you to worry about, ma'am, but I think we can safely say Chrissie won't be coming back to work here.'

'Oh, God! She *has* gone after him!' Grace muttered as they left the store. She was angry and exasperated but mingled with both emotions was concern for her sister. Would she be all right travelling alone? Would Pat

Kilroy really look after her? She was hurt too that Chrissie hadn't confided in her.

Georgie was just furious. 'We're going to the shipping office just to confirm it. They'll have a passenger manifest even if they don't remember her, and then we'll have to go home and tell Mam!'

'At least it's better than having to tell her that Chrissie is dead!' Grace reminded him.

The clerk remembered her well. 'She didn't tell me exactly when she would be travelling but she only wanted a single fare. Very pretty girl, she said she was going over to get married and I said he was a lucky feller. I'll check the manifest for last night's sailing. Is everything all right? She's not had an accident?'

'No, nothing like that, thanks. You've been very helpful,' Georgie thanked him after he'd read Chrissie's name on the printed list.

'What will we do? She'll have arrived in Dublin by now,' Grace asked her brother as they walked towards the tram stop.

Georgie exploded. 'She can go to hell for all I care! She's a selfish, pig-headed, hard-hearted, conniving little bitch! Hasn't Mam had enough worry and upset over the last few years without this? Chrissie didn't care that Mam would think the worst – that we all would – and be worried sick. She was only thinking of herself. Well, she's made her decision so she can damned well get on with it! I'm not going running after her to bring her back and neither are you. I'm finished with Chrissie!

Pat Kilroy is welcome to her and I don't think he's getting any bargain either!'

Grace nodded. Chrissie had been utterly selfish. Had it even crossed her mind just how worried they would all be by her disappearance? Mam had looked terrible when they'd left this morning, haggard and ill. Chrissie could have left a note or a message with someone, just to say she was safe and well, but no! Oh, and all the lies and deception! How could she have just gone off to work like that yesterday morning, so casually and with barely a peck on the cheek for her mam, knowing she wasn't coming back? She had to agree with Georgie in this instance. For all Chrissie knew half the police force could be out combing the streets of Liverpool for her by now while she was happily making her way to some small town in the Irish midlands without a thought in her head for any of them or of how they were feeling. It would be a long time before she would forgive her sister for this.

Chapter Ten

———————

BOTH SADIE AND POLLY looked up hopefully when Georgie and Grace arrived home.

Sadie struggled to her feet. 'Any news? Oh, please God, Georgie, don't let it be bad!' she begged.

'It's all right, Mam. Nothing has happened to her. She's not dead or lying injured in hospital,' Georgie began.

'Where is she? Where's she been all this time?' Sadie exclaimed as both she and Polly crossed themselves.

'Sit down, Mam, Grace will make us a cup of tea while I explain.'

Wearily Grace took off her coat and hat and made to put the kettle on. It had been a long and extremely anxious few hours and she felt drained. Heaven alone knew what her mam's reaction would be to the news Georgie was about to impart.

'Here, Grace, luv, I'll do that. You sit down, girl, you look fair worn out,' Polly offered. Grace did look exhausted and she felt heartily sorry for Sadie but by the look on young Georgie Devlin's face the worst was far from over. Chrissie Devlin was a madam and a half in her opinion and if she'd been her daughter she'd have given her a good hiding long before now. She certainly didn't let their Ellie get away with half of what Chrissie seemed to.

Georgie had taken off his jacket and cap. 'We talked to Avril Green, Mam. Then we went down to the offices of the B & I Line. Chrissie's gone to Ireland. She's run off to Pat Kilroy. Avril isn't a friend of Chrissie's but she saw her leave last night carrying a case and heading into town. It's true, Mam. We saw her name on the passenger manifest. She'll have arrived in Dublin by now, in fact she's probably on the train.'

'Oh, Mary Mother of God!' Sadie gasped, struggling with the relief that Chrissie wasn't dead and the shock of what her son had just told her.

'Well, the selfish, lying, stubborn little madam!' Polly exploded, Sadie had told her what Chrissie had supposedly been doing yesterday evening – clearly it had all been a pack of lies.

'I couldn't agree more!' Georgie snapped. 'As far as I'm concerned she can go to hell! Putting Mam through all that worry and heartache.'

Sadie looked pleadingly at Georgie. 'What can we do now?' Oh, it was just like Chrissie to do something like this and she was certain she would regret it.

It was Grace who answered. 'What can we do, Mam? By the time one of us arrives there the damage will probably have been done. She'll be living under the same roof as him and no doubt that will cause a terrible scandal. And she'd probably refuse to come home and we can't drag her bodily back. Even if we could what's to stop her running off again?' She didn't for one moment think that Chrissie would share the same bed as Pat Kilroy before they were married but if she was living in the same house, people would assume that she was. Chrissie was disgraced and there was no getting away from the fact.

'Grace is right, Mam. We'd get no peace. We'd never know when she'd run off again and there would be tears and tantrums morning, noon and night. I say leave her to it. It might not turn out to be too bad. She might well be happy there.'

'Oh, I wish your da were here, I really do! He would have sorted her out long ago. Where did I go wrong with her? Haven't I always tried to bring her up to be a decent-living girl and now she goes and does this?'

'You can't blame yourself, Mam. If anything is to blame it's the war. Things just weren't *normal* and there's not much sign of them getting back to it. Chrissie just couldn't accept that fact and I think she really believes she loves him,' Grace soothed.

'Sadie, there's a good deal of sense in what Grace is saying. If there'd been no war then Chrissie would have grown up gradually with Tom and yourself and even your poor Harold to keep her in check. She wouldn't have been working in munitions with all those women, listening to things she shouldn't hear about at her age and getting all kinds of ideas into her head. She wouldn't have been so discontented with everything. I agree with Grace and Georgie, leave her to it. She's made her bed, now let her lie on it. No doubt she'll be in touch soon, one way or another.'

Sadie shook her head, still very upset. She was thoroughly mortified by Chrissie's behaviour; they would be the subject of gossip by the entire street. 'Do you think we should send a telegram to Pat Kilroy?'

'Saying what? "Send Chrissie home immediately. She doesn't have my consent to get married"? Besides, we have no address – although I suppose Eileen Bateson would give that to us. Leave her to stew, Mam. At least we know she's safe and not lying dead in some back alley. According to Eileen he's a good lad. He'll do the decent thing by Chrissie. Or, who knows, she might even come to her senses and come home, though I doubt it.' Georgie was thoroughly sick of his sister's antics and still furious that she had caused his mother so much grief and anxiety.

At last Sadie nodded. If Chrissie loved Pat Kilroy so much that she had been willing to put them through so much unnecessary suffering, then maybe it was better to let her marry him. Eileen had assured her he was a good, steady, quiet lad. All she could do was pray that it would all work out for the best.

Chrissie was totally heedless of all the trouble she had caused as she made her way up O'Connell Street towards the General Post Office. She was feeling very pleased with herself. She had found out from a fellow passenger that she could get a tram to Heuston Station from where she would get a train to Tullamore. She had been also directed to the General Post Office and across the road she now glimpsed the rather grand-looking building that had once been the Imperial Hotel and was now the premises of Cleary's department store.

She was a little disappointed in what she had seen of Dublin so far. Oh, there were many fine buildings but as she'd walked from the docks she'd noticed that there were also slums and poverty and dirt. And even at this early hour there were men who were obviously the worse for drink. On this grey, damp March morning the city looked as dull and as shabby as Liverpool, although there were no bombsites, of course. Still, she wasn't staying here. She was going down to the country where things would be much, much better and where she was sure people worked and didn't spend their mornings in the pubs or begging on street corners.

She had decided to send Pat a telegram; it was cheaper than making a telephone call and a bit more reliable, the Post Office clerk had kindly advised after she had explained her position.

'Sure, won't the postman deliver the telegram as quickly as he can, whereas your one in the Post Office will take the message but might take half the day to get it out to your man and you'd be left waiting at the station for him.'

So she'd written 'Couldn't wait until Easter. Arriving Tullamore Station dinnertime today. Love Chrissie' on the form provided and duly handed over her money.

She then crossed the wide thoroughfare and made her way towards Cleary's. As she walked up the curving carpeted staircase to the first floor she was pleasantly surprised to see that there certainly didn't seem to be too many shortages here and the goods were definitely cheaper than in Liverpool. She spent the next hour browsing and finally decided on a smart cream rayon dress. It was a little light for the time of year but it did have long sleeves and she had her coat to go on top. The bodice was pin-tucked and fitted which showed off her neat waist and the bias-cut skirt was of a much longer length than the skirts she owned. It was trimmed on the collar and cuffs with brown velvet ribbon and had a wide brown belt. It was a bargain and she could afford a matching cream wool beret with a ribbon trim. She asked the assistant not to wrap them as she would wear them and was obligingly shown into a cubicle to change. Her now creased and grubby black shop dress and old cardigan were duly disposed of. As she studied herself in the long mirror she thought she looked very stylish and quite attractive. She combed her hair and applied a little lipstick, as she was looking a bit pale and tired. She hadn't managed to get much sleep at all. She did however begin to feel the excitement building up in her again. Only a few more hours to go now. Oh, she couldn't wait to see him again!

Back out on O'Connell Street she walked up to Nelson's Column where there seemed to be a large number of stationary trams. After making enquiries she was directed to a tram at the front of the line, took her seat and paid her fare. She didn't have a great deal of money left but she was sure it would be enough for a single train ticket to Tullamore.

To her relief it was and she was informed that she was in luck, that there was a train leaving in five minutes or thereabouts if they could get the firebox to stay alight long enough to get up a decent head of steam to start the engine.

On enquiring how long the journey would take she was rather confused by the non-committal reply that, 'Sure, it will take as long as it takes.'

At first she found the journey interesting for as the train left the grey suburbs of Dublin behind the scenery gave way to fields and patches of brown bog land. The sun was making a valiant effort to break through the heavy grey clouds and her spirits continued to rise. It certainly did look a lot better, quite picturesque really, with cattle grazing in the fields and quaint little cottages at the side of country lanes.

After several prolonged and unexplained stops,

however, she began to get bored. She tried asking the other occupants of the carriage the reason for the delay but the reply always seemed to have something to do with the effects of what they called 'the Emergency'. She vaguely remembered Pat talking about 'the Emergency' but she didn't equate it with the war that had just ended.

By the time the train finally drew into Tullamore Station it was well after noon and she was tired, hungry and a little irritable. The sun had long since lost its battle and a heavy downpour looked imminent. Adjusting her beret she took her case from the luggage rack and alighted, looking around at the few people who were waiting by the little station house. All the excitement that had bubbled up inside her disappeared when she realised that Pat wasn't amongst them. She had expected him to come peering into the carriages eagerly looking for her and a dart of fear crept into her heart. What if he wasn't coming? 'Pull yourself together, Chrissie! He's just a bit late, that's all. Maybe the telegram was delivered late,' she told herself firmly.

There were other people alighting from the train and being greeted warmly by friends and relatives. A section of the small yard was occupied by half-a-dozen bicycles and two carts between the shafts of which were sturdy-looking ponies, both were snatching at the vegetation beyond the yard wall. The station master was making his way towards her, waving, so she hurried towards him.

'Now, would you be Miss Chrissie Devlin, come all the way from Liverpool?'

'Yes. Yes, I am. Is there a message from Pat Kilroy for me?' she asked eagerly.

'There is so. You're to wait here for him. I'm to mind you. He'll be here in a small piece. He has a matter he has to attend to urgently first. Come along with me now, isn't there a good fire in the waiting room,' he urged, looking up at the sky. 'Sure, there's a wind getting up that would perish the crows, so it would.'

Chrissie followed him feeling hurt and let down. What was so urgent that it took precedence over meeting her? She'd been travelling for over fourteen hours and she was tired, cold and hungry.

The waiting room was a bare little room with a single wooden bench set against one wall but at least it was warm for a cheerful turf fire burned in the open hearth. She stretched out her hands towards the flames. The new dress was indeed much too light for this time of year.

She didn't have too long to wait before Pat arrived looking flustered and wearing wellington boots and an old jacket over a pair of stained overalls. An equally old and stained cap was pushed back from his forehead. She flung herself bodily at him.

'Oh, Pat! I've missed you so much and I was getting upset thinking you weren't coming to meet me!'

He held her tightly. 'Chrissie, I've missed you too

but sure to God what made you come now? I had to drop everything and come into town. I'd not even time to get changed. Does your mam know you've come at all?'

He'd been astounded when he'd received the telegram, which had come at an inconvenient time too. He'd been in the middle of helping Con deliver a calf and the poor beast wasn't having an easy entry into the world. All the way into town he'd been fretting, wondering if Sadie knew she'd come over.

'No. Oh, Pat, she wouldn't have let me come, you know that, and I was just so miserable that I couldn't stand it any longer! You are glad that I'm here?' She studied his face intently. There seemed to be something different about him. Of course he was in his working clothes but it wasn't that.

He smiled at her and took her arm. 'Of course I'm glad. Now, let's get out of here. I was late because I went to see Mrs Johnson, she has a bed-and-breakfast place here in town and you have to have somewhere to stay before you go back. We'll send your mam a telegram, she'll be heart-scalded with the worry.'

Chrissie stared at him. 'But I'm not going back! I came here to marry you, Pat.'

He was utterly dumbfounded. He'd truly thought she had just moved the proposed visit at Easter a few weeks forward. 'But, Chrissie, you know what your mam said. We have to wait.'

Tears sparkled on her eyelashes and her lip trembled.

'I don't want to wait! I *won't* wait! You do still want to marry me?'

He gathered her in his arms. 'Of course I do, do you think I'd be going back on my promise?'

Her shoulders sagged with relief. For a terrible moment she had been afraid he'd changed his mind. 'Then we'll get married. They won't follow me here and drag me back, they *can't*! I'm not a child!'

He was torn by his emotions. He did love her and wanted to marry her but he respected Sadie's wishes and he had thought he would have had more time to organise things. Now she had thrown everything into chaos – but she had travelled so far, alone, to be with him and she did look very tired. She was so vulnerable and appealingly beautiful. He nodded.

'Don't go upsetting yourself, Chrissie. I'll bring you to Mrs Johnson's place and get you settled and I'll get word to your mam that you're safe and that we're to be married as soon as possible. Sure, that should set her mind at rest.'

Chrissie beamed with joy. Oh, she knew she had been right to come. 'Do I still have to stay with this Mrs Johnson? Can't I stay with you?'

He shook his head, looking slightly bemused. 'Chrissie, we'd be the talk of the parish! A pretty young thing like yourself living with two bachelors?'

Chrissie blushed. 'Oh, I didn't mean . . . you know . . . sleep with you! I just thought I could sort of keep house?'

'There's only two bedrooms, Chrissie, and neither is really fit for a girl like yourself. I'd a mind to do mine up before we got married. No, you'd best stay with Herself until the wedding.'

Chrissie was a bit disappointed; she hadn't realised that they wouldn't be able to accommodate her. In reality she hadn't given it much thought at all. 'Can't I come and see what the house is like? After all, it is going to be my home, and I was so looking forward to seeing it.'

Pat smiled and nodded. It was only to be expected. But they'd have to tidy up a bit. 'I'll get you settled and then later on I'll come back and bring you out to the home place and you can meet Uncle Con. I'm sure you'll like him, he's a great old character, so he is. Then maybe we can go up to the church and see Father Doyle, he's the parish priest.'

Chrissie's spirits rose. She had known she could rely on him. Hadn't he already arranged for her to stay with Mrs Johnson? It must be a decent place if the woman took paying guests. She would get something to eat, she could get a wash and have a rest and then tidy herself up. Then she could look forward to seeing the house, meeting his uncle and the parish priest. She would also see the church where she was to be married. Oh, everything was looking rosy now.

Chapter Eleven

———◆———

COURT VIEW HOUSE, MRS Johnson's bed-and-breakfast establishment, wasn't far from the station and did in fact face the large, imposing, grey stone courthouse with its grand colonnade of Corinthian pillars. It was a medium-sized Georgian house that opened directly on to the street and the woman welcomed them warmly.

'Here you are again, Pat! Come along inside with you now, Miss Devlin, you must be worn out with all the travelling. 'Tis a desperate journey.'

Chrissie liked her immediately and followed her upstairs to a small but comfortable bedroom.

'I'll put on the kettle and bring you up some tea and soda bread and then I'll get Mary to cook you some rashers and an egg, you must be famished and it's a desperate day out there now.' She inclined her head towards the window against which a strong March wind was hurling a shower of heavy raindrops.

'I'll have to be getting back to Con now, Chrissie, but I'll come back for you after we've done the milking, about half past six. Have you a raincoat with you at all? And you'll need boots. That looks as if it's in for the day.' Pat glanced at her black leather high-heeled court shoes. They were not entirely suitable for the country.

Chrissie shook her head. 'I've only my coat and these shoes.'

'Then I'll bring you a mackintosh and some boots or you'll be soaked to the skin before we get to the home place,' he offered.

She'd nodded and thanked him but wondered why she would get so wet? Surely, they weren't going to walk out to the farm in this weather?

After she'd eaten, she went back upstairs and drew the curtains to shut out the now dismal afternoon. A fire had been lit and the room looked cosy. She'd taken off her new dress and hung it up, hoping the creases would fall out, then she'd lain down on the bed and pulled the quilt over her and had fallen asleep.

The fire had burned down to a white ash and the room was dark when she was woken by Mrs Johnson tapping on the door.

'Miss Devlin, 'tis half past five o'clock and I've brought up some tea.'

Chrissie got up and opened the door, rubbing her eyes, grateful that she hadn't slept longer. 'Wait, I'll switch on the light.'

'Ah, now, I'll light the lamps after I've set down this tray.'

The older woman set the tray down on a table in front of the window and deftly lit two oil lamps, the light from which bathed the room in a soft golden glow.

'Is there something wrong with the electricity?' Chrissie asked.

'Lord bless you, child! We don't have the electricity yet but there's some talk that we might get it next year when that power station that's over in Cloghan is up and running. Now, you have this tea while it's good and hot and I'll put down more turf on that fire.'

Chrissie was taken aback by this statement. How on earth did they manage without electricity?

After the tea Chrissie felt more awake and she washed her face and hands in the basin on the washstand. Then she put on her dress, brushed her hair and reapplied her lipstick. She certainly looked far better than when she had arrived, she thought, studying her reflection in the mirror that hung on the wall.

Pat arrived at just after half past six, swathed in a voluminous mackintosh from which rainwater dripped on to the tiled floor of the hall. 'I'll not come in further for the boots will have your floor destroyed entirely, ma'am,' he informed Mrs Johnson, who had opened the door to him.

'Pat, you're soaking wet! Surely you haven't *walked*?' Chrissie cried.

He smiled at her. 'Ah, 'tis only a small drop of rain. I've the trap waiting outside.' He held out a similar garment to the one which covered him and a pair of rubber boots, which were obviously going to be several sizes too big for Chrissie.

'The what?' Chrissie asked, looking mystified. 'Can't we get a tram?'

'Ah, would you listen to her, God love her! Can't you tell she's a city girl?' Mrs Johnson laughed and Pat grinned.

'Chrissie, there are no trams outside of Dublin,' he explained.

'Then how do people get around?' It was inconceivable to her that there was no public transport. She'd even been able to get a tram out to Kirkby and that was in the country.

'They walk or they have a bicycle or if they're lucky they have a pony and trap. If they're really grand they have a motor car but these days they don't get to use those contraptions much, there's not much petrol to be had.'

'So, I'm . . . we're to go in a pony and trap? Is that some sort of little carriage?'

He nodded. 'Except that it's not covered.'

Chrissie dutifully put on the waterproof coat, which swamped her, and the boots, which were indeed much too big and came up above her knees. She might as well have worn her oldest clothes, she thought, she must look an absolute fright. Still, she supposed it was better than getting absolutely drenched to the skin and arriving at the farmhouse looking like a drowned rat. Did it never stop raining? she wondered as she followed him out to where a bedraggled-looking skewbald pony stood patiently waiting in the shafts of what appeared to be a round cart on wheels. This must be the 'trap', she thought, wondering if there was somewhere to sit or would she have to stand all the way?

To her relief there was a seat and she tucked the mackintosh tightly around her, pulling the hood close to her face. It was a very strange sensation riding in a pony and trap, she thought, and she said as much to Pat.

'Ah, you'll get used to it in no time at all and I'll have to be teaching you to drive it yourself for after we're married you'll need it to come into town.'

Chrissie didn't like the idea of this very much for although there had been horses on the streets of Liverpool for as long as she could remember she had never had anything to do with them, apart from giving the milkman's horse the odd pat as it stood patiently waiting for its master. In fact if the truth were told she was a little afraid of them. They often bolted for no good reason and with fatal results. 'Won't you be able to drive me? I don't think I could manage this thing.'

'I won't be able to drive you all the time. 'Tis easy, the pony knows its own way about,' Pat replied, thinking he must make allowances for her. She was a city girl, born and bred, but he was certain she'd soon get used to living in the country.

Once the paraffin-fuelled streetlights of Tullamore were behind them it was very dark, the only light coming from the carriage lamp and the windows of the houses and cottages along the roadside. This at least she was used to, she thought, thinking of the blackout of the war years when walking home had been fraught with danger from unseen obstacles. Even the trams had had their headlights masked. She could make out the tall hedges and the black shapes of trees and bushes and as they crossed a stone bridge she heard the distinctive sound of water.

'Is that the Tullamore River?' she asked, hoping he would be impressed that she had remembered something of the geography of the place that had been explained to her when they'd walked in Stanley Park.

'No, 'tis the Grand Canal. Just a small piece down the road now and we'll be home. Are you cold?' He glanced at the hunched figure beside him with some sympathy. He was used to being out in all weathers but she wasn't.

Chrissie smiled at him bravely. 'Not too bad and this coat does keep the rain out.' She was trying hard not to complain too much.

At last he turned the pony into a wide gateway and she could see lights burning in a downstairs room of the house. Her spirits rose. This was it. This was going to be her new home and from what she could make out it was a two-storeyed stone house that looked substantial.

'Wait now and I'll help you down. This yard can be a bit muddy and we don't want you falling.' Pat jumped down and then carefully lifted her down. 'Hold on to me. I'll take you in and introduce you to Uncle Con, then I'll have to check on a couple of cows that are due to calve tonight.'

Chrissie felt a little apprehensive as Pat showed her inside. The kitchen was warm and lit by oil lamps and the light from the turf fire. It was larger than Mam's, she thought, but the floor was flagged and there were no curtains at the window, just a sort of lattice. Against one wall was a split dresser, crammed with crockery in no set order. Against another was a big table also covered with crockery – most of which needed washing. Various items of clothing seemed to be scattered around the room. Mam would have had a fit if her kitchen was so untidy, especially to bring visitors into.

'Here she is, Con. This is Chrissie, my fiancée.' There was a note of pride in Pat's voice.

Chrissie pushed back the hood of the mackintosh and smiled, holding out her hand. 'I'm very pleased to meet you. Pat has told me so much about you,' she said a little timidly to the bent old man who got up from his chair to greet her. The hand he offered was gnarled and calloused, the nails broken and none too clean. She affected not to notice.

'You're welcome, girl. Take off those wet things and sit down by the fire.' Pat was right, she was a fine-looking girl, if a bit small and on the fragile-looking side, he thought. He would have preferred her to have been bringing a bit of money into the family for she had no land to bring, of course, being a city girl. But Pat had set his heart on her.

Chrissie was very thankful to sit as near to the aromatic blaze as she could for Con had taken her wet things and also her coat and she wished she had had the sense to put on a cardigan over the thin dress. She had exchanged the boots for her black shoes.

'I'll put on the kettle and we'll have tea after Pat has seen to the beasts.' Con pushed a black kettle, suspended on a large hook, over the fire.

Chrissie cast around for something to say after Pat had gone out. 'It's a shame it's dark, I would really have loved to have seen around the place. Looked at all the . . . er . . . animals.'

Con cast her an amused glance. 'Most of the beasts are in the fields. We turn them out after milking. The chickens and geese are shut up for the night or the foxes will have them destroyed. Ah, but ye'll see them soon enough. Sure, it will be grand to have some help around the place. The poultry will be your responsibility and the spare eggs ye can take into town to Herself at Egan's Grocery; she'll take something off the bill for ye. Same as the butter ye'll be after making,' he said affably. It had always been the custom for the woman to do this thereby decreasing the amount of cash spent on tea and sugar and the like.

'Oh, I can't make butter! I just wouldn't know how to start.' Chrissie didn't like the sound of this. You bought butter from a shop, all wrapped up neatly in greaseproof paper. She knew absolutely nothing about poultry either.

'Ah, won't Pat learn ye and he'll learn ye to milk too,' Con informed her as he poured the hot water into the big brown teapot. Clearing away some of the dirty dishes with a sweep of his arm he set three clean mugs, taken from the dresser, on the table. A big jug of milk already resided there, as did a bag of sugar. He cut slices of soda bread, buttered them and found a clean plate. She had made no move to offer to help and she looked horrified at his last statement, which didn't bode well. For now she was a guest and would be treated as such, but when she came in the door as a wife she would be expected to work. 'I hear the pair of ye are off to see the Father above in Killina? 'Tis a mite late but then he's always available for those who need him.'

Chrissie brightened. 'Yes. I'm really looking forward to seeing the church and finding out exactly when Pat and I can be married. Then I can start to look around for a wedding dress and a veil. Are there some nice shops in Tullamore?'

'It's a grand enough town,' Con answered, peering at her closely. He was beginning to think Pat hadn't chosen wisely. Where did the girl think she was at all? Above with the gentry in Dublin? He hoped she had the money for all this finery she seemed intent on having.

He couldn't see what was wrong with the dress she had on now. It was far too fancy for sitting in a farm kitchen and those shoes would be ruined in no time.

'Ye were so set on it that ye didn't tell the mammy ye were coming, Pat tells me?' he continued seriously. That showed a marked lack of respect and a streak of wilfulness and he'd said as much to Pat.

Chrissie felt a pang of guilt at the censure in his voice but she wanted to make him understand why she had gone against Sadie's wishes. 'I was. Oh, they don't understand! They are so old-fashioned! I'm nearly nineteen, I've lived through a war and I know my own mind. I just couldn't have stuck it over there for another three years. You don't know what it's like with all the rationing and queuing and the bomb damage and things just don't seem to be getting any better. It's so depressing. If I'd have stayed I'd have been utterly miserable!'

He nodded. Not a word about her affection for Pat or of her missing him either. No, it was all about how she felt. She appeared to be self-centred too. Well, that was something that would have to change. You had to work together to make any kind of a living these days. This was a poor country.

'Ah, here's the lad now. Drink up this tea while it's good and hot. Then ye best go up and see Himself and get things sorted out. I know ye sent a telegram but I think ye'd better write to the mammy as well to explain and apologise, put the poor soul's mind at rest, for Pat

140

tells me she's had a heavy cross to bear these last years what with your brother and your da getting killed.'

Chrissie felt as though she was being told off and looked pleadingly at Pat.

He smiled reassuringly at her. 'Don't worry, Chrissie, I'll write too, when we get back and have something definite to tell her. Then you can post both letters first thing in the morning in the Post Office in town.'

Chrissie smiled at him but felt rather relieved when it was time to leave. The visit hadn't been the outstanding success she'd thought it would be and she wasn't entirely sure that Con approved of her.

Sadie had been relieved when the telegram from Pat arrived. Upset and heart-sore though she had been, she had worried about Chrissie making such a journey alone.

' "Letter to follow", he says,' she'd said, passing the telegram to Grace.

'A letter from Chrissie or himself? But knowing our Chrissie she'll leave it to him to do the explaining,' Georgie had commented coldly.

Mags was going over a list of guests for the wedding with Sadie and Grace when the two letters arrived by the last post the next day. 'I wonder what they've both got to say for themselves?' she mused. Like Georgie she had been furious with Chrissie for subjecting Sadie to so much worry.

Sadie opened Chrissie's letter first. It consisted of a single page and stated that everything had been arranged and she wasn't to worry, that she was sorry for the upset and that Pat would explain everything in more detail.

Grace shook her head as her mam passed the note over. Surely Chrissie could have made more of an effort instead of leaving it all to Pat?

Sadie read Pat's much longer letter carefully, frowning occasionally.

'So, what does he say, Mam?' Grace asked while Mags chewed the end of her pencil thoughtfully.

'That he's very sorry indeed that I have been so upset—'

'It wasn't his fault!' Grace interrupted but Mags frowned at her.

'I've really nothing to worry about. Chrissie is staying with a Mrs Johnson in town. She runs a very respectable bed-and-breakfast establishment and Chrissie will be with her until the wedding. Well, thank God for that! At least her reputation won't be ruined.'

'That was decent enough of him but then Eileen said he wouldn't go making a spectacle of them both throughout the parish,' Mags commented.

Sadie continued. 'They've been to see the parish priest and while he wasn't too happy at first, he's finally agreed to marry them at the end of the month, after the banns have been called. Then Chrissie will move in with himself and his uncle. He says he would be delighted if any of us would like to go over for the ceremony and he'll arrange accommodation, but he'll more than understand if we don't. He apologises again on behalf of Chrissie and himself for all the upset and says he promises faithfully to look after her. He's getting the place tidied up now for her moving in and hopes I can see my way to giving my blessing,' Sadie finished.

'Well, I hope she'll be happy now, I really do,' Grace said sincerely.

Mags nodded but said nothing. If she wasn't then Chrissie had no one to blame but herself and Pat Kilroy certainly sounded as though he would make a good husband. 'Will anyone go, do you think?' she queried.

Sadie shook her head sadly. 'How can we with your wedding so close? Don't we need every penny?' She felt that as Chrissie's mother she should be present but when all was said and done Chrissie had deliberately flouted her wishes and given no thought to her feelings. She would try to find a nice card and put some money in it and that would have to do. Like Grace she devoutly hoped that now Chrissie would be happy.

Chapter Twelve

———◆━◆◆━◆———

THE FOUR WEEKS HAD passed quickly for Chrissie.
At first she was disappointed that there wasn't a
shop in Tullamore where she could purchase a wedding
dress and it was just too far to travel to Dublin, but Mrs
Johnson had been a great help, informing her that Mrs
Scully at the Drapery would get her the material and
trimmings and that there was an excellent dressmaker in
William Street, a Miss McEvoy, who had trained up in
Belfast and was considered to be very stylish. Chrissie
had chosen and ordered the material and she had
already paid two visits to Miss McEvoy: the first to
choose the style and the second for a first fitting. Miss
McEvoy was also helpful regarding veils and
headdresses.

The wedding was to be small and quiet; Mrs Johnson

herself had offered to stand for Chrissie as matron of honour and Mr Johnson would give her away. The rest of the bridal party would consist of Pat, his Uncle Con and Michael Delaney, Pat's best man. After the ceremony they would all go into town for a meal at the Bridge House Hotel and then the new Mrs Kilroy would return to the farmhouse with her husband. It wasn't exactly what Chrissie would really have liked for the most important day of her life, but she was resigned to it. After all, although the party was small they were bound to cause a stir in the hotel. She might even get her picture in the local paper, for hadn't she travelled all the way from Liverpool to marry Pat and settle here? There couldn't be many brides in Tullamore who had come so far.

There was plenty to occupy her time: fittings for the dress, shoes to buy, flowers to order. Everything was being paid for by Pat, much to Con's disapproval.

'Sure, I've never heard of such a fuss and a bother! Has she no money of her own at all?' he'd asked.

'What little she had saved she spent on her fare and don't forget her ma is a widow. No, it's my duty to provide for her,' Pat had answered firmly. He didn't begrudge Chrissie anything for her big day.

'Then ye'd better tell her to buy some sensible clothes and shoes for around the place for the things I've seen her in will be unsuitable entirely and will soon be ruined and she can't expect ye to be spending out on her every week,' Con had advised.

Pat had passed the advice on and Mrs Johnson
helped Chrissie choose a couple of dark skirts and plain
blouses, a pair of good strong shoes and some
wellington boots. She had also advocated the purchase
of a thick, serviceable shawl.

Chrissie had stared at her in astonishment. 'A shawl!
Whatever for?' Only the very poorest women of the
Liverpool slums wore shawls and even then usually only
the older women.

'Won't you find it very handy and warm to throw over
your shoulders around the yard and the outbuildings?
You don't want to go ruining that good coat you have and
it will keep the rain and wind from having you destroyed
entirely,' Mrs Johnson urged. Although now living in the
town she had been brought up on a small farm near Clara
and knew what she was talking about.

Chrissie had finally agreed but had vowed never to
wear it beyond the farm gates. She wasn't going to have
people seeing her looking like an 'old shawlie' as Sadie
called the Liverpool women who wore the garment.

She had been out to her future home only twice and
had declined Pat's offer of a 'tour of inspection' of the
byre, barns and milking parlour as on both occasions it
had been raining. Instead she had concentrated on the
house which she had informed him needed quite a lot of
'sprucing up'.

'Ah, now what do you expect of two bachelors? It
will look grand by the time I bring you into it,' he'd
promised.

She had spent some time looking at curtain material. She'd admired the fancy glass shades for the oil lamps, pictures and new crockery in the hardware stores but hadn't yet suggested to Pat that they purchase any of these items. Mrs Johnson had offered to show her how to make rugs from old strips of material.

'They brighten the place up no end and you'll need something to occupy you in the evenings,' she'd advised.

'Oh, I know how to make them, but I expect Pat will be taking me into town quite often, he promised he would,' she'd answered, smiling. Sitting making rag rugs of an evening didn't sound like much fun at all. She'd spent too many evenings making them when she'd been younger. She'd had quite enough of sitting at home over the last months.

'I expect he will,' was the older woman's reply delivered without much conviction.

She was very relieved that the morning of the wedding dawned fine and bright. It was still a little chilly but at least it wasn't raining, which was indeed a blessing. Mrs Johnson helped her dress and when she stood before the long mirror in the woman's own bedroom she was delighted with the dress Miss McEvoy had made for her.

'Ah, 'tis a shame your own mammy can't see you, Chrissie! Aren't you the most gorgeous bride to set foot in the church at Killina for many a year.' The woman meant it. Chrissie was a very pretty girl and in the long white satin dress with the high collar edged with rows of lace, the train spread around her feet and the wreath of pink-and-white artificial flowers that held the long veil framing her shining curls she did look beautiful.

Chrissie swallowed hard. She *did* wish that Mam could see her but she cheered herself up with the thought that they were to have their photograph taken and she would send a copy to Sadie.

'And won't he be delighted with you altogether!' Mrs Johnson enthused. She herself was resplendent in her best burgundy wool costume, pale pink blouse and a matching hat, bought on her last trip up to Dublin six months ago.

Chrissie blushed. 'Do you really think so?'

'How can he not be? Now, we'd best be starting out, we don't want to keep them waiting.'

As she carefully followed Mrs Johnson down the stairs, Chrissie thought that this was the happiest day of her life. She couldn't wait to get to the lovely little church and see Pat's handsome face wreathed in smiles as she walked down the aisle towards him. A little shiver of excitement ran through her and her heart was racing. Never mind that it was a very small wedding and that none of her family was here to see her, this was *her* special day and she was going to enjoy every minute of it!

And enjoy it she did. When she'd driven along the Charleville Road people came out from the houses and cottages to wave and wish her well. The road was lined with trees on which the first tender green leaves were beginning to unfurl. As they crossed the bridge over the Grand Canal she thought how lovely everything looked with the sunlight sparkling on the calm water, the reeds beginning to grow along the banks with here and there a splash of colour from the water irises and a family of moorhens moving slowly along. The green fields beyond lay tranquil in the spring morning air. When finally they'd turned into the lane where the pretty grey stone church stood beside the convent, she was delighted to see beds of bright spring flowers to greet her.

To her surprise there had been quite a few people in the church for the Nuptial Mass and they had waited to wish the happy couple well. They had then driven back into town in the trap and she had waved delightedly to the people who called out to them en route. They had had their photograph taken at the entrance to the hotel, which, because it was on the town's main street, caused a bit of a stir. To her delight there had even been a reporter from the local paper, the *Tullamore Tribune*, who, after taking down some of her details, had assured her that the piece would appear in next week's edition. Father Doyle had accompanied them and had stayed for the meal. The hotel, which was furnished in the main with heavy, dark and rather old-fashioned pieces, hadn't been very full, it was patronised mainly by commercial travellers who had all gone back to their homes for the weekend, but many of the staff had come to wish her well and comment on how lovely she looked. She had thoroughly enjoyed the wedding breakfast of thick vegetable soup with soda bread, followed by roast chicken, ham, floury potatoes and vegetables, finishing with apple tart and creamy custard and she'd told Pat it was wonderful to have so much good food so readily available.

'I'll get fat if I go on eating like this!' she'd laughed.

'I'll love you just the same, Chrissie, and aren't I the envy of every man who sets eyes on you!' Pat had whispered to her as he'd taken her hand and led her out of the door at the end of the festivities.

She'd smiled up at him with shining eyes as he'd helped her up into the trap.

She'd thought it so romantic to be carried over the threshold into the house and she was quite surprised to find that the whole place had been freshly painted and was clean and tidy.

'Didn't Theresa and Caitlin Fahey, two of the neighbours, come in and give the whole place a good going over yesterday,' Pat confided.

She had taken off her wedding finery and had made some supper while Pat and Con went about their chores and after she'd cleared away they'd sat contentedly by the fire until Con had announced that he had to be up early in the morning, so he'd go up and get some rest.

As the evening had worn on Chrissie had begun to

get a little nervous, fidgeting as she sat beside the fire with Pat.

He reached out and took her hand and gave it a squeeze. 'Ah, Chrissie, there's nothing to be upset about. I'd never hurt you,' he said gently.

She smiled at him. 'I know that, Pat, but . . . but . . .'

'We love each other, Chrissie, and isn't it the natural expression of our love?'

She nodded, feeling a little less nervous.

She'd felt a little shy and embarrassed as she'd undressed but he seemed not to notice and then she forgot about everything as he took her in his arms. She was his wife now and she was so happy. She wasn't in the least bit sorry to have left both her family and Liverpool for him.

Sadie received the wedding photograph, accompanied by a brief note from Chrissie, the day before Georgie and Mags were to be married.

'She *does* look happy, Mam, and she looks lovely!' Grace pronounced enthusiastically. She was happy for her sister but she did miss her.

'She does that, luv. Oh, I hope she really has done the right thing. At least she had a beautiful dress and veil, he certainly isn't skimping on her and she's been married over a month now and she doesn't seem to have any complaints so far.'

Grace nodded. 'Will we put it back in the envelope, Mam, until after Georgie's wedding?' She knew that

Mags was disappointed at having to wear Eileen's wedding dress and the sight of Chrissie in all her new finery would only add to it.

'I think that would be for the best, luv,' Sadie said wistfully, wishing now that she could have been at Chrissie's wedding. Chrissie was after all the first of her family to get married. 'Now, we'd better get on, there's still plenty of things left to do,' she added firmly, putting the photograph carefully into a drawer of the dresser.

Grace had laid out their clothes for the next morning. Sadie had borrowed Polly Nelson's navy blue coat, which was fairly new. She had a cornflower-blue dress to go under it and Kate Nelson had trimmed her navy hat with light blue ribbon and had also managed to get an artificial flower, which she'd attached to the brim. The outfit had been pronounced a triumph under the present circumstances.

Grace, as Mags's chief bridesmaid, had an ankle-length dress of peach crêpe de Chine, borrowed from a friend of Kate's, and a wreath of peach flowers for her hair. The dress had long sleeves and a sweetheart neckline, which suited her. Mags had said they couldn't have bought anything as nice anywhere. Georgie was to wear his navy demob suit but Sadie had washed and starched his best shirt and his boots were so highly polished you could almost see your face in them, Billy had said.

'I just hope that lad behaves himself and doesn't go showing me up!' Sadie had remarked for Billy was to be his brother's best man. Then Sadie had sighed heavily, thinking that poor Harold would have been more suited to the role.

'He will, Mam. He's as proud as punch that Georgie asked him and isn't having one of his mates from the Army,' Grace had reminded her.

The bedroom that the newly-weds were to have had been painted and they'd made new curtains for the window and a rag rug for the floor. Grace had bought a couple of pictures from a second-hand shop, which helped to brighten the room up too. Although Mags had scoured the shops she'd been unable to get a new eiderdown and bedspread set. Instead Sadie had given the old eiderdown a good airing over the washing line and the pale-green-and-white check bedspread had been washed and ironed. Mags had moved her belongings in during the week, helped by Grace, and had confided that it would be much more peaceful living in Royal Street than at home, where her Aunty Flo and her five kids had the place like a bear pit most of the time.

'You wait until we're all trying to get out to work in the mornings with Mam yelling at our Billy to get out of the bed! It won't be very peaceful then, I can tell you,' Grace had laughed.

Mags had grinned. 'At least it's only Billy who won't get up, Aunty Flo has three of them that seem stuck to the mattress! Mam says she has a banging headache by the time nine o'clock comes. No, we'll be fine here and I can give your mam a hand with everything.'

Grace had smiled gratefully at her. It would be good to have Mags living here.

Grace went round to Mags's house early next morning. Her outfit had been carefully packed in tissue paper and placed in a large paper carrier bag. Mrs Draper answered the door to her, with curlers in her hair, looking very strained.

'Come on in with you, Grace. I'd go straight up to our Mags if I were you, it's like flaming Fred Karno's circus in the kitchen with our Flo trying to get them kids sorted out and Mr Draper suffering from a drop too much last night and me trying to keep the bouquets out of harm's way! God knows when I'll have time to get myself ready.'

'Why don't you put one of the older kids in charge of the flowers? That would give one of them a bit of responsibility and help keep them quiet. Then make a cup of tea, bring it up with you, have a few minutes' peace and then get dressed. You are the Mother of the Bride, don't forget. I'm sure Mr Draper can manage to get himself organised,' Grace suggested.

'That man couldn't organise a tea party! It's "Ethel, where's this?" and "Ethel, where's that?" ' Mrs Draper replied scornfully.

'Let your Flo sort him out or at this rate you'll be worn out before you begin and you won't enjoy the day,' Grace urged, thinking fleetingly that maybe Chrissie had been fortunate in having a small, quiet wedding. The noise coming from the kitchen was definitely increasing.

Mags's mother nodded firmly. 'You're right. I'll follow you up. We've all worked hard to make this day special for her. She's a good girl and I'll not have her fussed or upset.'

'Oh, Grace, I'm so glad you've come! God Almighty, what's going on down there? All I can hear is my Aunty Flo bawling at the kids, Mam bawling at Da and I can't get this head-dress on right!' Mags was flushed and nervous.

Grace unpacked her dress and laid it on the bed, then she turned her attention to her future sister-in-law. 'Calm down. I've told your mam to make herself a cup of tea and bring it upstairs and see to herself. Your Aunty Flo can sort your da and her kids out.'

'I hope to God they give her a new house soon, she's driving Mam mad!'

'Sit down on the bed and let me see to your hair and head-dress.'

Carefully avoiding Grace's borrowed dress, Mags did as she was bid and glanced for the tenth time that morning at Eileen's wedding dress that was hanging behind the door, covered with a sheet. 'It's so good of her to lend it to me but—'

'You'll look just as gorgeous as she did and hardly anyone who is coming to this wedding has seen it! You've got to have "something borrowed", you've got your "new" silk undies, your stockings are the "old" and the "blue" is the blue ribbon bows on your camiknickers. There's nothing in the shops to beat that dress or the veil, but your head-dress is new.'

Mags smiled, reassured. 'Is it bedlam in your house too?'

'Not too bad. I left Mam giving our Billy a lecture but don't worry about him. He's so delighted with himself that Georgie thinks he's grown up enough to be best man that he won't put a foot wrong.' Grace had deftly arranged the head-dress over Mags's dark hair. 'Are you nervous?'

'Just a bit. I keep hoping nothing will go wrong.'

'Nothing will. It's supposed to be the happiest day of your life, so enjoy it. Our Georgie is looking forward to it, I know that, and you've both waited so long for it that I know it will be great!'

Mags smiled at her through the mirror on the dressing table and Grace smiled back, giving her a quick hug. 'Now, let's get this dress on you and then I'll clip your veil in place. Your mam will be up soon and she'll want to see you dressed and ready, all nice and calm.'

'I hope she remembers to take her curlers out, she's been known to get halfway up the street before she's remembered about them.'

Grace laughed. 'She's that hat to get on, that should remind her!'

When Mrs Draper finally emerged looking very smart and considerably less stressed and with her curls peeping tidily from beneath the brim of her hat both girls were ready.

'Doesn't she look an absolute picture?' Grace enthused.

Mrs Draper sniffed and hastily dabbed her eyes. 'Oh, she does, Grace! Indeed she does! My little Mags . . . Oh, just wait 'til your da sees you!'

'Mam, don't, or you'll have me in tears too!' Mags cried, her eyes overly bright.

'I'll go down and get the flowers and make sure they haven't all killed each other in that kitchen, although it's quietened down a lot,' Grace commented, making for the door. Mags needed these few minutes alone with her mother. She wondered how her own mam was feeling right now as they set off for the church. Happy, proud and yet sad that her father, Harold and even Chrissie were missing for this wedding. Well, she couldn't do much about her da or Harold but she vowed if ever she got married she would have as many of her family as possible around her. Still, she somehow knew that her da and Harold would be watching over them today of all days.

Straightening her shoulders she made for the kitchen, determined that if there were any last-minute hitches she would sort them out. Nothing was going to spoil Mags and Georgie's day.

Mags arrived at the church with her father who carefully handed her out of the wedding car. Fortunately the church wasn't far away so they could use one car; petrol was still in very short supply. Grace and the younger bridesmaids and Mrs Draper had all walked the short distance. Ethel had already gone in but Grace and the others were waiting in the porch.

Mags smiled a little tentatively at Grace as she arranged the white satin train.

'Not still nervous, surely?'

Mags shook her head. 'Not really.'

'Well, I am. I'll be glad to get her down the aisle and pass her over to Georgie,' Mr Draper confided.

Grace laughed. 'So will I. I have to keep this lot in check. Right, there's the organ starting up. Off we go!'

Both Sadie and Ethel Draper were seen to be dabbing their eyes as Mags and Georgie made their vows. Grace thought her new sister-in-law looked radiant. She thought fleetingly of Chrissie and wished that she could have seen her sister married; she was sure that Chrissie would have looked just as beautiful as Mags.

When the service was over and the photographs had been taken the wedding party moved on to the parochial hall where Eileen Bateson had had her evening reception. Everyone had clubbed together to put on a decent wedding breakfast with what was available but Grace thought a little sadly that neither the decorations or the food were anything like Eileen's. Still, it was going to be a great day just the same, she told herself firmly.

After the speeches the tables were cleared and the older women sat together in a group while most of the men made a beeline for the bar that had been set up at the far end of the room.

'I just hope our Billy doesn't go mad and make a show of us,' Sadie muttered to Grace, her eyes firmly on her younger son who had a pint glass in his hand and was chatting to a cousin of Mags.

'He won't, Mam, he's been on his best behaviour so far but I know he's glad all the formalities as he calls them are over. Now let him relax a bit and enjoy himself. I'm going to.'

'At least that flaming Tommy Milligan isn't here, that's a blessing in itself. He's a bad influence on our Billy,' Sadie confided to Ethel.

'Oh, yer often get lads like that, Sadie,' Ethel agreed, sipping a glass of sweet sherry.

'Is there any sign of your Flo getting a house?' Sadie asked.

Ethel raised her eyes to the ceiling and leaned closer to Sadie. Grace sighed, knowing there would now follow the litany of complaints about Ethel's young nieces and nephews. She'd be glad when the dancing started.

Mags came and sat beside her, her bouquet discarded and her long veil removed.

'Have you left him already?' Grace laughed.

'He's having a pint with da, your Billy and our Trevor and I don't suppose I begrudge him that. He told me he was so nervous thinking about his speech that he could hardly eat.'

'He didn't look or sound nervous. Your da was in more of a state.'

Mags laughed. 'That's because Mam kept glaring at him for accidentally standing on the train of my dress when we were having the photos taken. She told him she'd be mortified if she had to give it back to Eileen covered in dirty footprints. But everything has gone so well so far, hasn't it?'

Grace smiled and squeezed her hand. 'It has and once the dancing starts everyone will say it's the best wedding they've been to for ages and that you looked just gorgeous! And when we get the photographs we'll send one to Chrissie and Pat.'

Mags nodded her agreement. At this moment she felt happy, proud and very contented with life.

Chapter Thirteen

⁂

IT WAS THREE WEEKS LATER when Chrissie received the stiff cardboard envelope that contained the wedding photograph. She thanked the postman and left him chatting to Con. The meal was cooking and the table was set so she wiped her hands on her apron and, having checked the pans simmering on top of the turf-fired range, sat down to open it. She smiled, thinking that Mags looked lovely in Eileen's dress, but at the same time felt a little dart of sympathy for she knew Mags really would have liked a new one. Grace too looked very attractive and Mam looked smart. Her smile widened as she looked at Billy, thinking she'd never seen him look so well groomed and more grown up than usual. When she went into town next she'd get a nice frame for it and put it on the dresser.

She glanced idly around the kitchen, tucking a wisp of hair behind her ear. Sunlight flooded into the room and it was very warm, due in part to the heat from the range. That was something she still hadn't properly mastered; what little cooking she'd done in Liverpool had been done on a gas cooker and it was far easier to judge and control the heat on that than on the range. Oh, there had been so much to get used to here, she thought. Being without electricity and piped water made life difficult to say the least but she hadn't complained, she was trying her best to adapt. There were times when she had to admit she missed her mam and Grace and she did try to write as often as she could but there always seemed to be so much to do and by evening she was worn out – they all were. Oh, she knew she shouldn't complain about Pat, he was patient with her, more patient than Con, but sometimes she felt left out as though she wasn't as important to him as she'd been in the first weeks of their marriage. She shook herself mentally. She was just being silly, she enjoyed living here. After the shortages in Liverpool it was wonderful to have an abundance of good food, she had some nice clothes, the bit of independence that driving into town gave her and he did take her out as he'd promised he would and on those occasions she enjoyed herself.

She looked at the photo again and bit her lip. She hoped that Mags had had a better wedding night than she'd had. It hadn't been what she had expected at all. In all her dreams she'd envisaged herself lying in Pat's arms while he whispered endearments and then being transported into a world of unimaginable ecstasy. It hadn't been a bit like that. All the fumblings had been embarrassing and for her penetration had been painful, and as for the panting and groaning – she'd been very conscious of Con trying to sleep in the adjoining bedroom! She just wished that someone had explained in more detail what she should expect. Mam had just skirted around it all. She knew that Pat had been just as inexperienced as herself but he didn't seem to find it awkward or embarrassing, he seemed to enjoy it far more than she did. She sighed; maybe it would get better in time. She wondered how Mags felt living with Mam and the family for she didn't find it easy living with Con.

She was brought out of her reverie by Con's voice.

'What have ye in the oven that's after burning?' he demanded.

With a look of horror on her face Chrissie shot up. 'Oh, God! The meat!' She grabbed the piece of sacking that served as an oven cloth, opened the door of the oven and yanked out the metal tray. The piece of meat was ruined. 'Oh, damn! I'll never get used to this range!' she cried in frustration.

Pat entered the kitchen and took in Chrissie's flushed face, the burned meat and the bubbling pans on the top of the range. He shook his head but his eyes were full of amusement.

'Sure, the dinner's destroyed entirely – again,' Con commented acidly.

Chrissie bit her lip and hastily pulled the pan of potatoes off the heat. 'Oh, I'm sorry, Pat! I got engrossed looking at Georgie and Mags's wedding photo.'

Pat took the meat tin from her. 'Never mind, Chrissie. There's plenty of bread and cheese and some cold ham. It's not the end of the world.'

She managed a wry smile. 'One of these days I'll master that thing, I promise. Sit down both of you while I cut the bread and get the cheese and ham from the larder.'

Pat washed his hands, still smiling to himself. She did *try*. There had been a few incidents like this but as he'd told Con, they had to be patient with her.

'Will we ever see the day when we get scones and buns?' Con muttered to his nephew.

'Ah now, go easy on her.'

Con shook his head. 'She's been here long enough to be coping better than this and 'tis a sin to see good food ruined. Ye have her spoiled altogether, bringing her to the hotels for tea and to the cinema and dances.'

Pat shook his head. 'You know as well as I do that all the outings will have to stop soon what with the hay-making and the turf. Summer is a fierce busy time.'

Con nodded as Chrissie came back into the room. 'Ah, sure this will be grand!' he said, being determinedly cheerful. 'And eat plenty up yourself Chrissie, we've to turn the hay this afternoon.' He helped himself to a big hunk of cheese and two slices of soda bread which she'd made on the griddle that morning. At least she could cope with that, he thought.

As Chrissie poured the tea she looked at Pat with puzzlement in her eyes. 'Why do I need to eat plenty?'

'You're to come with us too, Chrissie. Everyone has to help out at hay-making time. You'll enjoy it, out in the fields in the sunshine with the birds singing and the butterflies flitting hither and yon. All the neighbours come and there's mighty chat. The women really do enjoy it.'

Chrissie looked doubtful but then smiled. 'I suppose I'll give it a try, it might be fun.'

Pat had been right, she thought a few hours later. Everyone had come and there was a great deal of laughter and chatting. Stone jars of buttermilk and tea had been brought along and some of their neighbours had brought soda bread, scones and buns.

'Is it a bit like a picnic then?' she'd asked Theresa and Caitlin Fahey, the daughters of a neighbouring farmer, as they'd all ridden on the back of the ass cart up to the fields.

'Sure, I suppose ye could say that. But it's fierce hard work and ye do get parched,' Theresa answered.

'And ye get roasted by the sun too,' Caitlin added. 'Last year I got so many freckles ye could hardly see a speck of skin between them. I made sure I've a hat with a good brim on it with me this day.' She laughed, waving a wide-brimmed straw hat.

'Ah, but there's a grand day's chat to be had, so there is,' Theresa assured Chrissie as she jumped down to open the gate to the field. 'And wait until we go up to turn the turf, now that's what ye call fierce hard work.'

By late afternoon Chrissie couldn't imagine anything being harder work than turning the hay with the heavy pitchfork. Her back and shoulders ached abominably. Beneath her hat her hair was stuck to her scalp and beads of perspiration stood out on her forehead. The sun beat down relentlessly and her blouse was also stuck to her. She felt hot, dirty, smelly and exhausted. She just didn't know how the other girls and women found the energy to keep up the unbroken conversations, never mind the laughter.

When finally the men called a halt she stuck the pitchfork into the ground and leaned on it. Her head was thumping.

Pat put his arm around her. 'You look worn out, Chrissie.'

She leaned thankfully against him. 'I am! Oh, I just want to go home, have a nice bath and rest.'

'I know, I feel like that myself but it's been a grand day, you'll have to agree? All working together, having a bit of a laugh and a joke. We'll all be going up to give the Faheys' a hand with their hay at the end of the week.'

Chrissie looked at him in amazement. 'You mean I've got to go and work like this for them?'

' 'Tis expected.'

'But . . . but we were going to go into town to the cinema.'

Pat shook his head. 'I'm sorry, Chrissie, but we'll not be having the time nor the energy for outings for a while. These few months are summer are fierce busy.' Seeing the hurt and disappointment in her eyes he hastily added, 'But won't I give you the money for a new hat to sort of compensate.'

She felt a little mollified at his words and nodded.

They began to walk towards the ass cart, his arm still around her shoulders. 'At least we'll be working together and that's a good thing. And summer is a grand time here. In the long evenings we can take a walk along the canal bank. It's cooler then and there's plenty of wildlife to see and everything looks so peaceful in the evening light: the fields, the hedgerows, the river, even the bog.'

If we've the energy to take a walk, Chrissie thought and then gave a little shudder, remembering what Theresa had said about the hard work of turning the turf. 'Does it take long to turn the turf?' she asked.

'A good few days. Everyone does their own patch.'

'And will I have to help with that too?'

Pat nodded.

She looked up at him, her forehead creased in a frown. 'Don't you think I have enough to do keeping house and cooking? I'm worn out by evening.'

He looked a little taken aback. 'But, Chrissie,

everyone helps with these tasks during summer. Look on it as a grand day out, that way it won't seem too much like a chore at all.'

Chrissie didn't reply. Was that really what he considered a 'grand day out'? Well, she certainly didn't. It was just more work no matter how you looked at it, and no more proper outings until God knows when. Disappointment filled her. Life wasn't turning out the way she had expected it to at all. Her gaze followed the groups of women and girls who were all still chatting and her mood deepened. She didn't have much in common with them at all, really. The young unmarried girls went to dances and the cinema; the married women very rarely did. She was still young and she wanted more out of life than just endless days of back-breaking work.

As she lay beside a sleeping Pat that night she wondered just how he'd found the energy for love-making. She'd been so exhausted that she turned away from him, sleep already claiming her, but he'd pulled her to him and without any of the tender, romantic gestures she so craved had taken her. Then, when satisfied, he had instantly fallen asleep. She felt the tears on her cheeks. Tears of exhaustion, disappointment and disillusionment. Why couldn't he understand how she felt? She'd wanted romance and excitement. Why didn't he understand that? Didn't he realise that she was so tired, so very, very tired? All there seemed to be in life now was work, work and more work and in the months to come without even the occasional trip into town to lighten the load.

She shook him hard and he woke, muttering drowsily.

'What is it?'

'Pat, I have to talk to you!' she said as loudly as she dared for fear that Con would hear.

'Ah, Chrissie, can't it wait until morning?' he grumbled.

'No, it can't! I ... I want more than just to be a skivvy. I didn't marry you to be that. I married you because I love you.'

Pat looked up at her, puzzled. 'And I love you, Chrissie. You know that.'

'But you don't understand, Pat! I'm young. I want to go out and enjoy myself but I want *you* to take me out. I don't want to be stuck here every day, working myself into the ground. I've had years and years of working hard in that munitions factory, of doing without things. And ... and I want you to ... love me ... differently.'

Pat sat up and put his arm around her. 'Chrissie, I explained all about life here, you know I did. I told you how different it would be to Liverpool. And you do have so many things you didn't have there. Good food, nice clothes, a lovely peaceful place to live. Can't you try to get used to it for my sake?'

'But nothing is turning out the way I expected it to, Pat! I've not complained about the lack of electricity, gas or water or public transport. I'm trying so hard to be a good country wife, I am! But . . . but . . . things are getting too hard for me!'

'Chrissie, marriage is all about give and take, rubbing along together in good times and bad.' He was hurt and disappointed that she felt like this.

'I know that! But it's not what I expected or want!'

'What do you really want, Chrissie? Is it something that I can't give you?'

She was utterly confused and miserable now. 'Pat, I just want to . . . to enjoy my life more, can you understand that? I . . . I want you to be more understanding, more . . . romantic towards me.'

'You want me to bring you flowers every day, compliment you all the time? Take you out three or four times a week? Tell you I love you a dozen times a day? You *know* I love you, Chrissie! It's just not the way I am and it's just not possible to always be bringing you out. I try to give you everything, God knows I do! But obviously you want more than I can give. I'm sorry, Chrissie. Truly I am.' He turned away from her, unable to hide the anger and hurt.

She stuffed her fist into her mouth to stifle the sobs. Oh, why couldn't he understand how she felt? Why? As she closed her eyes the months of unrelenting work stretched ahead of her, taunting her. Oh, she was dreading this summer – but would the autumn be any better?

Chapter Fourteen

GRACE HAD PERSUADED MAGS to accompany herself and Kate Nelson to a dance to be held in Bootle Town Hall that was being advertised as a 'Halloween Ball'.

'It says there will be dancing, entertainment and a light supper,' Grace had informed them both, reading from the ticket as they'd all sat around the fire one dismal October evening.

'Light? That probably means there won't be much of it,' Sadie commented sagely.

'I've never heard of anyone having a special ball for Halloween before. All we ever did for Halloween was try to fish apples out of a bowl of water with our teeth or bite chunks out of those suspended on pieces of string and, before the war, maybe a toffee apple or two or some home-made cinder toffee to follow after you were well and truly drenched,' Georgie had commented, laying down the newspaper, which was full of the reports of the executions of the Nazi war criminals who'd been convicted at the Nuremberg trials, and long columns describing the increased fighting in Palestine. He'd sighed heavily; the world was still in a mess judging by what he'd just been reading, so why shouldn't people go out and try to enjoy themselves?

'You might as well go, Mags. You don't get out very often,' he'd urged.

She'd smiled at him. 'Neither do you, luv, and besides I'm a married woman now, not footloose and fancy free like these two. And I'm trying to put a bit of money by for Christmas.'

'Ah, go on with you. One night out won't break the bank and I'm going to watch Everton play on Saturday.'

'Come on, Mags. It will be something a bit different,' Grace had urged and finally Mags had agreed.

As the Thursday evening approached the usual question of what they were to wear arose. Grace didn't want to waste her clothing coupons on a new skirt or dress, she was saving them for a winter coat as her brown tweed one had seen better days and was looking shabby.

'I've got that peach crêpe de Chine I had for your wedding but it's a bit light for this time of year,' she mused. Kate's friend had kindly said Grace could keep it as she was sick and tired of it and Kate had altered it, making the skirt shorter and less full and also shortening the sleeves, but it had been well worn.

'It won't be cold in that place and it looks lovely on you, especially with that brooch pinned to the shoulder. I suppose I could wear my brown cord skirt but what will I wear with it? I don't have a wardrobe suitable for gallivanting off to balls these days,' Mags asked. All three girls were ensconced in Grace's bedroom where Grace had hung her only three presentable dresses on the wardrobe door for closer scrutiny.

'None of us have had a suitable wardrobe for flaming years! Why don't you wear my cream blouse with the lace collar and cuffs? I could ask our Ellie if she'll lend you that fancy belt she cadged off one of her friends,' Kate offered.

Mags brightened. 'That would be great, Kate, if you're sure you don't mind lending it to me?'

'Haven't we all been borrowing and swapping for most of our lives? At least it's handy being able to sew, and I can get a bit more in the way of materials now too.'

'Why don't you wear that dress you've just finished? The dark blue one with the new long-length skirt? Then we'll all be in the height of style,' Grace suggested.

Kate nodded then laughed. 'God, you sound just like your Chrissie. By the way, how is the "stylish" Mrs Kilroy these days? The talk of Tullamore I'll be bound!'

Grace laughed. 'She's great according to her letters.'

'Even though they're not very long,' Mags added.

'She was never a one for writing letters but Mam does get the occasional note from her. We haven't had one for a while. Her last letter said she was doing fine. Driving herself into town in the pony and trap and getting to grips with the poultry and the butter-making.'

'That doesn't sound as if it's up your Chrissie's street much. I never thought she was overly fond of animals, especially horses or ponies,' Kate commented dryly.

'I know but at least she's not written complaining about anything so maybe she really is settling down and enjoying being a country wife.'

Kate looked far from convinced but said nothing. 'So, that's all settled then. I'll get that belt off our Ellie and make sure the blouse is clean and pressed. What time will we leave?'

'We don't want to get there too early and be sitting around like wallflowers. If we get a tram at about a quarter to eight we should get there about a quarter past,' Grace advised.

'I wonder what the light supper will consist of?' Kate mused, idly picking at a loose thread on the sleeve of Grace's peach dress.

'Paste sandwiches and a few plain biscuits probably,' Mags surmised, without much enthusiasm.

'Oh, great! I just hope the entertainment and the dancing will prove more exciting and I hope there will be some decent fellers there too. At three shillings a ticket it's certainly not cheap. You can go to the Grafton on a Friday and Saturday night for three and six and that's the best ballroom in the city,' Kate commented.

'Well, it does say it's a ball,' Grace reminded her. 'Let's hope it lives up to its name.'

They were all surprised to find that the ballroom was quite full when they arrived, that the place had been decorated with balloons, streamers and papier mâché masks and that the 'light supper' was in fact Lancashire Hotpot served with pickled red cabbage.

'Well, that's a turn-up for the book, I never expected a hot meal here. I wonder where they managed to get all the meat?' Grace said.

Kate rolled her eyes expressively. 'It's probably all potatoes and veg with a piecrust on top and served with a teaspoon of red cabbage. You know what they say about Bootle?'

'It's where the bugs wear clogs and the kids play tick with hatchets,' Mags replied, using an old and derogatory saying that implied it was a very tough place indeed. Bootle, although geographically close to Liverpool, was a completely separate town and not a suburb of the city. Having miles of docks it had suffered very badly during the wartime bombing and even before the war had never been as prosperous as its larger neighbour.

'That's just an old saying. It can't be *that* bad otherwise Mam wouldn't have let us come traipsing all the way here to a dance,' Grace reminded them as they found a table near the edge of the dance floor.

Kate nodded, looking towards the bandstand. 'Oscar Rabin's is a decent-enough band and I've heard that their singer is rather good. The fellers aren't too bad either and there are quite a few Yanks here too, they're the only ones in uniform. They must have come all the way from Burtonwood, so surely that's a good sign?'

'I'm not so sure, they're the only ones with enough petrol to get them anywhere they want to go. Anyway, I thought they were all going home.' Mags wasn't at all interested in the men and she twisted her wedding ring around on her finger a little self-consciously, wondering if she were the only married woman here.

'They are but I suppose it will take a while to get them all back. Mam was telling me about that Betty Dodd who lived at the bottom of the street. Do you remember her, Grace? She married a GI and went out to Ohio. Apparently she's having the time of her life, according to Mrs Dodd. In her letters she goes on and on about her washing machine, her refrigerator and ice box, her "closets" – whatever they are – her telephone and driving herself to her local "market" where she's never seen so much food for sale in her life and you don't have to queue for anything. Her mam says it would make you sick listening to it all!' Kate rummaged in her bag and found her powder compact, checked her appearance in its mirror and after tweaking a few unruly curls, returned it to her bag. 'And now apparently she calls her handbag her "purse" and her purse a "wallet". Did you ever hear the like?' she finished, grimacing.

Mags raised her eyes to the ceiling, thinking that Betty Dodd was indeed fortunate.

As the evening progressed both Kate and Grace were asked to dance regularly. Mags was also asked but politely declined and was quite content to sit and watch. The band was good and she was glad that Grace seemed to be enjoying herself. She thought that Grace looked lovely. The peach dress suited her and she'd done her hair in a new style. She was also pleased that Grace had been asked to dance three times by the same young man for she had long wished that Grace would find someone special, just as she had. By the way her sister-in-law was chatting animatedly to him, it boded well.

'He looks nice. What's his name?' she asked when the dance ended and Grace returned to their table.

'He is. He's Scottish. His name is Sandy McBride,' Grace informed her, smiling and looking a little flushed. She had liked him. He was tall with reddish-blond hair and blue eyes and an open, honest-looking face. He'd told her he was twenty-four but when he smiled he looked much younger. He'd been a mechanic in the RAF, and had decided to stay on in the area as his parents had died during the war and his only sister had recently married a Canadian soldier and gone to live in Ontario. He now had a good job in the English Electric Company. 'I do have a bit of trouble understanding his accent at times though,' she laughed.

Mags grinned. 'Oh, you'll get used to that.'

Lyn Andrews

'I might not have time to. He might not ask me to dance again, but I hope he does.'

'I bet he will. Here comes Kate.' Mags frowned for Kate looked none too pleased. 'What's up with her?'

Kate plumped herself down in the chair next to Grace and took a long swig from her glass of orange juice. 'The flaming cheek! Do you know what that feller said to me? That I was the "cutest broad" he'd danced with all night and did I want to "quit this joint and take a ride with him in the jeep?" I told him where to get off in no uncertain terms! What kind of a girl does he think I am to go off riding in a jeep with a stranger? I know what he's after and God knows where I'd end up. Mam would kill me! And I don't like being referred to as a "cute broad" either. Flaming Yanks!'

Mags looked sympathetic. 'I thought you were getting on very well.'

'Oh, he's no manners at all! I asked him where he was "dragged" up, being sarcastic like, and like a thicko he says, "Honey, I was raised in Baltimore." So I told him that he might talk like that to the girls in Baltimore but he needn't think he could talk like that to me!' Kate fumed.

'Never mind. I think the hotpot is going to be served, shall we get in the queue? I'm quite hungry,' Grace suggested to calm her friend down.

After the supper was over the dancing resumed and Grace was hardly off the floor and nearly always with Sandy McBride.

'I'll have no leather left on the soles of my shoes at

this rate!' she laughed when he insisted they stay up for yet another foxtrot.

'I'll buy you another pair, Gracie, if you promise to let me take you home?' he'd laughed back.

'I came with Kate and Mags and it would be rude if I didn't go home with them,' she answered a little regretfully.

'And what if they both got asked to be taken home too? It could be arranged, I'm here with two mates,' he persisted.

She shook her head. 'Mags is my sister-in-law, she lives with us, and Kate lives next door so we'd all end up together anyway. Besides, our Georgie would kill any lad who had designs on Mags.'

He looked serious. 'I'm sorry, Gracie. I didn't know she was married and I wouldn't want you to think I'm that sort of a laddie.'

She smiled. 'Apology accepted.'

'But I would like to see you again. Could I take you to the cinema one night? You don't have a steady boyfriend, do you?'

'No, I don't and I would like to go to the cinema.' She did like him. There was just something about him that she found both attractive and appealing.

'Then will we say Sunday night? Where is the nearest cinema to your house?'

'The Astoria on Walton Road, but I'm not sure what's on and it's quite a journey for you.' He'd already told her he had lodgings in Norris Green.

'Och, that's not a bother. I'll meet you outside at half past seven and I'll see you home afterwards, if that's all right?'

She nodded. It was a date and she felt happy and excited at the prospect. If everything went well she might even ask him in to meet her mam and she'd never done that before.

'I thought that feller would have asked to see you home?' Kate commented as the dance ended and they left, Grace waving to Sandy McBride who made an extravagant gesture of blowing her a kiss, making her laugh and blush.

'He did but I said I was going home with you two. He's taking me to the cinema on Sunday night,' she informed them, pulling the collar of her coat up around her neck as a cold blast of wind coming up from the river made her shiver.

'Good for you, but you could have let him see you home. We wouldn't have minded,' Mags said. She hoped this would indeed be the start of a romance for Grace.

'No, we'd have caught an earlier tram and dashed up the street when we got off to give you a bit of privacy,' Kate added.

'No, it wouldn't look right. I don't want to rush things.'

Kate glanced at her with mild amusement. 'God, Grace, no one can accuse you of rushing things – unlike your Chrissie! You've turned down more dates than I can count.'

'That's because there wasn't anyone I really wanted to see again,' Grace answered seriously. It was true and she wasn't impetuous like Chrissie. When she got married she wanted to be absolutely sure it was to the right man but she wondered had she at last found him? Only time would tell, but she had really liked Sandy McBride from the first few minutes she'd danced with him.

This year, the first full year of peace, had seen both her sister and her brother married. Would it also be the year that she met her own Mr Right?

Part II

Chapter Fifteen

December 1947

THE COLD RAIN DRIVEN by a biting wind stung Chrissie's cheeks and she pulled her shawl closer around her head as she trudged across the yard to let out the chickens and geese and then feed them. Parts of the yard were ankle deep in mud for it seemed to have rained incessantly for over a week, turning the fields nearest the river into small lakes. The cattle were all in the byre now for winter and that made Pat's workload heavier, even though they employed a man to milk and four local men as labourers and glad they were of steady employment. In her opinion they were paid a pittance of a wage but at least it meant that she didn't have to help to milk. She shuddered with horror at the thought of having to sit on a three-legged stool in close proximity to such large animals, even though Pat had assured her they were docile enough. She had begged and pleaded with him over the matter for in truth she was terrified of cows and gave all the beasts a very wide berth, except for the pony.

The first time she had driven into town on her own – heavens, how long ago it seemed now! – had been very unnerving. She had expected the animal to bolt at every opportunity but it hadn't and gradually she'd got used to driving. And it was the only bit of independence she seemed to have these days.

The summers were all too brief here, she thought bitterly as she fumbled with the rusty hasp on the hencoop, her fingers stiff with cold. And through those few stifling months life was exhausting. There was hay to cut and turn regularly to dry. It was needed for winter fodder. There was turf to cut up on the bog and then bring down to be stacked and stored in the sheds for winter fuel and this in addition to all the usual everyday chores of a working farm.

Her first summer in Rahan she had stubbornly and resolutely refused to help with the turf, which had caused a serious row between Pat and his Uncle Con who was of the opinion that she was 'slacking'. Pat had argued that she wasn't used to such back-breaking work and he worried that she would fall sick. This had been met with the derisive comment that he should have married a 'fine, strong, local girl who knew what was expected of her'. Chrissie's eyes became hard as she thought of all this. Con had made it increasingly clear that he didn't like her.

She had only gone up to the bog once, taking the men their lunch and she had hated it. The sun had beaten down relentlessly on them all for there was no shade, not even a few trees to sit beneath while they ate. The flies had seemed of plague proportions to her and she had been bitten all over. She had cursed every step of the way home and vowed never to go again. She had insisted that they take their lunch with them each morning when they set out, even though it had caused yet another argument. She had kept her vow: this last summer she had not set foot on the bog even once.

The chickens and geese clucked and flapped around her as she threw handfuls of food to them; once that was devoured they then straggled across the yard to forage in the apple garden – as Con called the small orchard – and Chrissie watched them for a few minutes before turning back towards the house. She was freezing for the December morning was raw and a long day of endless chores stretched ahead. Her shoulders slumped and she felt weary and dejected. If the summers were hard here then the winters were worse: last winter had taught her that.

Beside the back door was the pump and the big stone trough that held the water they used in the house. She would have to fill up the buckets and take them into the kitchen before she could even think about starting to clean up. Two large baskets of turf stood beside the door; at least Pat had been thoughtful enough to bring them over from the turf shed but she would still have to drag them inside. Even the simplest task was such hard work, she thought. She had taken electricity, gas, piped water, shops and public transport so much for granted in Liverpool. You could even have coal, milk and bread delivered to your door.

She filled two of the buckets from the trough and heaved them into the kitchen, looking around the untidy room with annoyance. How did three people manage to make such a mess? She herself was tidy, Mam had insisted on it, but both Pat and Con were hopeless, littering the place with clothes, boots and newspapers. She had tried, politely at first, to make them hang up their coats and jackets and caps and to take jumpers upstairs, to leave the boots by the back door as she did and to fold up the newspapers and put them in a pile by the fire. All to no avail. Then she had resorted to arguing and nagging, thinking to herself that she sounded just like her mam in a bad mood. Well, this morning she was going to sit down with a cup of tea before she started to clean up, she vowed rebelliously.

She put down more turf on the fire and while the kettle boiled she took a clean mug and the sugar basin from the dresser, brought the jug of milk from the larder and spooned the tea into the pot. Then she drew the bentwood rocking chair closer to the fire.

Clasping her cold hands around the mug of tea she stared despondently into the flames. Oh, why had she come here? When had the rainbow dreams of an idyllic life of plenty faded into the mists of disappointment and disillusionment? She did love Pat, at least that's what she told herself, and she had tried so hard to be the perfect wife but somehow it had all gone wrong.

At first she had been happy, it had all been such a novelty last spring and he had taken her out every week. Sometimes they'd gone to the Grand Central Cinema or the Forrester's, which was Tullamore's second cinema. Sometimes they'd gone to the Bridge House Hotel or Coulton's or Hayes Hotel. She had become a regular client of Miss McEvoy and had been delighted that at last she had plenty of new and stylish clothes to wear when she went into town where she always encountered both admiring and envious glances. Con had put a stop to all that.

She frowned as she sipped her tea. He had complained that Pat was spending too much money on her, demanding to know why she needed to be 'dressed up like the gentry' when she was a farmer's wife. Surely she only needed one good outfit for Mass? To her chagrin Pat had reluctantly agreed with his uncle, saying by way of an explanation that they were saving hard for a Fordson Major tractor which would make life so much easier but which was very expensive. Then, as the weather had improved and the work increased, Pat had apologised that he could no longer spare the time for their outings into town.

'I won't mind if you go to the cinema on your own, Chrissie. Sure, I want you to have some bit of pleasure in life,' he'd offered.

'How can I do that? I'd be the talk of the parish! A married woman off gallivanting to the cinema on her own. Wouldn't I be labelled the "bold one" or worse?' she'd snapped back at him, unable to hide her disappointment.

She sipped her tea. After the war had ended she had sworn she was going to enjoy the rest of her life, but now there was nothing, *nothing* at all to enjoy.

This spring their outings had resumed, but all too soon the relentless summer work schedule had overtaken them, and they hadn't been out for months now, except to Mass. They'd slipped into a routine of what was literally 'bed to work'. She got up at half past six, winter and summer, she cleaned, cooked, ironed, fed the poultry and collected the eggs, which often meant hours of trekking around the barns and outbuildings and hedgerows. She made butter in the dairy, another back-breaking task with the hand churn, and she was so tired by the end of the day that she was glad to crawl into bed at ten o'clock. Only on a Thursday did the routine vary. On Thursdays she drove herself into town, taking the excess butter and eggs into Egan's Grocery where they helped pay for the flour, sugar, tea and other groceries she needed. Those few hours were her only form of relaxation and entertainment.

The second Tuesday of each month was market day when oats, hay, potatoes and turnips were bought and sold. The third Friday of each month was Fair Day when the farmers drove their animals into town from as far away as Moate, but she never ventured into town on those days. It was too busy, for people came from miles around; the streets were too dirty with the droppings of the hundreds of animals; and there were far too many drunks celebrating a 'deal well done'. Pat or Con went on Fair Days and always came home complaining about the prices they had had to pay or the pittance they were now receiving for their animals. Twenty pounds for a sow and her litter was a disgrace and the five pounds they had to pay for the licence needed to export their cattle was little more than daylight robbery.

She had wanted a new and exciting life and what did she have? A life of drudgery and boredom with no prospect of it ever changing and if she had children that would only add to her work. The long, dreary months of another harsh winter stretched ahead of her and she felt utterly wretched. Her tea had gone cold and the fire was burning down.

She didn't stir when the door opened. She was comfortable and much warmer now but she shivered slightly as the cold draught pervaded the room.

'So, 'tis sitting by the fire taking your ease while meself and Pat are out in the weather!' Con said sharply. He had no liking for Chrissie at all and she had caused many arguments between himself and his nephew, something that had seldom occurred before she'd come into the house. In his opinion Pat had saddled himself with a lazy, frivolous, spoiled and selfish wife.

Chrissie got to her feet, annoyed by his comments.

'How many times have I asked you – politely – to take your boots off at the door and not be trailing the muck and mud of the yard into the house?' she snapped, glaring at the trail of muddy footprints across the flagged floor.

He ignored her. 'Is there tea in the pot?'

She nodded curtly. 'I thought you were helping Pat muck out those beasts?'

Again he ignored her, pouring himself a mug of tea which he quickly drank and added the mug to the pile of dirty dishes already on the table.

Chrissie's irritation turned to anger and she made a snap decision. 'Well, you can tell Pat I'm going out! I'm going into town! I'm sick of this house!'

Con glared at her. ' 'Tis not Thursday and this place is a midden and the fire's half out. And what are Pat and meself expected to do for our dinner with you off gallivanting?'

'You can do what you did before I came here! I'm sick and tired of being stuck here all day. I'm nothing but a drudge and if this place is a midden it's because *you* make all the mess. I'm sick of cleaning up after you two. You think you work hard but it's nothing, *nothing* compared to the work I have to do and no thanks for it either!'

Con gripped the edge of the table, his knuckles white and his weather-beaten cheeks flushed with anger. 'Now ye listen to me, girl! Ye have a good home here, ye want for nothing. There's good food aplenty on the table, doesn't Tess Maher come every week to do the washing and Mrs Maloney every month to do all the sewing and mending? What did ye expect when ye came here? To be waited on hand and foot? Ye have a good man who denies ye nothing, who would spend his last penny on ye and the fancy ideas ye have. Ideas and notions above your station, to my mind. And what are ye, when all is said and done? Not an heiress, that's for sure and for certain. Ye didn't bring a dowry or anything of use with ye. A jumped-up, spoiled, ungrateful little brat from a Liverpool slum is what ye are and don't ye forget it!'

Chrissie was shaking with rage at the insults heaped upon her. 'I am not a spoiled, ungrateful brat and I don't come from a slum! My home was in a good part of the city; my family is respectable and hard-working! Our house was a palace compared to this . . . this . . . *dump*! We had electricity, gas, piped water and the place was always clean and tidy,' she yelled.

'Then ye should have stayed there! But I seem to remember ye couldn't wait to leave. Ye were sick and tired of the shortages and the hardships. 'Tis my opinion that ye used Pat as a means to get out and when the mammy refused her permission ye were so wilful and determined that ye came running after him.' He wagged a finger at her. 'Well, ye got him and ye'll be contented and grateful for your lot. Now get this place cleaned up and the dinner prepared for your husband. I'll hear no more talk of running off into town to waste the money Pat half kills himself to earn!'

Chrissie was near to tears. 'I hate you! You've always

resented me! You're a nasty, evil-minded old man! I'm going to tell Pat every single thing you've said to me and then he'll have something to say to you!' she screamed at him

Con grabbed her by the shoulders and shook her hard. 'Ye've caused enough arguments in this house, girl! There was never a cross word spoken before ye came in the door. Ye'll say nothing to Pat, *nothing*, do ye hear me?' He released her and she grabbed the arm of the rocking chair for support. 'Now get on with the work!'

The door slammed shut behind him and Chrissie slumped down in the chair. She was still shaking and her face was white with shock. No one had ever treated her like this before. Her da had never raised a hand to her in his life. Con hated her, she had seen it in his eyes, and suddenly she was afraid. What if Con became more violent towards her? She should tell Pat of his uncle's behaviour this morning but would that only make matters worse? Would Con deny it and would Pat believe him? And the next time she dared to complain, would Con take it as a good-enough reason to beat her?

She glanced fearfully around the room. She couldn't stay here, she *couldn't*, not now. She was afraid of Con. She felt that Pat didn't understand her, he didn't seem to care about what she wanted, what she needed. She'd tried to explain to him that summer night last year but he'd turned away from her and on the two occasions when she'd tried again she'd met with irritation and rebukes which had made her feel a little guilty. She'd write to Mam and tell her everything and beg to be allowed to come home. She didn't care what people would say, she couldn't go on living like this. She'd write at once and she'd give the letter to Jack Brennan, the postman, when he called. They would have to send her her fare for she had very little money of her own and she couldn't ask Pat for it. She passed a trembling hand over her forehead. Pat . . .

He had been so good to her but she knew that Con would do everything in his power to turn him against her. When she had first complained to Pat about Con's attitude towards her Pat had begged her to be patient with his uncle, he was an old man, set in his ways, who had worked hard all his life for the family. In the early days of their marriage Pat had always defended her, been patient with her, indulged her, but she'd noticed a change in his attitude: sometimes he was impatient and irritable. She'd put it down to tiredness, but now she wondered was Con behind it?

Ignoring the mess in the kitchen, she rummaged in the drawer of the dresser until she found paper and an envelope and a pen, then she cleared a space at the table and wrote a long and detailed letter to Sadie, a letter stained with tears of misery and disillusionment. When she'd finished, she wiped her face with her apron and began to clean up, vowing to go up to the little church at Killina that afternoon to pray to Our Lady that she would soon be released from this awful existence.

Chapter Sixteen

SADIE GRIMACED AND CAUGHT her breath at the now familiar sharp pain in her back as she carried the coal scuttle into the kitchen. The 'twinges' as she still referred to them were getting worse and harder to hide from her family. She was just getting older; it was arthritis, that's all, she firmly told herself but there were times when in her heart she feared it was something far worse. These cold December days didn't help either.

Georgie looked up. 'Mam, why didn't you tell me you wanted more coal bringing in? I'd have carried it for you.' He was still concerned about her health for although she no longer went out to work and both Grace and Mags helped in the house she hadn't put on weight and she often looked pale and tired.

'For heaven's sake, lad, I can manage! You get on

with your tea. I won't have it going cold while you run around fetching in coal.' The pain made her tone sound sharper than she had intended. 'Oh, I know you mean well, Georgie, but I'm not an invalid!'

He grinned at her and poured her a cup of tea. 'Well, sit down and have this, you look as though you need it. Our Grace is late tonight,' he commented. Mags worked late on Friday nights as they were always busy in the grocer's shop but Grace was usually in by now. Billy had already finished his meal and was getting himself spruced up to go out with Tilly Armstrong, his first real girlfriend.

'She was meeting Sandy in town; they're going to the cinema, the Gaumont, I think.'

Georgie nodded, stirring his tea. 'Do you think it's serious between those two, Mam? He's a decent bloke with a good steady job, she could do worse.'

Sadie looked thoughtful. 'I wish I could say it was but I just don't know, lad, and that's the truth. He seems very keen on her and I like him too. I know she's fond of him because I asked her straight out how she felt, but she says she doesn't know if she *loves* him.' Sadie shook her head. 'She says she doesn't feel the way Mags feels towards you, or at least how Mags described being "in love".' She sighed heavily. 'She said she certainly wouldn't up and go chasing after him like our Chrissie did with Pat Kilroy.'

'Grace was never like Chrissie, Mam. She always had more sense in her head, thank God!'

Sadie nodded her agreement. She still worried about Chrissie for the occasional brief note was all she ever received and she hadn't even had one of those for a while. She sipped her tea, thinking that like every other mother she knew, she still worried about them all. Billy had been promoted to the sorting office and thought he was a real 'big feller' now, although Georgie kept him in check. She hoped Grace had at last found her 'Mr Right' in Sandy McBride. She truly wanted to see Grace happy and settled. She was praying hard that Georgie and Mags would get a nice council house of their own soon – although it still didn't look very likely as there were so many families waiting to be rehoused. She got on well with them both and would miss them when they did go but it wasn't the best way to start married life, living here with herself and the rest of the family, there was very little privacy, and now Mags was expecting their first baby next summer. She smiled to herself. Her first grandchild, wasn't that something to look forward to?

She got to her feet as Mags came into the kitchen. 'Ah, home at last from that shop, Mags. Now sit down. Georgie will pour you a cup of tea. You look tired, luv,' she fussed.

Mags smiled at her as she took off her coat and hat. 'I'm fine, Ma, honestly. I'm not ill, just expecting.'

'Well, these early months can be difficult. I'll feel happier when you leave that job. On your feet all day with only half an hour for your lunch.'

'You do look a bit peaky, Mags,' Georgie ventured.

Mags tutted. 'Honestly! If I'm looking a bit peaky it's because I've been having to explain to customers all day that rations are being cut – again! Meat has gone down from two shillings' worth a week to a shilling's worth, potatoes are down to three pounds per person per week and bacon down to two ounces. I tell you, things are looking bleak for Christmas.'

Sadie nodded. 'And it comes to something when Princess Elizabeth has had to go off on her honeymoon without a trousseau because of the shortages.'

'Ah, but wasn't her wedding dress magnificent?' Mags replied dreamily, thinking of all the photographs in the newspapers of the wedding of the King's eldest daughter to Prince Philip of Greece the month before. It had been such a grand occasion that it had cheered them all up.

Sadie frowned. 'How are we expected to keep body and soul together on those rations? Things are getting worse, not better. Well, I'm going to write to our Chrissie and see if she can send over a goose and some butter and eggs and anything else she can get her hands on or it's going to be a right miserable Christmas. I'll send her the money. I won't have them thinking we're asking for charity.'

'Mam, it takes her all her time to put pen to paper these days so I can't see her making an effort to parcel up all that stuff and send it over. Besides, the eggs would be smashed to bits by the time they arrived. Don't I see every day the way parcels are handled?' Georgie remarked.

'She will when I tell her we have to look after Mags's health now,' Sadie replied firmly while Mags just grinned at her husband. His mam was determined to mollycoddle her but she wouldn't turn her nose up at roast goose for Christmas dinner.

Grace had had a pleasant evening – but then she always did, she thought as Sandy walked her to the tram stop. She'd enjoyed the film; it was Alfred Hitchcock's *Notorious* with Cary Grant and Ingrid Bergman.

'I wish I had gorgeous long blond hair like Ingrid Bergman, instead of these mousy curls,' she sighed.

Sandy laughed. 'You've gorgeous hair, Grace. In fact you're every bit as attractive as she is.'

'Oh, stop it! She's a film star! I'm a cutter in a place that makes flags.'

He squeezed her hand. 'Well, you're just as beautiful in my eyes.'

She smiled up at him. She really was very fond of him and they did get on well together. They'd never had the slightest disagreement – yet.

'Did I tell you that there's a good chance I'll be promoted in the New Year and it will mean a rise in my wages? Nothing definite has been said but it's been more than hinted at.'

'That's great, Grace, but wouldn't it have benefited you more to have the extra money before Christmas?'

She shrugged. 'I suppose so but I've a bit put by for presents. I've been thinking, Sandy, that I might save up and go to see Chrissie for a few days. I do miss her and it will be quite an adventure for me. I'll be entitled to a week's paid holiday next year and I know Mam worries about her.'

He looked at her with interest. 'We could go together, Grace, if you like? I haven't had a holiday in years and I've never been to Ireland. Besides, you'll need someone to look after you.'

Grace laughed. 'You make me sound like a five year old! Chrissie managed the journey on her own!'

'Och, you know what I mean. We'd enjoy it. Separate rooms, of course, and your mam would worry less if I were with you.'

That made sense, Grace thought, but was she ready to spend so much time with him? It was a commitment of sorts. She always felt comfortable, at ease and safe with him but she could never get Mags's words out of her mind. She didn't feel excited or nervous or ecstatically happy when he kissed her and she didn't feel dejected and miserable when they were apart, unable to wait for the moment they would meet again. They'd been courting for a year now and maybe she was being selfish and unfair to him in continuing to see him for she knew he loved her, he'd told her so.

'Let's wait and see, shall we? I might not get promoted at all or Mam might not want me to go, or Chrissie might not want to be bothered with me either.'

He nodded reluctantly. He hoped they would go; it might be just the right opportunity to ask her whether her feelings for him had deepened enough for her to consider marrying him. She hadn't told him she loved him, she'd said she was very fond of him but he'd realised that Grace was rather serious-minded about such things and he hadn't pressed the matter. He preferred to give her time; that way he would be certain that when she had definitely made up her mind, it would be a binding and resolute decision.

When she got home she found both Mags and Sadie were in bed, but Georgie was waiting up for herself and Billy.

'Was it a good film? Is Sandy not with you?' Georgie questioned.

'No, if he'd come home with me he'd have missed the last tram and I couldn't expect him to walk all that way home. Is our Billy not in yet?'

'What do you think? Mam told him he's to be in at eleven at the latest and it's half past now. You know how she worries about him and she's sure Tommy Milligan is a bad influence on him. She thought when he started going out with Tilly he'd settle down.'

Grace eased off her shoes and placed her cold feet on the hearth. 'He's not all that bad, Georgie. They never get into trouble. How is Mags?'

'Tired and harassed. Rations are being cut again and Mam says she's going to write and ask our Chrissie to send over a goose and other stuff for Christmas.

She worries that Mags isn't getting the right things to eat.'

Grace nodded. 'Mam's always worrying about one or other of us. I was telling Sandy tonight that I might get promoted and that I was thinking of going over to see Chrissie next year, on a sort of holiday. Until now I've not had the time and the money to spare, the weather should be better and I can set Mam's mind at rest.'

'I'd write and ask her first, Grace, but it might be a good idea for you to go. Put all our minds at rest that she hasn't made a mess of things – she tells us so little in her letters it's hard to know what's going on.'

'Sandy wants to come with me but I´.–. I don't know. I told him we'd wait and see. He might take it as some kind of commitment and I don't want that . . . just yet.'

Georgie sighed. 'I suppose you're right to be a bit cautious although I like him, he's a nice feller.'

'Mags might need some help after she has the baby, I don't want to put extra work on Mam, even though she's over the moon about being a granny.'

Georgie nodded. 'I wish she'd go and see the doctor about these so-called twinges, he might be able to give her something for them.'

'She won't. I've asked her. She says it's old age and she's not paying him three and six to tell her just that.'

'She won't need to pay soon, once this Welfare State thing gets going.'

'But she still won't go, you know how stubborn she

can be.' Grace got to her feet. 'Well, I'm off to bed. Don't be too hard on our Billy, he thinks he's really grown up now.'

Georgie shrugged but then grinned. 'Then he should be more responsible and act his age not his shoe size!'

Billy arrived fifteen minutes later, looking a bit sheepish.

'Oh, finally you managed to come home,' Georgie commented, looking pointedly at the clock on the mantel.

Billy flung himself down in a chair opposite his brother. 'Ah, don't start going on at me! You were always out late when you were my age. If you can't have a bit of fun when you're young it's a poor show.'

Georgie relaxed and grinned at him. 'I'm not going on at you. I just don't want Mam to worry and she told you to be in by eleven at the latest. She'd prefer you to be going out with Tilly, you know what she thinks about Tommy.'

Billy grimaced. 'You've got to go out with your mates now and then. Just because I've got a girlfriend it doesn't mean I've got to dump me mates.'

'You'd be an idiot if you did that. Good mates are hard to come by.'

'And besides, it's not serious or anything with Tilly. She's OK and we have a bit of a laugh, that's all.'

Georgie nodded. 'I suppose when I was your age that's all I ever thought about too, having a bit of a laugh.'

'I look at it like this, you've got to enjoy yourself while you're young because when you get older you have to get married and settle down and from what I can see there's not much fun after that. It's all worry and responsibilities.'

'You're right about that.' Georgie grinned at his brother. 'You're not as daft as you look, Billy Devlin. Go on, get up to bed and don't go making a noise. I suppose I'll have to tell Mam you were in on time, just to keep the peace.'

Billy flashed him a smile as he got up. 'Thanks, Georgie. You're a star.'

They all had to work on Saturday mornings, in fact Mags had to work all day. Wednesday afternoon was her afternoon off. Sadie went about her household chores as usual, occasionally glancing out of the window at the sky, which in her opinion threatened snow. It was certainly cold enough; when she'd come down this morning there had been ice on the inside of the kitchen window. She prayed they were not in for a winter like the last one when heavy snowfalls and sub-zero temperatures had brought the country to its knees. Thousands of people had been laid off by power cuts and as the coal trains had been unable to get through twenty-foot-high snowdrifts, homes had been without light or heat. Constant blizzards had brought all shipping in the Channel to a halt and the fishing fleets were kept in port. Doctors and nurses had done their rounds on horseback in the country areas. Oh, it had been terrible

– and then when the snow had melted there had been floods. No, she didn't want to go through another winter like that, not the way she felt this morning.

She cleared away and washed the breakfast dishes, tidied the room, built up the fire and then went upstairs to make her own and Billy's bed. Grace always did her own and kept the room tidy and so did Mags. When she finished she promised herself a cup of tea and a little rest before she black-leaded the range and then prepared the midday meal.

She'd just sat down when Polly Nelson knocked and then let herself in by the back door. Polly had always been a big woman but in middle age she had grown stouter and the heavy coat over numerous cardigans she wore in the cold weather made her look even more rotund.

'Holy Mother, it's bitter out there, Sadie! We'll have snow before the day's out.'

'Sit down, Polly, and take off that coat or you won't feel the benefit of it when you go out. I've just made a fresh pot of tea. You look starved.'

'I've been down to Ted Granby to see what I could get and it wasn't much, I can tell you. Two chops and half a dozen sausages to feed my lot for the weekend! In the name of God, I thought by now we'd have full and plenty. But there're some who can get these new French fashions, didn't I read that seven hundred of those Dior New Look costumes sold in one week! I ask you, what's the world coming to, Sadie?'

'Some people have all their priorities wrong, Polly, that's what it is.'

'Was that the post? You sit there, luv, I'll go,' Polly offered, thinking Sadie looked exhausted. And it was only eleven o'clock, she mused as she picked up two letters from behind the front door. Oh, it looked like milady over the water had written a decent letter at last, she thought, noting the word *Eire* on the stamp.

'One looks like a bill and the other a letter from your Chrissie,' she informed Sadie, placing them on the table beside her neighbour.

Sadie looked pleased. She'd been hoping for a letter from Chrissie.

Polly drank her tea while Sadie began to read the letter but she put down her cup as Sadie gave a low moan and what little colour there was in her cheeks drained away. 'Holy Mother of God! What's wrong, Sadie?'

Sadie passed the letter over, shaking her head in despair. 'I knew it, Polly! I just *knew* it! What am I to do with her?'

Polly read quickly and she pursed her lips. Chrissie was begging to come home. She hated her life. Everyone hated her, especially the uncle whom she said had attacked her, and she wasn't even sure that Pat still loved her. She was being worked to death and there was still no electricity or gas or even piped water. Polly folded the letter and gave it back to Sadie.

'You'd better see what your Georgie and Grace have

to say, Sadie, luv. Don't you go making yourself ill over it now. She might be exaggerating it all.'

Sadie nodded miserably. She would have to discuss this with Georgie and Grace when they got home. She had a fair idea already of what Georgie would say.

Chapter Seventeen

———◆———

BILLY AND GEORGIE ARRIVED first. Georgie was the overseer of the section of the sorting office where Billy now worked, so they finished together. Both were dismayed to find Sadie sitting at the table with her head in her hands. There was no sign of a meal having been prepared.

'Mam! Mam, are you ill?' Georgie was full of concern. 'Billy, go and get the doctor!'

'No! I'm not ill!' Sadie shook her head vehemently and looked up.

Billy, alarmed at the prospect of some possible forthcoming disaster and the lack of anything to eat, quickly went back out to see if there was any sign of Grace. To his relief she was making her way up the street towards him.

'Grace! Hurry up, there's something wrong with Mam and there's no dinner ready but she says she's not ill!' he called.

Grace began to run, fearing the worst. It was unheard of that there was no hot meal waiting for them on Saturday lunchtime, especially at this time of year. She followed Billy into the kitchen to find her mother still sitting at the table and Georgie reading what appeared to be a long letter.

'Mam? What is it? What's wrong?' she demanded, putting her arm around Sadie's shoulders.

'Chrissie!' Sadie croaked, dabbing at her eyes with the hem of her pinafore.

'Oh, God! What's happened to her? Is that letter from Pat? Has there been an accident?' Grace demanded of her brother.

Georgie flung the letter on the table, his cheeks flushed with anger. 'It's not from Pat, it's from Chrissie and there's been no accident! Read it, Grace!'

Grace scanned the lines, her eyes widening in horror. 'Oh, no! Surely, surely all this can't be true?'

'It's probably all a pack of lies! I can't see Pat Kilroy allowing anyone to lay a finger on our Chrissie. No, she's decided she doesn't like being married, doesn't like living in Ireland – she says so – nor does she seem to like having to do a decent day's work!' Georgie fumed, although despite his anger he was concerned for Chrissie. What if the old man had belted her? After all, they'd never met him.

'I knew this would happen! Oh, why wouldn't she listen to me when I begged her to wait? I've prayed every day that she hadn't made a mistake and that she'd be happy,' Sadie moaned.

Grace sat down. She didn't know what to believe. Like her brother she was certain Pat would never allow Chrissie to be ill treated, he had promised and she believed him.

'She wouldn't listen to Mam or to me. No, she went running off after him without a thought for anyone. She was the one who insisted on marrying him; well, she *is* married and there's nothing that can be done to change that. She'll just have to make the best of it.'

'But what if she runs off and leaves him?' Grace asked.

'She's begging Mam to send her the money for her fare. She obviously doesn't have money of her own and she won't get far without any. Mam, you'll just have to be firm with her. Point out that it was her choice, her decision and one that can't be changed now. She took her vows before God in church that she would love, honour and obey, until death. She's not even been married two years, and she's fed up already! She's probably been throwing tantrums and demanding he give her the earth and take her out gallivanting morning, noon and night when the man has a living to earn!'

Grace reread part of the letter, noting the tearstains on the paper. 'She says he did take her out and she had lovely things and she was happy and that she has tried to be the perfect wife, but his uncle put a stop to all that and is turning Pat against her. Now she's terrified of the uncle. What does she mean he "attacked" her? Did he beat her?'

'I can't honestly see Pat allowing that. I've often spoken to Eileen Bateson and she said Pat idolised Chrissie and was being very patient with her, her not being used to country life. She did say once that Con was a bit set in his ways but that he had always worked hard. If our Chrissie was spending money like water and gallivanting and not pulling her weight, then I can see the old man being angry with her. Earning a living from the land is a damned hard life.'

Sadie dabbed at her eyes again. 'Oh, I hate to think of her living in fear and being so miserable. It must be terrible to have no electricity or even piped water, it would make everything so much harder.'

Grace took her hand. 'Mam, if she had waited like we wanted her to do, gone for a visit as was planned, she would have been able to see all that for herself and it might have changed her mind, but she *wouldn't*.'

'Grace is right, Mam. If you can't face it, I'll write to her and tell her she has no choice but to stay and make the best of things,' Georgie said quietly, his anger fading a little.

'She knows you didn't approve and she'd feel worse. No, no, lad, I'll write. It won't be easy but I'll do it.'

'And if you like, I'll write too,' Grace offered.

'Thanks, Grace, but I'm her mam. It will be best coming from me.'

Grace got to her feet. 'Right. Let's get a meal started, our Billy looks as though he's going to drop in a faint with hunger! You sit there, Mam, I'll see to it.' She turned to her younger brother who had remained stunned and silent up to now. 'Right, Billy, go and fetch in another scuttle of coal and build up that fire. Georgie, will you put the kettle on and make us all a cup of tea? We could do with it.'

Both lads did as they were bid and as Grace put a pan of potatoes on to boil she muttered to Georgie that when Mags got home they were both going to see Eileen to try to ascertain if there could possibly be a grain of truth in Chrissie's accusations.

Mags was just as worried and distressed as Grace when she heard the news and after they'd had their evening meal both girls made the short journey to Eileen Bateson's home. Georgie had wanted to accompany them, for it had indeed started to snow, but Mags had been adamant.

'She's a good friend of mine and she'll be more open with us,' she had said firmly.

Eileen ushered them into her warm and comfortable parlour and then sat open-mouthed when Grace informed her of what Chrissie had said.

'Mother of God! Uncle Con wouldn't raise a hand to a woman, that he would not! And didn't I only have a letter from Pat last week and he saying they were all getting along fine. Sure, they don't go out much but the weather's not fit for it and he says Chrissie does get very tired and is glad to go to her bed early. He said she was coping very well, for a city girl and that she enjoys driving herself into town on Thursdays to do the bit of shopping. He does try to ease her work as much as he can. She doesn't milk or tend to the beasts, just the poultry. She has a woman who comes in each week to do the washing and another once a month to do all the mending – which is more than I have meself.'

'She's never mentioned that,' Mags said sharply. It was a luxury neither Sadie nor her own mam had ever had.

'It's always been the custom for those who could afford it and it gives employment to those who need it. In truth, Mags, I think she's exaggerating. Uncle Con would never beat her any more than Pat would.'

Mags nodded. She was angry for she believed her friend to be telling the truth. 'They probably had a row and Chrissie has blown it all up. I'm so sorry, Eileen, that we had to come to you with such a tale. Georgie says Mam has to write and tell her to pull herself together, she's not a child, she's a married woman whether she likes it or not.'

Eileen shook her head sadly. ' 'Tis Pat I feel sorry for, Mags. He truly loves her and by the sound of it she . . . well, she's not happy and that will make him miserable.'

'I'm sorry for him too, Eileen,' Mags agreed.

Eileen stood up. 'Well now, I'll get Himself to get out the car and take you home, you can't walk back in this weather, not in your condition, Mags. In these early months you have to take care of yourself. I suppose you should really consider giving up work. You're on your feet all day. I know you'll have to give up when you're six months but you might think about leaving a bit earlier. And with this snow and ice you might fall and that would cause complications that we don't want.' Eileen patted her friend's hand but wished with all her heart that she had never invited Chrissie Devlin to her wedding. She couldn't write to Pat about this, she couldn't interfere between man and wife.

Sadie spent the entire afternoon on Sunday composing her letter to Chrissie. It was the hardest letter she'd ever had to write but eventually she was satisfied.

'I'll post it first thing in the morning, Mam,' Grace offered for she had promised Georgie she would make an early start and walk with Mags to Peegram's to be certain her sister-in-law didn't slip. There was now a covering of snow everywhere and a sharp frost had made conditions underfoot treacherous.

The two girls walked slowly down Royal Street next morning, thankful that most people had thrown the ashes from their fires on to the pavement to give some grip.

'Honestly, Grace, you don't have to come the whole way with me. I'll be fine,' Mags said.

'Mam would kill me if anything happened to you and her grandchild! I can get a tram from Westminster Road into town. Remember you promised Georgie you'd go to your mam's and wait for him to call for you?'

Mags laughed. 'I hope this weather doesn't last or everyone will be worn out looking after me.'

They'd reached the pillar box and Grace took Sadie's letter from her shoulder bag and posted it. 'There, let's hope that brings our Chrissie to her senses.'

'Well, we can be sure of one thing. That's the end of the goose for the Christmas dinner. She'll be so mad that even if we went down on our knees she'd send us nothing!'

Grace nodded. 'Maybe if we write to Pat he'll send us one?'

'I think it's best to let things alone, Grace. We'll manage, we've had plenty of practice. Eight years of it now.'

'Please God next Christmas will be better,' Grace said fervently.

'Amen to that. Now come on, let's get going.'

Chrissie watched each day for the arrival of the postman, but there was no post on a Saturday or Sunday and that only added to her impatience. She hadn't spoken a single word to Con since the row and Pat had noticed her silence and the strained atmosphere.

'Chrissie, has there been some kind of a fight between you and Con?' he'd asked with concern. His uncle had said nothing to him but he'd noticed that the old man's glances at Chrissie were full of contempt.

She had shrugged. 'Nothing more than usual, I asked him to leave his boots by the door and he bit my head off.'

'I know he can be difficult, but he's set in his ways and sure you can't ask a man who is nearing seventy-six to change them. Cheer up, Chrissie, it will be Christmas in a week or two.'

'And what difference will that make around here? I suppose I'll be expected to spend the next weeks cooking and baking so you two can stuff yourselves silly! I don't expect we will be going into town to a dance or any other kind of entertainment and even if we were I've nothing decent to wear!'

He'd looked at her with hurt and disappointment in his eyes. 'Chrissie, what do you want? I'll gladly take you into town, there's bound to be a dance on somewhere, but you're always complaining that you're too tired to do anything of an evening.'

'I am! Wouldn't anyone be exhausted with the work I have to do?'

He'd made another attempt to cheer her up. 'Ah, we'll have a grand Christmas. I'll cut plenty of holly and we'll decorate the place up. I know Con is planning to slaughter a pig so there'll be pork and we'll have a goose as well, and don't we always have a bottle or two of port wine? And I've had my eye on something that will be a surprise for you. It will delight you.'

She'd made a half-hearted effort to look interested but she had prayed that by the time Christmas arrived, she would be far away from here. That she would once again be back in Liverpool.

The following Thursday when she arrived back from her trip into town Sadie's letter was on the table. When there was no one in Jack Brennan just left the mail there; the door was never locked. She hadn't enjoyed her outing for the weather was wretched with strong winds and driving sleet and by the time she'd arrived she was cold and wet through. With Christmas approaching the town had been very busy but she knew very few people and as she'd negotiated the crowded pavements she thought that even after more than eighteen months she'd made no friends. Oh, Pat seemed to know everyone and when she was with him all the world and its wife chatted to them but they spoke so quickly and the brogue was so strong that she found it hard to keep up with the conversations. Some of the local women did pass the time with her after Mass but she had little in common with them and she often thought they viewed her as stuck up.

She'd taken her butter and eggs into Egan's and had purchased the groceries she needed but instead of wandering around, peering into the shop windows as she usually did, she'd come straight home.

Dragging off her mackintosh, her coat and the woollen tam-o'-shanter, she took the letter and sat down in front of the fire. Oh, thank God it had arrived!

Now she could start to make her plans. She hugged the
envelope to her. She would say nothing to Pat – what
could she say? Next Thursday she would drive into
town as usual but she would take her case with her. She
would leave him a note, telling him she was sorry but
that she just couldn't go on living here and to pick up
the trap from the station yard where the station master
would mind it until he arrived. She intended to be on
the train by mid-morning which would get her to
Dublin in good time for the ferry. By this time next
week she would be on her way. This life would be
behind her. She would start again. Of course she would
still be married but even so, life as a married woman in
Liverpool was far better than life as a married drudge
here. She was only twenty, she would get a job and have
money of her own again. She would be able to buy
clothes and make-up and go out with Ellie Nelson. She
had had enough of men to last her a lifetime so she
wouldn't be looking for boyfriends, she just wanted to
enjoy life.

She tore open the envelope and scanned the lines of
Sadie's small, neat handwriting, and then she uttered a
strangled cry of despair. No! No! Mam couldn't do this
to her, she just *couldn't*! Mam was telling her she
couldn't go home, that this was her home now and Pat
her husband. She even doubted what she had told her
about Con's treatment of her, saying that Grace and
Mags had been to see Eileen who had sworn that the old
man would never raise a hand to her. Oh, why didn't

they believe her? Tears of shock and bitter disappointment poured down her cheeks. Sadie had written that marriage was for life, for better or for worse, promises made before God, and that she really would have to make the best of it. She said she was sure Pat saw that she wanted for nothing, didn't she even have a woman to do the washing and another to do the mending? She didn't know how well off she was for things were getting worse not better in England, the shortages were crippling.

This was all Georgie's doing, she was certain of it, no doubt encouraged by Mags. She could just hear him telling her mam what to write and now . . . now she would have to endure God knows what kind of a life. She wished she were dead!

She flung the letter into the fire and watched it burn, dashing away her tears with the back of her hand. Well, she wasn't going to stand for it. She would write again. She wasn't going to give up, she *couldn't*!

Chapter Eighteen

———◆———

CHRISTMAS IN BOTH THE house in Royal Street and the farmhouse in Rahan was a quiet affair. At least the weather was seasonal, Grace remarked, for it had snowed for the two days before Christmas Eve. Sadie was still worried about Chrissie and the fact that once more she would be hard put to provide a decent dinner. Coal was again in short supply although they were very fortunate that Eileen Bateson had persuaded her father-in-law to have an extra bag delivered to Sadie, mainly for the benefit of her friend Mags, so at least they would have a decent fire.

Grace and Mags had made paper chains with which they decorated the kitchen and Billy and his mate Tommy had taken a tram out to Fazakerley Terminus and then walked to Simonswood where they had cut large bunches of holly from the hedgerows. These had been divided between the two families.

Sandy had taken Grace to a dance at the Grafton Ballroom on Christmas Eve and he was to join them for dinner next day, he having supplied a large piece of cured ham in a tin.

'Mam's delighted that you got that tin of ham, where did you get it by the way?' Grace had asked as he'd walked her to the tram stop after the dance.

'Och, you can get all kinds of stuff in the place I work if you know the right people and have the money. I tried to get a chicken or a capon but you can't get fresh meat for love nor money, just tinned stuff. Wait until you see what I've got for you, Gracie.'

She'd looked at him in concern. 'Sandy, you haven't gone and spent a fortune on me, have you? I've got you something but it wasn't expensive.'

'Don't worry your head about it. You're worth every penny and who else have I to buy for? You've got the entire family.'

'Well, Mam's very grateful for the ham. We were hoping for something from Ireland but what with our Chrissie . . .'

Sandy had nodded. He'd been informed that things were not going very well in Rahan. 'Then I take it we won't be going on our little holiday next year?'

'Not much point. There wouldn't be much pleasure in it, would there?' Grace had answered.

Both Grace and Sadie were up early on Christmas

morning but Sadie insisted that Mags have a lie-in. Both she and Georgie were going to the Drapers' house at teatime and Mrs Draper was looking forward to the first peaceful Christmas she'd had in years, as her sister Flo had finally been rehoused. Everyone went to eleven o'clock Mass and then the gifts were exchanged. Grace was thrilled and astonished with Sandy's gift. No less than three pairs of Wolsey nylon stockings and a small bottle of Evening in Paris perfume. She hugged him, feeling that the pair of Argyle-patterned socks she'd given him was totally inadequate. Later on she would give Mags a pair of the nylons. She had seen the wistful look on her sister-in-law's face and she knew Sandy wouldn't object.

The addition of the ham to the small shoulder of lamb that Sadie had been able to purchase, together with roast potatoes and some carrots and parsnips, was declared 'a feast', even if there was no traditional plum pudding to follow. Billy's contribution was half a dozen bottles of Bent's Pale Ale for himself, Georgie and Sandy and a half-bottle of Madeira wine for 'the ladies'.

As Sadie settled down that evening in front of the fire to listen to the wireless with Grace and Sandy – Billy had gone off to Tommy Milligan's house where some effort was being made to throw a bit of a party, and Georgie and Mags were still at Mags's parents – she felt it had been quite a successful day but now she just wanted to rest and relax and try not to worry about Chrissie for a few hours.

* * *

Pat had made an effort to decorate the kitchen, he'd even given it a fresh coat of limewash first, and he'd bought a big red paper bell, decorated with bits of gold foil, which he'd hung above the fireplace. This was in addition to the bunches of holly and mistletoe. Chrissie had been very subdued, he'd noticed, but had stirred herself enough to bake mince pies and a cake. He was certain though that when she saw the gift he had purchased for her she would be delighted and more like her old self.

Con had killed a pig and had butchered it, salting most of it down, but hams now hung in one of the outhouses and his uncle was curing them over a fire of wood shavings. A leg had been kept aside for the holiday. Pat had asked Chrissie to pick out a good fat goose for the table but she had refused, telling him to choose it himself as he was the one who would wring its neck.

They all went to Midnight Mass at Killina, which Pat always thought of as being the real essence of Christmas, especially as the figure of the Christ child was placed in the crib during the service. Afterwards they shook hands and exchanged greetings with all their neighbours and even Chrissie seemed to brighten up a bit.

Chrissie had written again to her mother, this time stressing even more vehemently how miserable, how despairing and afraid she was and finishing with the words: 'Mam, if I have to stay here I will *die*! One way or another this place will kill me!' She had posted it the day before Christmas Eve when she'd gone into town with Pat for 'a bit of lunch', a rare treat and something he was hoping would cheer her up.

'It won't get there in time for Christmas, Chrissie. You should have sent it earlier. Will she be disappointed?' He'd asked when they'd stopped at the Post Office.

'No. I've already sent them a card. It's nothing important,' she'd replied off-handedly. If she could just get through this awful holiday, she'd thought, she was certain that this time Mam would agree to letting her go home.

She felt guilty when on Christmas morning Pat produced a large box, nicely wrapped, and kissed her, saying, 'Happy Christmas, Chrissie.'

Inside, wrapped in tissue paper, was what people called a tippet: a short cape that just covered the shoulders. This one was of soft brown velvet, lined with cream satin and fastened with a gilt clasp in the form of Celtic knots.

'It's . . . it's lovely, really lovely. You know how much I like nice things, thank you,' she said, kissing his cheek. 'But where will I wear it? It's far too grand for everyday use.'

'Sure, next year I was thinking we might go to the Galway Races, you could wear it then. The women do dress up for that.'

She smiled but encountered a scornful, sceptical glance from Con and the smile faded. She placed the garment hurriedly back in the box.

Throughout the Christmas dinner, which she had to agree was the best she'd had for many a year, comprising a thick vegetable soup, roast goose with carrots and parsnips and potatoes, followed by the traditional pudding and custard and accompanied by glasses of port wine, she was silent and preoccupied. Pat and his uncle discussed the state of the economy, particularly in relation to agriculture, and the possible outcome of the General Election and if Mr de Valera would continue as Taoiseach. Then their conversation turned to the news that on the first day of the New Year all the railways in Britain would be nationalised and that the year would also see the introduction in Britain of the National Health Service. No one would have to pay for medical treatment, it would all be free.

'And sure where are they going to find the money for all that? Doctors still need to be paid. And paid well. Doesn't Sadie write that things are still desperate there with half the country not having enough to eat?' Con commented.

'From increased taxes, I suppose, Con. I do hear that this Aneurin Bevan, the Minister of Health, has great plans altogether. 'Tis a pity we don't have someone like him here. Someone with a bit of a vision for the future.'

Con cut himself a slice of cake and looked thoughtful. 'More taxes we can do without, Pat. Sure, things are bad enough with fifty thousand people a year taking the emigrant ship, economic decline and strikes – even by the teachers.'

Chrissie got to her feet. She was bored stiff with this conversation. All Con ever did was complain – about everything! 'I'll clear away later. I'm going for a walk, I've a bit of a headache,' she announced.

Pat looked up; she did look a little feverish. 'Will I come with you?'

She shook her head. 'No. No, I'll be fine. I won't be long.'

'A good blast of fresh air always does clear the head,' Con opined. This was one of the few days in the year he enjoyed and took some ease. A day of little work, a good dinner, a glass of port wine and a chat beside the fire with his nephew. Just the way they'd always spent that special day and he was glad she was taking herself off out and would not be spoiling the hour banging dishes and pots around and with a puss on her face even though Pat had bought her that piece of finery that must have cost more than they could afford. And as for the idea of going off to the Galway Races, wasting hard-earned money gambling, just to entertain your one and she grateful for nothing, well, he'd have something to say about that!

Chrissie wrapped the heavy shawl around her as she trudged across the yard. Where the snow had thawed it was muddy and she avoided those places for she hadn't changed into her boots. The ground was hard and rutted and iced-over puddles cracked beneath her feet. She closed the yard gate behind her, hearing the snuffling of the beasts in the byre. She didn't care how she looked; there was no one about to see her. She walked up the track and on to the canal bank. The waters of the canal were frozen, the dead reeds at the edges stiff with frozen snow. The branches of the trees on the opposite bank stood out black and bare against the grey sky. The Lock House looked to be empty although she knew it was not. The Mitchell family who were the lock-keepers were probably all taking their ease after dinner.

She crossed the small stone bridge over the canal, glancing briefly at the two-storeyed white house with its dark green painted door that had been built nearly 150 years ago for the canal agent, an important man in his day. Oh, she prayed that this time her mam would ignore anything Georgie or Mags had to say. She couldn't go on like this, she would fall ill, she knew she would. People did fall into a decline and die. There was nothing to look forward to. She had no future. She was twenty years old and her life was over. In her heart she knew she had no one else to blame for her predicament but herself. Mam had begged her to wait and she should have taken heed of her. If she was utterly truthful she knew she couldn't blame Pat for her unhappiness. He had tried, in his way. It wasn't his fault that she couldn't endure living here. Couldn't endure the isolation, the harshness of rural life. And then there was Con. He'd never liked her, nor approved of her, and now she was sure he hated her. If there was another row she was certain he would beat her. He'd never been married, never been in love, didn't know how to treat a woman – and she wasn't even a woman, just a girl. Oh, it was all such a mess! And should she even be praying to God when she was going back on all the vows she had made?

She walked on, her head down, as all the regrets and questions swooped around in her mind, like the flock of crows that circled noisily above her in the trees beside the quarry. At her approach a heron resting on the bank took flight, but she didn't even notice it. She was engulfed by misery and despair – and yet there was just a tiny glimmer of hope. Hope that she would soon receive the news she longed for. Her mother's agreement that she could go home.

Chapter Nineteen

———◆◆◆———

SADIE RECEIVED THE SECOND letter in the week between Christmas and New Year. It had come at a very bad time for the pains in her back were worse and to add to her worries Mags had been confined to bed, having been sent home from work after getting a 'show'. Dr Schofield had been called and had given strict instructions that she must not set foot out of the bed for at least a week.

'But she will be all right? I mean, she won't lose the child?' Sadie had asked fearfully as she'd shown him downstairs.

'Not if she does as she's told, Mrs Devlin. Can I rely on you to see that she does?'

'Oh, indeed you can, doctor. It's no wonder this has happened. She's on her feet all day in that place and she's only a little slip of a thing.'

'Then it might be advisable if she were to finish early. She won't be able to work after she's six months anyway,' he'd advised.

Sadie had nodded. They would manage without Mags's wages and she didn't mind the extra work, as long as her grandchild survived. And then Chrissie's letter had arrived.

There was a family conference of sorts that night. Mags was still in bed and Billy had been dispatched to the Milligans' house for, as Sadie said, these things were not for a young lad's ears. Billy had been relieved to go, he wasn't entirely sure what was wrong with Mags but he was fully aware that their Chrissie was causing trouble – again.

'What am I going to do this time?' Sadie begged of Georgie and Grace. All three of them sat around the kitchen table; Chrissie's letter lay between them. 'I'm terrified that she *will* go into a decline or become so desperate that she'll harm herself!'

'Mam, I don't think she'd do that. She knows it's a mortal sin and a crime,' Grace said firmly. Oh, just what was wrong with Chrissie? she thought.

'I still think she's making a huge drama out of everything but Mags is getting really worried about her. She doesn't always agree with what Chrissie does but she does care about her and more stress is something Mags can do without at the moment.' Georgie was very concerned about his wife. 'You know, Mam, I'd go over and try to sort things out but I just can't leave Mags – not now.'

Sadie nodded. Georgie was indeed the best one to go to see Chrissie and Pat and at any other time she'd have urged him to do so, but not now. 'I'll have to go myself. I'll not rest easy until I see this all settled.'

Grace reached across the table and took her hand. 'No, Mam. You're needed here. You've enough on your plate looking after Mags and Georgie and Billy and you know how tired you get, even though you won't admit it. I'll go over. I'll go and see Mrs Phillips in the Welfare Department and explain and ask can I take my holiday entitlement or a few days without pay.' Although she sounded positive she felt very apprehensive about going. True, she wanted to see Chrissie and do what she could to help her sister but there was the long journey to deal with, then she would have to tackle Con which would be stepping into dangerous territory, and she had little experience of whatever was going wrong between Chrissie and Pat.

'What about your promotion? Won't you taking time off to go to Ireland affect that? It doesn't make you look very reliable,' Georgie asked. It didn't seem fair that Grace should put her chances in jeopardy.

Grace shrugged. 'I don't know, but they're usually good about domestic problems. Mam is going to worry herself into an early grave if this isn't sorted out soon and I'm not having that! It's not fair of Chrissie to dump her problems on Mam like this but she has so we'll have to do something about it. You can't go, Georgie, you've got responsibilities now. Mam, write and tell her I'll be over the first week in the New Year and ask her the times of the trains and whether someone can meet me at the station,' Grace said firmly.

Sadie looked relieved. 'You're a good girl, Grace. I'll write tonight and you can post it in the morning. We'll all chip in to help with your fare.'

'There's no need for that, Mam, I've a few pounds saved up. You need everything to keep the house going and if Mags is going to finish work early, you'll need every penny you can get, Georgie.'

Sadie sighed. 'It's good of you, Grace. You've taken such a weight off my mind and I know you'll do your best.'

'I will, Mam, you can be certain of that.' She smiled. 'And I'll try and bring some food back with me.'

Sadie nodded and managed a smile herself. 'That would be great, luv.'

Georgie poured a cup of tea to take up to Mags while he informed her of Grace's decision. He hoped Grace would indeed bring some food because a few decent meals would help Mags no end, he was certain. He just prayed that Grace wouldn't bring Chrissie too.

Grace explained the position to Mrs Phillips in Welfare next day and was very relieved when she was told that under the circumstances leave could be granted, without pay, of course, and subject to the approval of Mr Alfred.

'I'm so grateful, Mrs Phillips. It will only be for a week. I . . . I do hope that this won't affect my prospects. I do try to be reliable and conscientious at all times,' she'd added.

The woman had smiled at her. 'You're very reliable and conscientious, Grace, and I'm sure you won't be making a habit of it. The extra workload will be divided between the other cutters.'

That had cheered Grace up considerably for she wasn't looking forward to her trip. It would take a day or two to listen to what Chrissie had to say for herself and see just what things were like and hopefully to have a long chat with Pat and his Uncle Con. She intended to be fair and firm with everyone concerned – especially Chrissie – and hopefully by the end of the week it would all be settled and she could come home with good news for Mam. She'd go and draw out her savings at lunchtime and then book her passage on the ferry. It wouldn't be a pleasant journey at this time of year but that couldn't be helped.

Mags was sitting up in bed, knitting a shawl, when Grace went up to see her when she arrived home.

'How are you today?' Grace asked, sitting on the edge of the bed. The room was warm although it smelled strongly of paraffin for Sadie had borrowed a Tilley stove from one of the neighbours to heat the room. Billy had suggested they borrow a two-bar electric fire as paraffin heaters always stank but Sadie had dismissed that idea as being far too expensive.

Anyway, just whom did they know who would lend them one? she'd asked.

'Bored and I've a bit of a headache, probably from the stink of paraffin oil!'

'Shall I open the window a bit? It does smell awful.'

Mags nodded and shifted her position in the bed. 'Well, did you get the time off?'

Grace nodded. 'They were very good about it. I won't get paid, of course, but that doesn't matter. I've booked my passage for the Sunday night after New Year so I should get there about lunchtime on Monday, which is the fifth of January. I did think of going on Saturday but I wasn't sure if the trains ran on a Sunday or if there was just a skeleton service. I can't say I'm looking forward to it.'

Mags looked sympathetic. 'Neither would I. Oh, I wish I was back on my feet. Georgie should be the one to go, Grace. We're both worried about her but he'll stand no nonsense from Chrissie and probably Pat and the uncle would be happier to confide in him.'

Grace smiled and then grimaced. 'Well, they'll all have to make do with me.'

'You'll do fine, Grace. You're a born peacemaker and you'll be able to see just how things stand and if she's exaggerating everything.' Mags frowned. 'I was only thinking earlier that maybe your mam should have waited a day or two before writing to her.'

Grace looked puzzled. 'Why?'

'Because she'll have time to write back and tell you

not to go, or worse have upped and run off thinking you're going to read her the riot act, but maybe the mails will be delayed because of the holiday.'

Grace bit her lip. 'I never thought of that.'

'She's hoping that your mam will write and agree to her coming back, she won't be expecting to hear that that's not the case and you're on your way. She won't have told Pat that she's been begging to come, you can be certain of that, it's not her style.'

Grace knew that to be true and the last thing she wanted was to arrive to find that her sister had run off, leaving her to try to explain to Pat what had happened. 'Perhaps I'd better write and tell her that I'm *not* going to read the riot act and that she should tell Pat I'm coming on a bit of a holiday?'

Mags looked sceptical. 'A holiday in January?'

'I could say I haven't been feeling well, because of the lack of decent food? What other excuse can I give?'

Mags nodded and sighed. 'I suppose it will have to do. Honestly, Grace, what a flaming mess! Just what does she want from life? Just what did she expect of marriage? It's never all a bed of roses. Doesn't she know when she's well off?'

'Obviously not, but I don't think she knows *what* she wants.'

Mags sighed wearily. 'Then it's about time she did, Grace, and I hope she realises the sacrifices you're making: losing a week's wages and using your savings to traipse all that way to try to sort things out. I take it she does have room for you? She's never told us much about the house, except for all the things it doesn't have.'

'I suppose so. I've never been inside one but I think farmhouses are usually quite big. Didn't Eileen say there were ten of them reared there? She must have room but I'm not going to worry about that. Right, I'll let you get on with your knitting while I go and write to her.'

Chrissie read her mother's letter with a feeling akin to horror. Oh, the last thing she wanted was Grace arriving here, laying down the law and telling Pat that she wanted to leave him. There would be a huge row and both Pat and his uncle would heap accusations and recriminations on her head. She couldn't face it, she just couldn't, but what was she to do? She had no money and nowhere else to go.

It brought a little relief to her anxiety and panic when Grace's letter arrived. Grace stressed that she was not going to read the riot act; she just wanted to talk to her, to see for herself how things stood between Chrissie, Pat and Uncle Con, to try to sort out why she was so unhappy. She hoped she could resolve the problem. She was going to say nothing at all to Pat about Chrissie wanting to leave him and return to Liverpool. Chrissie was to tell him that Grace hadn't been feeling well lately, food was so scarce and the weather so cold, and that Mam had insisted she take a little holiday.

Chrissie was very thankful when she read that Grace was coming instead of Georgie, who couldn't be spared owing to Mags's present condition, and that Mam was needed at home. It was a blessing really; she missed Grace and Georgie would indeed have read her the riot act. He wouldn't have been in the least interested in what she had to say but he would have sided with Pat and Con. He would never have understood just how hard she had to work in this place; at least Grace would.

She burned both letters but informed Pat that evening that Grace was coming to stay with them for a few days.

He was surprised but pleased. 'Ah, won't that be grand for you, Chrissie, but sure, 'tis not really the time of year for a bit of a break.'

'She's not been feeling too well lately. Things really are desperate over there. I know what it's like having to do a hard day's work with an empty belly, it saps your strength. Oh, it was different during the war. It was a matter of pride, you never complained because you were doing war work, making shells for the lads at the front to use. Now there's not even that bit of pride to sustain you and the shortages grind you down.'

'Then aren't ye the fortunate one to be having three good meals a day, a good turf fire in the hearth and a decent coat on your back?' Con remarked. He just hoped that your one that was paying them a visit wasn't as ungrateful, lazy and sullen as Chrissie was.

Chrissie ignored him. 'It will mean that you will have

to share a room with Con. Grace will have to share with me. I just don't know how you all fitted in here when all your brothers and sisters were at home. Why wasn't the house built larger in the first place?'

Pat shrugged. 'That's the way Irish houses were built and how families lived and we managed well enough. Grace is only coming for a week, Chrissie. That's not a bother.'

Chrissie didn't reply. She wished it could be a permanent arrangement for these days she found Pat's advances almost unbearable.

Chapter Twenty

GRACE ARRIVED COLD, TIRED and hungry early on
Monday afternoon after what had seemed like an
interminable journey. Pat was waiting for her with the
trap and was obviously glad to see her. So Chrissie
hadn't had the courage to come and face her, she
thought wearily. It didn't bode well and obviously Pat
had no idea how things stood.

'Grace, don't you look perished with the cold? But,
sure, it's good to see you and thanks be to God you've
arrived safely. Here, let me help you up.' He took her
bag and helped her into the trap, wrapping a thick rug
around her knees.

She smiled at him. 'Thanks, Pat, and it's good to see
you again. I hope I'm not putting you out, descending
on you like this?'

'Indeed you are not! It will cheer Chrissie up no end to have company; she's been rather down lately; 'tis the winter weather, I expect. She didn't come herself to meet you as she's fussed getting the room ready. You'll be sharing with herself; I'm moving in with Con.'

This surprised Grace; obviously there were only two bedrooms. 'I *am* putting you out. I didn't think it would be a problem as Eileen said there were ten of you reared in the house at one time.'

Pat grinned. 'Sure, there were. It was a desperate crush but we managed and one by one they all left. Now, you settle back while I concentrate on getting us home in one piece. The roads are desperate in places: the frost was very heavy last night.'

Grace was quite content to sit and look around with interest as they left the town and drove out along the road to Rahan. Where the sun hadn't penetrated the frost was indeed heavy but it was a lovely winter day. The sky was a pale duck-egg blue and the air was sharp and clean. Wisps of blue turf smoke rose from the chimneys of the houses and cottages they passed and she thought how much pleasanter it smelled than the often choking fumes of coal and coke that contributed to the thick winter fogs they frequently had to endure at home.

Despite her weariness she had enjoyed the journey; the countryside looked quite pretty, she thought. A light covering of snow still remained, frost still sparkled on the hedgerows and as they crossed a bridge over the canal and the ancient, grey stone Rahan Church, set in the middle of a field, came into view she told Pat that the scene looked just like something you would see on the front of a Christmas card.

He laughed. 'I'd never have thought of it like that but then I see it every day of my life.'

When they reached the farmhouse she had come to the conclusion that despite the time of year and the daunting task that lay ahead of her, she was going to like staying here.

'She's here!' Pat called as he ushered her inside. 'Sure, the train was late but then when is it ever on time? Go on in to the fire, Grace,' he urged.

Chrissie gazed at her sister with eyes full of apprehension. 'Grace, come in.'

Grace smiled and hugged her and Chrissie relaxed a little. 'Sit down and warm yourself, it's bitterly cold out there and it's a long drive. I had to break the ice on the water trough this morning but the kettle's on and there's a hot meal waiting for us all.'

Grace looked around as she sat beside the roaring turf fire. It was a comfortable room and it didn't look as though they were short of anything. Things weren't quite as modern as in Mam's kitchen but it was warm and clean and fairly tidy. There were oil lamps and pictures and a bright rag rug on the flagged floor by the dresser and another at her feet.

Chrissie busied herself with the potatoes and the thick slices she'd carved from one of the smoked hams, knowing that she couldn't put the inquisition off indefinitely and praying that Grace wouldn't start asking questions immediately. Pat had obligingly taken Grace's carpet-bag upstairs.

Con came in and took off his heavy old overcoat, scarf and cap and remembered to hang them on the pegs by the door, instead of draping them over the back of the nearest chair. He glanced at the girl sitting beside the fire. She resembled Chrissie but her hair was darker, she was much thinner and as she stood up he realised she was also much taller. Despite the tiredness evident in her face there was no sign of the almost permanent frown that was present on his nephew's wife's face these days. She was smiling pleasantly.

'This is my Uncle Conor,' Pat announced, having come back downstairs.

He didn't look like the ogre Chrissie had described, Grace thought. He was an old man, a little stooped, his face lined and weather-beaten. She extended her hand and chose her words carefully. 'I'm very pleased to meet you at last and I hope my visit isn't going to disturb you too much. I'm sorry you've had to give up your privacy and share a room with Pat but I didn't realise, Chrissie never said that there were only two bedrooms.'

Con nodded and shook her hand. At least she was polite, he supposed that was something, and it didn't surprise him that Chrissie hadn't explained about the house. She was only here for a week, however, and he'd often shared a bedroom in the past: it was unusual not to.

'Right, I'll dish out this meal,' Chrissie announced, clattering the plates to hide her discomfort and apprehension.

Grace enthused over the potatoes and ham and the freshly baked soda bread and the big pat of yellow butter. Chrissie had never been the best of cooks, Mam had always done most of the cooking, but you couldn't go far wrong with the simple but wholesome food on the table. 'And to think that I can eat as much as I like! I can't remember when I could last do that.'

Pat smiled at her. 'Ah, we'll have you fattened up before you go back, Grace.' He'd never gone hungry in his life and she did look much thinner than when he'd last seen her. 'Things are still in a desperate state over there, so they are, according to the newspapers.'

Grace nodded, her mouth full, as Chrissie put another slice of ham on her plate.

The girl was half starved, Con thought; thank goodness Chrissie for once had managed to put a decent meal on the table. Often food was undercooked or burned to a crisp; her gravy was lumpy and what she served up as soup he considered only fit for the pigs.

'Will you rest this afternoon, Grace, or would you like Chrissie to show you around?' Pat asked, pouring Grace another cup of tea.

'Oh, I can rest later on. I'd like to see around the place, we can wrap up warm.' She laughed. 'And I'll have to get some exercise after eating all this or I'll be tortured with indigestion!'

'The yard is very muddy in places and there's really not much to see. And it gets dark early,' Chrissie said without enthusiasm, trying to buy time.

'I don't mind. It's a clear, crisp day and we won't go far. I'll help you to wash up and then we'll go for a bit of a walk,' Grace said firmly.

Pat and Con both went back to their work and after the dishes were washed and dried and Chrissie had put down more turf on the fire they put on coats, hats, scarves and gloves and ventured out.

'That was a great meal, Chrissie, thanks,' Grace said, linking her sister as they crossed the yard. 'Now, you can give me the guided tour and then we'll have to talk.'

Chrissie nodded but her heart sank, wondering just what Grace would say to her, although she took some comfort from the fact that her sister so far seemed to be her usual easy-going self. She showed Grace the barns, the byres, the pigsties and the empty milking parlour. They inspected the dairy and then the coops where the poultry was kept at night.

'So, how much of this land do Pat and his uncle own?' Grace asked, pointing over the fields.

'The orchard, those fields over there as far as the river, although you can't see it from here, some fields on the other side of the canal and a stretch of bog from where they cut our turf. Pat sells turf as well.'

'So they're not hard up then.'

Chrissie shrugged. 'I suppose not. They employ a few labourers too.'

They walked up the track and on to the canal bank where Grace judged them to be far enough away from the farm for her to start to question her sister.

'So, just what's gone wrong, Chrissie? Why are you so miserable that you want to leave Pat and come back to Liverpool? The house is comfortable, you have help and it's lovely here. At least I think it is.'

Chrissie bit her lip; so much depended on what she said next. She *had* to make Grace understand. Slowly she began to describe her life, how she spent her days, the feeling of isolation, and the fact that they went nowhere, except to Mass. That she had no money of her own to buy what she wanted and there was nothing in her life to look forward to. Everything was such a bitter disappointment; it wasn't what she had expected at all. Things were not as Pat had described them to her. He had painted a picture of an idyllic life where she would want for nothing and be taken out whenever she wished to go. But it hadn't proved to be like that and she was utterly disillusioned. And then there was Con.

Grace had listened in silence, sympathising to an extent. The work was hard and unrelenting, but then hadn't her mam's life been hard too, especially these last years? Much harder in some ways than Chrissie's. True, Chrissie was a city girl but that didn't excuse everything and she had come here and married Pat of her own free will.

'So, just what did happen? Did you have a row with

Con? Did he hit you? Just what did you mean when you said he'd "attacked" you?' she asked quietly.

'There was a row; Pat wasn't there. I told him I was nothing but a drudge. He said the place was like a midden and I told him it was himself and Pat that made all the mess, that I was sick to death of it, sick of *every-thing*! He . . . said I have ideas above my station. That I didn't bring any kind of a dowry with me and he called me a "jumped up, spoiled, ungrateful little brat from a Liverpool slum!" He called me a "slummy", Grace! I was furious! I yelled at him that we lived in a decent area, that our family is respectable, our house is a palace compared to that dump. He said I should have stayed there and that I should be grateful, *grateful*! I told him I hated him, that he'd never liked me, that he was a nasty, evil old man and then . . .' Chrissie was near to tears.

Grace was frowning. Whatever Chrissie had done or not done, Con had no right to call her a slummy. It was neither true nor fair and it was a great insult. 'Then what?' she pressed.

'He . . . he grabbed me by the shoulders and shook me – hard! I told him I would tell Pat and he threatened me.'

Grace stared at her. 'He shook you. He didn't hit you?'

Chrissie shook her head.

'And he threatened you?'

'He roared at me, saying I caused all the arguments and that I was to say nothing to Pat.'

'Or else what?' Grace asked.

Chrissie shrugged. 'He didn't say but I knew, Grace, I just *knew* that next time . . . next time he would hit me. He hates me, he really does, and I'm afraid of him.'

Grace was perturbed. She was struggling to be fair. Eileen had sworn that Con would never raise his hand to a woman and indeed he hadn't hit Chrissie, he had just shaken her. There had obviously been a huge row and he probably did resent her sister, especially if Chrissie had been constantly complaining and shirking. Had he just lost his temper? Had Chrissie in fact driven him to it? There was always more than one side to every story and she realised that she would have to hear Con's. Pat obviously knew nothing of any of this but maybe it was time he did?

They walked on a little way in silence until Chrissie spoke. 'So, you see why I can't stay, Grace? I'm desperate to get home.'

'And what about Pat? You said you loved him?'

'Oh, Grace, I really thought I did but . . . but all of you were right. I didn't know him. He was virtually a stranger. I know it's all my own fault and I really don't want to hurt him but I can't go on like this, Grace!'

'But you will hurt him, Chrissie. You'll hurt him deeply. Was there something specific? Was there a huge row, did he say anything to really upset you? And what about . . . well, the "bedroom" side of things?'

Chrissie sniffed miserably. 'There was one night, ages ago, after I'd had to help with turning the hay. I was exhausted but he insisted we . . . well . . . we made love. Oh, Grace, it's not at all the way I imagined it would be. It's all so . . . so one-sided. I did try to tell him how disappointed I felt but he couldn't or wouldn't try to understand. I think he's blaming me and since then things have just got worse and worse and then Uncle Con . . .'

Grace sighed. Of course she had no experience in such matters but she wondered fleetingly if Chrissie had expected too much? Had she relied too heavily on romantic dreams and stories? Yes, there had to be some romance in a marriage but there had to be passion too. 'Can't you talk to him again and try to impress upon him how you feel? It's not fair just to walk away and leave him without an explanation.'

Chrissie clutched Grace's arm tightly. Grace believed her! Grace had said she couldn't 'just walk away'! That must mean that she could go home! 'I'll tell him, Grace. I'll tell him tonight and then I can come home with you! You won't have to stay the week.'

Grace stared at her in disbelief and shook her head. 'No! You're his *wife*, don't you realise what that means? You can't run away, you have to try and sort this out between you and the only way you can do that is to tell him you are unhappy and why. Tell him that you are not getting on with Con and why. He loves you, Chrissie, he'll understand, and I'm sure he'll do everything he can to put things right. You say you've nothing to look forward to but look at all the things you have. The love of a good man, a decent home, no shortage of money or food or clothes, someone to do the washing and mending. Oh, I know you work hard and that there are so many things you're not used to but you have to try. You have to try to make this marriage work.'

Chrissie had now begun to sob. That one ray of hope, her chance of freedom, had disappeared with Grace's words.

Grace put her arms around her. 'I know I sound hard but life isn't easy and no matter whom you fall in love with, or think you love, there are no guarantees that marriage to that person will be happy. I'll talk to Pat and Con and then I'm sure that between us we can work things out. Life will get better, Chrissie.'

'It won't! It won't!' Chrissie sobbed. A terrible fear was creeping over her. There was no way out and when Grace dragged all this out into the open she was certain it would make matters worse.

'Hush! Hush now!' Grace soothed. She hated to see her sister so upset but she hoped she had got through to Chrissie that she had no option but to honour her vows.

Chrissie raised a tear-stained face. 'Grace, stay with me? I can't face a life here on my own, I *can't*! Please, please, Grace?'

Grace felt her heart plummet. She had her own life to live. She had her job, which she enjoyed, and the chance of promotion. There was her Mam to consider – her health wasn't good – and there was Sandy. And she too was a city girl with everything that implied. It just wasn't fair of Chrissie to ask this of her and yet her sister was so upset, so utterly miserable that she couldn't leave her like this.

'Dry your eyes. I'll stay on for a bit longer, that's all I can promise at the moment.' Silently Grace prayed that things could be sorted out after she'd spoken to Pat and his uncle.

Chapter Twenty-One

———◆◆◆———

CHRISSIE HAD CALMED DOWN considerably by the time they returned although she was still shaken. Grace unpacked and soon darkness was falling and the men came in from the yard. Chrissie went out to round up the poultry while Grace prepared the evening meal. She then helped Chrissie to serve it and afterwards to clear up.

'Grace, you must be worn out. You've hardly sat down since you arrived,' Pat commented.

She smiled. 'I am tired. If no one minds I think I'll go up.'

'And I'll come too. It's been a long day,' Chrissie added. She had no wish at all to sit here with Pat and his uncle. She was still upset by her talk with Grace.

Despite her weariness Grace didn't sleep well. She

tossed and turned, worrying about Chrissie and her own future. It also seemed strange to her that there were no streetlights nor any noises at all except for the occasional sounds from the byre, but that was something she was sure she would get used to.

Next morning she was up with her sister; she was determined to see just how hard Chrissie's day was and she intended to speak to both men, if at all possible. The sooner all this was sorted out the better, although she now realised that she would probably have to stay longer than a week for that to happen. She felt she owed that to Sadie and Chrissie and Pat.

The two girls worked quietly, sharing the chores between them, although Grace left the poultry to Chrissie for, as she said, she'd probably inadvertently frighten them or chase them off in all directions.

'You'd be hard put to frighten those geese, they'd terrify you the way they come at you hissing and flapping!' Chrissie had replied grimly.

By dinnertime Grace realised that her sister hadn't been exaggerating about the work and that life was more difficult in some respects than at home. But in others, because there were no shortages, it was easier. And during the war they had worked just as hard and often in far worse conditions.

'Chrissie, it's a lovely day, why don't you take a few hours off this afternoon? Mrs Maher has done the washing and I'll bring it in later on. You could go into town. I've got a bit of money, I could let you have a few shillings. Treat yourself to something,' Grace offered for she had to do something to get Chrissie out of the way and Georgie had insisted on giving her half her fare.

Chrissie brightened; it was so long since she had had money to buy herself something. 'Oh, Grace, that's really good of you.'

Grace smiled. 'Right then, after we've fed these hungry fellers you get yourself ready and let me deal with any questions as to why you are off gallivanting.'

Chrissie couldn't wait to get out and when she'd gone Grace wrapped her sister's shawl around her, pulled on Chrissie's boots and went in search of Con. She found him in one of the sheds, tending to a cow that had recently calved. She had seen Pat and another man moving fodder into the byre, they had waved to her and she'd waved cheerily back.

'Oh, has it just been born? Isn't it beautiful!' Grace said quietly, leaning her arms on the edge of the wooden stall, watching the black and white calf struggle to its feet. 'I've never seen one so young before. There are dairies in Liverpool where they keep cows, of course, and sometimes we used to go for milk when we ran short, but I never saw any calves.'

Con nodded, cleaning his hands with a handful of straw. 'A fine young bull calf it is but a city is no place to keep animals.'

'I suppose you're right. They should be out in the fields and there's certainly none of those in Liverpool. Lots of parks, though,' she added.

Con looked at her intently, certain she had more on her mind than idle chatter. 'That was a grand meal. Ye make a tasty nourishing soup, girl. Better than your sister's, and ye have a lighter touch with the bread.'

Grace sighed. 'Chrissie was never much of a cook. She had no interest in it. Mam tried to teach her but she always found an excuse to be doing something else. I enjoy cooking, I always tried to help Mam out and it's so much easier when you've got such a range of ingredients to hand and don't have to worry about trying to make something out of nothing and making it stretch. In fact it's a pleasure.'

Con was warming to her. She had a very different attitude to her sister and had seemed to take everything in her stride and without complaint. 'She's spoilt, is that one,' he commented.

Grace shook her head and took a deep breath. She wasn't looking forward to this but she had to get it over with. 'No, not spoilt.' She frowned slightly. 'I wanted to talk to you about Chrissie. She seems to think you resent her, that you don't like her. Is that true?' she asked quietly.

Con held her gaze. Was this why she'd come? Had that bold brat been telling tales? 'Sure, some of it is the truth. I don't like her attitude. I don't like the way she's been treating Pat and she's grateful for nothing. 'Tis my opinion that she's lazy and she's the worst waster I ever did meet. We work hard to make a living here; sure the country is poor and getting poorer. She doesn't want to pull her weight, she just wants to be off amusing herself and wasting money on fripperies and rubbish.'

Grace nodded but now she had to choose her words carefully. 'Con, she was never used to a life like this. When war broke out Chrissie was just twelve, still a child. She grew up living in fear, doing without all the things she'd been used to. I know life hasn't been easy for you but do you know what it's like to have to run from your home in the middle of the night to sit in a cold, damp shelter and listen to the hundreds of planes roaring overhead and the thunder of anti-aircraft guns? To shake from head to toe in terror for eight, ten, sometimes as long as fourteen hours as the bombs explode all around and the ground shakes and you never know if or when you'll be blown to smithereens? And that went on night after night for over a week. Thousands of people were killed, my da amongst them and some of the neighbours, men we'd known all our lives. People were left with nothing, absolutely *nothing* except the clothes they stood up in. And each morning we had to face the carnage and we had to go to our work to make munitions, through streets that were just rubble with water, sewage and gas pipes fractured and electricity and phone wires down and bomb craters everywhere. Do you know what it's like to watch your city burn, be systematically destroyed?' She paused, all the fears and grief of those years welling up again. 'My oldest brother's ship was sunk in the Atlantic and he drowned, Georgie was away for two years fighting and we didn't know if he'd come home safely. Chrissie grew up with all that and then it was over and she was eighteen. She felt she had been robbed, cheated out of her youth and so she just wanted to enjoy life.'

Con had listened intently to her, trying to imagine what they had gone through. 'And didn't ye grow up through all that too, Grace? Ye are not much older than her yourself. Ye were cheated of your youth too but ye don't have the same attitude as your one.'

She nodded. 'But I'm not like Chrissie. Mam always said I was more sensible, I found it easier to accept the hardships and get on with life. Chrissie thought things would get back to normal immediately – we all hoped they would – but they didn't. It was a bitter disappointment to her, she was depressed and then she met Pat at Eileen's wedding and, well, you know the rest. I'm not making excuses for her, I'm just trying to explain.'

He nodded slowly and shivered as a blast of cold air came through the open door.

'I hear there was a row between you?' Grace ventured.

'Sure, I lost my temper, said things that maybe should never have been said but she did ask for it! She's bold, so she is, and I shook her to try to get some bit of sense into her. Pat is a good lad; she wants for nothing. She has more than many women in this parish,' he answered a little sullenly, annoyed that he should have to explain himself.

Grace let the shawl fall from around her head and

pushed back the tendrils of hair that had fallen over her forehead. 'She's afraid of you now. She says you hate her and are turning Pat against her and she's convinced that if there's another row you will beat her.'

Con took a step backwards, his weather-beaten face full of outrage. 'I don't *hate* the girl! To hate is a sin and I swear before the Holy Mother of God that I would never beat her. Never in my life have I harmed a woman. I don't like the way she is treating Pat, I don't like the way she is carrying on at all but 'tis not my place to come between man and wife.' He was bitterly hurt that Chrissie had made such accusations against him and it showed in his eyes.

Grace nodded. 'Please don't get upset, Con. I believe you, we all do. I went with Mags to see Eileen and she was just as horrified as you. Chrissie has exaggerated it all.'

'Do ye mean to tell me that she's told these barefaced lies to the entire family?'

Grace nodded. 'I'm not going to lie to you, Con. She's written to Mam twice, begging to be allowed to come back. That's why I'm here, to try to sort things out. I've already told her she just can't walk away from everything and she'll have to accept it. She won't find it easy, that's why I had to find out if what she said about you was true and why I'll have to talk to Pat.'

Con had never expected this. 'Sure, it would break Pat's heart if she left him. He does dote on her.'

'I know. I told her that, but we have to talk – all of

us. Pat has to know she's not happy and why and then . . . then you'll all have to try to resolve matters. I think I might have to stay on longer than I intended. She's very upset.'

'Do ye want me to talk to Pat?' Con offered, still shocked.

Grace shook her head emphatically. Although the old man obviously knew his nephew far better than she did she felt that he might not approach the subject with the necessary tact. 'No, thank you. I think it's best if I talk to him, she's my sister. But I'd be grateful if this evening you could go up early and I'll send Chrissie off to bed too.'

He nodded and turned his attention back to the cow that was now suckling her calf.

Grace pulled the shawl up over her head. 'It's a grand little fellow and I'm sure he'll thrive. Now, I'd best go and bring in that washing before it starts to get damp.'

When she'd gone Con leaned against the side of the stall feeling old and tired. The girl was indeed sensible and wise beyond her years, all she had gone through seemed only to have strengthened her, not weakened her as it had obviously done to her sister. He wondered was there some weakness of the mind in Chrissie? Had those years been too much for her and she little more than a child? He prayed not, thinking of Pat. That would be too much for them all to bear. He would just have to leave matters to Grace and pray hard to St Jude that life would get better for everyone. He was glad Grace was staying on for a bit.

True to his word, after supper was over he bade them all goodnight and went to bed. If Pat was surprised he didn't say so. Grace had already told Chrissie of her conversation with Con and of her intention to speak to Pat this evening, so Chrissie too excused herself, leaving Grace and Pat sitting beside the fire.

'Will I make us a pot of tea, Pat?' she offered.

'Ah, haven't you done enough today, Grace? You've done all the cooking and even made a start on the ironing, besides helping Chrissie. Sit and take your ease. I'll put down more turf on the fire.' He obligingly threw more sods on the fire and poked it hard. 'And it was good of you to let Chrissie have a few hours to herself to say nothing of a few shillings and aren't you the one who is supposed to be having a bit of a holiday?'

Grace stared into the flames. 'I sent her off because I wanted to have a talk to your uncle.'

Pat sighed. 'I know himself and Chrissie don't see eye to eye, Grace, but I've tried to explain to her that he's an old man and set in his ways. He's always worked hard and times haven't been great, for sure in his young days they were desperate bad altogether. When he was born 'twas only thirty years after the great hunger had decimated the country, then there were the days of the Land League and the struggle to get rid of the landlords, the fight for independence and then the civil war. He's had a hard life.'

'He has indeed, Pat, but I tried to explain to him that we have had to live with terror and hardship and grief and that's why Chrissie wants a bit of enjoyment in life now. I know you love her, Pat, and that you've really tried to give her everything and that she wasn't prepared for this kind of life—'

'I didn't lie to her about this place, Grace, I swear I didn't!'

'Of course you didn't.'

'But haven't you seen for yourself that there's always a huge amount of work to be done around the place and it's not always possible to be going out and spending money? Sure, I have to say the bills from that Miss McEvoy were coming in thick and fast last year and Con began to complain.'

'She likes to look nice but I do realise that there has to be a limit. You didn't know about it, Pat, but there was a row between Chrissie and your uncle. He called her names and she called him names back and then he lost his temper and shook her.'

Pat frowned; he was deeply perturbed. It wasn't like Con to lose his temper like that. 'Why did neither of them tell me about this?'

'I don't suppose Con wanted to cause another argument, but Chrissie says she's afraid of him now.'

Pat was appalled. 'Sure to God, there's no reason for her to fear him! He'd never harm her.'

'I know, Pat, and I've told her so but . . . but she's not happy. In fact she is very miserable and upset.' She looked across at him and met his gaze. His grey-green eyes were filled with concern and a degree of hurt and she knew she couldn't tell him that Chrissie wanted to leave him.

'Because of Con? I'll speak to him.'

She shook her head. 'It's not just Con.'

'Is it me? Is it something I've done? Tell me, Grace?'

Grace blushed slightly. 'That's something you'll have to talk to her about. I know she feels that life isn't turning out the way she hoped it would, that she doesn't have much to look forward to and she's finding the isolation hard to cope with. She's been used to having lots of people constantly around her. I've had a good talk to her and . . . and I think I might have to stay for longer than a week. In fact she begged me to.'

'I'll talk to her, Grace, I promise. She should have told me all this herself.' He was upset and couldn't hide it. He was aware that relations were deteriorating between them, he felt hurt and humiliated when she constantly turned away from his advances and it was a real sorrow to him that there was no child on the way. If communication between them didn't improve he realised that there never would be.

She felt so sorry for him. He was a decent lad and he did love her sister, but she couldn't discuss such an intimate thing as their marital relationship. She'd done what she could. 'So she should. I've told her how lucky she is and that there are no guarantees of endless happiness in life. She is still very young, Pat. She'll grow up and learn to accept things; we just have to try to give her time. You know we all wanted her to wait before marrying and that's why, but Chrissie was too impatient and impetuous.'

'She does still love me, Grace? She hasn't changed her mind?'

There was such pain in his voice that Grace looked away, unable to answer for a second, but when she spoke her tone was quiet and firm. 'She can't change her mind, Pat, she knows that. We're Catholics and the vows of marriage are sacred and not to be broken. Just talk to her and give her time. Things will work out, I know they will and I'll do everything I can to help.'

He hadn't missed the hesitation and it tore at his heart. Was there something she knew that he did not? There was nothing he could say to her, if he pressed her he might hear things he would regret, words that would break his heart and shatter his life.

Grace rose. She felt utterly exhausted but at least she had started what she fervently hoped would be a process of understanding, reconciliation and hope for the future. 'Talk to Chrissie tomorrow. Things always look better in the morning, Pat. Tomorrow is another day. We'll all feel better then, I know we will.'

He nodded, but a tiny seed of doubt had been sown in his mind.

Part III

Chapter Twenty-Two

April 1948

GRACE CLOSED THE DOOR of the dairy behind her. Everything had been scrubbed down. The milk that was to be left to separate stood in big pans on the shelves, covered with muslin. It would be left for two days then the cream would be skimmed off. She would then churn it, skim it and churn it again. The butter would be washed and made into pats with the wooden paddles; it was a slow process but she enjoyed the time spent in the cool dairy, which she kept spotlessly clean.

She stood and turned her face upwards towards the dying but still warm rays of the sun. Almost four months had passed since she'd come here and it was very, very different to life in a city. She found it peaceful and, despite the hard work, relaxing to be away from the constant rush and bustle. If she was truthful it had also given her a breathing space. She had thought a great deal about her relationship with Sandy in the first weeks and had decided that she couldn't make a definite commitment to him. She didn't love him enough to marry him.

It was now April and finally it seemed that spring had arrived after the long months of cold and sometimes dismal weather. The heavy shawls and coats could now be discarded for lighter jackets and cardigans.

Con came out of the barn and crossed towards her. 'Have ye finished in there for the day, Grace?'

'I have indeed. But as you know well the work is never finished in this place.' There was no note of complaint in her voice and she was smiling as she walked beside him towards the house.

He smiled back. He liked her. She had settled well and she seemed to enjoy being here. There was hardly ever a moan from her and she worked hard. Far harder than Chrissie did. She did all the cooking, helped with the cleaning and she had taken over the butter-making from her sister. Chrissie still saw to the poultry and went into town with the eggs and butter and shopped, although sometimes Grace went with her. Grace also worked for a few hours each morning up in the laundry at the Jesuit College where she helped the nuns who did all the washing for the priests and their students. Grace's particular job was to wash and starch the white clerical collars and she was up and out early after breakfast and away like a dervish on the bicycle she'd bought second-hand in the town.

'Did the mammy say how things are going on over there?' he asked, knowing she'd had a letter from Sadie the day before.

'Well, Mags is blooming although she does get tired and there's still no sign of a council house for them as there's still thousands on the waiting list. But Mam says the weekly milk ration is going up a pint to three and a half pints, which will be a help.'

Con shook his head. 'Isn't it shocking to think that's all the milk for a whole week? Sure, we get through twice as much.'

Grace nodded. 'Georgie sent a few pages too but there wasn't much good news from him. From June people with cars will only be allowed to drive ninety miles a month and now the electricity is to be nationalised. Oh, and he says the government has voted to get rid of the death penalty – just as a trial.'

'I'd not be agreeing with that at all. Doesn't the Bible say "an eye for an eye"?'

Grace frowned. 'I suppose they'll just have to see how it goes.'

They had reached the house and Grace automatically took off her boots and left them beside the door. Con did likewise, although most of the time he forgot, which was still a source of great annoyance to Chrissie and sometimes to herself, although she said nothing.

'I told Chrissie to heat up that soup and put the potatoes on to boil and there's the pie I made and put in the oven earlier,' Grace informed him as she opened the door.

'Don't ye have us fed like kings? The food was never so good since Pat's poor mam, God rest her and be good to her, passed away. Ah, she was a grand cook was Carmel.'

Grace smiled. 'I'm sure she was.' She looked around the kitchen, which was clean and tidy. Chrissie had set the table and was stirring the soup. She seemed happier these days, Grace thought, but you never really knew. True to his word Pat had had a long talk with his wife but Grace had never learned just what had been said. Chrissie had remained stubbornly and uncharacteristic-ally silent on the matter and Grace hadn't questioned Pat, feeling it wasn't her place.

In that first week in January the atmosphere in the house had been strained. She knew that Pat and Con had had long conversations and a few arguments. She'd heard their raised voices after both she and Chrissie had gone to bed, but the old man did seem to be trying to be more patient with her sister. Because they shared the workload Chrissie now had more time to herself and complained less about being tired, but she wasn't too happy about her sister going out to work. But Grace had explained she had to earn some money towards her keep and for personal necessities. She had also urged her sister to make more of an effort to find friends of her own for she herself had forged new friendships.

'I've tried, Grace, I really have, but what do I have in common with the women around here? None of them are at all interested in the things I like to talk about,' Chrissie had cried defensively, so Grace had given up on the matter, hoping that in time Chrissie would become more outgoing.

During that first week she had written to her mother, informing her that she intended to stay longer. She had had to write to Mrs Phillips at Porter Brothers and also to Sandy. There had been many letters to Sandy in January and February as she tried her best to explain why her visit was being extended.

As the time passed she realised that she enjoyed life here. It was a very different existence, of course, but there seemed to be so many advantages. Despite the weather she loved the countryside. It was quiet and life seemed so much simpler. She was interested in the workings of the farm and the welfare of the animals, although Con had warned her not to get sentimental about them. They were the means of earning a living and some of them would end up on the dinner table. She had often helped Con with the calves and although she did not help with the milking, she enjoyed working in the dairy. Neither did she have Chrissie's fear of the cattle or pigs. Between them the sisters tended the kitchen garden where the vegetables and herbs grew and the 'pratie' garden where Pat had sown the potatoes.

Of course she missed her family but they all wrote regularly and at length, with the exception of Billy who had always hated putting pen to paper. When she knew she no longer had a job at Porter's and Sandy's letters became less and less frequent, she had asked Sadie to parcel up the rest of her clothes and send them over to her. She had been so fortunate to get the part time work in the laundry. Her friend Mary Scully had 'spoken' for her.

She'd met Mary one day when she'd been out for a walk, something she enjoyed but which she rarely had time to do. Mary had been struggling with three small children and a heavy bag of turf and Grace had gone to her aid. They'd chatted and Mary had invited her in for a cup of tea and they'd become friends. It was Mary who had begged Sister Assumpta, who was in charge of the laundry, to help Grace out. Sister Assumpta had once been plain Rita Carroll – Mary's oldest sister.

'Pat, leave the half-door open, it's a lovely evening,' Grace instructed as Pat joined them in the kitchen.

Chrissie frowned, thinking it wasn't *that* warm. She had never been able to understand just why Grace really loved living here or why she'd given up every-thing, her home and family, a good job, friends and even Sandy. Of course she was very glad she had done because life was so much easier now, at least from the workload position.

She was still far from happy. She had found it very, very hard to come to terms with the fact that she could not escape her predicament. She was still discontented and felt isolated but at least she had Grace to talk to and she didn't have to share a bed with Pat. Reluctantly she had faced the fact that she really didn't love him. Looking back she realised that when she had met him she had believed she loved him but she had been infatuated, flattered, swept along by events and by dreams of a new and romantic life. It was such a hard thing to admit but she couldn't push it from her mind any longer. It hadn't been true, enduring love at all and the loneliness, homesickness and difficulty of settling into life here had all played their part in making her acknowledge it. She just didn't love him the way he loved her. At times that made her feel guilty but she was trying her hardest to make the best of things. It was all she could do.

'Wash your hands and then come to the table,' she instructed her husband. 'What's wrong? You look so serious, has someone died?' she asked, catching sight of his expression.

He nodded. 'A lot of people have, Chrissie. Old John Fahey has just come into the yard to tell me the news he heard in town. A plane has crashed at Shannon Airport, they think there's as many as thirty dead.'

Pat, Con and Grace crossed themselves devoutly. Chrissie put down the soup ladle and she, too, blessed herself.

'May God have mercy on them all!' Grace said quietly.

'Amen to that. Ah, but sure I've no faith in those contraptions at all! If the good Lord had meant us to fly wouldn't He have given us wings?' Con remarked sadly, shaking his head.

'I suppose you could say that if He'd meant us to smoke we'd have been born with chimneys on our heads!' Chrissie countered, her gaze resting on the old man's pipe rack on the shelf beside the fireplace. 'It's terrible, of course. A terrible, terrible accident and very sad but we have to move with the times,' she finished.

'Will we go up to the chapel after supper? There's bound to be special prayers,' Pat suggested.

'We will so, 'tis only fitting,' Con said firmly, settling the matter.

They all went up to the little church in the trap to the Mass that was said for the souls of those who had died in the crash of the Pan-American Constellation aircraft. Both Grace and Chrissie were surprised that the congregation was so large; obviously news of the disaster had spread rapidly around the parish. As they came out Grace spotted Mary Scully and her family and went over to speak to them.

'Ah, 'tis shocking, so it is!' Mary said sadly.

Grace nodded. 'It is indeed. How are you, Liam?'

Mary's husband was carrying their youngest son. 'I was feeling grand in meself all day for I've had almost a full week's work – until I did hear the news.'

'I wonder will it affect the dance? The Father didn't

say so but sure then it might have slipped his mind altogether,' Mary mused.

'What dance?' Grace queried as they walked towards Con, Pat and Chrissie, who were standing at the church gates. The men were deep in conversation with another farmer. Chrissie stood silent, attempting to look suitably solemn but she was uninterested in what they were discussing.

'There's to be a dance in the school hall on Saturday May the first. Then on the Sunday, after Mass, there will be the procession around the church grounds in honour of Our Lady. 'Tis the month dedicated to the Mother of God,' Mary informed her friend.

'The first of May is Chrissie's birthday. Her full name is Christina Maria.'

'Sure, isn't that very fancy.' Mary glanced at Chrissie who caught her gaze. Mary smiled and Chrissie smiled back politely. She often wondered just what her sister and Mary Scully talked about? Grace was a single girl; Mary, although only two years older than her sister, was a married woman with three children. Grace had told her that the Scullys found it hard to make ends meet on Liam's wages as a labourer. She also knew for a fact that whenever Grace went to visit Mary, she never went empty-handed. There were always a few eggs, a pat of butter, some buns or scones, a few rashers and butter-milk for the children.

Grace smiled. 'Mam said she'd read about someone called Christina in the newspaper and she'd liked the name and of course Maria is the same as Mary. I hope they don't cancel it. It would do Chrissie and Pat good to get out.'

Mary sighed. These days she and Liam never got out for there wasn't the money to spare and who would mind the children? 'Maybe they won't, it's still a couple of weeks away and I know the committee have put a lot of work into the planning of the occasion.'

Pat greeted Liam cordially for they had been at school together. Con finished his conversation and the little group moved towards the trap.

'Mary was just telling me there's to be a dance in the school hall on your birthday, Chrissie. You and Pat should go, if it's not cancelled of course.'

Chrissie looked very interested and glanced hopefully at Pat. 'I haven't been to a dance for ages. What kind of an affair will it be?' This question was directed at Mary.

'Sure, it will be grand altogether. Wasn't I only chatting to Mrs O'Reagan last week and herself is on the committee? The hall is to be decorated and there's to be a bit of supper and the musicians are coming over from Clara. Father Doyle said it was not to go on too late because of the Mass and procession on Sunday morning, so they've promised it will be over by two o'clock at the latest and that the place will be tidied up.'

Con nodded his agreement. The school was opposite the church and the convent and it wouldn't be at all fitting if any unsightly mess was left or the priests and nuns were kept awake all night by the noise. In fact Father Doyle would probably make it his business to keep his eye on the entertainment to ensure nothing got out of hand and that there was no drink taken on the premises. He usually felt it was his duty for the school was run by the Presentation Sisters who educated the girls. The boys were educated in the National School not far from their own home place.

'Oh, can we go, Pat?' Chrissie asked.

'Why not? It all sounds grand,' he replied, smiling at her.

Chrissie was delighted, already thinking of what she could wear. Now that the weather was warmer she could pull out the dresses Miss McEvoy had made when she first came to Rahan. She would have liked something new but she realised that that was out of the question.

Pat turned to Grace. 'Why don't we bring you too, Grace? 'Tis a long time since you had a bit of entertainment in your life and we might even persuade Con here to come as well. Make it a family outing; sure, most of the parish will be there.'

Con shook his head. 'Ah, I'm too old for such goings on. I'm best off at home by the fire with the old pipe.'

Grace considered it for a second, then she caught the expression on Mary's face and she too shook her head. 'I don't want to be cramping your style and I'd feel such a wallflower. Why don't I mind the children for you, Mary? You and Liam could have a night out.'

Mary smiled at her and looked a little embarrassed.

'That's kind and thoughtful of you, Grace, but this lot can be like a bag of cats when they get tired and the angel Gabriel himself would find it fierce hard to mind them, and then we'll have to be up for the procession next day. Thanks all the same, 'tis much appreciated.'

Grace nodded, regretting she had made the offer for she realised now that her friend could not afford it.

'So then, that's settled. We'll bring you with us, Grace, and you'll not be a wallflower at all for if the lads around here are eejits enough not to ask you to dance then I will meself,' Pat said firmly.

Mary and her little family bade them goodnight, they would walk home, and Pat helped Chrissie and Grace up into the trap while Con unhitched the pony.

'Oh, I'm looking forward to it already. It sounds as if it's going to be great. Now, what will we wear?' Chrissie enthused, already determined that she would be the best-dressed woman there and the centre of attention.

'Do ye think it's fitting to be chatting about frocks and the like when 'tis a Mass for those poor souls we've just been after attending?' Con said reprovingly.

Chrissie said nothing but inwardly she thought he was taking things too far; after all they had known no one who had died in that crash. It was miles away in Limerick.

'No, it's not, sorry. We've time enough to think about the dance,' Grace said in a contrite tone, not wishing for the subject to become yet another bone of contention between Con and Chrissie. If Mary and

Liam had said they would go she wouldn't have minded missing the event but now she too began to look forward to it; it was months since she had been to a dance. The last time had been on Christmas Eve last year – with Sandy. She felt a little stab of regret for she felt she had treated him badly. She had begged him not to go on waiting for her, not to consider her if he met someone else. He had hinted that he had in the last letter she'd had from him and she'd received no more since. Even though she felt a little guilty when she thought of him, she told herself that truthfully she hadn't loved him and that eventually she would have had to have been straight with him. It wouldn't have been fair to carry on stringing him along, living in hope of something that could never be – marriage. It just wasn't in her nature to do something like that.

Chapter Twenty-Three

To Chrissie's relief the dance wasn't cancelled and as the day approached both Pat and Grace noticed that she became more animated than she'd been for a long time. She spent hours trying on everything she considered suitable, finally settling on a rose-pink two-piece costume. The skirt was full and reached almost to her ankles. The jacket was short, nipped in at the waist, and the collar and cuffs of the three-quarter-length sleeves were trimmed with a deeper shade of rose satin.

'Won't you get a bit warm in that?' Grace asked as Chrissie viewed herself in the long mirror on the inside of the wardrobe door.

'If I do I can take the jacket off, there's a little sleeveless top that goes underneath it in the same coloured satin. It matches perfectly. I'm going to wear those pearlised clip-on earrings Ellie Nelson gave me and that link of pearl beads.'

Grace had picked up the brown velvet tippet from the bed. 'I thought you'd wear something that would go with this. It's lovely and I know you haven't worn it yet.'

'There's nothing that goes well with it. It is lovely but I don't know . . .' She frowned. 'I think it makes me look smaller and dumpier somehow.'

Grace had started to hang up the discarded clothes that were piled on the bed. 'It would look nice with this.' She held up a cream dress of fine lawn that had short sleeves trimmed with lace and a square neckline, also edged with lace. It too was fitted and the bodice was pin-tucked but the skirt wasn't full. 'Brown and cream go well together.'

Chrissie shook her head. 'That's not fancy enough; I want to look really stunning. I only wear that to go into town when it's a hot summer day. Why don't you wear it or have you already decided what you're going to put on?'

Grace laughed. 'There's not much to choose from. My wardrobe is still firmly stuck in the "utility" mode and I don't have a Miss McEvoy! I don't think this is plain at all, she's done a great job.'

'Then wear that. It will suit you. It will be much shorter on you, you're taller than me, but as you've just said all your skirts are the utility length. You can wear the little brown cape over it,' she offered.

'I couldn't do that, Chrissie! Pat bought it specially

for you for Christmas and I bet he paid quite a bit for it too and you've not worn it yet.'

'Oh, I'm sure he won't mind, Grace. I'll ask him, if you like? Surely he can't object? You do enough work around here and you never go out. You don't even come with me into town very often and that's not what I'd call a proper outing, let alone entertainment.'

'No! No, I've got a coffee-coloured cardigan that's quite nice. The dress isn't fancy, so the cardigan will be more appropriate.' Sometimes Chrissie could be very tactless, Grace thought. She was sure that Pat would feel hurt that Chrissie seemed to think so little of his gift that she would lend it to her sister before she'd even worn it herself.

She tried on the cream dress and liked it. It certainly wasn't as opulent as the outfit Chrissie intended to wear but then she wasn't setting out to be the belle of the ball. On her it did only come to just below her knee but she didn't mind that.

'Don't the pair of you look just gorgeous? You'll take the sight from the eyes of everyone up there,' Pat exclaimed when they came down on the appointed Saturday evening. His birthday gift to Chrissie had been a pair of small gold hoop earrings, bought especially for her to wear this evening. She'd said they were beautiful and that he was very good to her but that she would save them for another occasion as she'd already decided on the pearlised ones. He'd been disappointed but had said nothing.

He turned to his uncle. 'Won't I be the envy of everyone, Con, walking in with these two gorgeous creatures?'

'Ye will indeed. Ye look very well, Grace.'

Chrissie shot him a sharp look for he'd not complimented her and she knew she looked far more stylish than her sister.

'That's praise indeed. Thank you, kind sir!' Grace laughed, sweeping him a mock curtsey.

Con grinned. 'Ah, get off with ye, making a mock and a jeer of an old man! And don't ye be letting them lads up there with their fancy talk go turning your head!' He thought she looked far nicer than Chrissie, who in his opinion was over-dressed for a country dance. Chrissie looked small and dumpy and fussy in that outfit. The skirt was too long and too full and the satin on the collar and cuffs cheapened it, and in his opinion the jewellery looked trashy. By comparison Grace looked tall and elegant, the colour of both the dress and light cardigan suited her, as did the simple style. She wore a small gold crucifix on a chain around her neck and a pair of tiny gold stud earrings. She'd done something different with her hair, he mused, although he wasn't quite sure what. It made her look softer, more attractive. 'Get off with ye all and give me some bit of peace,' he instructed. He was looking forward to a few hours alone with his pipe and the newspaper and maybe later on he'd have a drop of Jameson's with hot water. He hadn't felt too well these last couple of days, he was getting old and the work seemed to take its toll more.

The hall was already fairly full when they arrived and their entrance caused quite a few heads to turn. Pat found them seats and then brought them each a glass of lemonade. The dancing was already under way to the fiddle, accordion, bodhrán and tin whistle of Johnny Hickey and the Ballycumber Boys and Grace was the first to be asked up to dance.

Pat nodded and looked a little smug. 'There, wasn't I right? Didn't I tell her she wouldn't be a wallflower at all? Now, finish up your drink, Chrissie, and we'll get up and take a turn around the floor ourselves.'

As the evening wore on the hall became more and more crowded and Chrissie noted that there were quite a few men who had taken drink, although there was nothing remotely alcoholic on sale in the building. They must either have been to the pub before they had come or had a bottle or a flask concealed in their pockets. Both Father Doyle and Father Porag, the curate, spent a good deal of time circulating and chatting and generally keeping their eye on things.

It had become very warm and she had discarded the jacket of her costume, placing it on the back of her chair. Grace, too, had taken off her cardigan and Chrissie thought her sister would have looked better if she'd had a few bangles to wear. It would have taken the rather bare look away from her arms. She herself had her watch and a gilt-coloured bangle that had originally belonged to Ellie Nelson but had been swapped for something or other during the war years. Grace wore just the very plain and simple wristwatch her father had bought her for her fourteenth birthday.

She glanced around her, sipping her drink. The dancing finished as the interval for 'tea and a bite to eat' was announced. After the initial interest her appearance had caused everyone seemed to have become engrossed in pursuing their own entertainment and her enjoyment and enthusiasm had worn off. Grace had hardly been off the dance floor while she had had to be content to stick mainly to sedate waltzes with her husband. She frowned, with the noise and the heat her head was beginning to ache a little.

'I've been danced off my feet and I'm exhausted!' Grace laughed as she joined them. 'And I could murder a cup of tea.'

'Aren't you proving a huge success? These lads are no eejits and sure I thought Martin Kenny and Seamus Bracken were going to come to blows over you.'

Grace punched him playfully on the arm. 'Oh, stop that, Pat Kilroy! You're exaggerating. They were very polite to each other and I *did* dance with them both – eventually. Now, I'm going over for a cup of tea and a sandwich. Are you coming, Chrissie?'

'Pat, will you bring me something, please? I've a bit of a headache,' Chrissie replied, an edge of curtness in her voice.

Pat looked concerned. ' 'Tis probably the heat. You

don't feel faint, do you? Would you like me to take you for a bit of a walk along the road? The fresh air will help. Then we'll have the tea.'

Chrissie had no desire to go out for a walk, by now she felt that she would really like to go home but she didn't want to ruin their evening. She shook her head. 'No, it's not that bad. A cup of tea will help.'

Grace and Pat walked across the room and joined the queue that had formed for tea and sandwiches, chatting amiably together, and Chrissie felt the familiar sense of isolation creep over her. Everyone else here had known each other almost all their lives. She was an outsider, she didn't belong, she didn't fit in and if she was honest with herself she didn't want to make an effort to do so. This wasn't her home, it wasn't her country, they weren't her people and she'd never be happy or contented here. Yet Grace seemed to fit in perfectly, she didn't appear to think of herself as a stranger, she was accepted. Look at her now chatting to everyone, even Johnny Hickey from the band whom she'd never met in her life before. She wondered why her sister seemed to be so at ease and so popular.

'Isn't that a gorgeous outfit? Did ye have it for a grand wedding in England before ye came here?'

Chrissie's reverie was broken and she looked up to find Maura Dunne, a girl Grace had also become friendly with, beaming down at her. Maura was what was called a 'fine big strap of a girl' by Con, although privately she thought a saying she'd heard in town

291

suited the girl more: 'beef to the heels like a Mullingar heifer'. She was tall, big-boned and heavy, but she was the daughter of a substantial farmer who lived out on the road to Mucklagh, which was probably why Con approved of her. Maura was wearing a dress of a shade of puce that definitely did not suit her and her hair had come loose from its pins and was straggling untidily. Her face was flushed and there were beads of perspiration on her forehead and Chrissie thought she looked most unattractive, yet it was obvious that she hadn't been short of partners in the dancing. Probably because she would go to whoever married her 'with a farm of land', she thought scathingly.

Chrissie tried to look polite. 'No, I didn't have it for a wedding in Liverpool. I had it made here, in Tullamore.' A wedding in England, she thought irritably. Didn't the girl realise that it had been impossible to obtain such an outfit in Liverpool or anywhere else in the country? There had been a war on, for heaven's sake!

'Did ye now? I never realised such a thing could be got in Tullamore. Who made it for ye?' Maura persisted. It was very stylish. She'd never seen anyone in the entire parish wear anything like it.

'Miss McEvoy in William Street. She learned her trade in Belfast, she's very good.'

'And does your woman charge much for an outfit like that? Does she provide the material too and is that included in the price?' This was proving very interesting to Maura. If this Miss McEvoy wasn't too expensive then she might be able to prevail upon her da to let her have something made, something just like this.

'She can send to Dublin for material or you can ask Mrs Morris at the Drapery to get it for you. I suppose she *is* quite expensive and trimmings are extra.'

Maura was about to ask Chrissie exactly how costly was 'quite expensive' when Pat and Grace returned, carrying cups of tea and a small plate of ham sandwiches.

Chrissie was relieved. 'Oh, lovely! My throat is as dry as dust.'

Pat handed his wife her tea and smiled at her companion; he knew her father well enough. 'How are you, Maura? I saw you doing a lively hornpipe around the floor with Tom Delaney.'

Maura laughed as she got to her feet. 'And wouldn't that feller have ye killed, he's two left feet, so he has.'

Grace grinned at her. She found Maura good company. She was an easy-going girl, always laughing. 'I'm glad he didn't ask me to dance then or there would have been two of us with two left feet and we'd have made a right spectacle of ourselves. I can't follow all the steps of half these dances, I'm just used to waltzes and quicksteps and the occasional foxtrot.'

'I'll learn ye, Grace. Ye'll pick them up in no time and ye can learn me how to quickstep, if we can find someone who will play one for us. Now, I'll get a cup of tea myself. 'Tis thirsty work, dancing.'

'Isn't she what you call a "gas", Pat?' Grace laughed as her friend disappeared.

Pat nodded.

'What were you talking about?' Grace asked her sister.

'Clothes,' Chrissie answered curtly.

Pat raised his eyes to the ceiling and grimaced in mock despair. 'What else?'

Chrissie's headache increased as the dancing resumed and she refused to take to the floor with Pat. 'Ask Grace, she seems to be without a partner at the moment.'

'She won't be for long. Is there anything I can get for you? A glass of water?'

Grace looked at her sister more intently, she did look a bit pale and it was stuffy in here. 'Is it very bad, Chrissie? If you want to go home I really don't mind. My shoes are beginning to pinch and these dances are so fast it's exhausting. I'm just not used to it. Where on earth they all get the energy to go on like this until the early hours of the morning I don't know. And Seamus Bracken was telling me that sometimes they don't finish until four o'clock!'

Chrissie nodded although she felt a little guilty for she could see from his face that Pat didn't really want to leave yet. He seldom went out either and by local standards this was a big occasion. 'Oh, would you really not mind, Grace? It's beginning to thump.'

Grace stood up and took her cardigan from the back

of the chair. 'We'll go then. There's nothing worse than having a banging headache, it makes you feel really wretched and you just can't enjoy yourself.'

They made their excuses to the two priests and various other friends and neighbours and Chrissie felt very relieved as they walked towards the trap. All she wanted to do was take off this costume, her own high-heeled court shoes and the earrings that were pinching the lobes of her ears and crawl into bed.

When they arrived home the oil lamps were still burning in the kitchen.

'I thought Con was going to bed early but he must still be up,' Pat remarked. 'I'll see to the pony, then I'll be in.'

Grace stepped down and then turned to help Chrissie who was having a bit of difficulty with the ankle-length skirt. 'Mind you don't get your heel caught in it or you'll fall,' she warned.

The kitchen was warm although the fire had burned down, Chrissie thought as she went in. There was no sign of Con. 'He must have gone to bed but wouldn't you have thought he'd have put out two of those lamps?' she said irritably. Then she gave a cry as she caught sight of the old man half lying, half sitting on the floor between the dresser and the table. 'Grace! Oh, my God! Grace!'

Grace had followed her sister in and now she rushed and bent over Con, feeling for a pulse at his wrist. She was just as shocked but she managed to stay calm. 'Con? Uncle Con. Can you hear me?' she asked.

Slowly he half opened his eyes and she breathed easier. 'Chrissie, go and shout to Pat to come in as quickly as he can! Uncle Con, let me help you. Here, lean against me. What happened? Did you fall?'

He tried but seemed unable to move.

Grace was worried, he'd managed to open his left eye but the other remained half closed and that side of his face looked sort of lopsided.

Con tried to speak but the words were badly slurred. 'Can't, can't move the fathe . . . lipth . . .'

'Don't try to speak. Pat will help us get you to bed and then go for the doctor.' She was beginning to realise that the old man had had a stroke. Old Mrs Nelson, Polly's mother-in-law, had had three strokes before she'd died. She prayed that Con wouldn't go the same way; he would hate to be paralysed.

Pat at last burst into the room, followed by Chrissie who was white-faced and shocked.

'Grace, what's the matter with him? Is it bad?'

She looked up at him and nodded. 'I think he's had a stroke. Will you help me get him to bed and then go for the doctor?'

Pat was instantly beside his uncle, his face serious. 'Now, just take it very slow and easy, Con. Let Grace and meself get you up and to your bed then I'll be away for Dr Wrafter, he's nearest. Thanks be to God we came home!'

'I should have stayed,' Grace said quietly as they helped Con up, Pat taking nearly all his uncle's weight and determining that he would carry the old man bodily up the stairs.

'*I* should have stayed, Grace. I should have realised that he's getting old but—'

'Maybe we shouldn't blame ourselves. He said he was fine and we didn't want to disappoint Chrissie,' she said firmly. It wasn't Pat's fault, he'd only been trying to give her sister a treat on her birthday.

Chrissie stood gripping the back of a chair watching as they got Con to the stairs, then Pat lifted him and carried him up, followed by Grace. Her initial shock was beginning to fade. How could any of them have known he would take ill? He'd been his usual self. Just how ill was he? she wondered.

Chapter Twenty-Four

———◆◆◆———

DR WRAFTER WAS A STOCKY, middle-aged man with dark hair that was greying at the temples and a very down-to-earth and practical nature. He informed them that it wasn't too bad, he'd seen far worse, and said they should make Con rest and that in time, please God, he would recover. He would call again that evening but he told Pat that at his time of life Con should have been taking things much easier and would have to now.

'Sure, that's something that's easier said than done. He's worked hard all his life, you know that,' Pat said gravely as he'd shown the doctor out.

'Well, if he doesn't he'll end up killing himself and I'll tell him that too, so I will,' was the stark reply.

Grace was very relieved to hear that it was more than

likely Con would recover. 'He'd have *hated* to have to be an invalid for the rest of his life.'

She settled Con comfortably in bed and then made a pot of tea and although it was well after half past two the three of them sat around the table. Chrissie had stirred herself enough to make up the fire. She was still very shocked and she too had thought about old Mrs Nelson and how Polly, and sometimes her own mam, had looked after her. If Con were paralysed then who would look after him? He'd need nursing and probably for a long time and she just *couldn't* do it! She just couldn't face it! Pat couldn't expect her to, it was just too much to ask. Grace would have to do it or maybe Eileen would come over, she was an experienced nursing sister and Con was her uncle too when all was said and done.

Pat shook his head slowly, still looking anxious. 'He'll be like the divil himself to take care of. We'll have a job to keep him in the bed at all once he starts to feel better and gets a little use in his limbs again.'

'That could take some time. I got the impression from what the doctor said that it wasn't going to happen overnight,' Grace replied. She sighed. She had become quite close to the old man and was concerned about him.

It had been a worrying couple of hours, she thought. First the shock of finding Con, then the realisation that his condition was serious and then the visit from the doctor; now they were all tired. But the night wasn't over yet. There were still practical decisions to be made.

'I'll do as much for him as I can but it's going to be hard on you, Chrissie, I'm afraid.' Pat reached across and took his wife's hand. 'I'm sorry, it hasn't been a great birthday for you at all.'

Chrissie looked at him with rising panic and snatched her hand away. 'Pat, I . . . I can't look after him! I can't nurse him!'

Pat stared at her. Her words took a few seconds to sink in. 'But . . . but who else is there?' he asked as the realisation that she was refusing began to dawn on him.

Chrissie looked at Grace. 'Grace! Grace, I just can't do it!'

'But neither can Grace.' Pat was becoming angry. 'She has her work up at the college, she works in the dairy and she works hard in the house too. You can't expect her to give up her little bit of a job, 'tis the only money of her own she has. You're not being fair on her, she has to have some independence, Chrissie!'

'But what about my independence?' Chrissie cried and then fixed her gaze pleadingly on her sister. 'I can't do it! I can't feed and wash and shave him and . . . and I *can't* empty . . . chamber pots or change . . . dirty bedding! Oh, Grace, I'd be sick, I would! I'd throw up! If you can't do it then can't we ask Eileen to come? She's a proper nurse, she's used to all . . . *that*, and he's her uncle too?'

Grace had been taken aback by Chrissie's refusal, but now she realised she should have anticipated some such protest. It didn't make her any less annoyed with and disappointed in her sister though. 'Oh, for heaven's sake, Chrissie, don't be so *stupid*! Eileen is a married woman now, her responsibility is to her husband. How can she drop everything and come running over here for the Lord alone knows how long? Have some sense! And you talk as if you're expecting me to stay here for ever and I hadn't really planned on that.'

Pat too had been astounded by his wife's words. He was deeply hurt. She was flatly refusing to lift a finger to help an old man who was sick and could do little to help himself. An old man who had welcomed her into this house and, apart from some totally justifiable complaints about her extravagance, worked hard to help to provide her with a good standard of living. After his parents had died and his siblings had emigrated, his uncle had been his rock and he was devoted to the old man. Her attitude was nothing short of callous, without a shred of care or pity, and it shocked him to the core. Did she really hate Con so much?

'Grace is right. Eileen has to put her husband first; she can't come and you can't expect Grace to put her life on hold. You'll just have to do it, Chrissie. I've promised I'll do as much as I can for him.' His voice held an edge of harshness that had never been there before.

Grace noticed it but Chrissie didn't. She got to her feet, knocking the chair over backwards, her face set. 'No! You're out in the yard or the fields all day! I won't do it, I CAN'T! Don't you understand? It will make me ill! My stomach is churning now, just at the thought of it! You . . . you can't *make* me do it!' Seeing the anger in his eyes she turned and fled upstairs, slamming the bedroom door behind her. Throwing herself on the bed, she burst into tears. She *wouldn't* do it! They'd have to drag her into that sickroom!

Grace sighed heavily and rubbed her temples for her own head had begun to ache. 'Leave her, Pat. I'll nurse him. He has his pride and I won't stand by and let Chrissie humiliate him by making it obvious that she doesn't want to help him. That . . . that what the poor old soul has suffered disgusts her. I'm so sorry, Pat, really I am, for the way she's acting. I'm ashamed of her and Mam will be too. She's my sister and I thought I knew her well but . . . I'm shocked and hurt and angry too! I don't mind giving up my job or staying on to nurse him, I'm fond of him and it will be worth it to have him back on his feet and able to get around again. He *does* have his pride and he won't be happy having to be nursed by anyone but we'll manage it between us.'

Pat nodded slowly. She had put his own feelings into words, not only about Chrissie but his uncle too. 'Maybe Sister Assumpta will give you a bit of time off, under the circumstances.'

Grace managed a wry smile. 'Would it even be fair to ask? We don't know how long it will take him to recover. It could be months.'

Pat frowned. It just wasn't fair on Grace. She never complained about anything, she was always good-natured and she had given up a good job, her life in

Liverpool and even Sandy to try to ease Chrissie's life and make her happy. He wondered tiredly if anything would ever make Chrissie happy? God knows he'd tried hard enough, as had Grace, and this was the way she repaid them both. 'I'll see if I can manage him myself for those few hours.'

'Pat, how can you? There's so much to be done of a morning in the yard.'

'Maybe I could ask someone, one of the neighbours, to sit in with him.'

Grace shook her head. 'No, Pat, what would they think? What would they say? Two women in the house and neither of them able to see to him. That would humiliate us all and I won't have that.'

'Then I'll take on another labourer. Tom Healy has been with us this long time now, he can stand in for myself. Between us we'll manage, Grace. It won't be for ever and I won't have you giving up your bit of independence. You have your pride too, Grace, and aren't you entitled to it?'

She nodded. 'We'll give it a try. I'll warn them in the laundry that I might have to give notice, but thank you, Pat.' She stood up and began to clear away the dishes.

'Ah, leave those, Grace. Let Chrissie do them in the morning, 'tis the least she can do.'

She didn't miss the new note of bitterness in his voice and she wondered had her sister gone too far this time? Had she pushed Pat's understanding and sympathy to the limit? She hoped not. 'I'll go up then, Pat. I'll look in on Con before I turn in and if you need me to help with him in the night call me.'

He nodded and she went upstairs. She prayed her sister had fallen asleep for she was just too upset to try to cope with Chrissie now. All she wanted to do was get some sleep too.

Pat sat for a while longer, staring into the embers of the dying fire. Life was going to be difficult over the next weeks and maybe months and the seed of doubt that had been sown in his heart as to whether Chrissie still loved him or not began to grow. And did he still love her as much? he asked himself. He had seen another side to her this night, one he had never suspected she possessed. Maybe it had been there all the time and he'd been too blind to discern it. He'd excused so much because he loved her but what now? He shook himself mentally and got to his feet. Things were bad enough without venturing down that particular road, he told himself firmly.

As the days and weeks progressed and the weather grew warmer Con did improve slowly. He wasn't an easy person to nurse but Grace was firm, considerate and patient with him, meeting his complaints and irritability with humour. He had his good days and his bad ones but gradually his speech became clearer and he regained the use of his limbs.

'You're just so impatient, that's your trouble, and you're going to have to learn to take things easy. You know what the doctor told you,' Grace told him for what she thought must be the five hundredth time as at the beginning of June Con managed slowly, and with her assistance, to come downstairs for the first time.

'It's a glorious day. I've put a comfortable chair by the door so you can sit in the sun and watch what's going on,' she said breezily, holding his arm as he shuffled slowly across the kitchen.

' 'Tis not going to be easy to sit and watch others work,' he muttered, although he was relieved to escape at last from the bedroom for he'd been very afraid he would spend the rest of his days there.

'No one said it would but you'll have to get used to it. Now, you just rest while I get the vegetables peeled for the supper.'

'Where's herself then?' Con asked for Chrissie was nowhere to be seen.

'It's Thursday, she's in town. I expect she'll be back later on,' Grace replied.

Con nodded. Lately he'd begun to notice that there was a difference in his nephew's manner towards his wife. A coolness that had never been there before. When he'd been sick he'd hardly seen Chrissie. She had come in occasionally to see him but that was all. Pat had tended him in the mornings, telling him he was not to worry, that he'd taken on another lad and that Tom Healy was overseeing the work and was well able for it. Grace had tended him in the afternoons and evenings after she'd come back from the laundry, and she too had told him not to worry for Chrissie had again taken over in the dairy and was busy with the chores too, which was why she didn't come up too often, so he was being no bother at all. He must rest and get well again.

He knew nothing of Pat's angry silence, met with stubborn resentment by Chrissie, that had gone on for over a week until Grace, unable to stand the atmosphere any longer, had told them both that things were bad enough without them constantly glaring at each other and would they please, for her sake and that of poor Con, make some kind of effort to at least be civil to each other. What was done was done, there was no taking back the things that had been said but everyone had to *try* to get along. After that relations had improved little by little but they were far from being back to normal and Grace doubted they ever really would be.

'Is that the post?' Grace asked, hearing the familiar, slightly tinny sound of Jack Brennan's bicycle bell as he rode into the yard.

'It is so,' Con replied, thinking it would be grand to have a chat at last with Jack and hear the latest news of the parish. The postman not only collected and delivered mail, he also kept his eye on everyone and knew everything that was going on, usually as it happened.

'Well, now, there you are yourself, Con! Isn't it grand to see you on the mend? You'll be back on your feet in no time at all now, thanks be to God!'

' 'Tis thanks be to Him indeed and the good minding I've had from the family,' Con replied, crossing himself.

Grace came to the door, wiping her hands on her apron. 'How are you Jack? Anything for me today?'

'There is so, Grace. Two letters from England, no less. I have to say the family do keep you well informed of what's going on. There's many a one would be only delighted to hear so often from those who have gone off to live and work across the seas. Now, Con, tell me how you're feeling?'

Grace took the letters from him and left them to their chat. One was from her mother and the other from Georgie, which was unusual. When he wrote he usually enclosed his letter with either that of Mags or Mam. She ripped open the envelope and then gave a delighted cry. Mags had had a little boy. He'd been born at half past six in the morning and had weighed six pounds two ounces and they were going to call him Thomas Harold, after his grandfather and his dead uncle. Mother and baby were doing well and he was as proud as punch. Billy couldn't get over the fact that he was an uncle. He'd taken Billy and Tommy Milligan out to the pub with Alf Nelson from next door and some of his mates to 'wet the baby's head' although Mam hadn't been very pleased about it as both lads were under age.

She read his words again. She was an aunty! Oh, she longed to see little Thomas Harold Devlin, and she wondered whom he looked like? Trust Georgie not to mention that. She opened Sadie's letter and scanned the lines. According to her Mam, Mags had had a long and arduous labour and was still tired and confined to bed.

The baby was a little angel, Sadie wrote. He had a mop of dark hair like Mags and blue eyes, but as all babies were born with blue eyes that might change. He definitely had Georgie's nose. He was to be christened next week and it was such a pity that neither Grace nor Chrissie could be spared to be godmother but both Mags and Georgie understood how things were over there, so Mags had asked Eileen Bateson who was delighted. Billy was to be godfather and she intended to give him a good talking to about his duties and responsibilities to the child, for he was showing little signs of responsibility these days. Grace smiled, thinking of her younger and somewhat harum-scarum brother and then felt a pang of disappointment at being unable to be godmother herself. She sighed. It just couldn't be helped and Sadie promised that they would send a photograph so Grace and Chrissie could see their new nephew.

Grace glanced towards the door; the two men were still deep in conversation so she continued to read. Sadie had more news. Kate Nelson was getting engaged to the lad she'd been walking out with since Christmas and Polly was pleased but had confided that their Ellie was jealous, although she wouldn't for the life of her admit it. And Mrs Bradshaw's daughter Doris was expecting in the autumn, the same time as Princess Elizabeth, and it would be her first child too. It had been announced that they were to get twelve extra clothing coupons per person until the end of September, which had delighted everyone, but especially Kate Nelson. However, there was bad news too, as usual. The dockers were on strike and there was talk of the troops being sent in to unload the 232 ships now being held up because the meat ration had dropped to sixpence' worth of fresh meat and sixpence' worth of canned meat per person per week, which was nothing short of diabolical. Indeed Mr Attlee, the Prime Minister, had said 'We must feed the people' and he'd told the strikers that 'this strike is not against capitalists and employers. It is against your mates.' And she for one was inclined to agree with him. She finished by saying that she continued to pray for Con and hoped his improvement continued, that she was thankful that Chrissie and Pat were on better terms and that Grace should take care of her own health.

Grace folded both letters and left them on the table for Chrissie to read when she got home, then went to break up the conversation still going on at the door. She didn't want Con to get overtired.

'Sorry to interrupt but I've had great news. Mags, my sister-in-law, has had a little boy. I'm now an aunty.'

Con beamed at her, still a little lopsidedly. 'Isn't that a great piece of news altogether? Congratulations, Grace.'

'A blessing indeed, thanks be to God!' Jack added, thinking he had another bit of news to impart on his rounds.

'They're going to call him Thomas Harold after my da and my oldest brother. Both were killed in the war –

the Emergency,' she added for Jack's benefit. 'And guess what, Con? Eileen is to be his godmother.'

Con nodded slowly. He knew Eileen would be delighted but he also realised that had Grace still been in Liverpool that honour would have been bestowed on her.

'Right then, I'll be away now or would you be wanting to write a bit of a note to congratulate them? I'll wait if you do,' Jack offered.

'No, I'll write tonight because Chrissie will want to add a few lines too and she's not back yet, but thanks just the same. Now, I'll get you inside out of this sun, it's very strong, and I'll make you a cup of tea, Con. I think you've had quite enough excitement for one day.'

Con grimaced at her and then looked despairingly at Jack. 'Do ye see how she treats me? Ye'd think I was a child, so ye would.'

Grace laughed. 'Oh, we treat you shockingly, I'm sure! We have you spoiled.'

He smiled as she helped him up. 'Ye do indeed and I'm grateful for it, Grace.'

Impulsively she kissed his cheek. 'It's no more than you deserve after a lifetime of hard work for this family's benefit.'

He looked pleased but a little embarrassed. 'Aye, but there's some more grateful than others,' he said gruffly.

Chapter Twenty-Five

'MAGS, YOU'D BETTER FEED that child before we have the photograph taken, we don't want him to be shown for posterity bawling his little head off,' Sadie advised as they all returned from the church after the ceremony. Earlier Polly Nelson had helped her to prepare the christening tea that was to follow the official photograph.

Mags dutifully took her baby from the arms of his godmother and went upstairs to feed him. She felt a little tired but wasn't that only to be expected? she asked herself. She wasn't getting much sleep.

'I thought he was very good, he didn't even cry when Father Weaver poured the water over his head. He's a grand little fellow,' Eileen said smiling as she helped Sadie off with her lightweight jacket. 'And don't we all look smart?'

Sadie nodded. They had all made an effort, even Billy, who was now in the process of removing his stiff collar. 'You leave that collar alone, meladdo! Do you want to look like a real scruff on the photograph?'

'Ah, Mam! It's half choking me and it's too hot for collars and ties,' Billy protested.

'Just hang on for another half an hour, lad, then when the photographer has gone we can both get changed. I feel half choked myself,' Georgie urged his brother.

Sadie had put the kettle on. 'Well, we've time for a quick cup of tea at least.'

'Sure, Grace can't wait to get the photograph, she said so in her last letter,' Eileen informed them. 'It's a pity neither she nor Chrissie could be here,' she added, although she really had no wish to see Chrissie for she had heard of Chrissie's refusal to lift a finger to help Con. 'But then I suppose if they could have come I wouldn't have been godmother,' she added.

'You'll make an excellent godmother, Eileen, although I know it would have been Grace that Mags would have asked. At least Con is coming along just fine now, thank God.'

Eileen nodded. Thanks to Grace and Pat, she thought. 'Did I tell you that Pat has decided to buy a tractor? They're very expensive but they've been saving up for ages and he says it will be a huge help, especially for Uncle Con when he's able to do a bit of work again. He hates being idle.'

'He'll have to be careful, Eileen. You know as well as I do that he could have another stroke, God forbid.'

'Do they know how to drive? Those things must take some handling,' Georgie asked, thinking Pat couldn't be short if they were buying something as expensive as a tractor.

Eileen shrugged. 'Who is there to teach them to drive it? But sure, they'll get the hang of it and Pat says it will prove a godsend and will soon pay for itself.'

Sadie, catching sight of a man passing the window, finished her tea. 'Right, here comes the photographer. You two lads smarten yourselves up and I'll go and see if Mags is nearly ready.'

Eileen cleared the dishes while Billy straightened his tie and Georgie checked his appearance in the mirror.

Halfway up the stairs Sadie had to stop. The familiar sharp, stabbing pain in her back made her gasp and she gripped the banister rail tightly. 'Pull yourself together, girl, it will pass, you can't ruin the photograph. It's costing enough,' she told herself firmly.

Mags was on her way down and was startled to see her mother-in-law clinging tightly to the banister, her face drawn and contorted with pain. 'Ma! Ma, are you all right?'

Sadie nodded and with an effort drew herself upright. 'I'm fine. Just a twinge of my rheumatism.'

Mags was concerned. 'You don't look fine and your rheumatism shouldn't be playing up at this time of year.'

'I'll be just grand, as Eileen would say. The

photographer feller has arrived, I was coming up to tell you, so we'd better get ourselves down there and put on our best smiles. Is he asleep?'

Mags nodded, smiling down at her infant son who was resplendent in the christening gown that had been her own and which her mam had carefully treasured all these years.

They submitted to being moved around and told to 'stand a bit closer, no, not *that* close'. Billy thought that the photographer was being very fussy and that it was all a great palaver just for a photo. Mags, holding the baby, and Sadie and Eileen were sitting down with Georgie and himself standing behind them.

'Right. Now can we all smile, please? Let's look as if we're delighted to be here. It's a happy occasion, not a funeral,' was the instruction.

They all obliged although Billy was certain he would come out looking like a fool. Then it was all over and done with and the feller was packing away his stuff.

'Now can I take off me collar and tie, Mam?' he begged.

Sadie sighed. 'Oh, suit yourself. You can go and ask Tommy if he wants to come up and share this bit of a tea. Polly and her girls are coming in.'

Delightedly, Billy almost tore off the offending collar, discarded his jacket and went in search of his best mate.

Georgie went up to change and Mags placed the still sleeping baby in his crib. Eileen had taken off her hat and the jacket of her linen costume and Sadie went to fill the kettle in the scullery.

'Eileen, would you have a word with Ma? I found her hanging on to the banister rail and she looked awful. She said it was her rheumatism but I'm certain it's more than that. She might listen to you with your medical knowledge; she won't take a blind bit of notice of me.'

Eileen frowned. 'Has she been to see the doctor? He's more qualified than I am.'

'She won't hear of it.'

Eileen wondered how on earth she was going to broach the subject with Sadie but she nodded for she could see her friend was worried and she knew Sadie had been having these 'twinges' for a while.

She didn't have to make polite but probing enquiries about Sadie's health for as the older woman returned with the kettle, she suddenly groaned and had to put the kettle down quickly.

'Mrs Devlin, what's wrong? Have you a pain?' Eileen asked.

'Just another of my twinges,' Sadie replied, grimacing.

Eileen was instantly beside her. 'Sure, that's not a twinge!' She gently ran her fingers down Sadie's spine. 'Tell me where it hurts.'

Sadie gasped and bit her lip as Eileen pressed gently at the base of her spine.

'I'd say that is something a bit more serious than rheumatism. It could be a number of things, maybe sciatica, but I'm no expert. You'll have to go and see the doctor, Mrs Devlin,' she said in a tone that brooked no argument, a tone that many of her former patients had come to know only too well. 'You don't have to pay now, not with the new National Health Service, and is there any point at all in suffering when you don't have to?'

Sadie sat down and nodded, slowly. She knew in her heart it wasn't rheumatism but she was afraid of what it could be. Yet Eileen was an experienced nurse and maybe the girl was right. Maybe it was just something like sciatica. 'I'll go tomorrow morning.'

'Promise or I'll put Thomas in his pram and take you there myself!' Mags threatened.

Sadie managed a smile. 'I promise.'

'I'll come round tomorrow afternoon to make sure you've been,' Eileen added. She wasn't absolutely sure but she thought she had felt a small lump on one of the vertebrae and it worried her.

'At least then I'll be able to write and tell Grace that you've been. It will put her mind at rest too, you know she always asks about your health,' Mags reminded Sadie.

Sadie frowned. 'There's no need to go worrying Grace, she's enough on her plate as it is, Mags. You just tell her I'm fine, which I will be. I don't want you writing telling her I'm going to see the doctor, is that clear?'

Reluctantly Mags nodded. In her opinion Grace had a right to know but if Sadie didn't agree there was nothing she could do. She looked pleadingly at Eileen who gave a quick nod. Mags smiled back. Sadie hadn't forbidden Eileen to write and tell Grace.

The photograph of the christening group arrived at a very fortuitous time, Grace thought as she carefully took it from its wrappings. It might lighten the atmosphere a bit. The situation between Pat and Chrissie hadn't really improved and when her sister had heard that Pat intended to buy a new Fordson Major tractor she hadn't been very pleased even though she was aware that they had been saving hard for one.

'He can afford to buy one of those things, which cost a small fortune, but if I dare to mention that I need a pair of new shoes there's a huge row!' she grumbled.

'Chrissie, I know they are expensive but it will save so much time and effort, especially for Con. You know how irritable he gets. He hates it that he can't do everything he used to be capable of doing. He feels useless, he's told me so.'

'He's always been irritable and he'll just have to get used to the fact that he is *old*!' Chrissie had snapped back.

Grace had become annoyed. 'He's not an old horse to be put out to grass! He's worked hard and if he can still feel he's doing a day's work he'll feel better in himself. And do you really need another pair of shoes?'

'Oh, you're getting as bad as them, Grace, you really are! You always used to care how you looked but these days you don't.'

Grace had shaken her head. 'I do, Chrissie, it's just that life is different here. There's no need to be dressed up to death all the time. We wore those awful overalls and turbans when we worked in munitions, you couldn't call them stylish, but they served their purpose. The clothes we wear here serve their purpose too.'

'We had no choice then, now we do,' Chrissie had replied sullenly. It just wasn't fair that Pat was going to spend pounds and pounds on a piece of machinery and she couldn't have a pair of summer shoes. Since the dance, life had reverted to being dull and tedious and the longing to go back to Liverpool had increased. She'd had a letter from Ellie Nelson telling her all about the dances she'd been going to and how great a time she was having. Ellie had mentioned Kate's wedding plans briefly, saying the only thing she was really looking forward to was being a bridesmaid and having a new dress. Now that Pat was intent on the tractor there would be no new dresses for her, Chrissie had thought bitterly.

Pat came into the kitchen as Grace was poring over the family group. 'I see it's arrived then?'

Grace smiled at him. 'They all look rather stiff and formal except for our Billy, he's grinning like a prize eejit! You can't really see much of little Thomas, he's all done up in a christening gown and a bonnet. I always think little boys should wear something more, well, boyish, but it's the custom.' She handed Pat the photograph in its frame.

He smiled. 'Sure, I see what you mean about Billy

320

but Eileen looks well, so she does.' He became serious. 'Were you very disappointed, Grace?'

'You mean about not being godmother? Not at all. I couldn't leave you here to see to Con on your own, now could I? It was out of the question.'

His expression became resentful. 'Chrissie could have helped out, you could have gone, Grace.'

She laid a hand on his arm. 'Pat, let's not start thinking like that. I'm sure Mags will have more children and now that Con is doing so well, I'll be able to be godmother to the next one. And you'll have the new tractor, which will help.'

He fiddled with the string that had been around the parcel. 'Grace, these days I'm after thinking that nothing I can say or do will make Chrissie happy.'

'Oh, Pat, don't say that! You are so good to her and so patient too.' She was becoming alarmed. What was he trying to tell her?

'I'm losing the patience, Grace. There are times now when I just can't be bothered. Often I find myself wondering if she cares for me at all and I ask myself do I still care for her?' It was the truth, he thought. 'Chrissie hates it here.'

'Oh, Pat! She is trying but she'll always be a city girl no matter how long she lives here. I'm sure she still loves you, I really am! It's just taking her a long time to get used to this life. Do you want me to talk to her?'

'No! No, there's nothing you can say, Grace. You can't make her love me any more than you can make me

321

love her the way I used to. I've changed, I know now that I feel differently about Chrissie.'

Grace regarded him sadly. Oh, what a mess it all was for she was sure he was telling her that he was sorry he had married Chrissie. 'She's your wife, Pat.'

'I know and I'm after thinking that's the pity of it!'

She stared after him as he turned on his heel and walked out. What had he meant by that? She pressed her hands to her cheeks. He was just hurt and angry with Chrissie but he must still love her a bit, surely?

'Are ye sick, Grace?'

Con's question banished the thoughts from her mind and she thought fleetingly how much his speech had improved. 'No, it's just the heat in here. I've a stew in the oven and the bread on the griddle.'

' 'Tis a good job it's a stew for I'm in to tell ye that Pat and meself are off to collect the new tractor so we'll be late in for supper.'

She smiled at him. 'Won't the pair of you be the envy of every farmer in the parish? They'll be coming from miles around to have a good look at it. I'll be worn out making tea for them all.'

He grinned back. 'Ye will so but isn't it costing us every penny we have saved?'

'Now, Pat has said it will pay for itself and it will save you both hours of back-breaking work.'

The old man nodded his agreement. ' 'Tis a pity there are no pieces of machinery that would save ye hours of work, Grace.'

'You know that we're going to get electricity soon from the power station in Cloghan, that will be a huge help. Now, get off with you. I'll take the stew out for a while.'

He left and she took the meal out of the oven in the range, hoping that when they arrived home with the tractor there would be no arguments or tantrums from Chrissie. Then she opened the letter that had arrived with the parcel. It was from Eileen and she was disturbed to learn that Eileen had thought long and hard about writing to inform her that she had insisted that Sadie go and see the doctor with the pain in her back. It definitely wasn't rheumatism, Eileen wrote, and they were sending Sadie for some tests. This new Health Service was wonderful for it meant that Sadie wouldn't have to pay a penny for the tests or any treatment she might need. Eileen promised to keep her informed for Sadie had forbidden Mags to mention anything at all about it. Oh, that was just typical of Mam, Grace thought. Eileen said she was sure it was nothing serious, but it was another worry. The war had taken a heavy toll on her mother's health and she wondered should she go back for a visit, just to see for herself? She'd write and ask Eileen did she think a visit would help?

Chapter Twenty-Six

———◆◆◆———

ILEEN WROTE BACK TELLING Grace there was no need for her to come over to Liverpool. For one thing the results of the tests would take time and for another Sadie would know that someone had informed Grace of her visit to the doctor and probably Mags would get the blame for it. Grace had written again, begging Eileen to let her know the minute the results were known. Concern for her mother's health was never far from her mind.

As summer turned to autumn and the days grew colder and shorter Chrissie became more and more miserable and bad-tempered. Yet another long winter stretched ahead and she wondered how she would stand it and she frequently burdened Grace with her woes.

Grace had toyed briefly with the idea of trying to persuade Pat to let her sister go to Liverpool for a short visit. It might cheer Chrissie up and she would be able to report back on their mother's health. All the tests had proved inconclusive but Sadie still suffered from the pain in her back and Mags had written saying she didn't look at all well. But Grace had soon dismissed the idea, fearful that Chrissie, having once again tasted city life, might refuse to come back and that would only cause Sadie heartache and worry. She had also wondered if Pat would have cared if Chrissie had remained in Liverpool. He had said nothing more about his changed feelings towards Chrissie and for this she was grateful but these days it was obvious to everyone on the farm that Pat and Chrissie had little time or affection for each other. Pat was silent and morose in his wife's presence, only with Con and herself was he anything like his usual self. Chrissie, if she spoke to her husband at all, was offhand or snappy. It upset Grace to see them both so unhappy but she had to admit to herself that Chrissie just wasn't temperamentally suited to life here. Pat had tried; he'd done everything in his power to make her sister happy. Many a man would have lost all patience long before Pat had done. No one could blame him for the present situation.

During the long winter evenings Con and Pat sat either reading or discussing the state of the agricultural industry or of the country and Chrissie sat staring into the fire, lost in a world of her own and oblivious to everyone around her. Grace busied herself knitting jumpers for Mary's children.

As December arrived with heavy frosts and bitterly cold winds and Christmas was again approaching Pat finally admitted to himself that he didn't love Chrissie and that he should never have married her but there was no way out. He could never divorce her. Divorce might be the current trend in England now, or so it was reported in the newspapers, but the Catholic Church would not tolerate such a thing and there was no reason at all for the marriage to be considered for annulment. Over and over he asked himself where had he gone wrong? When had it all started to fall apart? There were times when the feeling of being hopelessly trapped in a marriage that was no marriage at all brought on black moods of depression. He couldn't unburden himself to Con either for he didn't want the old man to worry, it might bring on another stroke, yet there were times when he thought his uncle understood the situation only too well. He tried to put all his energies into his work and most of the time that helped.

The new tractor had indeed caused quite a stir but the novelty had gradually worn off. Con in particular was delighted with it and did far more work than Grace felt was good for him but any comments she made on the subject he dismissed out of hand.

Two weeks before Christmas Grace made up her mind that something would have to be done to ensure that the approaching holiday wasn't a tense, cheerless affair. She broached the subject with Con the following afternoon while Chrissie was upstairs lying down with a headache.

'We are going to have to do something, Uncle Con, to make sure that this Christmas isn't a total disaster.'

The old man stared at her hard and then nodded. ' 'Tis as clear as the nose on your face that those two have no time for each other. I'm no fool, Grace, and neither are ye, but what can we be doing?'

'I thought we could perhaps invite a few of the neighbours for supper on Christmas Eve? And maybe Mary and Liam and the children and Maura Dunne, she's always good company?'

Con considered the suggestion and nodded slowly. ' 'Tis a good idea, Grace.'

'It would perhaps cheer Chrissie up a bit and at least she and Pat would have to make some kind of an effort to be pleasant to each other.'

'I'm after thinking she hasn't much time for young Maura.'

'Well, she can just put herself out to be nice to Maura, there's no harm in the girl. We'll decorate the kitchen up for the occasion. We could even have a tree; I can make some decorations for it and get a bit of tinsel. Mary's children will be delighted with it. Maybe I could even get them a small toy each.'

'Ye don't want to be spoiling them. Sure, they'll come to expect it every year. Would not a few sweeties do?'

Grace tutted. 'Uncle Con, don't be such a misery! Christmas is a time for children.'

Con puffed on his pipe. 'The only childer's laughter in this house will be that of Mary and Liam Scully's. I'd hoped I'd live to see the day when I'd have a great-nephew or -niece.'

Grace sighed. 'I know but isn't that all the more reason to have Mary's children here? Oh, we'll put on a great spread! Why can't we have the Christmas dinner on Christmas Eve for a change?' she enthused. 'We'll get bunches of holly and mistletoe and there's that big red paper bell you had last year and Chrissie and I can get dressed up. We'll have a grand time.'

He grinned at her, catching her enthusiasm. 'And we'll have the port wine and a drop of Jameson's but not too much for we've to go to Midnight Mass. We'll ask the Dolans and the Kennys and old John Fahey, he's on his own now that Maggie's above in the churchyard, God rest her soul. And if your one can get herself dressed up to the nines it might take the puss off her face for a few hours. Ah, sure, we have to do something, Grace, and it's little enough but it is the festive season.'

Grace smiled at him and gave his hand a quick squeeze. 'Between us we'll bring a bit of "festivity" into this house if it kills us!'

At first Chrissie wasn't very enthusiastic about the idea but Grace finally persuaded her that it was just what was needed to cheer them all up and give them something to look forward to.

'Wear something really nice, Chrissie. After all, you will be the official hostess, not me. You are the mistress of the house.'

'I'll have Maura Dunne asking me where I bought my outfit and how much it cost,' Chrissie replied but she was smiling. Grace was right. A party was just what she needed to raise her spirits. She hadn't been looking forward to Christmas up to now and she knew there would be no expensive gift from Pat this year, probably no gift at all.

'I'll come into town with you tomorrow and we'll get the groceries and some tinsel and a few cheap little toys and some sweets. Pat and Con can get the greenery and a tree and see to the drink. Then maybe on Christmas Day you and me can walk over to Mary's and spend a few hours with them, it will make a change and you know the old saying "a change is as good as a rest".' She was trying to find ways of avoiding having to spend uncomfortable and silent hours in this house, knowing that after the party Christmas Day would be an anticlimax.

Con relayed all the information to Pat that evening when both girls had gone to bed. Pat felt relieved. He had been wondering what kind of Christmas it would be.

'And will ye be spending a fortune on herself this year at all?' Con asked bluntly.

Pat thrust his hands deep into the pockets of his jacket. 'I will not. She's never worn that bit of a velvet cape I got her last year nor the earrings I bought her for her birthday.'

'I know, lad, that ye are disappointed in her and I can't blame ye for it but ye have to make some kind of a fist of it, ye married her.'

Pat bent and poked the fire vigorously to hide the bitterness in his eyes. In his own way Con was telling him that he knew he no longer loved Chrissie but that there was no way out. 'I did and more's the pity.'

Con nodded thoughtfully. He'd suspected as much. 'Sure, I've often thought that your one never fitted in here, never tried to, never even wanted to try. But we have to put on a show of "happy families" for the neighbours. In the morning I'll go up with one of the lads and cut the holly and ye can take the tractor up to the field by the river, there's a few little fir trees growing in the bohreen. Grace has set her heart on having a tree for those childer of Mary Scully.'

Pat nodded. It would all help to make the occasion more cheerful.

Next morning Grace thought she detected a change in the atmosphere, a change for the better, and she smiled as she put on her heavy coat, scarf and hat to accompany Chrissie into town. Chrissie, she noted, had made more of an effort with her appearance this morning.

'Right. Now, have we got the list of everything we need?'

Chrissie nodded. 'But I don't know where we are going to get small cheap toys from. There isn't a toy shop.'

Grace frowned. She remembered Mary telling her that most people made things themselves or had toys made by a carpenter, if they could afford it. Little toys costing a penny or tuppence had always been available in Liverpool. Spinning tops and whips, wooden hoops, paper dolls and skipping ropes were the favourites. 'If we can't find anything maybe I can get Con to make a hoop and a top and whip and I could ask Mrs Moloney if she could make a rag doll.' She was determined that Mary's children would all have some little gift.

Chrissie shrugged. She wasn't the least bit interested in toys. She was wondering what she would get for Pat. Something practical, she thought, nothing that could be construed as a token of affection. And there were the gifts for the family in Liverpool too.

Con had come into the kitchen, dragging a bucket of turf and looking half frozen.

'Uncle Con, couldn't one of the lads have brought the turf in? Warm yourself by the range. We're off now but I've left a rabbit stew in the oven and there's fresh soda bread and some buns so you won't go hungry. We've a lot of shopping to do and we'll probably be late getting back.'

'Get off with the pair of ye and stop fussing about me. Young Dinny is coming with me to cut the green stuff. I'll leave it in one of the sheds until ye sort out where ye want it.' He, too, felt more cheerful this morning.

'Has Pat gone for the tree yet?' Grace asked.

'He'll be off in a while when they've finished feeding the cattle.'

'Will you ask him to pick a nice one, not too big or it will take up too much space.'

Con cast his eyes to the ceiling. 'Will ye just *go* and leave the greenery and tree to meself and Pat! Sure, there isn't a forest of trees to choose from at all.'

They spent the morning shopping for groceries and gifts and they managed to get some tinsel. Chrissie bought a new tweed cap for Pat. Grace bought him a scarf and for Con she got two pairs of thick socks but the search for little toys proved fruitless.

'I told you we'd get nothing,' Chrissie said. She was a little disgruntled for she'd seen a lovely blouse in the Drapery, which would have looked very smart with her best skirt for the party, but she had no money to spare.

'What's that woman selling over there?' Grace asked, noticing a few people standing around a dark-haired woman who was bending over what looked like a large basket on the pavement on the other side of O'Connor Square.

'Probably crubeens – pigs' feet,' Chrissie replied without much interest.

'Let's go and have a look. I don't think it's food at all.' Grace took her sister's arm and pulled her across the square.

'She's a tinker woman. Heaven alone knows what she's got in that basket,' Chrissie informed Grace, noting the very dark hair and eyes and the olive skin.

'Pegs, ribbons, bootlaces! Come and look, ma'am, all very cheap.'

Chrissie pulled at Grace's arm but her sister ignored her.

'Do you have any little toys? Something cheap?' Grace asked the woman.

'I don't, ma'am. What kind of things did ye want? Sure, I suppose ye could do something with these pegs and a bit of ribbon,' the woman suggested, not wishing to lose the chance of a sale.

Grace looked thoughtful and Chrissie regarded the woman more closely. She wasn't as young as she'd first thought. 'I suppose we could paint a face on the top of the peg and make a sort of dress with a bit of material and some ribbon,' Grace mused, 'but I was thinking of some little toys for boys too. Hoops or spinning tops or even a little horse carved from wood.'

'My lad Johnny could make ye those things, ma'am. He do be gifted at the carving.'

Chrissie sighed. Once Grace set her mind on something there was no moving her.

'Could he make me two little horses? I'd like them for Christmas Eve, Mrs . . .?'

'Mrs McDonagh, ma'am, and he will and he'll paint them too, so he will.'

'And they won't be expensive?'

'Not at all and he'll bring them out to ye, ma'am, at no extra charge.'

'That will be grand. I'll take a dozen pegs, we need

some for the washing, and I'll make some of them into little dolls, so I'll need some ribbon too, please, Mrs McDonagh.'

Delighted, the woman measured out a few lengths of ribbon and counted out the hand-whittled pegs and Grace passed over the coins in payment.

'And where will I tell Johnny to bring the little horses, ma'am?'

'Out to Kilroy's Farm. Just by Mitchell's Lock on the Grand Canal at Rahan. I'll pay him when he brings them and thank you, Mrs McDonagh. You've been a great help.'

'Are you really going to try to make those pegs into dolls?' Chrissie asked as they walked away.

'I am. I could see what she meant straight away. You wait until I've finished with them, Mary's little girl will be delighted.'

'Will we get a cup of tea before we start back? I'm freezing and it will warm us up for the journey home.'

Grace nodded, knowing Chrissie always treated herself to a cup of tea at one of the hotels when she came into town. It was the high point of her sister's week. Perhaps today she deserved it, for when they got home there was a great deal of baking and cooking to be done, to say nothing of decorating the kitchen and making decorations for the tree from pipe cleaners and bits of cardboard and coloured paper. But all that should be fun – if only Chrissie would join in.

Chapter Twenty-Seven

———◆———

WHEN THEY FINALLY ARRIVED home there was no one around and Chrissie went straight upstairs to take off her outdoor clothes. Grace tidied away the groceries, put down more turf and then washed up the dishes. Con and Pat and the labourers had obviously been in for the midday meal and she surmised that the holly and mistletoe and the tree were in one of the sheds.

When Chrissie finally came down she announced that she intended to write the Christmas cards they'd bought to send to the family in Liverpool and to wrap the gifts ready for Jack Brennan to take next day.

Grace wrapped her heavy shawl around her and put on her boots. 'I'm just going to see what they've done with the greenery and what kind of a tree Pat has cut for us, then I'll make a start on the baking. We can start on the decorations this evening.'

In the small shed beside the byre there were two large bunches of holly, laden with bright red berries, and a single bunch of mistletoe, which was less plentiful. There was no sign of a tree and she wondered if Pat had put it somewhere else. She tried every shed, outhouse and barn but could find no tree.

'What on earth has he done with it? Has he even cut it yet?' she asked herself aloud. She shrugged; maybe he'd been delayed this morning and was out cutting it now. It wasn't like Pat to forget. She trudged back to the house to find Chrissie sitting staring into the flames of the fire. The Christmas cards and gifts had been abandoned in a pile on the table.

'Well, the holly and mistletoe are out there but there's no tree yet.'

Chrissie just nodded.

'What's the matter?'

'Oh, I've another of my headaches coming on.'

Grace sighed. 'You do seem to have a lot of them lately, perhaps you should go and see the doctor?'

'I'll take an aspirin and have a lie down. We don't have a free National Health Service here, remember?'

Grace nodded. It was probably the stress of living a life she hated that was the cause of Chrissie's headaches and there was nothing any doctor could do to cure that.

She cleared the table, placing the cards and gifts on

the dresser and had started to mix the ingredients for the Christmas cake when young Dinny Coghlan who helped about the place almost fell into the kitchen, his face red with exertion.

'Dinny! What's the matter? Oh, my God! Is it Con?' she cried, suddenly fearful that the old man had had another stroke.

Dinny was panting. 'No, no, Grace! 'Tis . . . 'tis Pat. Sure, hasn't the tractor turned over and him in it, up in the bohreen! Con and meself went up to see how he was getting on with the tree, he was away a fierce long time, and we—'

Grace had torn off her apron and grabbed her shawl as a terrible thought hurtled into her mind. 'Is he—?'

Dinny shook his head. 'He's not been killed, Grace, but we don't know how bad he's hurted. I've to bring all the help I can to get it lifted off him.'

Grace pushed him out into the yard ahead of her. 'Go on then, Dinny! Run! Run and get Mr Mitchell from the Lock House and then go up the canal line and get every man and boy you can find! Hurry!'

The lad ran across the yard while she headed for the orchard and the fields beyond.

'Oh, please God, don't let him be too badly hurt,' she prayed as she ran, her heart hammering against her ribs and her breath coming in painful gasps. It wasn't easy running across the frozen ground and twice she stumbled and fell, but she dragged herself up and continued onwards. By the time she reached the bohreen, the little lane between two fields, she was perspiring and breathless. Ahead of her she saw the tractor lying on its side and Con desperately pulling and heaving, trying to move it.

'Uncle Con, stop! Stop, you'll kill yourself!' Grace screamed at him.

The old man turned towards her, his face grey with shock and his futile efforts to move the tractor even an inch. 'Grace! Oh, Jesus, Mary and Joseph! Thanks be to God you've come!'

Grace pushed past him and climbed up on to the wheel. With a huge effort she hoisted herself up, clinging to the side of the machine. She could just see Pat. He was lying on his side. His left arm and leg appeared to be trapped under him and there was a gash on his forehead. A trickle of blood ran down his face.

'Pat! Pat, can you hear me?' she called to him.

'Grace! Grace, I . . .' His voice was weak.

'Don't try to talk, Pat. Lie still, help is on its way. We'll get you out as quickly as we can. Dinny's gone for help and Con and I are here. Lie still.'

'My . . . arm . . . and leg, Grace.'

Desperately she pulled herself up further. If she could climb over the side she could maybe put her shawl over him. He must be in shock and she knew he must be kept warm. She tore off her shawl and inch by inch she pulled herself upwards. At last she managed to reach him and she gently tucked the shawl around him.

'Grace! Grace, have ye managed to get to him?' Con called, his voice cracking with fear.

'Yes. I've covered him with the shawl but I don't know how bad he is. He's conscious and says it's his arm and leg. Is there any sign of help yet?'

Con stumbled to the end of the bohreen and then called back. 'I can see Dinny and Martin Mitchell coming now and there's others behind them. Tell him we'll have him out soon now.'

'Uncle Con, when Dinny gets here tell him to go for Dr Wrafter. Tell him to take the trap and to hurry!' she called back, uttering a prayer of thanks that help was at hand.

With the help of the dozen men who had come with Dinny and Martin Mitchell – who had had the fore-sight to bring ropes – the tractor was slowly hauled upright. Grace had remained at Pat's side and as the machine moved she held Pat to stop the movement causing him more pain although he groaned in agony at each jolt.

'Come down now, Grace, and let Martin and meself see to him,' Con urged.

'Shouldn't we wait for the doctor? We could be doing more harm than good. I think both his arm and leg are broken, we could make it worse if we try to move him. I've got him wrapped in the shawl and I've torn a piece off my petticoat to stop the bleeding from his head.'

Con was frantic with worry. 'It could be half an hour

before the doctor gets here, Grace. Sure, he'll be frozen and that will do him no good at all.'

Grace bit her lip and thought hard. 'Send someone back to the house and bring all the blankets and quilts and get Chrissie to fill a hot-water bottle and bring it here.'

Twenty minutes later Dinny drove the trap, pulled by a sweating pony, up the bohreen. With him was a serious-looking Dr Wrafter. Grace had piled all the blankets and quilts around Pat who was grey-faced with pain and shivering with shock. There had been no hot-water bottle or any sign of Chrissie.

'You did the right thing, Grace, not to move him. Let me take a look at him and I can decide how we're to get him down. These accursed things may be labour-saving but they're downright dangerous. We must thank God he wasn't killed!'

Grace stumbled away to let the doctor see to Pat and found that she too was shivering uncontrollably.

Con and Martin Mitchell helped her down and the lock-keeper put his own coat around her shoulders.

Dr Wrafter informed them that there seemed to be no internal injuries. Under his watchful eye and following his explicit instructions, Pat was moved and brought down from the tractor. The doctor immobilised his leg and arm as a stretcher of sorts was made from the blankets. Grace covered him with the quilts and he was carried slowly and carefully back to the house.

Con walked beside her, his arm around her shoulder. 'Ye did well, Grace.'

'Thank God there's nothing wrong inside him, Uncle Con. The doctor will set his broken bones and stitch up his head but if he had been bleeding inside . . .' Suddenly she broke down and began to sob.

Con tried to calm her. 'Hush now, Grace, 'tis the shock, that's all. Thanks be to God, he'll get over this.' He tried to sound optimistic; he'd had a terrible shock himself.

Grace was told to remain in the kitchen as Pat was carried upstairs.

'But I can help, really I can!' she pleaded with the doctor.

'You can boil up some water for me to clean that wound on his head and tear up as much linen as you can spare. I'll need bandages to splint up that arm and leg. I'll give him something to ease the pain and make him sleep. I'll send word down when you're to come up. Now, lads, easy with him!' Dr Wrafter advised.

Grace turned to Chrissie who was standing by the dresser, her hands to her cheeks. Her face was white and she was shaking.

'Chrissie! Why didn't you bring the hot-water bottle?'

'I . . . I filled it, Grace, I did!' She indicated the stone bottle lying on the table. 'But . . . but . . . then I just couldn't move! I couldn't . . . I couldn't see him like . . . that! I can't stand the sight of blood!'

Grace's nerves had been stretched to breaking point. 'Oh, for God's sake, Chrissie, what's wrong with you? It was a terrible accident, he could have been killed!'

Chrissie burst into tears. Grace never yelled at her. She'd never spoken to her like this before. 'Grace, I'm sorry! I just can't stand the sight of blood and broken bones and . . . Oh, you know I don't mean to be horrible but . . . I can't do it!'

Grace relented a little. 'I didn't mean to yell, Chrissie. It's not just you who's had a terrible shock, we all have. Pull yourself together now and boil up some water while I cut some sheets into strips. When the doctor has gone and we've got him comfortable and settled, we'll have a cup of tea with a drop of Jameson's in it.'

Chrissie sniffed and wiped her eyes. At least she could do the practical things, like boiling water and helping Grace with the bandages, just as long as she didn't have to do any of the nursing.

The next half-hour was hectic for while the doctor, with the aid of Con and Martin Mitchell, tended Pat's injuries, the other men sat around in the kitchen discussing the accident and the effect it would have on the day-to-day workings of the farm. Grace had taken up the hot water and the bandages and had then made tea for the neighbours. It all served to take her mind off herself but as she passed around the mugs her hands were still quivering.

Chrissie said little as she tidied things away and made

up the fire, but listening to the neighbours she began to wonder how they would manage. There were only a few cows to be milked each day at this time of year but every beast had to be fed and the sheds mucked out. How was she to escape helping out with all that? She was afraid to be around such large animals, she wasn't even very happy when she had to feed the pigs. And this surely was the end of the Christmas Eve party and that had been the one thing she had had to look forward to.

At last the doctor took his leave, giving Grace a list of instructions. He had deduced that Pat's wife was not going to be much help, the girl looked too dazed and disorientated. The neighbours left too, promising to help out as much as they could in what time they had to spare, and finally Grace, Chrissie and Con were left alone in the kitchen.

Grace placed a mug of tea, to which she had added a drop of whiskey, in front of the old man. He looked exhausted. 'Drink that up now and then I think you should have a rest. You look ready to drop yourself.'

He sipped the tea. 'Ah, I'm fine, Grace. 'Tis just the shock of it all.'

'Uncle Con, the last thing we need now is you getting sick. We're all going to have to work ten times as hard until Pat is fit again.'

Con nodded but then looked at Chrissie. 'Are ye not going up to see your husband?'

Chrissie stared at him and then dropped her eyes. 'I'll go up later to see he's . . . comfortable.'

Con glared at her. 'Then I take it ye are not going to nurse him? Sure, 'tis only as I expected.'

Not wanting an argument Grace intervened. 'I've already told her that you and I will do it. She has no stomach for nursing, Uncle Con. She's never been able to stand the sight of blood, she can't help it,' Grace excused her sister.

Con didn't reply for a few seconds then he looked at Grace. 'Go on up and see him, Grace. He's been asking for ye and what the doctor has given him will have him asleep soon.'

Grace put down her mug of tea and went upstairs and Con turned his attention to Chrissie. 'Ye are no use to anyone, girl! Ye should never have come here. Ye don't love him and I'm thinking ye never did. Ye used him as an escape from the life ye were tired of, but ye'll have to work now. Grace and meself can't do everything. So there'll be no more "headaches". I don't know how the mammy put up with ye through the hardships and horrors of the Emergency, that I don't.'

Chrissie slammed down her mug and grabbed Grace's shawl from the back of the chair. 'And I wish I had never come here either! I hate it! I hate everything about this place and I hate you too! I'm going out and I may never come back!'

Con shook his head sadly as she slammed the kitchen door behind her. She'd be back, she had nowhere else to go for she was friendly with no one, but she was going to be even more difficult to live with from now on. His shoulders slumped. He was too old and too tired for all this worry and hardship but the next months had to be got through somehow.

Pat was lying on his back, his heavily bandaged arm resting on a pillow, his left leg also cushioned with pillows, a white strip of bandage around his forehead. Grace moved quietly to the bedside and took his good hand in hers.

'Pat, I won't stay long. I just came to see if you were comfortable?'

He opened his eyes, he was feeling very drowsy but thankfully the pain was easing. 'Grace. Grace, I'm . . . sorry about the tree.'

She smiled at him. 'Oh, Pat, forget about the blasted tree! I'm sorry I asked you to cut one. If I hadn't this would never have happened. I feel so guilty, you could have been killed.' She couldn't stop the sob in her voice.

He squeezed her hand. 'No, Grace, it was not your fault, don't be thinking that. I . . . I should have taken more care. I was probably going too fast, hit a boulder or a rut and the next thing . . . It happened so fast. I'm sorry to have ruined the Christmas.'

'Will you stop thinking like that! The only thing that matters now is that you get fit and well again.' She could see he was struggling to stay awake. 'You sleep now and don't worry about anything. Con and I will manage with the help of the neighbours. You know everyone is only too willing to help at times like this.'

'Grace. I . . . I'm . . . glad it was you who . . . came to . . .' He fell silent as sleep overtook him.

She looked down at him and bit her lip. If he'd been killed she knew that she would have been inconsolable. She was fond of him – as a brother-in-law. It could never be anything more than that.

Chapter Twenty-Eight

———

CHRISSIE HAD RETURNED WHEN it had grown dark. She had wandered aimlessly along the roads weighed down with the unhappiness of her plight. Whichever way she turned there was no way out for her. If she went back to Liverpool Mam would send her back. She had no money to speak of; she had no friends here who could help her. Con had made his feelings quite plain and even Grace had shouted at her. Pat no longer cared for her, she knew that. All she could see ahead of her was misery and never ending work. All she had wanted out of life was a bit of pleasure and excitement. Had that been too much to ask for? As the familiar thudding began above her right eye she turned dejectedly for home although she dreaded it, knowing that there would be no sympathy for her and no understanding either.

Grace had asked where she was and Con had replied curtly that she'd gone out.

'Did you two have a fight?' Grace asked wearily. The last thing she needed now was open hostility between her sister and the old man.

'Didn't I only tell her a few home truths? She'll have to pull her weight now, Grace. There're fierce hard times ahead for us until Pat is on his feet again.'

'You can't do it all, you remember what the doctor told you and I need you to help me with Pat, I can't nurse both of you. This time I will have to give up my job at the laundry, there's too much to do and Chrissie will have to do more too.'

'Didn't I tell her that?' Con said with some satisfaction.

That evening after supper, when Con and Grace had made sure that Pat was still asleep and comfortable, they sat down and made a list of all the jobs that were to be done and divided them up.

'There's still too much for you to do, Uncle Con. I know you have Tom Healy and young Dinny Coghlan but shall I ask Mary if Liam can come to help out full time? I know he'd be glad of the work and she'll be grateful for the regular wage.'

Con agreed. Liam Scully was a reliable worker.

'Chrissie, you will have to take over in the dairy again and can you see to the pigs?' Grace ventured for she was fully aware of her sister's fear of large animals. 'There will be extra washing too, we can't leave it all to

Tess Maher and it's not the best time of year to get things dry.'

Chrissie nodded silently. She had expected as much. She wasn't a bit happy about having to see to the pigs but she wasn't going to complain and bring on another tirade from Con; her headache was so bad that she couldn't stand that.

'Christmas will have to be a quiet affair now, I'm afraid, and I feel so guilty about that damned tree.'

'Ah, Grace, 'twas not your fault at all. Weren't you only thinking of Mary's childer? 'Tis a blessing that we hadn't mentioned it to anyone so there will be no huge disappointment.'

Grace nodded and got to her feet. 'Well, I suggest we all go and get some sleep, it's been a long, exhausting and worrying day. If you need me in the night, Uncle Con, call me,' she added.

They struggled through the days that followed. The weather didn't help, Grace thought. Heavy snow had fallen for two days. The yard had become slushy and it was bitterly cold in the sheds, the dairy and the milking parlour. The hens and geese had a hard time foraging for food and the ducks could get nothing from the canal for it was frozen solid. Heavy frost at night on top of the snow had made the roads almost impassable and Con had tied sacking around the hooves of the horse that pulled the farm cart for he had sworn he would never drive the tractor again.

Reluctantly Grace had given in her notice to Sister Assumpta, after explaining the situation and emphasising that they needed an extra pair of hands around the farm and in the house. She could see by the expression on the nun's face that she did not fully approve of herself, an unmarried girl, helping to tend to Pat, but she didn't care. 'Needs must,' she had muttered to herself as she'd left the College. She had also written a brief note to her mother informing her of the accident and had received a reply asking would it be of any help to them if Billy were to come for a few days over the holiday? She had been grateful for the offer but had replied that Billy wasn't used to this type of work and besides they would need help for longer than the few days her brother could spare.

Thankfully Con helped Pat with the more intimate things, which it would have been both inappropriate and embarrassing for her to have done. She made certain that Chrissie went to see him at least once a day but she knew they spent the time in uncomfortable silence, although she often caught Pat watching her.

'Grace, I'm sorry you have had to give up your job and I know you are working twice as hard as you used to, Con has told me,' he said to her one morning as she helped him to sit up.

'Oh, I don't mind and maybe it's for the best. We're all pulling together now – even Chrissie.'

He nodded slowly although he doubted Chrissie did as much as Grace. 'Do you think I might be able to get downstairs for Christmas dinner, just for the day that's in it? You'd go mad up here, so you would. Not that I'm complaining.'

She smiled at him. 'I think we could bring you down for a few hours.'

He caught her arm. 'Grace, I have to get back on my feet, you understand that, don't you?'

She looked concerned. 'You will, but you can't rush it. Broken bones take time to heal and it's not fit out there for man nor beast and we can't risk you falling.'

'But *you* have to go out. Take care you don't slip, Grace.'

'I'll take care. I promise.'

He still held her arm. 'Grace, I . . . I've had plenty of time to think while I've been lying here and there's something I have to say.

'You know how things stand with Chrissie and myself. I know now that I don't love her. I should never have married her; I should have sent her home to Liverpool. She's never even tried to fit in here. I made excuses and allowances for her but it was no use – you're more at home here, even Con knows that. I've made the biggest mistake of my life, Grace.'

'Oh, Pat! I'm so sorry about you and Chrissie. No one can blame you, you've tried so hard but—'

'Grace, it's you I've been thinking about.'

She felt her heart flutter and she became flustered. What was he trying to say?

'Grace, I think . . . I think it's you that I—'

'No! Pat, don't say it. Don't even think it. It . . . it would be wrong, terribly wrong! Chrissie is your wife even if you no longer love her and she's my sister. There can't be anything between us except friendship!'

'I know all that and it's an impossible situation for me, Grace. I can't help how I feel.'

'You'll just have to try to put . . . all thoughts like that out of your mind, Pat. It's something that can never, never be.'

He nodded slowly, feeling utterly confused and miserable. He knew she was right.

Grace turned and left the room but once outside she leaned her back against the door and put her hands to her cheeks. Should she have expected this? Had she unwittingly encouraged him? She had helped nurse him and she did care for him but . . . but deep in her heart was there more than just affection? She shook her head. No! No, there could never be more than that, never! She mustn't even think like that!

Pat leaned back against the pillows and stared up at the ceiling. She was right, nothing could ever come of his feelings for her. The whole thing was a social taboo and had been from time immemorial, but he wished with all his heart that he had never married Chrissie, that it had been Grace who had first caught his eye at Eileen's wedding. But it was too late now, much too late. A tear trickled slowly down his cheek as a wave of black despair washed over him.

* * *

The day before Christmas Eve Chrissie was carrying two heavy buckets of turf from the shed where it was stored when she was surprised to see a strange young man crossing the yard towards her. Grace was in one of the smaller sheds, which they were using to do the extra washing. Con had rigged up a hearth so they could heat up the water for the wash boiler and the turf was needed there.

'Would you be the mistress here?'

Chrissie looked at him closely. He was tall and well built and quite handsome with dark eyes and dark hair, most of which was covered by his cap. He wore a heavy overcoat that had seen better days.

'I'm Mrs Kilroy. Can I help you?'

'I brought these. You asked Ma if I'd carve them for you. I'm Johnny McDonagh.' He took a small carved horse from each of his coat pockets.

Chrissie put down the buckets and took them from him. She'd forgotten all about them. They were very well made and even had a saddle carved into them. 'They're beautiful!' she exclaimed.

He smiled at her, revealing white even teeth. 'Thank you, ma'am, but I'd be grateful if you could pay me for my fine work and 'tis a long trek out here.'

'Oh, yes! Could you wait here while I see my sister? She'll give you what's owed.' She reached down for the buckets but to her surprise he stopped her.

'A fine-looking girl like you shouldn't be dragging these heavy buckets. I'll be after carrying them for you. Where is it you want them? Up at the house?'

Chrissie felt flattered and smiled up at him. It was so long since anyone had called her 'a fine-looking girl' and she was acutely aware she looked far from her best. 'No, it's over in that shed, thank you. They're to heat up the water for the wash boiler.'

'Have you no one to do the washing, ma'am?' he asked, picking up the heavy buckets with no effort at all.

'We do but there's extra these days.'

'Do you need any extra help about the place? I'd be only too glad of a few days' work, ma'am.'

Chrissie looked thoughtful as she walked beside him. 'I'll see what my sister thinks, she . . . she knows more about what's needed on the farm than I do.'

Grace was poking at the small fire beneath the copper boiler and she looked up in surprise to see the young man with her sister.

'Grace, this is Johnny McDonagh. You remember you asked his mother to ask him to carve the little horses? He's brought them and they're beautiful. Look.'

Grace smiled as she took them. 'You're gifted, Mr McDonagh, I have to say that. We'll drop them into Mary's before Christmas.'

'Mr McDonagh has offered to come and help us out, Grace, and I think it's a good idea. We are both worn out.'

'I'm able for any work. Anything at all,' he exclaimed, seizing on Chrissie's words and the opportunity of some paid work. 'I won't even mind that it's Christmas or that the weather is desperate.'

Grace looked thoughtful. If he was willing to come and work on Christmas Day it would mean that Con could have a day's rest and he looked strong and fit. 'You wouldn't mind coming out here? Have you had far to travel?'

'From just outside the town and it's no bother, I have the old horse tied to the yard gate.'

'And your family won't mind you working on Christmas Day?' Grace pressed.

He laughed. 'Not at all. Ma knows me well enough, I'm me own man.'

'We'd be very grateful and we would give you some dinner,' Grace offered, thinking he looked very pleasant. 'I'll have a word with Uncle Con regarding what you're to be paid. He sees to that side of things.'

'Will I take him over to see Con? He's in the byre,' Chrissie asked.

'Thanks, Chrissie. I'll have to get on with this.' Grace reached for the turf bucket.

'Here now, let me tip this on to that fire for you,' he said.

As they crossed towards the byre Chrissie looked up at him and then dropped her eyes, her cheeks flushing. He was looking down at her admiringly. 'I must look a terrible mess.'

'You look grand, ma'am, and very young to be mistress here, if I may say so?'

Chrissie smiled. 'I suppose I am.'

'I'm thinking you're not Irish?'

She shook her head. 'No. I'm from Liverpool.'

'And how did you meet Himself then?'

'At a wedding.'

'I've been to Liverpool. 'Tis a grand city and they have a fine racecourse there.'

'Yes, out at Aintree, but we lived further into the city itself.'

He didn't miss the note of longing in her voice and he wondered how a city girl could settle here.

'Do you miss it at all?' He was watching her expression closely. Even in her yard clothes she was a very pretty girl.

'I do. Oh, indeed I do. I was never cut out for this life and nothing had prepared me for it.'

They had reached the byre and Con stopped his work and came to meet them.

'Uncle Con, this is Johnny McDonagh. He's very kindly offered to help out on Christmas Day.'

Con glared at them both. 'We can do without the "help" of tinkers! We'd be missing half the poultry if we so much as blinked!'

Johnny stiffened. 'We don't like to be called tinkers. We prefer to be known as travellers and I'd not be touching a feather of your poultry nor anything else!'

'Ye can "prefer" as much as ye like! I was being polite when I called ye a tinker!'

Chrissie glared at him. 'Grace has already agreed that he should come and help out.'

'Has she indeed? Well, I'll not be having a tinker on

358

the place.' Con wondered if Grace had indeed agreed to this mad suggestion or was it all Chrissie's idea?

'We can't go back on a promise. You'd better speak to Grace.'

'I will indeed,' Con said grimly, marching off towards the washhouse.

'I'm sorry about him but Grace will sort it all out. Will you still be willing to come and work?'

'I will so. Ah, take no notice of the old feller – I don't. People don't trust us. They don't understand us because our ways are not their ways.'

Chrissie nodded. She understood. She had come here as a stranger and she hadn't been accepted. 'So, we'll see you on Christmas Day?'

He grinned at her. 'You will so. Now I'll be off before the old horse is accused of stealing the few leaves that are left on the bushes.'

Chapter Twenty-Nine

———◆———

GRACE HAD PREVAILED UPON Con to overcome his prejudice and allow Johnny McDonagh to work for them for Christmas Day. They were all exhausted and in no position to turn down help, no matter where it came from, she had urged. Finally he had agreed.

Pat slowly and awkwardly made it downstairs for a few hours, aided by Con and herself. He said he would enjoy the change but it was obvious that the effort had exhausted him.

'I've nothing to give you,' he said after Grace gave him the scarf, which she said was a bit of a useless gift now. He had been intending to buy her something, he thought sadly. He'd already opened Chrissie's gift and thanked her.

'The best gift you can give me . . . give us all, is to get well,' she replied.

'Ye never said a truer word, Grace,' Con agreed.

'I'll get stronger every day, you'll see.'

'But don't you try and rush things,' Grace warned but she was smiling. She had made an effort with the table, setting it with a clean white cloth over which she had laid strips of red crêpe paper. She had polished up the cutlery and the glasses and had laid out the best delft. In the centre she had placed a little arrangement of holly.

'Sure, doesn't this all look grand, very festive,' Con remarked.

Grace smiled. 'It's a grand day, having Pat down for his meal.'

Chrissie had made an effort with herself, putting on a black wool skirt and a pink paisley print blouse and the pearlised clip-on earrings. She put out a dinner and covered it with a clean cloth and took it out to Johnny McDonagh who was working in the byre.

'If I'd had my way there'd be no food given to the likes of that lad out there!' Con muttered. 'Ye make sure Chrissie counts every bird when she puts them in for the night.'

'Now, Uncle Con, we've been through all this. It's good of him to come today and he seems to be working well,' Grace chided gently.

'Isn't he being well paid for it?' was the ungracious reply.

* * *

Johnny McDonagh came again on St Stephen's Day and once more Chrissie took him out a meal.

'Ah, ma'am, I didn't expect anything today. 'Tis good of you.'

'You can't be expected to work all day in this weather with no food inside you,' she replied, smiling.

He'd grinned back. 'You'd brighten up the dullest winter day, if I may say so?'

She laughed but she was delighted. 'You are a flatterer, Mr McDonagh!'

'Will you call me Johnny?'

She nodded as she watched him eat.

'And have you any children, ma'am?'

She shook her head.

'I thought you would have.' He was curious and wondered how long she had been married.

Chrissie sighed and suddenly she felt the need to confide in someone outside the family and the community who would not judge her. Who better than a stranger who probably wouldn't criticise? 'My husband and I . . . we . . . we don't get on. When I met him he told me how wonderful life here was and I was so fed up with everything in Liverpool, all the shortages and the drabness . . .'

He'd stopped eating and was looking at her closely. 'Did you love him?'

She sighed. 'I thought I did but . . . but after I came here . . . things changed.'

'He changed towards you?' he queried.

'Not at first. I hated it so much I begged my mam to let me go home but instead Grace came to live here. Things . . . things really got unbearable after Uncle Con had a stroke. Oh, I don't know why I'm telling you all this! I don't know you very well at all but it's such a relief to be able to confide in *someone*.'

'Sometimes it helps to talk.'

She nodded.

'I'm thinking that the old feller gives you a hard time?'

Again she nodded.

'And do you never get out to enjoy yourself?' He felt sorry for her, stuck out here with that old one and a husband she didn't love and who probably didn't love her when she was still only young. She was far too pretty to be buried here.

'No.' She sighed and realised that she had better go back to the house or someone would come looking for her. 'I'd better go now or I'll be accused of stopping you from working.'

'You can come and talk to me anytime you like, ma'am, if it helps,' he offered.

She smiled at him. 'Thank you, Johnny, I will but would you stop calling me "ma'am". It makes me feel so old.'

'What can I call you that's not disrespectful?'

She could see his point. 'My name is Chrissie, you can call me that when there's no one else around. I suppose I'll have to put up with "ma'am" for the rest of the time.'

'If there's to be a "rest of the time". Your man in there has no liking for me and neither will the other lads when they come back to work.'

Chrissie frowned and tilted her chin stubbornly. She liked him and she didn't care what anyone else thought. She would make sure he was given employment and Grace would back her up. She felt she had made a friend in Johnny McDonagh. 'Take no notice. There will be work here for you.'

She was relieved that Grace took her side when she suggested that Johnny be given a few days' work a week. Con argued but in the end he had to agree to give it a try although privately he vowed to have a word with Tom Healy, Liam and young Dinny, instructing them to watch McDonagh like hawks. You could never totally trust a tinker no matter how good a worker he was.

After that Johnny came three days a week, usually Friday, Saturday and Sunday, and Chrissie always found time to talk to him. Grace noticed that her sister was far more amiable and made more of an effort with her appearance on those days.

'Be careful, Chrissie, or people will start to gossip,' she warned.

'Oh, for heaven's sake, Grace! People will gossip about absolutely anything! I can talk to him and he doesn't pass any comments and he doesn't disapprove of everything I do or say. I've found a friend, that's all.'

Grace sighed. 'I'm just thinking of you, Chrissie.'

As winter began to ease its grip and the early wild spring flowers began to appear in the hedgerows Pat got stronger. The splints came off his arm first and eventually his leg but the doctor warned him against trying to do too much too quickly.

'Take it slowly at first. The crutches will help, but it will be a while before you can discard them and have the full use of your leg again. Do you intend to go on driving that death-trap of a machine?'

Pat grinned. 'I do so, didn't it cost a small fortune? Too much to let it rust away. I'll be more wary of it in the future though.'

Dr Wrafter shook his head. 'See that you are, next time you might not be so lucky. I'd advise having someone else with you, particularly if you are a good way from the yard.'

'Maybe you should take that advice when you do start using it again?' Grace suggested. The doctor's words had brought a flutter of fear to her heart.

'Sure, there won't be any need for that, I'll take more care,' Pat promised.

'Well, we have plenty of help. I'll see he doesn't go rushing things,' Grace promised as she showed the doctor out.

Pat stood at the kitchen door and watched the doctor leave then he looked out across the yard. The long period of inactivity had made him restless and sometimes depressed, especially when he thought of the situation between himself, Grace and Chrissie. Chrissie did seem to be a bit happier these days, which eased the atmosphere. He longed to be able to get out of the house and be useful again. He saw Johnny McDonagh crossing the yard and frowned. He shared his uncle's views on the lad although he had to admit that he worked hard and that so far nothing had gone missing, but he'd be glad when he moved on. It shouldn't be long now, he thought, they seldom stayed long in one place.

Grace came and stood beside him. 'You're not thinking of going out there, are you? The ground is still muddy.'

'No. I was just watching McDonagh and wondering when he'll move on. They've been camped on that bit of land outside the town beside the river for a few months now, so Con tells me.'

'You can't blame them for not travelling in winter but I can't understand why they have to keep on moving. I would hate living like that.'

'So would most people but it's the way they are. Still, he'll be off soon.'

'That won't please Chrissie. She seems to get on well with him.'

Pat frowned. Chrissie was leaving herself open to gossip and that didn't please him.

'He might stay until you are able to get out and

about again.' Grace hoped he would. The last thing she wanted was for Pat to try to go back to work too soon and in the next weeks she knew things would get busier. Once the cows had been turned out of the byre and all the sheds would have to be cleaned and then there were the calves to be fed and the field by the river would have to be ploughed and sown with barley. Con was adamant that he was not going to do that with the tractor, he would do it the old-fashioned way – with the horses.

'I doubt it, Grace, but we have Liam.'

'I don't want to worry you, Pat, but Con is doing too much and he's insisting that he ploughs that field himself and that's hard work. I'm sure if we were to ask him Johnny McDonagh would stay on.'

Pat shook his head. 'I don't think he'd stay. They please themselves, Grace. I'll talk to Con. Tom Healy is well able to do the ploughing.'

She left him leaning on the half-door and went back to her chores.

Pat stood in the pale, weak sunlight and surveyed the yard again and the fields beyond. It seemed to have been a long, bleak winter and the milder spring would be more than welcome. He noticed the yellow catkins on the hazel and the tiny cluster of primrose buds beneath the hedgerow that bounded the small orchard and the sight lifted his spirits. He felt stronger each day and by the time the blossom was out on the blackthorns he hoped he would be fully recovered.

* * *

That evening after supper as Grace and Chrissie were washing up Grace mentioned the conversation she'd had with Pat.

'Pat says that Johnny will be leaving us soon. They'll be moving on, they always do.'

Chrissie looked up, startled. Johnny had said nothing to her about moving on. Her heart plummeted. She didn't want him to leave. She had grown very fond of him – more than just 'fond', if the truth were told. A flush of pink crept into her cheeks as she remembered the first time he had kissed her, over a month ago now.

'Don't go back inside yet, Chrissie,' he'd pleaded when she reluctantly told him she would have to leave.

'I want to stay, Johnny, but the men are keeping a close eye on us,' she'd replied.

'Ah, to hell with them all!' He'd reached out and gently stroked her cheek. 'Aren't you wasted on that husband of yours?' he'd said as he took her in his arms and kissed her. She had responded, feeling a wave of happiness wash over her. She hadn't felt like this for so long. As his lips moved from her mouth to her neck she stroked the dark hair at the base of his neck while he murmured endearments, telling her she was the most beautiful girl he'd ever seen, how warm and soft her skin was, how he loved the sweet smell of her hair, how he'd fallen in love with her and how much he wanted her. Oh, he'd been so tender and so romantic and she'd responded to his caresses with a passion she had never felt before. When he'd finally released her she had promised him she would spend time with him every day and she had kept that promise. She was certain now that she was in love with him and it was a much deeper feeling than anything she had ever felt for Pat. She had felt a little guilty at first when she thought about Pat but then she told herself he didn't love her now and Johnny did. Everything in their relationship was so very, very different to hers with Pat. There was no embarrassment or reluctance, there was love and romance and passion. He didn't criticise her or make her feel inadequate, in fact he told her she was perfect in every way. She was no longer an eighteen-year-old girl, she would be twenty-two soon; now she was a woman. Oh, he couldn't go and leave her. He *couldn't*! She couldn't even contemplate what her life would be like without him!

She pulled herself together. 'I'll have a word with him, Grace. I'm sure he'll stay on if I ask him to.' She tried to keep her voice steady. Grace must never suspect that there was anything other than friendship between herself and Johnny.

'It might help if he would, Chrissie. Uncle Con is doing far too much and I'm terrified he'll have another stroke and that this time it will be worse.'

Chrissie nodded. 'He'll be here first thing in the morning, I'll see him then. The last thing we need is Uncle Con making himself ill, there's enough to do around here as it is.'

Grace nodded. 'Thanks, Chrissie, but don't say a word about it to either Pat or Uncle Con.'

'I won't,' Chrissie said firmly. It was the last thing she would do for she knew only too well that both men would be glad to see the back of Johnny. Given half a chance they would send him on his way. Well, she simply couldn't let that happen.

Chapter Thirty

———————

I N THE END CHRISSIE WAITED until Sunday to see Johnny for the yard was quieter on Sundays. Despite the cold wind she did not bother with either a coat or a shawl. He was working at the back of the barn but looked up and smiled when he saw her.

'Come here to me, Chrissie, you'll catch your death of cold. I've missed you, I've not held you in my arms for days.'

She went quickly and willingly to his arms. 'I had to wait until it's quieter, I have to talk to you. There's no one else around?'

'No. Just meself.' He kissed her hungrily.

'Johnny, they're saying you'll be leaving soon. Is it true?' She looked up at him pleadingly.

He nodded slowly; he could see she was upset.

'It is. They're getting restless now.'

'Oh, please can't you stay on? I don't think I could stand it here if you went. There would be nothing left for me in life, nothing to look forward to each day.'

He sighed and kissed her forehead. 'Ah, Chrissie. You always knew I'd be moving on one day. 'Tis our way of life.'

'But not yet. Please? Please, Johnny, I couldn't bear life here without you! You said you loved me and you know I love you!' She kissed him passionately. It was true, she couldn't stand the thought of him going away.

He sighed. 'I do love you, Chrissie, so I'll stay on, just until the beginning of April. I'll have to go then for we always go to England for the horse fairs.'

A month, Chrissie thought. Only another month and then her life would be utterly miserable again. She clung to him. 'Please, can't you stay longer?'

He shook his head. 'I have to go, I'm sorry, but I'll be back in the wintertime. We always spend the winter months here.'

Almost a year, Chrissie thought with rising panic. Could she stand it that long? All through the summer months and the autumn? No, it just didn't bear thinking about. And he'd said they were going to England. Oh, how she longed to go home. 'Then take me with you, Johnny, please, take me with you! You know how much I hate it here. You know they don't care about me. I want to be with you!' She was very near to tears.

He held her away from him a little. He hadn't

expected this. 'Chrissie, the travelling life is not for a girl like you. You know nothing of our ways.'

'I'll learn, I will!' she cried.

'You're used to the comforts of a grand house like that beyond. You'd find our ways a hardship.'

'I wouldn't, Johnny! I lived through six years of war, remember? Through bombings and shortages and working with explosives – wasn't that hardship?'

'But you hated it, Chrissie. You told me so and wasn't that why you married Himself?'

'But it wouldn't be the same with you! Oh, please, please take me with you? I'll die if I stay here, I *will*!' She clung to him, sobbing. She couldn't lose him, she *couldn't*! 'I'm not a girl now. I've grown up! I know my own mind!'

He stroked her hair. He was fully aware of how she would be greeted if he turned up with her on his arm: with suspicion and hostility. She would never be accepted. But he pushed the thoughts away. She was young and pretty and very desirable and she hated her life here. She could return to her family in Liverpool when she'd had enough of the travelling life as she would do – in time. He was very fond of her but he knew that when the time came for him to marry it would be to a girl of his own kind, one his family would choose. That was their way. 'Hush now, Chrissie. I'll take you with me, I promise. I'll stay on until the beginning of April and then we'll go.'

She raised a tear-stained face but her eyes were

shining. She would finally be escaping from this place. 'You won't regret it, Johnny! I'll stay with you, I'll work and I'll start to try to save some money for when we leave.'

He smiled at her. 'A sort of dowry is it?'

She nodded. 'Yes. I have a few nice things I could sell too. That would help.'

He held her closely. It would help for she wouldn't be able to bring even half of the fancy clothes she wore. There would be neither the room to store them nor the occasion to wear them.

To both Con and Pat's surprise Johnny McDonagh stayed on even after the rest of the travellers moved on, heading towards Galway.

'Sure, what is that feller up to? I heard the rest of them packed up and left three days ago and a desperate mess they left behind them,' Con wondered aloud.

Grace had had mixed feelings when Chrissie had reported that Johnny McDonagh had agreed to stay another month. The extra pair of hands would be welcome but she knew Chrissie was friendly with him and that disturbed her at times. She would just have to keep an eye on her sister. 'Maybe he stays where the work is? He probably likes the bit of steady money – and he's good with horses,' she added.

'They all are but he'll be little use in the fields, he couldn't plough a straight furrow to save his life,' was the terse reply.

Grace tutted and shook her head. Con was still insisting on ploughing with horses.

Mags buttoned up Thomas's little coat and adjusted his knitted hat and then fastened him securely in his pram. At nearly ten months old he was beginning to be a bit of a handful but she idolised him.

'Make sure you tuck that blanket around him, Mags, or he'll kick it off and he'll get cold,' Sadie instructed as she tidied up the kitchen.

'You could nail it down and he'd find a way to kick it off and I'm sick of having to stop and pick up his mittens when he pulls them off and throws them out of the pram,' Mags laughed, buttoning up her own coat. 'Why don't you leave that until I come back? Sit down and have a quiet cup of tea and a rest.'

Sadie cast her eyes to the ceiling. 'A quiet rest with our Billy and Tommy Milligan in and out of here like a fiddler's elbow!'

'What are they up to anyway? Why aren't they at work?' Mags asked. It was Saturday and they both usually worked the morning.

'They're supposed to be on some sort of training scheme but I have the feeling they've other plans. I tell you, Mags, the older that lad gets the less sense he has!'

'Oh, he's not bad, Ma. He'll settle down. Now, have you got the list?'

Sadie took it from the dresser and handed it to her daughter-in-law. 'It's a blessing that things are getting better at last, there's even talk that chocolate and sweets will be off the ration soon.'

'I hope so. Won't it be great to be able to go into a shop and just buy a bar of chocolate? I'm going to buy the biggest bar of Fry's Chocolate Cream I can find. It's my favourite.'

Sadie looked at her with interest. 'You're not having cravings are you, Mags?'

Mags laughed. 'No, I'm not! Haven't I got my work cut out with this one here?'

'Well, get off with you. I'm going up to the church later on. There's a special Mass for that Hungarian cardinal that those Communists have put in prison. It's a living disgrace, that's what it is, to throw a man of God into jail. No one believes he's guilty of trying to overthrow the government or all those other things they accused him of.'

'Cardinal Mindszenty, you mean? They said he admitted to everything but they either tortured him or had him drugged, so Georgie said.'

'That's what everyone is saying, even President Truman. I heard that on the news on the wireless. And Pope Pius said they used "secret influences", which is as good as saying they tortured the poor man. We all have to pray they release him soon.'

Polly Nelson, who was on her way in, helped Mags manoeuvre the pram out of the kitchen door.

'I'll call in on Eileen when I've done the shopping, Ma,' Mags called.

'Will you ask her if her father-in-law can deliver a couple of hundredweight of coal, Mags? We're getting low and the weather doesn't show much sign of getting warmer,' Sadie called back.

Polly sat down in a chair by the table. 'I've come in for a bit of peace and quiet, Sadie. Our Kate and Ellie are driving me mad with the arguments over these blasted bridesmaids' dresses. Our Mary isn't at all bothered but that Ellie would try the patience of a saint!'

'What's wrong now?' Sadie asked, knowing only too well the arguments that went on next door for the walls were very thin.

'They finally agreed on the colour, after about six rows, but now our Ellie says she doesn't want long sleeves. She's just being downright awkward, the little madam. I ask you, short sleeves for this weather? She's as jealous as hell but she won't admit it. Alf said if there're any more bust-ups he's not paying for the damned dress and she can just be a guest like everyone else. He's sick of the fighting.'

Sadie poured her a cup of tea. 'I don't blame him, luv. When a man gets home from his work the last thing he needs is a pair of daughters squabbling.'

'That's just what he said to me, Sadie, and I told the pair of them not to be giving him excuses to go off to the pub for a bit of peace and quiet. I'd like to know how they'd all manage if I took meself off to the pub when I was sick and tired of them all.' Polly fulminated.

'Oh, it'll all come out in the wash, as they say, Polly.

Your Kate will have her big day, despite everything. I'm going up to Our Lady Immaculate's later on, are you coming?'

Polly nodded. She'd add to her prayers for the poor Hungarian cardinal those asking the Holy Mother to let Ellie see sense. 'Have you heard from your Grace lately, Sadie?'

'Last week. She's fine but they seem to be very busy. I wonder sometimes if she'll ever come home. It's a hard life, Polly and you can bet our Chrissie doesn't do her fair share.'

'How are Pat and Chrissie getting on these days?' Polly probed.

'About the same, I think. At least Pat is getting stronger and Grace says he'll soon be able to do a day's work again.'

'Thank God. He could have been killed.'

Sadie nodded. She suspected that if he had been Chrissie would have been on the next boat back to Liverpool.

'Did she say how the uncle is?'

'Doing far more than is good for him but he'll take no notice of anything she says. Still, soon the weather will be getting warmer and that will be a blessing for us all.'

Billy came in, shrugging on his jacket. 'Mornin', Mrs Nelson. I'd better be off now, Mam.'

'You should have left half an hour ago, meladdo. Is Tommy calling for you?'

'We don't have to be there until later. Tommy's meeting me at the bottom of the road,' he replied, pulling his cap further down over his forehead. He was convinced it made him look older and more worldly-wise.

Sadie started to get to her feet but sat down suddenly, the colour draining from her face at the intensity of the pain in her back. She couldn't seem to get up.

'Mother of God! Sadie! What's wrong with you, luv?' Polly cried.

'Terrible pain! Can't . . . can't . . . get up!' Sadie gasped.

'Billy, shift yourself, lad, and run after Mags! Tell her to get back here as quickly as she can! Sadie, don't try to move, luv. Just sit back.'

Sadie leaned back in the chair, beads of perspiration standing out on her forehead. She'd gone to see the doctor and he'd given her some tablets which had helped but the pain had never, never been as bad as this and it terrified her that she seemed unable to move.

Billy ran out and Polly got a cushion and gently eased it behind Sadie, hoping it would help.

Mags arrived, flushed, panting a little and very worried. Billy had just yelled that his mam was in awful pain and couldn't get up out of the chair. She left the baby in his pram outside the door.

'Ma, what's wrong?' she gasped.

'I think someone had better go for the doctor, Mags. She's in terrible pain, so bad she can't get up.'

'Do you think between us we can get her on to the sofa?' Mags was really worried.

Polly was doubtful. 'We can try.'

'Billy, go for the doctor and then go and get Eileen too. She might be of some help.'

'No, I'd go for Eileen first, she'll get here faster and she can tell us if we should move her or not,' Polly advised.

Billy looked from one to the other questioningly. His mam had never been as bad as this before.

'Yes. Yes, go for Eileen first. We'll wait to see what she says. Go on, hurry!' Mags urged the lad.

The two women did what they could for Sadie until Billy arrived back with Eileen who had had her husband drive them to Royal Street.

'Mrs Devlin, can you move your legs at all?' Eileen asked.

Sadie nodded, biting back a groan as the slight movement caused intense pain.

'Would she be more comfortable lying down, do you think?' Mags asked.

'I think we should leave her as she is until the doctor arrives. After he's examined her he'll advise us what to do,' Eileen said firmly. 'But a hot-water bottle might help a bit until he arrives. I'll boil up the kettle. Mags, you'd better go and bring Thomas in, it was just starting to rain.'

As Mags went out to the pram Eileen went into the scullery with the kettle. She didn't like the look of Sadie at all. Mags had told her that the pain in her mother-in-law's back was no better, despite the tablets the doctor had given her and she hoped he wouldn't be long.

He arrived at last and examined Sadie and then told Polly and Mags that she could be moved to her bed and that he would leave some medicine that would ease the pain and make her sleep.

'I . . . I'll not be paralysed, doctor, will I?' Sadie asked, close to tears with pain and fear.

'No, Mrs Devlin, but you must rest. You will have good days and days that won't be as good. Rest will help. Now, these ladies will help you and I'll call to see you on Monday after surgery.'

Eileen showed him into the hall. 'Am I right in thinking she has a growth on her spine, doctor?'

He nodded slowly. 'She has, I'm afraid.'

'It's cancer then,' Eileen said flatly. It was the worst of news.

He nodded again. 'I don't know if or how far it has spread. I can't tell you how long she has. A few months perhaps.'

Eileen shook her head sadly. 'Should the family tell her?'

'I'd say not. She's been through enough these last years. But of course the final decision must be made by them. I'll give her morphine to ease the pain but it's not an easy death, God help her. Tell the family not to hesitate to call me should they need me.'

Eileen nodded slowly. 'Thank you, doctor. I'll tell

Georgie when he gets home. I'll be better able to explain it to him.'

She sent Billy off to his course, telling him that his mam would be fine, and when Mags and Polly came down she deftly managed to evade their questions.

'I'm always telling her she should rest more. The war really took it out of her. Mags, you just knock on the wall for me, luv, if you need me,' Polly instructed as she left.

'Eileen, just what is it?' Mags asked when Polly had gone.

'I'll put the kettle on. Mags, you see to Thomas, give him his dinner and then when Georgie gets home I'll explain it all to you both,' Eileen said firmly.

Georgie was home on time and Eileen sat them both down as she explained with a very heavy heart that Sadie was not going to get better and that it was only a matter of time before she would pass away. She had had to give families bad news many times in the past but when it was such close friends it was much, much harder.

'I'll do everything I can. I'll come and nurse her when she gets to the stage where she's unable to leave her bed,' Eileen promised.

Mags clung to her husband sobbing quietly. She was very fond of her mother-in-law. Sadie had struggled on through the war years, she wasn't old and now when life was just getting easier . . . Oh, it wasn't fair!

Georgie felt cold and numb. His mam was going to die and he would have to watch her getting worse day by day. He'd seen men suffer and die before but that had been in battle. It had been quick and often it had felt impersonal, somehow. It had shocked him but it hadn't affected him like this. This was totally different.

'She . . . she doesn't know?' he finally asked of Eileen.

She shook her head. 'No, and the doctor is of the opinion that she shouldn't be told, but it's up to you.'

'It wouldn't help if she knew, it would only be worse for her,' Mags added.

Georgie nodded. 'I don't think I could face telling her something like that. We'll say nothing but what about Billy?' He looked to Eileen for guidance.

'I don't think you should tell him either, he's too young and he might not be able to hide his feelings,' she suggested.

'Eileen's right, Georgie, he might get so distressed that he'd blurt it out.' Mags again dabbed at her eyes. 'What about Grace and Chrissie?'

'I don't think we should tell them just yet. If she deteriorates quickly we'll send for them. Grace has had enough to cope with lately both with Con and then Pat. I think we should leave it for a while,' Georgie decided.

Mags looked confused. 'I don't know, Georgie, perhaps Grace should be told. She would want to come home, I know that, but I think you're right. Chrissie would probably go to pieces and be no use to anyone. We should let Pat get back on his feet properly first anyway.'

'And if Grace came home now your mam will know there is something very wrong with her,' Eileen added. She sighed. 'When the time comes, Georgie, I'll write to Grace, if you like? I can probably explain it to her better.'

Georgie reached out and took her hand. 'Thanks, Eileen. You're a good friend to us all. We're going to need all our friends now.'

Chapter Thirty-One

◆◆◆◆

THE TIME COULDN'T GO quickly enough for Chrissie; she counted each day and began to save what money she could. She sold what good jewellery she had and a few of her more expensive outfits. It had been easy to smuggle them out and take them into town. She tried to remain her usual silent and downhearted self but that wasn't easy, especially as she felt that Grace was watching her closely.

Had she but known it Grace was too preoccupied worrying that Pat was trying to do more than he was capable of, as was Con, for as the month progressed and the evenings became lighter they both seemed to spend far more time out in the yard than she deemed was wise.

When the day arrived Chrissie felt a sense of overwhelming elation. At last! At last she would leave here and this life she hated to start a new and exciting future with the man she truly loved. It would be an adventure to go travelling and see so many new places and not be stuck here in this backwater for ever. She had packed a bag and surreptitiously given it to him the evening before. She had a small amount of money, not as much as she had hoped for, but it would tide her over. Tomorrow she would be on her way with the rest of the travellers, heading for the boat to Holyhead. Remembering the upset she had caused when she'd left Liverpool to come here she wrote a note for Grace and left it on the top of the chest of drawers in the bedroom she shared with her sister. She had hidden her coat and hat in one of the sheds and after supper she announced that she was just going for a walk to clear her head.

'Put a shawl on, it's quite chilly out there,' Grace called to her.

Chrissie nodded and took the shawl from its hook by the door. She'd leave it behind in the shed. Johnny had promised he would be waiting for her at the end of the laneway that led on to the road into town. She wished she could give Grace a hug and say goodbye properly for Grace had always been good to her and she would miss her. She glanced for the last time around the kitchen of the house that had been both her home and her prison and then she left, closing the door firmly behind her.

Pat settled down to read the *Farmers' Journal* and Con filled his pipe, after putting down more turf on the fire.

Grace picked up her knitting.

'Aren't ye always making something for one or other of those childer,' Con remarked, amiably.

Grace smiled at him. 'It helps Mary out and gives me something to do of an evening. I can't sit and do nothing.'

'Ye should have a bit of rest, Grace. Ye work far too hard.'

'As do you both. Is there to be any increase in the price of milk, Pat?' she asked.

He shook his head. 'No, but things should improve if this programme of economic development works. Sure, I hope the Secretary of the Department of Finance knows what he's doing. We could certainly all do with some "economic development".'

Con nodded sagely and Grace concentrated on decreasing for the armhole of the cardigan.

An hour later she began to get worried for there was no sign of Chrissie. 'I hope Chrissie is all right, she never usually stays out this long.'

'Will I go up to the bridge and see if there's any sign of her?' Pat didn't particularly want to leave the warmth of the kitchen but he too was beginning to feel uneasy.

Grace put aside her knitting. 'I'll go. You've been on your feet for long enough. I'll take the candle lantern.'

She went as far as the bridge but could see no sign of her sister. She even peered down into the deep dark waters of the lock, praying Chrissie hadn't fallen in, but she could see nothing suspicious.

'There's no sign of her. I'm getting really worried now,' she announced when she returned.

Both men got to their feet ready to go out and search the roads and laneways but a memory was stirring in Grace's mind. The memory of the day her sister had run away from Liverpool. Had Chrissie done the same thing again?

'Wait. I'll just go up and see if . . . there's anything missing.'

Pat and Con looked at each other in mystification.

On reaching the bedroom Grace lit the oil lamp and instantly her gaze fell on the folded piece of paper. She snatched it up and read it and then she sat down heavily on the bed. Chrissie said she was so very sorry but she couldn't stand this life any longer, it was slowly driving her mad. She had fallen in love with Johnny McDonagh and she was going off with him and his people. Grace was not to worry for this time Chrissie knew her own mind and even though people would condemn her she didn't care. She would write from time to time so Grace would know she was well and happy. She asked Grace to tell Pat she was sorry.

'Oh, Chrissie! How could you?' Grace groaned. She knew that this was yet another decision her sister would live to regret. How could she not worry about her? Chrissie would hate the travelling life and all its discomforts when the novelty of it wore off and she realised that she didn't love Johnny McDonagh either. And what was she to tell Pat? Oh, it wasn't fair that Chrissie should leave it to her to break this utterly humiliating news to him.

At last she heard Con calling to her and she went downstairs.

'Well?' Con questioned.

Grace bit her lip and handed Pat Chrissie's note and then sat down and covered her face with her hands.

Pat read it and his expression hardened. For Chrissie to run off like this was bad enough but to run off with the likes of *him*!

'Sure, what is it? What's she done now?' Con questioned, alarmed at the expression on his nephew's face. He could see that Grace was very upset by the contents of that note.

Pat handed it to him. 'She's disgraced me, Con!'

Con read it slowly and then his eyes blazed with anger. 'She's disgraced us all! The sinful, ungrateful, conniving little bitch! A whore to a tinker is what she is!'

Grace looked up. She had never heard Con use language like that before and she saw Pat wince.

'So she was carrying on like a bitch in heat right under our noses! And *him* laughing at us all the time behind our backs! 'Tis no wonder he stayed on when the rest of that tribe upped and left!' Con was furious at the humiliation of Chrissie's betrayal.

'And I . . . I thought she was just friendly with him. I should have watched her more closely but I never suspected, truly I didn't,' Grace groaned.

'It's not your fault, Grace. How were you to know?' Pat said quietly.

'Oh, Pat. I'm so very sorry. You gave her every-thing, you tried so hard to make her happy and this . . . this is how she has treated you. How *could* she? How could she forget everything she was ever taught? Mam didn't bring her up to do such terrible things,' Grace wailed.

Con was pacing the floor, shaking his head. 'She's made an eejit of you, Pat. She's made eejits of us all! How are we ever going to hold up our heads in this parish again when 'tis known she's run off with a tinker? But she'll regret it, so she will. They'll not be delighted to have her tagging along with them. She'll come running back to us – but she'll not set foot in this house again!'

Pat threw the note into the fire and sat down. ' 'Tis done. She's gone and there's an end to it. We'll go on as before,' he said firmly. He was smarting at what Chrissie had done but he wasn't sorry she'd gone. 'We'll say she's gone back to Liverpool – for her health. There's no need to broadcast that she's gone off with him.'

'But what if she's seen with him?' Con demanded, still fuming.

'It was almost dark when she went out, 'tis hardly likely anyone would see her and by now they'll be well away.'

'But they always come back for the winter,' Con persisted.

'Sure, we'll cross that bridge when we come to it.'

Grace stood up. 'I think we all need something a bit stronger than tea.' She took the bottle of whiskey and three glasses from the press. As she placed them on the table her hands were shaking. 'Oh, what am I going to tell Mam? She'll be sick with the worry of it! I could *kill* Chrissie, I really could!'

'Tell her nothing, Grace, for now. Give us all time to think.'

'I don't want to think about it at all, Pat! I'm so thoroughly ashamed of her.'

'We'll work something out in the morning. Things always seem clearer in the mornings.'

'You . . . you're taking it very well, Pat.'

He shrugged. 'Maybe I knew in my heart that one day she'd go and if the truth be told I'm not sorry. You both knew how things were between meself and her.'

'Ye don't mean it's glad ye are she's gone off with him?' Con demanded.

Pat shook his head. 'You know I don't mean that, Con. Now, let's have this drop and get to bed. What's done is done and 'tis no use sitting here debating it all night.'

When the two men had gone up Grace washed up the glasses and damped down the fire before turning out the lamps. This was the worst possible thing Chrissie could have done for she knew that sooner or later she would have to tell her mother.

* * *

Grace awoke next morning with a headache. She hadn't slept well at all and she suspected that neither had Pat nor Con. She dressed and went down to start breakfast for both men were already up and out in the yard. She knew they would have to talk, they would have to concoct a story to explain away Chrissie's sudden absence and she hoped that no one would connect the disappearance of Johnny McDonagh with that of her sister.

When the two men came in, accompanied by Tom Healy, she caught the warning look Pat gave her.

'Sit down with you all and get your meal. I've a great deal to do this morning,' she said, placing the big brown teapot on the table and putting down three bowls of porridge and the jug of cream.

Con poured himself a mug of tea but then pushed the bowl away. 'I've no appetite this morning, Grace.'

'You can't do a day's work on an empty stomach, Uncle Con,' she scolded. He didn't look well. He looked tired and drawn but then they all did, she thought.

He stood up. 'I'm feeling sick in my stomach.'

'Go on up to your bed. Tom and me will manage well enough with young Dinny and Liam,' Pat urged.

Con leaned heavily on the table and then Grace cried out sharply as the old man slumped forward.

'Pat! He's really ill! Catch him, quickly!' she cried as Con began to slide to the floor.

'Will I be sending Dinny for the doctor?' Tom Healy asked anxiously as Pat half carried Con to a chair and Grace bent over him.

'Yes. Yes, please, Tom and tell him to hurry.' She looked up at Pat. 'I think it's another stroke.'

' 'Tis no wonder. I'll carry him to his bed,' Pat said grimly.

Dr Wrafter examined Con and then told them both that this time it was a more serious stroke.

'But he'll recover, like last time?' Pat asked anxiously.

The older man shook his head. 'There's no knowing, Pat. He could have another at any time.'

'I've been telling him for weeks and weeks he was doing too much,' Grace said, biting her lip. It wasn't just the heavy workload, she knew that. It was the shock and humiliation of Chrissie's behaviour but she couldn't tell the doctor about that.

'He'll need constant nursing, Grace.'

'I'll see to him. I did the last time,' she reminded him.

'You'll have to bring down the bed for you can't nurse him through the night.'

Grace looked pleadingly at Pat, not knowing what to say.

'We'll bring down the bed. I'm afraid Chrissie has gone to Liverpool to her mother. Chrissie hasn't been well in herself these last weeks,' Pat informed the doctor whom he knew would be wondering where Chrissie was.

The doctor raised his eyebrows but said nothing. She'd chosen a fine time to go with Pat himself only recently recovered from that accident. 'I'll call in to see him tomorrow but if he gets worse send for me.'

They spent the rest of the morning making Con comfortable in the narrow bed that had been brought down and pushed against one wall of the kitchen, out of the draught of the door. It made the room seem very cramped and Grace decided that some of the furniture would have to be moved out.

'It's not the best solution. It's far from peaceful in here at times but there's no help for it. At least I'll be close at hand to see to him. How are we going to manage, Pat? I have all the chores Chrissie did as well as my own and you'll miss his help in the yard.'

Pat nodded. 'I know, but we'll get through somehow, Grace.'

'This is her fault, Pat. You know that. He was so very angry and upset.'

Pat nodded. She was right but he didn't want to think about Chrissie at all. 'All that matters is that he recovers,' he said firmly.

As the days passed somehow they did muddle through although they were both constantly exhausted. Kathleen Dolan and Lizzie Kenny, two of the neighbours, came from time to time to help Grace out and Con slowly began to recover his speech but not the use of his limbs. This caused him to become restless and frustrated and Grace pressed him to try to be patient.

'If you get all fussed and upset you'll only make yourself worse,' she pleaded. 'Easter will soon be upon us and then the better weather, you'll improve then. Try and be patient, Con.'

He'd nodded but didn't look convinced. Last time he'd begun to recover much more quickly.

On the afternoon of Easter Monday, 18 April, Pat came into the kitchen smiling. 'I have some news that will cheer him up, Grace. The best yet.'

Grace looked up at him and smiled. 'What?'

'Today we've become a Republic! The Republic of Eire and not a part of the British Commonwealth either.'

Grace looked at him speculatively. It had been discussed frequently and she knew an act had been passed by the Dáil, which had obviously come into force today, but she didn't take an active interest in politics. 'Tell him then if it will cheer him up,' she urged.

Pat sat down beside his uncle. 'Con. It's come at last. After seven hundred years we're free of the Crown. We're now officially the Republic of Eire.'

The old man's face lit up. 'Thanks be to God I've lived to see this day, Pat! Sure, I never thought I would. But what about the six counties of the North?'

Pat shook his head. 'There's no reunification, Con. The government in Westminster has said that in no event will Northern Ireland cease to be part of Britain without the consent of the Parliament at Stormont, but only time will tell. Mr de Valera is our new President. We should be celebrating.'

'Could he take a small drop of Jameson's, do you think?' Grace asked, thankful that the old man really did seem to be very happy at the news.

Pat smiled at her. 'I think he could manage it all right. I think we'll all take a drop for the day that's in it. This will be bound to speed his recovery, Grace.'

She poured three small tots of whiskey and added a generous amount of water to her own for she really preferred port wine. Pat held the glass to Con's lips. 'Here's to the new Republic and here's to us!'

Con nodded and sipped the drink while Grace smiled at them both as she lifted her own glass. For a few moments they could be happy, she thought. They could all forget the trouble and heartache Chrissie's departure had brought for it was a momentous day.

In the early hours of the following morning Con had another stroke and died peacefully in his sleep.

Chapter Thirty-Two

———◆◆◆———

'HOW ARE YOU FEELING today, Ma?' Mags asked Sadie as she brought her up a cup of tea. As the doctor had said, Sadie had her good days and her bad ones. It had been hard to accept that she wasn't going to get well and it seemed strange not to have her in the kitchen going about her chores. The heavier workload had fallen on her and Georgie had finally said that they would take Polly Nelson into their confidence. Polly had been shocked and upset when they'd told her but she had promised she would help Mags on the days when Sadie was unable to get up. Obviously, her mother-in-law didn't feel too bad today, Mags judged, for Sadie was sitting up in bed.

'I think I could come down today, Mags. I don't feel too bad at all. The pain isn't as fierce this morning.'

Sadie wasn't a fool: she was aware that there was something seriously wrong with her but she had great faith in Dr Schofield and the medicine he'd given her did ease the pain. She prayed daily that when the weather got warmer she would be able to get around more. The extra rest seemed to help.

'I'm glad to hear that. You have this tea and then I'll help you to get dressed.'

'Oh, you go on down, Mags, I'll be able to manage just fine.'

Mags smiled. 'You really are feeling better today.'

'Did our Billy take that letter for Grace, like I asked him to?' Sadie queried.

'He did, but I had to put it in his hand as he went out the door.'

'That lad would forget his own head if it wasn't fastened on! I worry about him, I really do,' Sadie muttered darkly.

'Well, he'll be off to do his two years' National Service later this year, that should settle him down,' Mags reminded her.

Sadie was settled comfortably in the chair by the range when Mags finally had both herself and Thomas ready to go out to do the shopping. 'Polly is coming in for a chat while I'm out, so you won't be sitting here on your own, Ma, and I'll be as quick as I can.'

Sadie frowned. 'Polly seems to be in and out a great deal these days, Mags.'

'She comes in to escape. You know the wedding is

only a few days away now and they're still driving her mad,' Mags replied. It was true but it was also a good-enough excuse not to arouse Sadie's suspicions, although what she would use as an excuse after Kate's wedding she didn't know.

Polly was glad to see her old friend and neighbour up and she relayed the latest on the arrangements for her eldest daughter's wedding.

'I'll be glad when it's all over and done with and so will Alf, I just hope when the other two finally get themselves wed there won't be as much fuss and bother,' she finished.

'There will if your Mary gets married before Ellie.'

'Oh no there won't! I've told our Ellie I'll stand for no more of her nonsense!' Polly said firmly. 'But God help the feller that gets *that* one!'

'There's the post, Polly, would you get it for me?' Sadie asked, seeing the postman pass the window.

Polly obliged. 'It's from either your Grace or Chrissie, I can tell by the stamp.'

'It won't be from our Chrissie, I haven't had a word from her in weeks.'

Polly poured them both a cup of tea while Sadie read the letter.

'Ah, Polly, the poor old man has died. God rest his soul,' Sadie announced, crossing herself devoutly.

'That's a shame, luv,' Polly concurred.

'He had another stroke and went in his sleep. They've sent a telegram to Eileen. He's being buried today.'

Polly nodded. 'And does she say how Pat is taking it? He was very fond of the old feller.'

'He's upset of course but he wouldn't have wished him to be paralysed and neither would she.'

'I wouldn't wish that on me worst enemy. Didn't I have me work cut out with old Ma Nelson? You remember, Sadie, how we had to wash her, feed her, change her, turn her regularly so she wouldn't get bed sores and she hated it? No, it's a blessing God took him. How is Pat getting on himself?'

'He's a lot better now.' Sadie was still scanning the lines of Grace's letter, then her face lit up. 'Here, Polly, she says she's coming home!'

'Really? For good or just for a visit?' Polly enquired, wondering if someone had informed Grace of her mother's illness.

'For good. I suppose she feels she'll only be in the way now. Pat and Chrissie will want to have the place to themselves. They've never been on their own in all the time they've been married, they might get along better.'

'Does she say that?'

Sadie shook her head. 'No, but she says she can't really stay now. It wouldn't be right.'

'She liked it there. Do you think she'll get used to living here again?'

'I'm sure she will, she can make a life for herself now and she'll be a big help to Mags. And she's never seen little Thomas,' she finished, thinking it would be good to have Grace home again: she'd always been far less trouble than Chrissie and Sadie had missed her. And it looked as if Chrissie didn't mind being left on her own with Pat, which was a blessing in itself. Maybe Chrissie had at last grown up and was shouldering her responsibilities.

'So, when will she arrive? Will it be in time for our Kate's wedding? They were good friends.'

'No. She's coming next week, Polly. She has things to sort out.'

'Ah, that's a shame. Never mind, I can tell her all about it,' Polly said amiably.

After the shock of Con's death and the removal and burial Grace had realised with a heavy heart that she could no longer stay for she and Pat would be alone in the house.

The days that had followed the old man's demise had seemed like a blur with the neighbours in and out and all the arrangements to be made. She constantly found herself turning to speak to Con before she remembered he was no longer there. She missed him but Dr Wrafter had said it was for the best for in his opinion Con would never have recovered.

'At least the poor old soul lived to see the Republic declared and I know it was one of his dearest wishes,' the doctor had said to Pat as he'd signed the death certificate.

She knew Pat was very upset for Con had been his constant companion, friend and mentor. When the wake was over and everyone had departed she began to clear away all the dishes. She realised that Pat had had a few drinks more than was usual, although he was by no means drunk, and she urged him to go to bed.

'It's been a long and harrowing day, Pat. You go on up.'

'Not yet, Grace. Put down those dishes. I . . . I have to talk to you.'

She sighed as she placed the dishes in the sink and wiping her hands on her apron she turned towards him. She knew this had been coming.

He looked closely at her. He had to tell her what was in his heart. 'What are we going to do, Grace?'

'I'm going to have to go back to Liverpool, Pat. I can't stay. It wouldn't be right.'

'So you'll be after leaving me too. First Chrissie, not that I miss her, then Con and I *do* miss him and now . . . you.' His voice cracked with pain and grief.

'I'm so, so sorry, Pat, but I can't stay and you know why.'

'I know I love you, Grace. I began to realise it after the accident. I pushed it away but after . . . after she ran off I couldn't deny it to myself any longer.'

Grace twisted her hands together and said nothing. What could she say? What did he expect her to say? She too knew that her feelings for him were growing but she had fought desperately against them.

'And what about you, Grace? Do you feel anything for me at all?'

'Pat, don't ask me that, please? I . . . I don't know how to answer you without there being more hurt and disappointment.'

'So you don't love me?'

She knew she should say 'no' but she just couldn't speak, it was as though her throat had closed over. She looked up at him and the expression in her eyes gave her away.

Before she could stop him he had taken her in his arms and was kissing her.

All her resolve crumbled and she kissed him back, clinging to him tightly. She had never felt like this with Sandy and she knew now that she would love Pat Kilroy until her dying day. But at last it was she who pulled away.

'Pat, I . . . I do love you, I can't deny it, but we can never be together. You must realise that.'

'Don't say that, Grace, please!' he pleaded.

Tears sparkled on her lashes and her heart felt as if it were being torn in two. 'I know, but this moment is all we have – all we'll ever have.'

'No, Grace! I won't let you go! We can go away from here.'

She shook her head, the tears now slowly trickling down her cheeks. 'I won't let you sell this place, you love it just as much if not more than you love me, even though you might not realise it. It's your land, your heritage, everything your family worked and fought and even died for. It's where you *belong*, Pat! If you left it we wouldn't be happy. I have to go back to Liverpool; we have no choice. It can never be, Pat. We both have to acknowledge that and try to make new lives for ourselves. It won't be easy – it will be terribly hard, but we *have* to!'

She began to sob quietly and he held her to him. He knew she was right. Chrissie had deserted him but she was still his wife and always would be, there was no getting away from that fact. She would have to go back to Liverpool and he would have to try to get on with his life as best he could. It was a bleak and bitter future. He kissed her again and then reluctantly released her.

She sat down a little unsteadily and wiped her eyes. 'I'll go back early next week, Pat, after I've helped you to sort out Con's things. I'll write to Mam tomorrow.'

He stood staring down at her his eyes full of misery. He was losing her – for ever. 'Wait there, Grace, just for a moment.'

She looked at him questioningly but he went upstairs. She looked around the kitchen. Oh, how she would miss all this! She had been happy here until Chrissie had gone. She would miss everything about this place and the friends she had made here, but most of all she would miss him.

He returned with a small box, which he handed to her. 'I want you to have this, Grace. It belonged to my mother.' He was struggling with his emotions. 'It will be something to remind you of me and the love I'll always have for you.'

She opened it. Inside was a gold wedding ring engraved with a design of Celtic knots. 'It's . . . lovely.' She managed a bleak little smile. 'I'll wear it on a chain around my neck. I'll wear it always, I promise. You have my heart, Pat, but I wish I had something to give to you, something tangible.'

'I have a photograph of you. The snapshot Martin Mitchell took of us both last summer when we brought the last of the turf down from the bog, remember? He'd just got that camera and wanted to try it out. I'll get a frame for it and put it on the dresser.'

She fought down the sob that rose in her throat. Oh, this was so very, very hard. 'Goodnight, Pat. God bless you and take care of you – always.' The last word was no more than a whisper as she fled towards the stairs.

Chapter Thirty-Three

CHRISSIE TURNED HER FACE up towards the warm rays of the sun and leaned against Johnny's shoulder. She'd been so happy these last weeks, happier than she'd ever been in her life. Sitting here beside him as they drove along the leafy lanes of the Welsh countryside made her feel so contented. She didn't even care that she was viewed with suspicion by his family and the rest of the travellers; she'd almost got used to it. Nothing mattered except the fact that she loved him and he loved her. She had not a single regret about leaving Pat and her life in Rahan. The days were long and full of sunlight and laughter and she enjoyed seeing different places. It was much better than being stuck in one depressing place all the time. Life was now so different, carefree and exciting.

'Where will we be stopping tonight?' she asked, glancing up at Johnny and thinking how handsome he looked for the sun had darkened his skin.

He smiled down at her. 'Just outside the little market town of Denbigh. Sure, we should reach there before dark. 'Tis a grand little place, there's a ruined castle on the hill. Will we take a walk up there tomorrow?'

'I'd like that. I always think those places have such a dreamy air about them.'

He laughed. 'Ah, Chrissie, you delight me! You're such a romantic.'

'And what's wrong with that? You are one of the most romantic people I know. You say such lovely things to me when . . . well, at night,' she replied, thinking of the rapturous hours when she lay in his arms.

He bent and kissed her on the forehead. 'Ah, wouldn't any man be moved to poetry when he had such a gorgeous woman in his arms?'

She sighed, thinking she was the luckiest person in the world to have found such happiness and she was looking forward to climbing a hill to a ruined castle with him tomorrow. It would be a few hours away from everyone else.

After a few minutes she realised that the pony's pace had slowed and she saw one of the men walking back towards them.

'What's up ahead, Willie?' Johnny asked.

'A bit of a track but we've heard that there's an auld feller with a few horses he might sell lives at the end of it. Will ye be after coming along with a couple of the lads and meself?'

Johnny passed the reins over to Chrissie. 'I will so. You drive on, Chrissie.'

She looked at him in astonishment. 'But I've only ever driven a trap.'

He grinned up at her. ' 'Tis the same principle. Ah, you'll be fine. The old nag knows her own way, she'll just amble along after the caravan in front. It'll be no bother to you. We won't be long, we'll catch you up.'

Chrissie was a little uncertain. He'd never left her alone to do the driving before. 'You're sure you won't be long?'

'I promise. You'll hardly know I've gone at all.' He turned away and followed Willie McVeigh.

Chrissie shrugged and gave the reins a flick. She supposed she couldn't expect him to stay at her side every hour of the day and night, she didn't want to appear possessive, and he'd promised he wouldn't be long. After all, what was so difficult about following the caravan in front for a while? 'Make sure you drive a good bargain, Johnny!' she called after him.

He turned and grinned at her. 'Sure, don't I always!' he called back, blowing her a kiss.

Grace's journey back was utterly miserable. She hadn't been able to face letting Pat take her to the station so Martin Mitchell had driven her. They had said a heart-breaking last goodbye that morning and she hadn't even been able to look back or wave as the trap had been driven out of the gateway. They had told everyone who needed to know that she was returning to Liverpool reluctantly to look after her mother and hopefully facilitate Chrissie's return, although that would depend on her sister's health.

Only when the train at last pulled out of Tullamore Station and the green fields and brown bog land, quiet and peaceful in the April sunlight, slid by did she break down. She was alone in the compartment and by the time the train reached Clara she had regained some of her composure.

On the ferry she slept little; her mind was churning, trying to find the words to explain to her family the real reason why she was returning to Liverpool, and when finally the familiar buildings of the waterfront came into view she realised with a terrible sense of finality that she would never go back to Ireland: it was now no longer a part of her life or even a part of her own country as it had been for so long.

The city didn't look much different, she thought as she made her way towards the tram. The bombsites were still there; the buildings that were still standing were coated with soot. The dockers on their way to work at this time of the morning all looked weary in their drab working clothes. She knew conditions were slowly getting better. Most things were off the ration now, derelict buildings were being pulled down and new houses were being built to replace those destroyed in the Blitz, and of course there was the new National Health Service. These thoughts, however, did little to lift her spirits.

Mags was up and dressed when she arrived home. She hugged her sister-in-law and then looked at her closely. 'Grace, you look worn out and I don't think it's just the travelling.'

'Oh, Mags. I'll tell you all about it later. First, I'd love a cup of tea and a cuddle of my nephew.'

'I doubt you'll get much of a cuddle, he's like a little eel these days. He'll be walking soon, I know he will. He's already pulling himself up and hanging on to the furniture. I have my work cut out with him I can tell you.'

She poured Grace a cup of tea and smiled as Grace scooped little Thomas up in her arms. True to form he began to wriggle and Grace laughed and set him down on the rug.

'I thought Mam would be up? How is she, Mags?'

Mags looked at Grace sadly, thinking this was a fine homecoming for poor Grace, but she had to tell her before she saw Sadie. She sat down.

'She's not good, Grace, I'm afraid.'

'What? Why?' Grace demanded.

'Oh, Grace! I've only just come to terms with it myself. She's got cancer. There's no cure and Dr Schofield says she might only have months to live. She doesn't know and she has good days and bad ones.

413

Eileen has been so good. She's offered to come and nurse her when . . . when she gets really bad.'

Grace shook her head in disbelief. Mags was telling her that Mam was . . . dying! It couldn't be true! Why hadn't they told her? 'Mags, you really should have let me know! If anything had happened to her and I wasn't here . . .'

Mags reached out and took her hand. 'Grace, we thought . . . we agreed we would send for you if she deteriorated quickly and you had so much on your plate. I'm devastated myself, as is Georgie. We haven't told Billy.'

Slowly Grace nodded. Everything was taking on a dreamlike quality. Life was turning into a nightmare. She had lost Pat, Con was dead and now . . . now her poor mam was to follow him. If she stopped to think about it all she would go mad. 'Mags, now I'm glad I came back but I have bad news too. I couldn't stay in Ireland because . . . because Chrissie has run off again but this time she's gone off with someone. A man called Johnny McDonagh, he's a tinker.'

'Oh, my God!' Mags cried, horrified.

'She's humiliated Pat in the worst possible way and it . . . it killed Uncle Con. He was so angry and upset it brought on the stroke. I don't know where she is but she's with the "travellers", as they like to be called.'

'How could she do such a thing? We all thought things weren't too bad! Mother of God, how are we going to tell Ma?'

'I don't know. Maybe we shouldn't tell her at all, I don't want it to have the same effect on her as it did on Uncle Con,' Grace replied, her voice full of fear.

Mags instantly put her arms around her. 'Oh, Grace, it's been a terrible time for you. No wonder you're so upset and to come home and find out about Ma . . .'

'There's something else . . . something has happened.'

'What?'

'Promise you won't be shocked? I couldn't bear that but I have to tell someone.'

'For God's sake, what is it? What's happened, Grace?'

'I . . . I've fallen in love with Pat! I . . . I didn't mean to, I've tried so hard to deny it to myself but . . .' She broke down.

Mags was stunned. This was something she had never expected. This situation was a serious taboo but her heart went out to her sister-in-law. 'And what about him? Does he know this?'

Grace nodded. 'He loves me too but we both know it's something that has no future, something that can never be. That's why I had to leave.'

Mags held her as she cried brokenly. Oh, what a mess, she thought. What a terrible, terrible mess and poor Grace was by far the worst off. She had given up everything to go to Ireland to try to help Chrissie. If Grace had stayed here she would never have fallen in love with Pat, a man she could never have – a man Chrissie had callously discarded and for such a one as this Johnny McDonagh! Chrissie thought of no one but herself and she left a trail of wrecked lives and broken hearts behind her.

It was little Thomas catching the edge of the tablecloth and dragging everything to the floor that brought them both up sharply.

'Oh, you little terror!' Mags cried, lifting him up.

'He's not hurt, is he?' Grace asked for the teapot had broken.

'No, thank God! Oh, you could have been scalded! What am I going to do with you? You're going in your high chair whether you like it or not while I clean this mess up!'

The incident served to steady them both and they soon had everything cleared away. Mags gave the baby a Farley's rusk to keep him quiet.

'Mags, what happened? I heard all the noise. Grace! Grace, luv, I didn't hear you arrive!' Sadie stood in the doorway, her dressing gown clutched to her.

'Oh Mam, it's . . . it's so good to see you!' Grace managed to keep her voice steady as she hugged her mother but her heart turned over as she realised how thin her mother had become.

Mags too had pulled herself together. 'It was this little terror here. Pulled the tablecloth off, he did. We were just having a cup of tea, and then I was going to send Grace up to you. She's not been in long and she's exhausted.'

Sadie looked at her daughter more closely. 'You do

look tired, luv, and have you been crying?'

'She was telling me about poor Con. She got a bit upset,' Mags said quickly, throwing Grace a warning look.

'Poor soul, God rest him. I know you were fond of him, Grace,' Sadie sympathised.

'Now that you're up I'll make a fresh pot of tea but I'm going to have to use your best teapot, the other one smashed. Meladdo there was responsible for that. I'll get one to replace it from Appleton's. I was going to call on Eileen too. Would you like to come, Grace?'

'I think she'd be better off getting some sleep. She's had a hard time of it lately, Mags,' Sadie advised.

Mags had gone to replace the teapot leaving Grace alone with her mother.

'I really am glad you've come home, Grace. I've missed you so much, luv.'

Grace took her mother's hand. 'And I've missed you too, Mam.' She had to fight to keep her voice steady, thinking how much more she would miss her mother when she'd . . . gone.

'So, tell me how are things over there now? Pat must be missing the old man sorely.'

Grace nodded, swallowing hard. 'He does, but I . . . I felt it was time for me to come home.' She couldn't sit and weave a web of lies about Chrissie and Pat.

Sadie nodded. 'It might be the very thing they need now, Grace. Time on their own. Let's hope it's the making of them. And you have your own life to lead, luv. You can't play nursemaid to their marriage for the rest of your life, it wouldn't be fair on you. Have you any plans?'

'Nothing definite yet. It's just nice to be home.'

'It's a pity I'm not my usual self. I don't know exactly what's wrong, something to do with my back, and I can't get around like I used to. I suppose there's some long, complicated medical term for it. Dr Schofield has given me some medicine for the pain, which it does help, but it makes me sleep a lot. He's been very good and I have great faith in him.'

'I'm sure he knows what he's doing, Mam, and you need to rest, haven't you worked your fingers to the bone all your life?' Grace hoped her mother hadn't noticed the catch in her voice.

'That's just what Polly says. She's in and out a lot, she's a real help and a good friend. She says it's the only bit of peace and quiet she gets, sitting with me for a few hours.'

Grace managed a smile. 'I bet she's glad all the fuss of the wedding is over.'

'She is. It was a pity you missed it. She'll tell you all about it, no doubt. Well, you look as if you can hardly keep your eyes open. Go and get a few hours' sleep.'

'I will, Mam. I'll be fine once I've recovered from the journey.'

* * *

Grace had gone to bed and Polly was sitting with Sadie when Mags went out first to do the shopping and then to visit her friend. Eileen was both furious and upset at the news Mags had to impart. Furious with Chrissie and upset for Pat.

'I'll have to see what Georgie says about telling Ma,' Mags said when at last Eileen had run out of expletives to call Chrissie and expressions of sympathy for her brother.

'It will do her no good at all to hear all this, Mags, that it will not!'

'I know but she's no fool and I'd hate her to learn of it by accident.'

Eileen nodded; there was no easy answer.

Billy was delighted to see Grace when he arrived home. 'You being here might take her mind off nagging the daylights out of me,' he said, grinning as he hugged his sister.

'That's a fine thing to say, Billy Devlin! Not, "Hello, Grace, it's great to see you",' Mags chided but Grace managed a smile.

'I'd be worried if he was that polite. And you must be giving Mam something to nag you about.'

He rolled his eyes. 'She's always saying that Tommy is a bad influence and I should get a more responsible mate. Is me tea ready?'

It was Mags's turn to roll her eyes. 'He thinks of nothing else other than his belly. We'll wait until

Georgie gets in. I've already fed Thomas and Grace has taken your mam hers on a tray. She's been up most of the day and she's tired now. Go and wash your hands then at least you'll be ready to come to the table,' she instructed Billy, who grimaced.

Georgie greeted Grace with a hug and a 'welcome home' and when the meal was over, the dishes washed, the baby asleep and Billy had departed to Tommy Milligan's house he looked questioningly at his wife.

Mags nodded. 'I've told her. I told her as soon as she got in this morning.'

'We thought you had enough on your plate over there,' Georgie said, 'but I'm glad you've come home, I really am.'

'I'll just nip up and see that Ma is asleep. She should be, she's had a tiring day and she's taken her medicine.' Mags knew that when Georgie heard about Chrissie there would be raised voices and she didn't want Sadie to hear anything.

'You should have let me know, Georgie. I would have come home sooner,' Grace said quietly.

'I honestly didn't want to put more worry on your shoulders. You seemed to have enough with Pat and Con. Sorry.' Perhaps they had made the wrong decision, but they had been trying to do the right thing.

Mags returned, and she gazed steadily at her husband. 'You'd better make a big effort to keep your voice down, Georgie. Ma's just dozing off and what I've got to tell you now is going to make you very mad indeed.'

Grace watched her brother's face turn almost puce with anger as Mags told him of Chrissie's betrayal and desertion.

'Well, that's *it*!' he spluttered at last, trying to keep his voice under control. 'That's the end for that little bitch! I never want to see her again. She's disgraced not only Pat, she's disgraced us all! If she ever has the damned effrontery to show up here I'll show her the door. She'll get tired of him or he'll get tired of her sooner or later. The tinkers'll not accept her, she's not one of them and never will be. They'll turn him against her and I can't say I blame them. She's a bloody disgrace, that's what she is. Thank God Da isn't alive to see how she turned out although he must be spinning in his grave as must our Harold!'

'But what are we going to do about Ma? Do we tell her or not? I went to see Eileen this afternoon to let her know and she thinks it won't help at all, but Ma's not a fool and she'll be expecting a few letters at least from Chrissie.'

Georgie looked solemn. Mags was right. 'We'll have to stall for as long as we can. *That* one never wrote much anyway.'

He felt very sorry for Pat Kilroy and wondered how he would manage without his uncle, his wife and Grace, although he doubted that his wayward sister had ever really worked hard. He sighed heavily. 'Have you thought of what you are going to do, Grace? Mags and Polly can see to Mam during the day and Eileen has promised to come . . . later on. It's not fair to expect you to have no life of your own. You've had to leave a life you enjoyed and that's for the second time already.'

Grace managed to smile at him. 'I didn't really mind the first time and I can't expect you to keep me. I'll have to get some sort of job although I can't go back to Porter's. Really, I could do with something part-time and local so I'm on hand if . . . if . . .' She couldn't finish.

'Maybe you could get something in one of the local shops? They won't pay as well as the ones in town but it will be something,' Mags suggested. She agreed with her husband. A job, even part-time, would keep Grace's mind occupied. 'I'll ask when I go shopping. I can tell everyone how steady and reliable and hard-working you are and so can Eileen.'

Grace nodded, feeling the weight of all her conflicting emotions descending again. The future looked bleak, but there was nothing she could do to change anything. She would just have to accept her lot.

Chapter Thirty-Four

———◆———

GRACE MANAGED TO GET a part-time job in Frost's on County Road, mainly owing to the influence of Eileen who had an account there. It was a small department store and Grace served in the household department, which stocked linens, towels, bedspreads and a selection of curtain materials. She worked a half-day on Wednesday and all day Thursday, Friday and Saturday, which were the busiest days. On her days off she helped Mags in the house and often took little Thomas with her when she went to do the shopping. It gave Mags a bit of a break and as the weather improved she sometimes took him to the park.

She found it very hard to get used to life in a city again. She missed the peace and quiet, the fields and hedgerows, and when she took the baby to the park her longing for the countryside became more intense. She missed Pat dreadfully too and there were many nights when she either lay awake tossing and turning or cried herself to sleep. She told herself over and over that she must put all thoughts of him out of her mind, that she must try to build a new life for herself, but it didn't help much.

Mags tried to bolster her spirits, knowing how unhappy she was, for Grace had told her how much she missed the countryside. She didn't need to impress upon Mags how impossible her love for Pat was and Mags prayed that time would help Grace get over him. It was just a pity that Kate Nelson was married now, otherwise she was certain Kate would have coaxed Grace to go out more. The other two Nelson girls were younger and in her opinion a bit on the flighty side.

As the summer months wore on it became obvious to everyone that Sadie was failing. The doctor increased the strength of her medicine as the pain became worse and at the end of August Mags and Grace went to see Eileen.

'How is she, Mags?' Eileen asked as she ushered them both into the parlour with little Thomas. It was a sticky, sultry day and Eileen had opened all the windows.

'Oh, Eileen, she's getting much worse. That's why we've come. We've left Polly sitting with her. She hasn't been able to get up for the last three days now.' Mags settled her little son down on the floor and gave him the toys she had brought with her to keep him occupied.

'I can't bear to see her in so much pain. It breaks my heart. If I could take that agony on myself I would. She's little more than skin and bone,' Grace informed her with a catch in her voice. 'When we were small Mam was plump and pretty and now . . .'

Eileen patted her hand sympathetically. 'I know, Grace. That's what the disease does. It's a desperate, horrible thing!' She felt so sorry for Grace, she had had so much heartbreak to contend with without now having to watch her mother die in such a painful way. 'I'll make us all a cup of tea or would you prefer something cool? 'Tis so hot and sticky.'

They opted for some home-made lemonade and Eileen brought it in a jug with three glasses.

'We'd better get down to the practicalities,' she said briskly as she poured out the drinks. 'I can come for a few hours each morning and afternoon or would you prefer me to come in the evenings and stay?'

'We can't ask you to do that. You've a husband to look after, it's not fair on him,' Mags reminded her.

'Oh, Joe understands. I've already told him I've promised.' Eileen knew that it wouldn't be for long.

'Mags and I can see to her during the day, on the days I don't work, and there's always Polly. She's promised we can rely on her,' Grace informed Eileen.

'Yes, on the days Grace works Polly will help me,' confirmed Mags.

Eileen nodded. 'There's no question of her going into hospital?'

Both girls shook their heads emphatically but it was Grace who answered. 'No. No, we wouldn't even consider it. We told Dr Schofield that when he suggested it. She . . . she's going to go in her own home and with her family around her.'

'Then I'll come after I've given Joe his supper and I'll stay all night. You can't be doing without your sleep and nursing her during the day too. I can sleep during the day: I often did the night shift when I was working, I'm used to it. I'll come up this evening.'

'Thanks, Eileen. I don't know how we'd manage without you and we'll never forget all your kindness.'

Eileen smiled at Mags. 'Sure, isn't that what friends are for?' There were some very hard days and nights ahead, she knew that. 'And what about young Billy? He hasn't been told yet?'

Mags sighed. 'No. He's going to have to be told and it's not the best time for him. He has to go and do his two years' National Service at the end of September.'

'Do you want me to tell him?' Eileen offered.

Mags shook her head. 'Thanks, but no. Georgie will tell him. He's going to have to take some hard knocks when he goes in the Army so he really could do without . . . without losing his mam.'

'Poor lad, his carefree days are over. Make the most of this little one's childhood, Mags. It doesn't last long,'

Eileen urged, taking down two little ornamental brass bells from her mantelpiece and giving them to her godson to play with.

'He'll give us all a headache with those,' Mags said.

'Sure, won't the weather do that? A good storm would clear the air. Dare I ask has anything been heard of herself?'

'No. Not a word,' Grace replied. 'God knows where she is.'

'I had a letter from Pat yesterday. He says he's managing. He's had to take on more help but there are always plenty of lads looking for work, the country is still in a desperate state altogether. He said he misses Uncle Con at every turn and I suppose it's only to be expected but time will help to heal that. I'm going to send him some money and ask him to have Father Doyle say a few masses for Sadie.'

Mags rose. 'We'd better get back. I don't like to leave her for too long. Will you give those little bells back to your Aunty Eileen now, Thomas?'

The little boy hung on to them.

'Ah, let him take them with him, Mags. I'll collect them tonight. You don't want a tantrum.'

'You spoil him. He'll have to learn he can't have everything he wants,' Mags chided gently.

'Sure, he's only a baby!' Eileen said a little wistfully for although she'd been married a while now there had been no sign of a child of her own. Her sisters and brothers in America and Australia seemed to produce them regularly and with no bother at all, so why couldn't she?

After supper Georgie took his brother aside and told him as gently as he could that their mother wasn't long for this world.

'Why? Why, Georgie? She's not old enough to die! Only old people die!' the lad sobbed. He couldn't envisage a life where there was no mam putting his meal on the table, insisting he put on a clean shirt or collar or chiding him for his many transgressions.

'I don't know, Billy. Maybe God thinks she deserves some peace. She's had a very hard time of it, struggling on through the war. She's . . . she's going to Da now and Harold and you know how she misses them.'

Billy was inconsolable. 'But what about us? We'll miss her!'

Georgie was struggling to keep his composure. 'Of course we will, but she's in terrible pain, Billy, and has been for a long time. We can't wish any more on her, can we?'

Billy shook his head and wiped his face with his shirtsleeve, something Sadie would have had a fit about had she seen it, Georgie thought sadly.

'And, Billy, you've got to be brave about it. She doesn't know. You can't go breaking down in front of her,' he urged, thinking his brother had a lot of growing up to do in the coming months.

Billy sniffed. 'I'll try, Georgie.'

'And there's something else she doesn't know either.'

Billy looked at him fearfully. Things couldn't get any worse, could they? 'What's that?'

'That our Chrissie has run off and left Pat. That's why Grace came home; with the old uncle dead she couldn't stay on living in the same house. It wouldn't have been proper.'

Billy looked at him, puzzled. 'Where . . . where's she gone?'

Georgie looked grim. 'I don't know and I don't care! She's run off with someone else, some tinker feller! She's a living disgrace to us all! We're not going to tell Mam, she'll only get upset and start worrying and that won't help but I never want to see our Chrissie again.'

Billy nodded. 'I won't say nothing to her.'

'Good lad. Now go and wash your face. Eileen Bateson will be here soon. She's going to come and nurse Mam through the night so Mags and Grace can get some sleep. They'll look after her during the day and Mrs Nelson will help too.'

'Can I go and see her before Eileen comes?' Billy asked pitifully.

'Of course, if you think you can face it. If you can't just yet, everyone will understand, Billy. It takes time to really sink in.'

Billy squared his shoulders. 'I'll be all right, really I will, Georgie.'

Georgie watched his younger brother go into the scullery and sighed heavily. Billy's carefree, irresponsible days were over, just as his own had been the day they'd got the news that Harold's ship had been lost. He'd grown up a lot that day and in all the days that had followed.

Mags came into the kitchen. 'You've told him?' she said quietly.

He nodded and then covered his face with his hands, his shoulders shaking.

Mags went and put her arms around him. 'Oh, luv, I know it's hard. It's so hard on all of us. We all love her and don't want to lose her.'

Georgie leaned his head against her. 'I've lost my da and our Harold and now Mam. Oh, Mags, sometimes everything looks so bleak!'

Mags stroked his hair. It must be terrible for him, she thought. She was so fortunate that her parents were still alive and she'd not lost anyone close during the war years. Even her Aunty Flo had been widowed before war had broken out. She had to try to bolster his spirits. 'Look at the good things, luv. We've got each other and Thomas. Grace is home now and everyone's standard of living is steadily improving. Even Billy won't be giving us much cause for concern when he goes in the Army.'

Georgie nodded, making an effort to pull himself together. 'We do have a lot to be grateful for, Mags, but the next weeks are going to be hard.'

'I know but we'll get through, Georgie. Hush now, Billy's coming and we don't want him to get even more upset.'

Eileen was as good as her word and she came every evening at half past six and stayed until either Grace or Mags got up in the morning. Dr Schofield came regularly too and he confided to Grace that they were indeed fortunate to have someone of Mrs Bateson's experience to help them through this difficult time.

As the days passed Sadie lapsed in and out of consciousness and Eileen explained that it was the strength of the medicine that had this effect.

'At least she doesn't seem to be in such pain, thank God,' Grace had replied, thinking that there could hardly be anything worse than having to watch her mother slowly losing her grip on life.

Billy was much quieter and didn't go out with his mate Tommy Milligan. He went up each evening to sit with Sadie for half an hour before Eileen came. Sometimes she could chat for a little while and sometimes she couldn't and for the first time he fully understood what it meant to lose someone. Both his da and his elder brother's deaths had been quick. They had come as a shock and he'd been upset, but he'd been much younger then. He'd accepted the fact that Harold was never coming home, as he'd also come to accept that his da would never again give him a telling off or a clip around the ear. They'd both died bravely too, something he was proud of. But his poor mam was slipping slowly away from him day by day. He was watching her go and that was very different. The time he spent with her became something precious.

Sadie was perfectly lucid one afternoon when Grace went up to see her.

'Let me fix those pillows, Mam. They've slipped a bit and you don't look comfortable.'

'Has Polly gone?' Sadie asked as Grace lifted her slightly and moved the pillows.

'She has for now.'

'She's been a good friend and neighbour, Grace. We've shared the good times and the bad.'

'I know, Mam.'

Sadie caught her hand and held it but her grip was weak. 'I've not got long now, Grace. I know that.'

Grace bit her lip, not knowing what to say and fighting back the tears.

'Don't get upset, luv. I'll be . . . glad. I know your da is waiting for me and . . . and . . . my lad. I'm tired, Grace. It's been so . . . hard.'

Grace could only nod, knowing if she tried to speak she would break down.

'Georgie and Mags will be all right and the Army will sort Billy out, make a man of him. He's not a bad lad. Chrissie and Pat will make a . . . go of it too. It's you, Grace, I worry about.'

'Oh, Mam! Don't worry about me!' Grace managed to get out. The mention of Pat's name only added to her misery.

'I wanted to see you . . . settled, luv.'

'I . . . I will be one day, Mam.'

'Don't . . . don't make the same mistake as Chrissie,'

Sadie pleaded, then fell silent. She was exhausted.

'Oh, Mam, I won't. I . . . can't . . . because—' She stopped herself.

'Find a good man, like your da, and then . . .' Sadie's voice trailed off.

Grace bent and kissed the thin cheek, the skin of which was just like parchment. 'I'll wait until I've found one, I promise,' she whispered. She longed to throw herself into her mother's arms and tell her that she had already found the man she loved and that he was a good man but that she'd never be able to marry him. She longed for the comfort her mother could once have given her but now could not.

They were all with Sadie when she breathed her last early the following morning. Grace, Georgie and Mags, Billy, Polly Nelson and Father Weaver. It was Eileen who had sent for the priest. Mary Nelson was looking after little Thomas downstairs.

'She's at peace now. May God have mercy on her soul,' the parish priest said quietly.

Georgie put his arm around his wife who buried her face in his shoulder. Grace held a quietly sobbing Billy in her arms while her own tears slid down her cheeks.

Polly dabbed at her eyes with her apron and nodded to Eileen and they both went downstairs, Polly to tell Mary to take the baby out for a walk in his pram, Eileen to put the kettle on; they'd all need a cup of strong sweet tea for there were arrangements to be made. Later on

Polly would go and collect a few pence from each of the neighbours towards a wreath. Sadie Devlin had been well liked and respected in Royal Street. The whole street would be in mourning, all the curtains would be closed and would remain so until after the funeral as a mark of that respect.

Chapter Thirty-Five

———◆◆◆———

CHRISSIE CAME DOWN THE steps of the caravan and looked around frowning. They'd been travelling for six months now and this place certainly couldn't be called 'picturesque'. They were on the outskirts of the industrial town of St Helens: factory chimneys seemed to dominate the skyline and the smoke from both them and the hundreds of back-to-back terraced houses almost blotted out the weak October sunlight. They were heading back towards Liverpool and then to North Wales and the port of Holyhead and the chill of autumn was in the air. It had been a long and tedious journey from the last in what seemed like an endless round of horse fairs in Yorkshire. She had certainly seen a lot of the country, she thought, but they never seemed to be allowed to stay in what could be called 'decent' places. It was always somewhere like this.

'Chrissie, have ye that fire made up and the water on yet?'

Chrissie turned and stared at Bridie McDonagh. She'd come to thoroughly dislike Johnny's mother who was always nagging her; and his sisters who openly showed her nothing but contempt.

'I'm waiting for Johnny to fetch the water for me,' she answered sharply.

'Why could ye not fetch it instead of having him running after ye like one of the curs? 'Tis not right. 'Tis woman's work.' Bridie had no liking for Chrissie and didn't bother to hide it.

'Because I hurt my back carting the firewood yesterday and he was going to water the horses anyway.' Chrissie poked at the embers of the fire with her foot. It wasn't much to ask and he certainly didn't do a great deal to help her.

Bridie turned away and shooed before her a group of shouting and laughing children who were followed by half a dozen mangy-looking dogs, and Chrissie sat down on a three-legged stool and attempted to revive the fire. The place was a mess, she thought: kids, dogs and horses everywhere, to say nothing of washing thrown over the few straggly bushes to dry and the rubbish they always seemed to accumulate, would make even the prettiest of meadows look terrible. And this site was just a piece of wasteland on the edge of a town. She was tired. She was constantly tired for she worked far harder now than she had ever done in Ireland, and she felt permanently grubby and untidy. All her clothes were ruined by the life she now led; she had nothing remotely decent to wear when she ventured into a town. Her hair had grown and she'd tried to cut it herself with disastrous results. She ran her fingers through it; she would have to just scrape it back for she hadn't been able to find her hairbrush this morning.

'I've brought you two buckets. Make them last or you'll have to go and get more yourself. I'll not be at your beck and call all day.'

She looked up at Johnny. Oh, he was still handsome, she thought, but looks were superficial. He wasn't the person she had believed him to be, but then if she were brutally honest with herself she hadn't known him well at all when she'd run off with him. After the first month she had noticed a change in his attitude towards her. He was less considerate, less romantic and it had got worse these last few weeks. Now she knew that he was selfish and impatient and could be arrogant and offhand at times. Like the rest of the men and boys all he thought about was horses, food and his own comfort, in that order. These days she came very low down on his list of priorities.

'Well, don't be expecting any clean shirts. I can't carry heavy buckets. Unless you want me to be laid up permanently and then you'll get no meals either,' she answered sullenly.

He stared down at her with dislike. He never should have agreed to bring her along; it had been sheer madness. He'd quickly grown tired of her. She was lazy and spoiled and expected him to put her first. She knew nothing of their ways and she was terrified of horses. That fact alone had caused him a great deal of embarrassment amongst his kin.

'You'd still better be getting the washing done today, we're moving on tomorrow morning, so you'll have to be packed up and ready.' He turned away before she could answer him back. That was another thing that embarrassed him. She didn't know her place. She always argued with him and his ma and she refused to accompany his mother and sisters into the towns and villages when they went selling pegs and bits of finery.

'Oh, for God's sake, we've only just got here! I'm sick to death of having to pack up!' Chrissie yelled after him. This was a worse life than anything she had ever known before. She hadn't been accepted at all. She was still watched with suspicion and resentment by the travellers and wherever they went they were all shunned. People everywhere mistrusted them. In some places they had encountered outright hostility and on two occasions the police had come and forced them to move on. She had never felt so humiliated in all her life as she'd been then. Even at the last fair a gang of men had shouted abuse at her. It had been awful. She'd wanted to scream back that she wasn't one of them but all she'd been able to do was

run away and they'd laughed and jeered at her. She'd
got no sympathy from Johnny either. He'd told her she
would just have to get used to it.

He turned back towards her now. 'You wanted to
come with me. You were the one who pleaded not to be
left behind. I warned you, so I did.' They'd had this
argument so many times before that he was bored.

'You never said it was going to be like this!'

'I did so. I told you you'd find it a hardship but you
said you knew all about hardship.'

Chrissie glared at him. Oh, how everything had
changed. At first, she hadn't cared that no one
welcomed her with open arms, because he'd warned
her about that. She'd found the caravan 'cosy and
quaint' and told him so. He'd laughed saying he'd
never heard one called that before. She'd even taken a
turn at driving the horse that pulled it. Everything had
been a novelty then; now she hated the cramped
caravan where there was barely room to move and very
little storage space and she longed for a proper house
with decent facilities and some comforts. Like a fire in
the hearth, a bedroom with wardrobes, a kitchen where
there was no need to take such care about which dishes
were used for eating and those used only for such
things as washing. And at first he'd been good
company: he'd been attentive and loving and their time
together had been wonderful – but only at first. Then
he'd begun to spend more and more time with the
other men, leaving her isolated once more, for the

other women didn't speak to her much, except to order her about. She'd had to learn to stand up for herself.

He narrowed his eyes. He was sick of her. 'Sure, you're nothing but a burden to me, Chrissie! A burden and an embarrassment. When we get back to Ireland you can take yourself back to the place you came from – if they'll have you!'

Chrissie got to her feet bitterly hurt and furiously angry. 'I hate you! I hate you all! You won't have to "burden" yourself with me any longer. You can pack this damned heap of junk up yourself. I'm going to Liverpool. It's not that far and you can give me the money for my train fare! I have a decent family to go to which is more than I can say for you!'

He threw a handful of coins at her, his eyes blazing at the insult. 'You can go to hell, Chrissie, for all I care! You'll be no loss at all!'

She picked the coins up from the ground as he walked away and then noticed that his mother had witnessed the row.

'Ye are a bold, ungrateful trollop and ye'll be no loss! Didn't I tell him a hundred times it was wrong what he'd done? He should never have brung ye with him, ye are not one of us and never will be. Get ye gone!' Bridie snapped.

She stormed up the steps of the caravan and grabbed her bag and began to stuff a few things into it, then she snatched up her shawl.

Bridie was standing with a small group of women and children and she glared at them defiantly.

'I'll not even say goodbye – it's good riddance!' she yelled and pulling the shawl up over her head she marched away with as much dignity she could muster.

By the time she reached the station she was beginning to feel miserable. It had started to rain and it had been a long walk and she was sorry she'd even bothered to bring a bag. Everything in it could only be considered rags. She could hardly remember the days when she'd been dressed in the height of fashion. Now she barely had a shoe to her foot. She'd been only too aware of the hostile glances, the looks of contempt, as she'd walked into town. Everyone thought she was a tinker woman. Oh, she knew she had behaved very badly indeed, running off with him, but she'd been at her wits' end then. She laughed bitterly to herself. She'd still been an eejit of a girl then. If only she'd known what life on the road was like. She would apologise for everything she had done and she would turn over a new leaf, she would! She had at last learned that there was far more to life than just dressing up and going out. She'd hurt so many people in that quest for enjoyment. Well, now she'd get a job and she'd save. She would help Mam in the house and she wouldn't even want to go gallivanting around. She'd even help Mags with the baby. He was over a year old and she hadn't even seen him.

She wasn't looking forward to facing Georgie but when she told him of the terrible time she'd had and promised to try to make amends, surely he'd forgive her? She was still only twenty-two; she would make a new life for herself. She would become steady and reliable. If they would just take her back she would show them all that finally she had grown up.

She was very relieved when she learned that she had enough for her train fare to Lime Street Station. She didn't know exactly how far St Helens was from Liverpool but it would have taken her ages, maybe even a whole day, to walk. There was nothing left for tram fare from the station home but that couldn't be helped.

As it was nearly mid-morning the train wasn't busy and she was glad to find an empty compartment. She'd caught a glimpse of herself in one of the mirrored advertisements that adorned the station walls. Now she realised why people had looked at her with contempt. She looked terrible. She did indeed look like a tinker. Her hair was tangled and needed washing. Her clothes were creased and grubby. She had no stockings and even her shawl was of the type they wore. Mam would have a fit at her appearance. She prayed that no one would recognise her as she walked up Royal Street: Mam would be mortified.

By the time the train pulled into Lime Street she was hungry and thirsty and feeling very apprehensive. She had managed to doze a little but her back still ached and now she had a long walk ahead of her.

Before she went out on to Lime Street she went into the ladies' waiting room. She didn't even have the required tuppence for a 'wash and brush up' and the attendant eyed her suspiciously.

'I 'ope yer're not intendin' ter stop in 'ere long, girl? This place is fer respectable women,' the woman said grimly.

'No. I'm just going to try to tidy my hair. I'm going home to Royal Street to my family. I . . . I've fallen on hard times, you see,' she answered as politely as she could.

'Is that a fact? Well, I 'ope yer're not lookin' fer a 'andout from me!'

'I'm not,' Chrissie answered curtly, her cheeks growing pink. She wasn't begging! She did the best she could with her hair and then adjusted the shawl. The shawl! Oh, the shame of it! Con had once called her a 'slummy' and now that's just what she looked like.

She left the station and walked on past the Empire Theatre and up London Road. She stopped when she reached T. J. Hughes and looked in at the window displays. They'd never take her back in there! Well, nor did she want them to. She'd find somewhere else. Half-heartedly she noticed that there was so much more in the shops now than when she'd left England.

She moved off slowly, retracing her steps and heading for Byrom Street but by the time she'd reached it she felt slightly sick. She realised she'd had nothing to eat since early that morning and now it was early afternoon. As she trudged along Scotland Road she looked hungrily into the window of the shops that sold food. Oh, she wished now that she'd had the sense to take a few shillings from the box *he'd* kept his money in. She could have had a wash at the station, she could have got a cup of tea and something to eat and she could have caught a tram home. She still had the length of Scotland Road and Kirkdale Road to walk, then up Everton Valley and she was exhausted!

She stopped at the junction of the two main roads and leaned against the wall of a pub. If she just had something to eat – *anything*, even a dry crust – it would help.

A policeman turned the corner and eyed her without favour. 'Move along, girl! You're not loitering on my beat! And it's an offence to beg.'

Chrissie stared up at him, near to tears. 'I wasn't begging, sir, I'd just stopped for a rest. I've travelled from St Helens and, I've walked from Lime Street. I'm going home to Royal Street. I'm a decent girl, sir, I am! I know what I . . . look like, but . . .' She was too tired and humiliated to go on.

'What were you doing in St Helens?' he asked more kindly.

'Trying to get work. There're plenty of factories there and I heard there were jobs but . . . but I had no luck,' she lied. She didn't want to admit that she'd been living with the travellers. 'I spent the last of my money on the train fare.'

'How long is it since you've eaten?' She wasn't a beggar or a streetwalker, he could see that now, but she looked half-starved and as if she'd been sleeping rough.

'I've had nothing since early morning, sir.'

He dug into his pocket and brought out a sixpence and handed it to her. 'There's a pie shop just down the road. Get yourself something to eat or you'll be falling down in a faint and then I'll have the trouble of sending you to the hospital.'

'Oh, thank you!'

'Get off with you now or it will be dark before you get home.'

The shop not only sold pies and pasties and assorted pastries but there was a little room at the back where you could eat them if you wanted to. She bought a pie and a pasty and asked for a mug of tea. She sank down thankfully on one of the wooden benches and devoured the food and at length a young girl brought her a small pot of tea and a mug. When she'd finished she felt much better and at last got to her feet, reluctant to leave the warmth and comfort of the place. Still, there really wasn't that much further to go now, she thought.

The dusk of the autumn evening was beginning to fall when she resumed her journey and she hugged her shawl closer to her for the air was damp and chilly. She'd asked the young girl to dump her bag in the nearest bin. She wasn't carrying it any further; it wasn't worth it for the rubbish that it contained.

It was almost dark when she finally reached the top of Royal Street and she heaved a sigh of pure relief. She'd made it. Oh, everything was so familiar – dearly familiar. The big soot-blackened Methodist church on the corner, on the railings of which the banner she and Ellie had made when Georgie had come home had been fastened; the steep cobbled roadway that led down to Walton Road and the Astoria Cinema. The neat houses with their bay windows. Tommy Milligan's house, the Bradshaws', the McMurrays', the Sheills' and then Polly Nelson's and then . . . With what energy she had left she quickened her steps and finally began to run. She was home.

Chapter Thirty-Six

———◆———

G RACE SLOWLY STIRRED THE pan of scouse for the
evening meal. The table was set but it still seemed
strange to be setting it just for three. Billy had gone
down to the training camp at Aldershot two weeks ago.
They'd all gone to see him off and he looked strangely
neat and tidy and a bit self-conscious and ill at ease in
his uniform.

'You'll be just fine, Billy. And both Mam and Da
would be proud of you. I know it's not the same thing as
going off to fight for King and Country but if we ever
need soldiers again – God forbid – you'll all be trained,'
Georgie had said as he'd shaken his brother's hand.

'I just hope he will be fine, he's taken Ma's death
hard,' Mags had said with concern as they'd waved him
off.

They'd had two letters from him and he said he was enjoying it, the discipline was a bit hard to take but he supposed he'd get used to it and he'd made quite a few mates already. Grace sighed. She still couldn't get used to Mam not being here. She missed her so much. The house was sometimes unbearably quiet, she thought. Especially of an evening. She still hadn't settled back into city life even though she'd asked to be taken on full time at work. There was no need for her to spend days at home now and it would take her mind off the absence of both her mam and Billy but most of all it would help her to stop constantly thinking of Pat. It was six months now since she'd had to leave him but it seemed like six years and even though Mags had assured her that 'time would heal' the longing for him hadn't faded at all.

She turned down the gas under the pan, leaving it simmering slightly. She cut the thick slices of bread to go with the meal and then made up the fire. It was getting colder now so a good plate of scouse would warm Georgie up when he got in.

Mags had been bathing little Thomas and she came in with him wrapped in a big towel. 'I'm soaked! I tried to take those plastic ducks you bought him away because he splashes them – and me – but he yelled blue murder. When I've got him ready for bed I'll have to get changed.'

'Give him to me and get that blouse off before you get a chill,' Grace instructed. 'The pan is on a low light, it won't burn.'

Mags handed the baby over and Grace sat down beside the range with him on her knee. He looked like a fat little cherub, she thought fondly as he played with the ring Pat had given her and which she wore on a chain around her neck, although he was far from being an angel most of the time. Mags always said he looked absolutely gorgeous – when he was asleep!

Mags returned having changed the damp blouse for a knitted jumper and took the baby from Grace to get him ready for bed. They both looked up in surprise at the sound of the door knocker.

'Who on earth can this be at teatime?' Mags wondered. It wasn't Georgie or Polly, they always came in the back way, and besides Polly would be getting the evening meal ready herself, as would most other women in the street.

Grace frowned, hoping it wasn't the priest doing his rounds. If it was he would have to be given tea in the parlour and Georgie would be in any minute and he'd be hungry. 'I'll go. But if it's anyone selling things they'll be sent off with a flea in their ear, calling at this time of day!'

Nothing could have prepared her for the sight that met her eyes when she opened the door. At first she didn't recognise her sister, thinking it was someone begging. Only when the shawl slipped back from Chrissie's head and the light from the lobby caught her features did Grace realise who it was.

'Mother of God! Chrissie!'

Chrissie burst into tears. 'Grace! Oh, Grace, I've come home! I'm sorry! I'm so, so sorry for all the trouble I've caused!'

Grace stood staring at her in disbelief. Chrissie looked terrible. She'd never seen her sister look so downright scruffy, no wonder she'd taken her for an unfortunate beggar.

'Please, Grace, can I come in?' Chrissie cried for Grace hadn't uttered a word nor had she made any move to bring her indoors.

Still shocked, Grace automatically opened the door wider and Chrissie stepped thankfully into the hallway.

'Grace, who is it?' Mags called from the kitchen.

Grace finally found her voice. 'You'd better go on in but don't expect to be greeted with open arms, Chrissie.' So, she'd left Johnny McDonagh too, she thought wearily. Well, it had been a foregone conclusion and only a matter of time.

Chrissie turned and grasped her arm. 'I . . . I don't but I couldn't stand it any longer, Grace! It was far, far worse than living in Rahan. They all hated me!'

Grace nodded slowly. Just what had Chrissie expected?

'But I've changed, Grace, I have!'

Grace just couldn't find the words of acceptance and comfort her sister seemed to expect. Chrissie had wrecked too many lives. Instead she pushed her gently towards the kitchen.

Mags stood up and her eyes widened. 'What the—?'

'She's left him and come home,' Grace said flatly.

Mags groaned. 'Oh, God! Chrissie, what's wrong with you? You can't go on doing this to us!'

Grace bit her lip. Now she could see clearly in the brighter light just how much her sister had changed in the last months. She was dirty, bedraggled, her clothes little better than rags but, worse, she looked older, careworn and somehow . . . defeated.

'I'm sorry, I really am! I haven't anywhere else to go and I . . . I just wanted to come home.' Chrissie was again crying. She'd known it wouldn't be easy but she had expected a bit more sympathy.

Before Mags could reply the scullery door opened and Georgie stood in the doorway. He stared at Chrissie, shocked and unable to believe his eyes, then anger flooded through him.

'What the hell is *she* doing here?' he demanded.

'What do you think? She's left him too,' Mags answered.

'Mags, take Thomas up to bed,' Georgie instructed quietly, knowing that a row of mammoth proportions was in the offing for he'd sworn that Chrissie would never be allowed to come back here again. She'd caused too much heartache and he couldn't forgive her for not getting in touch with them since she'd left Pat.

Mags nodded. She had no wish for her little son to be upset by what was surely to follow, even though he wouldn't understand.

'I . . . I couldn't stand it, Georgie, I *couldn't*! You've

451

no idea what it's like living like . . . *that*. Everything is so cramped and untidy and dirty. People hate you, really *hate* you. They look at you as if you're dirt. The police move you on and . . . and I've even been spat at!'

'What did you expect, Chrissie? As usual, you didn't *think*! You ran off and left Pat without a single thought for how he would feel or how he would face people. You've had to suffer humiliation so now you know how he felt. You've never thought about anyone except yourself! You've left a trail of ruined lives and broken hearts behind you but I don't expect you gave that much thought. Nothing mattered to you except your happiness! You didn't care that you shamed us all with that . . . that lowlife. You're no better than a whore, you who were brought up in a decent home. You're a *disgrace*!'

Chrissie hadn't expected such unforgiving fury. 'I . . . I realise that now, Georgie, I do and I'm so, so sorry, believe me!' she beseeched him.

'No, you don't realise and you never will. You were responsible for the old man's death, Chrissie. Con had another stroke the day after you ran off. You robbed Pat of his uncle.'

Chrissie shook her head, her shoulders heaving. 'I didn't mean to, Georgie. I didn't know he'd die. I didn't!'

'Again you didn't *think* what effect it would have had on him. When I heard what you'd done I vowed you'd never set foot in this house again. I don't care where you go, Chrissie, but you're not staying here. I mean it!'

'I've nowhere else to go, Georgie! Please, Georgie, please? I . . . I want to see Mam. Mam will know I'm sorry, she'll know I've changed, she'll believe me!' Chrissie pleaded. Sadie would never turn her out.

Grace's heart softened towards her sister. 'Chrissie, oh, Chrissie – Mam . . . Mam's dead. She died at the end of August. She had cancer.'

Chrissie looked at her in horror, her knees buckled and she sank down on to a chair. No, It couldn't be true . . . her mam couldn't be *dead*!

'If you had thought about anyone other than yourself and got in touch with either Grace or me we could have let you know how ill she was.' Georgie's voice cracked with the pain he still felt at his mother's death. This was what had turned him irrevocably against his sister: her callous, selfish attitude towards Sadie. He'd never forgive her for that.

Chrissie was sobbing brokenly now. Oh, if only she could turn back the clock. If only she could go back to the days before she had so foolishly run off to marry Pat Kilroy. She had thought life was dull and tedious then, she had felt cheated out of her youth by the war, she had wanted so much to enjoy the rest of her life but she had known nothing . . . nothing! Now Mam was dead and buried and her brother hated her, she'd heard it in his voice.

Grace put her arm around her shoulders. 'Why didn't you get in touch, Chrissie? You promised you would and we would have found a way to tell you about Mam.'

Georgie paced the floor, his anger increasing for she had all but ruined Pat Kilroy's life. 'Because she didn't care, she was too bloody selfish. Don't take her side, Grace! Don't forget you gave up your life here to go and try to help her but did she care? No. She's never really cared about anyone except herself.'

'I did! I did care about Mam!' Chrissie wept.

'You had a fine way of showing it, Chrissie. Well, it doesn't change things, you've caused enough trouble. You're not staying here to cause more.'

'I won't! Oh, I promise I won't!' Chrissie cried.

'You will. You're not staying here!'

Chrissie shook off Grace's arm and stood up. 'Georgie, please? If I have to go down on my knees and beg, I will. I've nowhere to go and no money. Look at the state of me. I only had my train fare. I had to walk the rest of the way. A policeman gave me the money for something to eat, I was faint with hunger!' Her voice was shrill with desperation.

Georgie turned his back on her. 'You can beg in the street for all I care. You've brought nothing but disgrace on us all. I disown you – I never want to see you again! Get out!'

Chrissie recoiled physically from his words and, uttering a despairing wail, pushed past Grace and ran out of the room.

'Oh, Georgie! Please, please don't send her away,'

Grace begged, her face white with shock. She hadn't thought he would turn Chrissie out, not when he could see that her sister was almost hysterical. 'Please go after her. She can't walk the streets. She's had a terrible shock, she didn't know about either Con or Mam and you only have to look at the state of her to see that. She . . . she's destitute, Georgie,' she implored him.

Mags finally came downstairs; Thomas was asleep even though you couldn't have failed to hear the shouting. 'Where's she gone?'

'I told her to go. I told her I wasn't going to let her stay here and cause us more trouble,' Georgie said.

'Oh, Georgie!'

'I'm right, Mags, she *would* only create more strife in the end. She'll find someone to take care of her – she always does. Or she can go back to him.' Georgie's tone was resolute.

'Mags, she's no money and nowhere to go,' Grace entreated him. Oh, she knew her brother was enraged and she herself would find it hard to forgive Chrissie but she couldn't see her sister homeless.

Mags sat down at the table, consternation in her eyes. 'Georgie, maybe . . . maybe you should reconsider? She could get into even worse trouble if she's at her wits' end. We can't leave her to roam the city streets penniless, God knows what would happen to her. At least if she's here we can try to keep her on the straight and narrow and she just might have finally learned her lesson.'

Georgie looked from his wife to his sister and then threw his hands in the air in exasperation. 'I give up! I can't fight both of you! Do whatever you want but don't come complaining to me when she starts wreaking havoc or runs off again with some feller who takes her fancy and makes us the talk of the neighbourhood.'

Grace looked at them both and then turned and ran from the room, down the lobby and out on to the street. She had to go after Chrissie. Matters couldn't be left like this. Mam would never rest in peace.

Chrissie stumbled onwards, blinded by tears, down towards Walton Road. She was crying hysterically and she was shaking and she had no idea where she was going. She couldn't even think clearly. Oh, why hadn't Georgie believed her when she'd said she was sorry, that she'd change? Why was he being so cruel? Why? Mam was dead and he'd said she had been responsible for Con's death too. He'd said she had broken too many hearts and now she knew she *had* but what could she do? Where could she go now?

Grace caught sight of her at the bottom of the street and began to run faster. 'Chrissie! Chrissie! Wait! Stop, please, stop!' she screamed but her sister had turned the corner.

Chrissie ran on. She hadn't even heard Grace's cries. She could hear nothing but the pounding of her own heart and Georgie's words beating mercilessly in her head. She didn't hear the desperate, warning shouts of the carter or the two policemen who were racing after the bolting carthorse. She didn't hear the thudding of the wrecked cart as it was bounced and jolted against the cobbles but as the pounding became louder she dimly realised it wasn't in her head any longer and she at last looked up. And then she stopped, petrified, unable to move a muscle as the huge dark shape, the black mane flying, eyes rolling white with terror, bore down on her.

Grace turned the corner in time to see her sister go down beneath the hooves of the terrified animal. She screamed Chrissie's name and then someone caught her and held her to stop her from falling to the ground. She looked up and caught sight of the face beneath the helmet but it was rapidly blurring. 'She ... she's ... terrified of big animals,' she whispered before everything went dark and she passed out.

Chapter Thirty-Seven

AS GRACE CAME TO SHE struggled to get up; her head was swimming and there seemed to be a great deal of noise in the background.

'Steady now, luv. Take it easy for a minute or two.'

The policeman was bending over her, his face full of concern. 'Chrissie! Is . . . is she . . .'

He shook his head sadly. 'I'm so sorry, there was nothing any of us could do. She just stood there, she didn't seem to hear us shouting at her to get out of the way.'

Grace stared up at him, her eyes wide with disbelief. 'She . . . she's . . . dead?'

He nodded and helped her to her feet. 'You knew her?'

She felt cold and numb and she had started to tremble. 'She's my sister.'

The constable took off his heavy cape and wrapped it around her. It was bad enough her having to witness such a terrible accident but the fact that that poor girl had been her sister made it far worse. 'Where do you live, luv? We'd better get you home.'

'Just . . . just up Royal Street. I . . . I ran after her. There was a terrible row and she fled. Oh, Chrissie!' She collapsed against him, sobbing.

He put his arm around her and guided her towards the bottom of the street. Behind them a small crowd had gathered around the police sergeant, another constable and the ashen-faced carter who now hung on to the bridle of the quivering, foam-flecked but stationary horse as the sound of an ambulance could be heard as it hurtled along Walton Road, bell ringing. 'It's all right, luv. Let's get you home. The sergeant and the ambulance men will take care of everything. There's nothing you can do now.'

Mags was standing on the doorstep, her forehead creased in a worried frown, her coat around her shoulders. She'd been so upset and concerned about Grace running after Chrissie that she'd insisted on waiting and watching. On catching sight of the two figures coming towards her her hand went to her mouth. Dear God, what now? she thought. She ran the few steps towards them.

'Grace, what's wrong? Are you hurt? Where's Chrissie? Did you find her?' she cried, looking up into the serious face of the constable.

'She's had a terrible shock. We'd best get her inside.'

Mags guided them both into the house, a feeling of dread creeping over her.

'It's Grace and a . . . a policeman,' she informed Georgie as they entered the kitchen.

Mags eased Grace down into a chair. Her stomach was churning with fear for she'd never seen her sister-in-law in such a state. Grace was trembling, her face was ashen and she was weeping uncontrollably. And where was Chrissie?

'What the hell has happened? I'm her brother George Devlin.'

'Chrissie was your sister too?' the constable asked. At moments like this he hated this job.

Georgie stared at him; he hadn't failed to notice that the man had spoken of Chrissie in the past tense. His mouth had gone dry and there was a lump of fear in his throat and he could only nod.

'I think you'd better sit down, sir. It's bad news, I'm afraid. The worst.'

The colour drained from Mags's face as the constable informed them of the accident. She looked pityingly at Georgie as he groaned and dropped his head in his hands. How was he going to live with this? she thought in horror. Chrissie had been distraught, hysterical almost, so much so that . . .

'She just sort of froze, sir. We were all yelling at her but she didn't seem to hear, she just stood there . . .'

Georgie looked up, his eyes haunted. 'God forgive

me, it's my fault. There was a row and I told her to get out.'

Through the mist of shock and grief Grace heard the pain and guilt in his voice. 'How could you have known what would happen? I screamed at her too but she . . . she was terrified of big animals, especially horses, and it all happened so quickly. If only I'd have left sooner or run faster . . .' She was racked by sobs once more.

The constable took the situation in hand. 'Now there's no use in blaming yourselves, that's going to help no one. The sooner these blasted animals are off the streets the better, there's countless people injured every year by them and the carter's in a dreadful state over it. God knows what caused the horse to bolt but it was an accident, pure and simple. The poor lass was in the wrong place at the wrong time. There will be an inquest and the Coroner will confirm that it was an awful accident. Now, is there anyone I can fetch to help you?'

Mags pulled herself together, taking some comfort from the man's words. 'Polly Nelson, she lives next door, please.'

'Right, I'll go and get her and if you can make a cup of strong sweet tea, Mrs Devlin, that would be a help.'

The next hour was all a blur to Grace. There seemed to be people in and out of the kitchen. Polly and Alf, two more policemen, Father Weaver and finally Dr Schofield who gave her a sedative and instructed that she go to bed. It was Polly who helped her upstairs.

'It's a terrible, terrible thing, luv, but you must try

and sleep. She's at peace now, Grace. She's with your mam and da,' she comforted her.

As the sedative took effect Grace tried to cling to those words. In all the nightmares that lay ahead when she would see her poor terrified sister go down under the hooves of that huge animal, she would console herself that at last Chrissie was at peace, that there was no more pain.

When Polly went downstairs the police had gone and so had the doctor, only Father Weaver remained in the kitchen with Mags and Georgie.

'She's asleep. Oh, Father, what a shocking thing for the poor girl to have to witness.' Polly herself felt numb.

'It was but Grace has always been a strong girl, she'll get over it in time and with God's help. Now, I think it best if we leave you two to try to get some rest. You have Thomas to see to, Mags, you have to think of him and believe me neither of you are to blame.' Mags, in great distress, had told him how Chrissie had left Pat and run off with Johnny McDonagh and had then left him and come home, knowing nothing of the death of either Con or Sadie. In between sobs she'd told him of the row and of how Georgie had told his sister to leave. It had all saddened him greatly. 'Chrissie, may God have mercy on her, was a troubled girl. I doubt she would ever have found peace and contentment on this earth. You all did your best for her and she brought you great distress and sorrow. You can't go on living under a cloud of guilt, you have to put it aside or it will destroy your little family. God is good and time will heal. I will pray for you all and you can leave all the . . . arrangements to me.'

'Thank you, Father,' Georgie replied, trying to take some comfort from the priest's words. He was utterly devastated and at this moment he felt he would never be free of the remorse that now overwhelmed him.

'Would you like me to write to her husband?'

Georgie shook his head. 'Thank you, Father, but no. I'll do that and I'll have to let Billy know too.'

Polly and the priest left together and Mags put her arms around Georgie. 'We'd better try and get some rest although I know there will be little sleep tonight. I . . . I just can't believe she's . . . dead! Poor Chrissie, she was so unhappy. Georgie, I know you really *did* care about her. You were angry and you had a right to be considering the way she'd behaved, but we couldn't ever have imagined that . . . that this would happen! You have to believe that; we both do. Father Weaver was right, she brought us so much misery and worry but we . . . we didn't wish her . . .'

He held her tightly. 'Don't say it, Mags! We neither of us wished *this* on her! We can never turn back the clock but at this very moment I wish we could. I'd give anything to be able to say to her, "Chrissie, stay, this is your home no matter what you've done," but . . . but I can't, Mags. I can't!' His tears fell into her dark curls and sobs shook him.

'We'll have to have faith in Father Weaver's words.

We can't live under a cloud of guilt and I won't let it destroy you. We've all been through so much these last years, Georgie, we can't let this tear us apart.'

'I know, Mags, but it will be easier said than done.'

She kissed him on the cheek, tasting the salt of his tears. 'I know. Oh, I hope Grace will be all right, it's so much worse for her, she saw it happen.'

'At least she will have the consolation of knowing that she tried to help Chrissie. She ran after her; she was always trying to help her.'

Mags nodded sadly. Both she and Grace had pleaded for Chrissie but it didn't matter now. They all had to learn to live with this tragedy and it wouldn't be easy. Tears slid down her own cheeks. Poor, poor Chrissie. All she had wanted out of life had been some happiness. She had wanted to enjoy her life and that life had been cruelly cut short. She had been thoughtless, headstrong and often insensitive but she had been so very young – only twenty two – and that was far too young to die. It would take them all a long time to get over losing Chrissie, especially Georgie, but she would do everything in her power to help him.

Epilogue

'ARE YOU READY, GRACE?' Pat called up the stairs while glancing at the clock on the mantelshelf.

'I'll be down in a minute, will you tie that puppy up in the shed or I'll never get Conor out without him insisting it comes too and we can't be having it following us up to church,' Grace called back as she buttoned her little boy's coat up.

The child gazed up at her pleadingly. 'Mammy, why can't Spot come too?'

'You know why. Dogs can't go to church and if we tied him up outside he'd howl the place down and then Father Doyle would get cross.' She took his hand and smiled down at him; he was so like Pat. 'Now, come on down with me while your daddy gets out the trap.'

Every year on the anniversary of Chrissie's death they had a special Mass said for her in the church at

Killina: the church where both Chrissie and herself had been married and where little Conor Joseph Kilroy had been baptised.

Once they were outside the door Pat bent down and picked his son up and lifted him into the trap. 'Up you get now and if you're good I'll let you hold on to the reins with me for a little while.'

Grace climbed up beside him and they started out, leaving the darkening farmyard behind them. For October it wasn't too cold, she thought, not nearly as cold as it had been the night Chrissie had been killed. Her poor sister, she thought sadly as they drove between the silent fields. They had never found out what had caused that animal to bolt but such occurrences had been fairly frequent. At least there were not as many horses to cause mayhem on the city streets these days, she thought, lorries were replacing them. Of course it hadn't mattered to any of them in the days and nights that had followed. They had all been devastated but Georgie most of all; to this day he hadn't fully forgiven himself.

'How could any of you have known what would happen?' Polly had said on numerous occasions.

Pat had said the same thing to his brother-in-law. He'd come over for the funeral; he'd insisted. Billy had been granted compassionate leave and he had taken it all very well under the circumstances. It had taken Grace herself a long time to get over the trauma and until recently she had suffered nightmares.

She held little Conor tightly as they left the laneway and drove out on to the road to the church. He protested and begged to be allowed to hold the reins.

'Not until we get over the bridge and past the Thatch,' Pat said firmly. From there it wasn't far and the road would be quiet.

Grace tucked the rug more firmly around the child. He was impatient to learn everything and followed Pat around like a little shadow and Pat idolised him. He'd said it was the happiest moment in his life when she'd placed his son in his arms.

Before he'd returned to Ireland after the funeral he'd asked her to write to him and she had agreed. They'd kept in touch for over a year, their letters gradually becoming more and more intimate until finally he'd written and asked her to marry him. When she had returned to Rahan to be married Georgie, Mags and Thomas had come with her. They deserved a break, she had urged. A change of scenery would do them good and as Billy had had to continue his National Service, they were the only family members she would have present. Eileen and Joe Bateson had come over too but it had been a very quiet affair, not that she'd minded that.

They reached the church and as Pat helped them both down and tied up the pony, she was touched to see that Mary and Liam were there with the children and that Theresa and Caitlin Fahey had come to remember Chrissie.

'You never forget, Mary. It's kind of you.'

Mary smiled at her. 'Ah, Grace, how could I forget? You've been a great friend to me.'

Grace gave her a quick hug. 'And you to me.'

'We'd better be after getting this lot inside before they start any trick-acting and have us disgraced,' Mary urged, holding on tightly to the hands of her two lively sons, who couldn't always be relied upon to behave.

As Grace knelt to pray she thought she would always remember how good Father Weaver had been about Chrissie. He had told her that he was certain that before she died Chrissie would have begged forgiveness from God for all she had done. Hadn't she already told them she was very sorry and had intended to change her ways? And she'd come home to her family. Grace hadn't been convinced of that but she had clung to his words for she couldn't bear to think that her poor sister had died with sins on her soul that would remain unforgiven. She would always remember his wisdom too, for he had said that they should not judge Chrissie harshly. She was just as much a casualty of the war as Harold and her da had been. It wasn't only the men who had had to fight who had suffered. Those years had changed so many people and they had changed Chrissie too. If there had been no war he was certain her values and expectations would have been totally different. She believed that. Chrissie had felt cheated; she had wanted to make up for her lost youth so much that she had let it become almost an obsession. Her search for that bright dream of happiness had been futile and had caused so much desolation but she couldn't judge her sister for in the end Chrissie's quest for pleasure had cost her her life.

She felt Pat take her hand and she looked over the head of their son and smiled at him. They had found joy together and she was content with her life here. Her adopted country was still poor, there was still mass emigration but she prayed that that would one day change. There was a new young Queen on the throne of her country but at last the war in Korea was over. Billy had had to go and fight but he had come through it unhurt and with distinction. He had made the Army his career; he was now Sergeant William Devlin of the Queen's Lancashire Regiment and they were all proud of him.

She thought sadly of her mam and da, of Harold and of Chrissie as she remembered them all in her prayers, but she had to look forward to the future with hope. Life went on. She thought back to what she had said to her mother on that Sunday when Victory in Europe had been announced. That hope had been the last thing out of Pandora's box and it was the best thing. She thanked God that she had the gift of hope; what a precious gift it was. She would keep it in her heart for ever.

Far From Home

Lyn Andrews

As the daughter of a blacksmith in 1920s Ireland, sixteen-year-old Kitty Doyle knows little of the ways of the world. But she has to grow up fast when the arrival of a stepmother means she is forced to leave her family home and take up a position as a maid at Harwood Hall.

Kitty's new life takes her across the water to Liverpool – but hard times are just around the corner. Strong-minded and independent, Kitty soon secures employment in a grocer's shop, where she also captures the attention of the owner, Stanley Ellinson. Stanley's much older than Kitty, though if she married him, she'd want for nothing. And the boy back home who won Kitty's heart has already betrayed her . . .

FAR FROM HOME brings vividly to life the streets of old Liverpool and of Ireland during a tumultuous era. At its heart is Kitty Doyle's determination to fulfil her dream: of having a home she can call her own.

Praise for Lyn Andrews' unforgettable novels:

'An outstanding storyteller' *Woman's Weekly*

'Gutsy . . . a vivid picture of a hard-up, hardworking community . . . will keep the pages turning' *Daily Express*

978 0 7553 3195 6

headline

Friends Forever

Lyn Andrews

In 1928 Bernie O'Sullivan and Molly Keegan catch their first glimpse of the bustling city they're about to call home. Both seventeen, and best friends since childhood, the girls have left Ireland behind to seek work and an exciting new life in Liverpool.

The girls are dismayed to discover that the relatives they are to stay with have barely two pennies to rub together; the promised grand house is a run-down building in one of Liverpool's worst slum areas. Desperate to escape the filthy streets, Bernie secures a position as a domestic servant, while Molly is taken on as a shop assistant. Soon they have settled in new rooms and find themselves in love with local men. For both, though, love holds surprises and the danger of ruin in an unforgiving world.

Bernie and Molly have tough times to face but the bond of their lifelong friendship gives them the strength to rise to every challenge and to hold on to their dreams.

Praise for Lyn Andrews' unforgettable novels

'A compelling read' *Woman's Own*

'Gutsy . . . A vivid picture of a hard-up, hard-working community . . . will keep the pages turning' *Daily Express*

978 0 7553 0840 8

headline

Now you can buy any of these other bestselling books by **Lyn Andrews** from your bookshop or *direct from the publisher*.

FREE P&P AND UK DELIVERY
(Overseas and Ireland £3.50 per book)

Far From Home	£6.99
Every Mother's Son	£6.99
Friends Forever	£6.99
A Mother's Love	£6.99
Across a Summer Sea	£6.99
When Daylight Comes	£6.99
A Wing and a Prayer	£6.99
Love and a Promise	£6.99
The House on Lonely Street	£6.99
My Sister's Child	£6.99
Take These Broken Wings	£6.99
The Ties That Bind	£6.99
Angels of Mercy	£6.99
When Tomorrow Dawns	£6.99
From This Day Forth	£6.99
Where the Mersey Flows	£6.99
Liverpool Songbird	£6.99

TO ORDER SIMPLY CALL THIS NUMBER

01235 400 414

or visit our website: www.headline.co.uk

Prices and availability subject to change without notice.